KATHA PRIZE STORIES
best of the
~90s~

# KATHA

# BEST OF THE NINETIES
# KPS 11

The best short fiction published
in fifteen Indian languages in
ten volumes of KPS, chosen by
Adoor Gopalakrishnan, Govind
Nihalani, Gulzar, Rituparno
Ghosh and Sharmila Tagore

Edited by
Geeta Dharmarajan

Katha
New Delhi

## KATHA

Copyright © Katha, 2002

Copyright © for each individual
story in its original language is
held by the author.

Copyright © for the English
translations rests with KATHA.

KATHA
A-3 Sarvodaya Enclave
Sri Aurobindo Marg
New Delhi 110 017
Phone: 2652 4850, 2652 4511
Fax: 2651 4373
E-mail: kathavilasam@katha.org
Internet address: www.FictionIndia.com

KATHA is a registered nonprofit society
devoted to enhancing the pleasures of reading. It works in the fields
of story, storytelling and story in education.
KATHAVILASAM is its story research and resource centre.

Cover design: Geeta Dharmarajan
Cover photograph: Mahesh Bhatt
Logo design: Crowquill

In-house editors: Chandra Ramakrishnan, Gita Rajan, Shoma Choudhury
Typeset in 9 on 13pt Bookman by Sandeep Kumar, Suresh Sharma
at Katha and printed at Usha Offset, New Delhi

Distributed by KathaMela, a distributor of quality books.
A-3 Sarvodaya Enclave, Sri Aurobindo Marg, New Delhi 110 017

3 5 7 9 10 8 6 4 2

ISBN 81-87649-70-4 (paperback)     ISBN 81-87649-57-7 (hardback)

*☙ Praise for earlier volumes of Katha Prize Stories ❧*

## Volume 10

This volume of *Katha Prize Stories* will definitely be a prized possession for those even faintly interested in contemporary creative writing in India.
*– The Telegraph*

These are 17 short stories, each one like a polished jewel. Crafted rough yet honed to perfection. The translations have in them the same urgency that the writer tries to convey through his story. These are stories of desire, of want, of love, anger, distrust and disgust. Human emotions all universal in their theme. A salute to Katha for sharing with us what we may have missed otherwise.
*– The Hindu*

## Volume 9

Profound, poignant and pulsating, the present collection of short stories published during 1998-99 is another testimony to the truly commendable work that Katha has been doing since its inception.
*– First City*

... the Indian ethos and the vigour and intensity of the writers shine through this collection.
*– The Hindu*

## Volume 8

A fistful of gems to treasure and share with friends.
*– The Hindustan Times*

... the *Katha Prize Stories* series have undoubtedly more than established the importance of regional fiction. Its publishers can justifiably take credit for creating a growing interest in regional literature.
*– The Hindu*

## Volume 7

Katha deserves a round of applause ... for unearthing a cache of talented translators and revealing the wealth and diversity of literature that lies hidden and unappreciated in this amazing land of ours.
*– Indian Review of Books*

Each story describes a different world, yet speaks of something universal. They draw heavily from the immediate surroundings for both the setting and the imagery ... Together, the kaleidoscopic view of these "worlds" brings home the concept we know as India.
*– Business Standard*

## Volume 6

... *Katha Prize Stories* make available a small share of the regional gold mine denied to most readers.
*– The Indian Express*

Since its inception in 1990, the *Katha Prize Stories* series has become something of an institution in the world of Indian literature ... Katha's work is of tremendous significance in building a new India ...
*– Business Standard*

## Volume 5

... a brilliant and stunning patchwork quilt, every piece standing out and holding its own because of its colour, its texture, its unique design.
*– The Pioneer*

... a rewarding experience for the reader ... the choice of stories has been made with admirable circumspection. *– Outlook*

## Volume 4

Translation is the essence of national integration. The discovery of the wealth of Indian creative writing through translation is an inspiration. Katha is part of this discovery. *– India Today*

... the Foundation justifies its claim to being a "research" organisation ... Volumes 3 and 4 ... are products of the "amrita manthans" of 91-92 and 93-94 ... the series of *Katha Prize Stories* attains the standard of perfection that Katha Vilasam strives for. *– The Book Review*

## Volume 3

Katha's pioneering efforts to bring out translated versions ... moisten the barren patch of short fiction in English ... *– The Indian Express*

... it has ... become a matter of prestige for writers, translators, nominators, journals to find their names included in that year's Katha collection. *– The Economic Times*

## Volume 2

Prize Catch ... The best of India translated. *– India Today*

... a publishing feat ... the stories have the earthy vitality of a live language and the advantages of a refined narrative technique. *– The Daily*

## Volume 1

Fastidiously hand-picked with an accent on the inherent heterogeneity and cultural complexity of contemporary India ... *– Sunday Chronicle*

The conception and execution of the *Katha Prize Stories* series surely represents a unique and special moment in Indian publishing history ...
*– The Economic Times*

# ❦CONTENTS❦

## THE NOMINATING EDITORS

Asomiya
PANKAJ THAKUR

Bangla
DEBES RAY

English
RUKMINI BHAYA NAIR

Gujarati
GANESH DEVY

Hindi
RAJENDRA YADAV

Kannada
D R NAGARAJ

Maithili
UDAYA NARAYANA SINGH

Malayalam
SUJATHA DEVI

Marathi
VILAS SARANG

Oriya
PRATIBHA RAY

Punjabi
KARTAR SINGH DUGGAL

Rajasthani
VIJAYADAN DETHA

Tamil
S KRISHNAN

Telugu
AMARENDRA DASARI

Urdu
ANISUR RAHMAN

# FOR THE STORIES IN THIS VOLUME

## THE WRITERS

Amar Mitra    V Chandra Sekhar Rao

Dilip Chitre    Maitreyi Pushpa

Manoj Kumar Goswami    Nataraj Huliyar

Nazir Mansuri    Prem Parkash

Ram Swaroop Kisan    Sundara Ramaswamy

Surendra Prakash    Vandana Bist

M T Vasudevan Nair    Vibha Rani

Yashodhara Mishra

## THE TRANSLATORS

Dilip Kumar Ganguli    Jayeeta Sharma

D Krishna Ayyar    S Krishnan

Mahasweta Baxipatra    Manu Shetty

Meenakshi Sharma    Nikhil Khandekar

N Pranava Manjari    Raji Subramaniam

Reema Anand    Renuka Ramachandran

C Revathi    Shyam Mathur

Suhas Gole    Vidyanand Jha

## THE JOURNALS

Aarsee    Andhra Jyothi

Desh    Gadyaparva

Gulmohar    Hans

India Today    Jagati Jot

Jhankara    Journal Emporium

Lankesh Patrike    Sandhan

Zahn-e-Jadeed

# ᱛᱷTHE KATHA AWARDS᙮

The KATHA AWARDS were instituted in 1990.

Katha requests an eminent writer, scholar or critic in each of the regional languages to choose what she/he feels are the three best stories published in that language, in the previous year.

Our Nominating Editors sift through numerous journals and magazines that promote short fiction. Many of them consult their friends or other Friends of Katha in the literary world to help them make their nominations. The nominated stories are translated and from these are chosen the Prize Stories.

Each author receives the KATHA AWARD FOR CREATIVE FICTION which includes a citation, Rs 2000, and publication (in translation) in that year's *Katha Prize Stories* volume.

The editor of the regional language journal that first published the award winning story receives the KATHA JOURNAL AWARD.

The translators are handpicked from the list of nearly 3000 names we have at Katha. Each of them gets the KATHA AWARD FOR TRANSLATION which includes a citation, Rs 2000, and the chance to translate a prize story.

The A K RAMANUJAN AWARD goes to a translator who can, with felicity, translate between two or more Indian languages, as Ramanujan himself was able to. A K Ramanujan was a Friend of Katha and this award was instituted in 1993.

The KATHAKAARI AWARD goes to a writer who renders the stories from our folklore and oral traditions into the written form, thereby making the stories available to future generations.

The KATHAVACHAK AWARD goes to a storyteller who with creativity and elan recreates folk tales from the oral tradition as stories to live our lives by.

Every year or so, Katha holds a literary workshop. The award winning writers, translators and editors are invited to it.

## ACKNOWLEDGEMENTS

We thank each of the Friends of Katha, people who have always so generously and spontaneously supported us.
Our heartfelt thanks to

Aateka Khan, Abdul Naseeb F Khan, Abdus Samad, Abid Hussain, Abraham Verghese, Aditya Behl, Afsar Ahmed, A K Datta, Ajeet Cour, Ajit Thakor, Alka Nanda, Allam Rajaiah, Amar Mitra, Amarendra Dasari, Ambai, Ambar, Ananda Rao, Anantha Murthy U R, Anil Gharai, Anil Vyas, Anisur Rehman, Anjali Nair, Anjana Desai, Ansari A M, Anupama Prabhala Kapse, Aparna Mahanta, Aparna Satpat, Apratim Baruah, Aravind Dixit, Arun Mhatre, Aruna Bhowmick, Aruna Vyas, Arundhati Deosthale, Arup Kumar Dutta, Arupa Patangia Kalita, Arvind Passey, Asad Zaidi, Asaduddin M, Asha Bage, Asha Damle, Asha Kardaley, Ashita, Ashok Srinivasan, Ashok Vajpeyi, Ashutosh Roy, Atreyee Gohain, Atulananda Goswami, Avaneesh Bhat, Ayyappa Paniker, Azhagiyasingar,

Bageshree, Bahubali Bhosge, Baldev Singh, Baran Rehman, Basappa, Bezboruah D N, Bhagirath Misra, Bhupen Khakhar, Bhupendranarayan Bhattacharyya, Bhushan Arora, Bibhas Sen, Bimal Kar, Bimbisar Irom, Bindu Nambiar, Bipin Bhise, Bipin Patel, Bolwar Mohamed Kunhi, Bonita Baruah, Brinda Bose, Brinda Charry,

Chandana Dutta, Chandra Prakash Deval, Chandrakant Keni, Chandra Sekhar Rao V, Chandrika B, Charudatta Bhagwat, Charusheela Sohoni, Chary S N A, Che Yoganathan, Chetna Sethi, Chitta Ranjan Das, Cho Dharmam, Chudamani R, C K Hota,

Devinder Kaur Assa Singh, Damodar Mauzo, David Davidar, Debes Ray, Debshankar Jha, Devika Khanna, Dhananjay Kapse, Dharmanand Kamath, Dhoomketu, Dhruba Hazarika, Dhruva Shukla, Digish Mehta, Dilip Chitre, Dilip Kumar Ganguly, Dipankar Basu, Dipli Saikia, Diptiranjan Pattanaik, Diwakar S,

Elizabeth Bell, Enakshi Chatterjee, Era Murugan, Fakir Muhammed Katpadi,

Ghanshyam Dass Hotumalani, Gagan Das, Ganesh N Devy, Gauri Deshpande, Gautam Sengupta, Geeta Ramsundar, Geeti Chandra, Ghanshyam Dass, Gita Jayaraj, Gita Krishnankutty, Gnani, Gopa Mazumdar, Gopichand Narang, Gopinath Mohanty, Gopini Karunakar, Gourhari Behera, G P Deshpande, Gracy, Gulam Mohammed Sheikh,

Harekrishna Deka, Harikrishanan, Harish Trivedi, Hatkanagalekar,

Hephzibah Israel, Himanjali Mitra, Himanshi Shelat, Hina Nandrajog, Hiranmoy Karlekar,

Imran Hussain, Indra C T, Indira Chandrasekhar, Indira Goswami, Indira Parthasarathy, Indu Ashok Gersappe, Irathina Karikalan,

Jagannathan N S, Jai Ratan, Jasjit Mansingh, Jatindra Kumar Nayak, Jaya Mohan, Jayant Bendre, Jayant Kaikani, Jayant Kumar Chakravorty, Jayeeta Sharma, Jeelani Bano, Jhaverchand Meghani, Jiwan Pani, Jyoti Ramachandran,

Kalyan Raman N, Kalyani Dutta, Kamala N, Kanji Patel, Kanti Patel, Kasturi Kanthan, Kaveri Rastogi, Keerti Ramachandra, Keisham Priyokumar, Khalid Javed, Khushwant Singh, Kranti Sambhav, Krishna Ayyar D, Krishna Barua, Krishna Chawla, Krishna Paul, Krishnan S, K S Duggal, Kula Saikia, Kunkna Dangi Adivasis,

Lakshman R K, Lakshmi Kannan, Lalita Vivekanand, Lamabam Viramani, Lankesh P, Laura Sykes, Leela Ponnappa,

Madhavan N S, Madhurantakam Narendra, Madhurantakam Rajaram, Mahasweta Baxipatra, Mahesh Nair, Maitreyi Pushpa, Makarand Paranjape, Malashri Lal, Malati Mathur, Manjeet Kaur, Manju Kak, Manoj, Manoj Kumar Goswami, Manu Shetty, Maya Sharma, Meena Kakodkar, Meenakshi Mukherjee, Meenakshi Sharma, Meghana Pethe, Milind Bokil, Minakshi Sen, Mini Chandran, Mithra Venkatraj, Mitra Mukherjee Parikh, Mitra Phuken, M L Sardesai, Mohammed Khadeer Babu, Mohammed N P, Mohan Parmar, Mohinder Singh Sarna, Motilal Jotwani, Mozzam Sheikh, Mridula Nath Chakraborty, Mukundan M, Mukta Rajadhyaksha, My Dear Jayu,

Na D'Souza, Nagaraj D R, Nagma Zafir, Naiyer Masud, Namwar Singh, Nandana Dutta, Nandita Aggarwal, Nandlal Jotwani, Narayan Hegde, Narendra Nair, Nataraj Huliyar, Naveen Kumar Naithani, Nazir Mansuri, Neer Kanwal Mani, Neerada Suresh, Nikhil Khandekar, Nirmal Verma, Nishikant Chaudhary, Nissim Ezekiel, Nivedita Menon, Nrisingh Rajpurohit,

Olivinho Games, Paavannan, Padma Sharma, Padmanabhan T, Pankaj Bisht, Pankaj Mishra, Pankaj Thakur, Paul Zacharia, P A Kolharkar, Perumal Murugan, Phul Goswami, Prabha Dixit, Prabhakaran N, Prabhavati, Prabodh Parikh, Prachi Deshpande, Pradipta Borgohain, Prakash Narayan Sant, Pranava Manjari N, Prasad G J V, Prasenjit Ranjan Gupta, Pratibha Ray, Pravin Patkar, Preeti Ratra, Prema K M, Prem Gorkhi, Prem Parkash, Priya Vijay Tendulkar, Priyakshi Rajguru, Priyamvad, Priyamvada K E, P R S Oberoi, Puduvai Ra Rajani, Pugazh, Puloma Pal, Purna Chandra Tejasvi,

Raghavendra Rao K, Raj Mohan Jha, Rajendra Yadav, Rajendrasinh Jadeja, Rajesh, Raji Lakshmiratan, Raji Subramaniam, Rajmohan, Rakesh Chaudhary, Rama T S, Ramachandra Behera, Ramachandra Sharma, Ramachandran C N, Raman Jaiswal, Ramakrishnan N, Ramanunni K P, Ramkumar Tiwari, Ramswaroop Kisan, Ramya Srinivasan, Rana Nayar, Ranga Rao, Rani Sharma, Ranjit Singh, Ranjita Biswas, Ranju Mehta, Rashmi Baruah, Rashmi Chaturvedi, Rawindra Pinge, R P Mishra, Reema Anand, Rekha, Rentala Nageshwara Rao, Renuka Ramachandran, Revathi C, Revathi Iyenger, Ritu Bhanot, Ritu Saksena, Robin S Ngangom, Roomy Naqvi, Roschen Sasikumar, Rukmini Bhaya Nair, Rukmini Sekar, Rukun Advani, Rupashree M S, Ruth Vanita,

Sacheen Pai Raikar, Sachidananda Mohanty, Sadi Bhushanam, Sadia Mehdi, Sadique, Sadiq-ur Rehman Kidwai, Sajid Rashid, Saleem Kidwai, Samita Jana, Sandhya Bhandare, Sangeeta Mehdiratta, Sangita Passey, Sanjay Chauhan, Sanjay Sahay, Sanjeev Palliwal, Sanjoy Ghose, Sanju Ramachandran, Sara Rai, Sarah Joseph, Sarala Jag Mohan, Sarat Bar Kakati, Sarat Kumar Mukhopadhyay, Sarita Padki, Sasi Bhushanam, Satchidanandan K, Satjit Wadva, Savita Goswami, Sethu, Shalini Sinha, Shama Futehally, Shamsul Haq Usmani, Shankaranarayanan K, Shanti S K, Shantinath K Desai, Sharada Murthi, Sharada Nair, Sharada Prasad H Y, Sharada Rao, Sharma A S K V S, Sharma K K, Shaukat Hayat Sheeba Chowdhary, Sherrif K M, Shirish Dhoble, Shirish Panchal, Shirshendu Chakravarthy, Shiva Prakash, Shivanath, Shyam Ponnappa, Shyam Mathur, Shyamal Gangopadhyay, Sithara S, Soharab Hossain, Sonali Singh, Sreevalli Radhika T, Sri Ramana, Srinivasan N, Subashish Ray, Subrabharatimaniam, Suchitra Bhattacharya, Sudha Naravane, Sudhakar Ghatak, Sudhakar Marathe, Sudhanshu Mohanty, Sudarshanam R S, Suhas Gole, Sujatha Devi, Sujit Mukherjee, Sukanya Dutta, Suma Josson, Sumangala Bakre, Sumedha Parande, Sundara Ramaswamy, Sugra Mehdi, Suparna Biswas, Surendra Prakash, Sushant Kumar Mishra, Sushil Ansal, Sushmita Mukherjee, Sutinder Singh Noor, Sutradhari, Swami, Swapna Jose, Swapnamoy Chakraborti, Syamala Kallury, Syed Mohammed Ashraf,

Tarapada Ray, Tarunkanti Mishra, Thanjai Prakaash, Thomas A J, Thomas Joseph, Tridip Suhrud,

Udaya Narayana Singh, Umapathy D, Unny E P, Upendra Nanavati, Urmila Bhendre, Urvashi Butalia, Usha K R, Usha Tambe,

Vaidehi, Vakati Panduranga Rao, Vanajam Ravindran, Vandana Bist, Vasudevan Nair M T, Vatsala P, Venkat Swaminathan, Venkatachala Hegde,

Vibha Rani, Vidya Pai, Vidyanand Jha, Vijay Mohan Singh, Vijaya Ghose, Vijaya Rajadhyaksha, Vijayadan Detha, Vijayalakshmi M, Vijayan O V, Vilas Sarang, Vinod Meghani, Vishnu Nagar, Vishwapriya Iyenger, Vivek Shanbag,

Yashodhara Mishra, Yogendra Ahuja,

Zakia Zaheer, Zamiruddin Ahmad.

## Journals

Aajkaal, Aajkal, Abhiyan, Andhra Prabha Sachitra Vara Patrika, Andhra Bhoomi, Andhra Jyoti, Andhra Prabha, Antikaa, Anushthub, Aarsee, Baromas, Bibhab, Binjaro, Chitrangi, Daar Se Bichhre, Dainik Pratidin, Dalit, Dastak, Desh, Dinamani Kadir, Dipavali, Gadyaparva, Galpa Sarani, Goriyoshi, Gulmohar, Hans, India Today, Jaag, Jagat Jot, Jhankara, Journal Emporium, Jugantor, Kala Kaumudi, Kalachuvadu, Karmaveera, Katha Desh, Katha Disha, Kathegallu, Kavitasaran, Krantik, Lankesh Patrike, Loksatta, Malayala Manorama, Manaosai, Mathrubhumi, Mauj, Miloon Saryajni, Nagmani, Navina Virutcham, Pahal, Parab, Parishkrit Varta, Prajavani, Prantik, Pratikshana, Rajasthan Patrika, Sadhana, Sahitya, Samaas, Sandhan, Saptahik Hindustan, Saptahik Sakal, Sathangai, Shabkhoon, Sharadiya Ananda Bazar Patrika, Sharashjya, Sheeraza, Shree Vatsa, Sipoon, Soughat, Subhamangala, Sudha, Sutradhar, Tanazur, Udayavani, Unnatham, Vi, Vipulshree, Wakhal, Zahn-e-Jadeed.

We thank our friends from the media who have been with us through the years, actively supporting us in all our endeavours, especially Sadanand Menon of *The Economic Times* who first brought Katha to the public eye with his review of *Katha Prize Stories 1*. We also thank all the bookshop owners who have helped us in promoting and selling our books. Our corporate partners, in particular Ansal's Charanjiv Charitable Trust, Ford Foundation, India Cements Limited, India Habitat Centre, India International Centre, Punjab and Sind Bank and The East India Hotels Limited, deserve our heartfelt thanks for their willing help and cooperation,

And last but not the least, we would like to thank all the people in Katha who have been associated directly and indirectly with the production of the *Katha Prize Stories* series over the years.

## ✍ Languages are not vegetables ... ≈

No, languages are not vegetables to be preserved but that's what a certain hegemony will have us believe, they who shake their heads gloomily, predicting that all Indian languages will die and one will reign supreme, English. And they'll have us artificially preserving our languages, forgetting strengths we have, like our stories, those that have helped keep our many languages gloriously alive. Creative and fun, ever changing and constantly challenged, they ably communicate our deep stories, our silences. When has it ever been anything else for us in India?

So the question that we in Katha constantly ask ourselves ... how much power do we want to give to statements that claim that English will destroy our living languages – the 400 or so that we presently speak and joke in – taking with them not just the cultures but also the still undiscovered wealth within each. How confidently and with how much self-esteem can we prove to ourselves that when in the next 50-odd years about 90 per cent of the world's 6000 languages grow probably extinct, ours will not. How positively can we remind ourselves that Hindi is the world's second most spoken language, and Bengali the fifth, among the world's top 10 languages.

No, if we billion people have a say, our languages will survive. And the story will continue to be that tensile backbone that will hold us together. The book you hold in your hands, *Katha Prize Stories: Best of the Nineties*, will hopefully bolster that confidence.

And so let's celebrate our writers and those Friends of Katha who have consistently and with never-wavering spirit found the best for us.

Spotting and staunchly supporting the best, reading up to hundred journals in any given year, doing this as a labour of love – this is what our Nominating Editors have done, year after year after quick-following year. And we have no words to thank those who, over the years, have made the difficult final choice from a selection that's probably gone through at least three rounds of rigorous selection already. The eclectic tastes of editors of diverse magazines and journals (ranging from a popular commercial weekly that sells in the lakhs to a quiet little magazine with a dedicated band of readers) have only added to the richness of each year's collection. From our first pride of award-winners to now, we did not even *try* to represent all the bhashas. This was determined by the quality of the stories and what the Nominating Editors vouched for. I remember that in 1989, the first of the Katha Award nominations brought hope with it. And this has continued each year. That year, many of our editors told us that surveying the scene for this collection made them aware of the extent of excellent short stories in their respective languages. And this has been reiterated to us, many times over the years. A case for celebration, that.

Thoughts are ephemeral. Language slips through the crevices of the mind to create a ripple that is almost atavistic, taking its source not in the word itself but in something experienced long ago, to create a story, a thing of magic. This is the magic that India has woven with consummate ease for the last 3,000 years and more. That's precisely why the short story can never be a "minor" art form in our country. And, just as importantly, the best of them help us, as one of our friends said, to "stop and examine the code by which we live." Over the years, many of the stories in *KPS* have jolted me out of my middle-class complacency, got me to think about our own chameleon-like entanglement with the everydayness of our diurnal lives that leaves little time or energies for the larger values.

But Katha's interest in the short story has never been fuelled by some kind of misplaced sympathy to try and save a genre which has been an intrinsic part of the storyteller's repertoire in our country for many years. We knew that in many of our languages people were writing excellent stories. Only, these were not reaching beyond the four corners of each language. Out of this conviction, nearly fifteen years ago, was born Katha Vilasam, the short story research and resource centre, and this series.

Over the years, we have strived to foster and applaud what we believe are important: Stories that will stand the test of time, stories that are honest, well-told and creative, and yet touch on the perpetual human predicaments, the moral and psychological conundrums, which are so much a part of life and living. And in this volume, *Katha Prize Stories: Best of the Nineties*, if the stories still ring true, are relevant after maybe ten years, the full credit goes to the writers, some established, others emerging, who saw and translated their vision with the keen singular eye of an appreciator of the world around us, with the deftness of a master wordsmith. We thank our writers for giving us of their best.

To the translators go our admiration and gratitude for bringing us our writers' best in living translations. In 1991, in my preface, I had noted that ... We see this as a book primarily for the Indian reader who wants to read what is being written today in the various languages which she/he cannot read. We could not see italics as the magic device one sometimes wishes for that can give meaning to the word it singles out from the narrative. We have tried to use Indian words as naturally as possible. But we did worry over what and how many words to gloss. We have used the footnote rather than a fullfledged glossary, and this too, grudgingly, only to explain those words which the context does not elucidate, or where a little more information would make the story more accessible. Also, we have tried not to reduce words to a standardized Hindiized usage. For instance, kumkum in north Indian languages is kunku in Marathi, kumkuma in Telugu and kumkumam in Tamil. And these stay so in the English translation.

Each continuing year, the *Katha Prize Stories* have helped us take our mission goals forward, as we agonized and mulled over the problems of translation and the politics of language – who gets translated, how, why – even as we tried to delve deeper, find the many different ways in which we can make up for the lack of dialects and registers in English, the frustratingly uniform lingo of the "convent-educated." More, it has helped us be proactive about reaching out to school and college students, to readers and emerging writers, in the hope that, together, we could rejuvenate the deep springs of creativity within us, with the strength that is story. And it has been a learning process all the way, starting with paying attention to something as irritating and finally so Indian as the dancing tenses, the easy mercury-like movement between the past and the present, the very clever use of a simple syntax or a definite article to create a certain atmosphere of innocence, to trying to bring these into English. I cannot say the ensuing translations have succeeded fully; but we, translators and editors, continue to strive, for your reading pleasure.

Choosing the best is never easy. Add to this the immense difficulties caused by India's many languages. But what we have managed to find are willing readers, critics, lovers of literature, people who do not admit, probably even to themselves, that they have had to extend themselves more than they really can. And it is in this same spirit that the five friends of Katha came into reading the award-winning stories of the ten exciting years of the '90s. And words will not suffice to thank this year's nominating editors – Adoor Gopalakrishnan, Govind Nihalani, Gulzar, Rituparno Ghosh and Sharmila Tagore for choosing the stories you hold in your hands.

Quintessentially Indian, each one of these stories is wrapped in a certain magic that tries to communicate a culture, the "codes, beliefs and acts of our daily life," a way of speaking that belongs to a special little place in the world created by a language called Malayalam or Tamil, Gujarati or Urdu – to name only a few of the languages represented here – and yet is shared by all of us who are Indian. Each of our selectors this year expressed again and again, their admiration for the stories, and how difficult it was to choose just one from each language for the 90s. Given the option, we would have loved to have included more, many more, almost all the stories from each one of our volumes. We take this opportunity to thank, with all the love we can muster, all the people who have stood by us over the years, helping us move into the 21st century with excellent stories that challenge our idea of life and living, enrage and outrage us, shame us or bring us the mercy of tears.

We hope the book pleases. And we hope too that it will do its little bit to help us recognize the strength of our bhashas and each one of their unique literary offerings. We hope that great stories will continue to bloom in our many languages, even though the best nestle, like water in the palm of the hand, fragile, full of here-one-minute-gone-the-next-minuteness. As I read these stories again, filled with the memories of long hours of editing and arguing and decoding of words and phrases and nuances, I continue to find the same some tantalizing, the same others appealing with their direct and telling narration. Strange. But they – like the many, many more we hope to bring you in the coming years – come from some of the 21 languages Katha will be working in that'll enrich the 21st century. And, as we move on, we hope to grow into more multi-lingual, multi-caste and -class classrooms, breaking that resounding culture of silence.

This is our promise to ourselves and our readers across India and the world. We hope the rich khazana of rememberable stories will in planned and sudden ways help dissolve some of the unnecessary baggage we have carried over hundreds of heavy years. These things of the blood were built and nurtured by story. And with story we will, inshallah!, recreate and reinvent ourselves, give ourselves that maturity to choose what of the old we want to keep, what of the new we want to accept.

1988 seems so far off. Yet it seems like just fifteen minutes away! And as Katha jumps with its usual buoyancy and finger-in-every-pie creativity into its fifteenth year, I pray that the Katha experiment will continue to keep you in a delightful embarrassment of literary riches away from even imagining a world without the language/s you've always seen as yours, the one that's rooted you and given you an identity, be it Tamil, Telugu, Malayalam; Marathi, Gujarati, Konkani; Asomiya, Boro or Tenedyie ...

But we cannot do it without you. Won't you join the adventure?

December, 2002                                    Geeta Dharmarajan

best of the
90s

**DILIP PURUSHOTTAM CHITRE**

The Full Moon in Winter

Commencing as an innocuous reunion of old collegemates, the story turns into a surreal erotic encounter that culminates into a devastating nightmare as the victim tries desperately to liberate herself from the asphyxiating hold of the psychological aberrations caused by the old Tease.                    **– Govind Nihalani**

I saw Antya approaching in that special rolling walk of his. He was wearing his lawyer's black jacket and had with him his briefcase laden with papers. He broke into a broad smile when he saw me and waved his hand in greeting. We met outside the Bombay High Court and getting out onto the University side, we crossed Mahatma Gandhi Road and went down the opposite street to our usual bar. We ordered two quarter bottles of gin before either of us said a word.

It was noon and very hot. Having gin wasn't such a good idea really but it was an old habit of ours – to drink when we met. Thirty years back when we were in college together, the State of Maharashtra had not yet come into existence. Mr Morarjee Desai, the Chief Minister of Bombay, was determined to impose prohibition. We drank country liquor on the sly. Our entire group met at clandestine hooch joints in various parts of the city. We are past fifty now. There are distilleries all over Maharashtra and not only is there no prohibition but drinking has become a socially acceptable vice. Those of us who had once broken the law to drink country liquor of the first-distillate variety were the brave pioneers. No way can we give up an old habit.

Antya is the oldest friend to have stayed in touch. He's a lawyer and I am a writer. I have taken up various occupations to earn my living while I carried on with my writing. Antya invariably helped me out when I was in difficulties. I've not been able to stick to either a house or a job for any length of time, while Antya has lived and worked on steadily. We've managed our families each in our own way. Antya and I have continued to meet, and when we do, we drink and we talk not only about ourselves but about everything under the sun. No other friendship gives me as much. Since our college days we have spent time like this, watching the happenings

Dilip Purushottam Chitre won the Katha Award for Creative Fiction in 1991, for this story. *Gulmohar* received the Journal Award for first publishing this story in Marathi.
The Katha Translation Award went to Suhas Gole.
This story first appeared in English translation in *Katha Prize Stories 1*, 1991.
We thank Vilas Sarang, our nominating editor, for choosing this story for us.

in the world and making learned comments on them. It is our way of savouring the world. All these years of discussion have made us realize how different we are from each other and yet how similar. The liquor is only a pretext.

I was uneasy today. Every friendship has its own unwritten codes. I do not tell Antya when I am in difficulty. There are many things about my life that he knows nothing about. He might, at best, be able to imagine them. I have lived not only in various parts of India, but in Europe, America and Africa. And I have moved about in spheres as diverse as clerkdom, government service, journalism, teaching, advertising, cinema and art. I am intense by nature and I have been involved with more women than most. This has been the cause of great complications and tensions in my personal life but I have resolved them in my own way. Antya may or may not have known this, but until I've raised the issues, he has never said anything on his own in this or any other matter. He will not badger me with questions – it is not his way. He won't even think I am being secretive.

"Do you remember Lalita Honavar, Antya?"

"You mean the one from college – *The Full Moon in Winter*?"

"Yes, that's the one."

"Whatever made you remember her after all these years?"

"I'll tell you. But first tell me what you remember about her. You have a wonderful memory."

"Well, her father was an ICS officer. Quite the Englishman. Got involved in some scandal or the other and committed suicide."

"What about the girl?"

"Great looking but so cold that no one ever thought of making a pass at her. That's what earned her the title The Full Moon in Winter. Snobbish. Only spoke English. Never mixed with anyone. And her subject – Sociology! She was either a year senior or junior to us – she wasn't in our class in the first year."

"What else?"

"Nothing more. This is the first time her name has cropped up after all these years. What's up?"

"Nothing. I've had a phone call from her."

"Oh?"

"Yes."

"What about?"

"She's the President of some women's organization. She has invited me to give a talk. She said on the phone that she had a feeling we had gone to the same college and asked me if I remembered her name. And like a fool I said, Yes, of course."

"You shouldn't have done that. Why, the bitch never so much as looked at anybody. Thought she was the best. You should have done the same thing now. Well, what then?"

"I met her. She's as old as us – over fifty – but looks every bit as she did at college. Probably dyes her hair. Hasn't married. Still a Miss."

"What use is that to us so late in our lives? You are a grandfather and my children are adolescents."

"I'm just informing you."

"What's the point?"

"She wanted to know if I've kept in touch with anybody from college. So I told her about you. She was very surprised to hear that we still meet regularly, and she was curious to know what we did when we met, what we talked about. I told her that we sit and drink, listen to old records, talk about old times and practically everything else."

"Then?"

"She said, How fantastic! I would love to join you one evening if I am invited. Just to observe two friends talk. I've never experienced such a thing myself! I was a bit taken aback. I said, Yes, of course, but I think you'll be disappointed. There's nothing in it really. But she insisted and I told her I would let her know after I had spoken to you."

"My dear chap, how's that possible? Are our meetings stage shows to be commissioned by whoever wants them?"

"But she's rung up thrice after that."

"So?"

"Are you free this Saturday?"

"What? Oh, well, yes."

"I have called her to my place. Said I'd confirm it after I spoke to you."

"God! But it's all right – she'll get bored and leave on her own."

"It'll be the usual thing. As you know there's no one at home now. We'll have a cold buffet: I'll get it from somewhere. It's settled then?"

"If you say so. But to tell you the truth, I still can't believe it."

That settled, we drank gin to our heart's content and having talked as usual, went back home.

I was to be alone in the house all of next week. My wife, son, daughter-in-law and grandson are in Pune. That's where we mainly live these days. When I come to Bombay on work I stay in a friend's flat. He has gone abroad and has left the keys with me. The flat has all the amenities including a phone. It's centrally situated – at Worli – an affluent locality, and peaceful, so I can concentrate on my work. As I grow older, I too have begun to look for all the maximum comfort and convenience I can get. The hectic pace that once used to add to my excitement has become hateful. Besides, there's this ischaemia hanging like a sword over my head.

I do not go out much. I cook my own food. But I love cooking. Trying out new dishes gives me great pleasure. For the last few days I have been busy doing some preliminary work on a film. I am preparing a detailed shooting script from a screenplay I'd written earlier. The location for the shooting, the cast and even the dates have been decided on. It remains now to decide on the tenor of each scene and divide the shots on that basis – the angle for each shot, the distance between the camera and the subject, the lighting, whether to keep the camera still or moving, the direction and speed at which the camera is to move, the movement of the characters and their gestures and actions, the highs and lows of the dialogue and the timbre of the voices, the props and things needed for the scenes, the costumes and their colour, the other sounds to be recorded apart from the dialogue, the background music, and the points at which it starts and ends, the order of the prints for editing and their stacking. I try and put down as many minute details as possible. Many of these will be altered at the last moment but I believe that if the whole team can have a clear picture of what the film is finally going to be like, each one can put his heart into the work and give his best.

I had invited Lalita Honavar for Saturday evening but I began to hate myself for it. Antya was coming and she was coming, which meant that the whole of Saturday would be spent getting things ready and taking care of the guests. Drinks and late night would mean that all of Sunday morning would be spent lazing around. That would be two whole days gone. But it was too late to cancel the programme now.

Putting together a cold meal is even more difficult than making a hot one. A hot meal goes down even if it is not very tasty but preparing a meal to go with drinks is more difficult. I had to get butter, mustard and mayonnaise for the sandwiches, boiled eggs and boneless chicken, ham and steamed pomfret with the bones removed, onion cut to order, tomatoes, pink radish, mint and garlic chutney, boiled chana and minced coriander leaves, beside farsan, roasted peanuts and chana, slices of cheese, apple, cashew nuts, two bottles of gin, a dozen bottles of soda, fresh lime juice and lime cordial, angostura bitters, orange and pineapple juice, chilled beer in case anyone wanted it, and Riesling wine. I'd barely finished organizing all this and had put on my silk kurta after a bath when Antya arrived.

"What! All this for that cold woman? Looks like a feast! Haven't we always managed on just gin and chana?"

"Enjoy yourself Antya, enjoy yourself. I've been given an advance for the film."

"That's interesting. You've actually received your payment on time, have you?"

"How am I to know whether I'll get the rest of the instalments? But the producer was in a great hurry."

"Fine. Now tell me, when is this female coming?"

"Seven thirty. There's still an hour left. Do you want to change? Have a wash?"

"Okay. I want to take off my coat and tie. By the way, how much do you pay for this flat?"

"Why should I pay? This is Bharat's flat and he's gone to America."

"Who's this Bharat?"

"Bharat Patel. He's originally from Uganda – he came here during the Idi Amin days. We got acquainted, and the acquaintance grew."

"Why don't you put on some music? Do you have anything classical?"

"Vocal or instrumental?"

"Vocal. Put on a concert tape. Do you have anything by Panditji?" Panditji is Krishnarao Shankar Pandit. We have been his admirers since we were children.

It's a first class concert. 1965 vintage. Starts with a khayal, a chees and a tarana in the raag Yaman. Then the Nand raag. Followed by a tappa in Kafi. Then Shankara. Then a thumri in Tilang, followed by a chatrang in Malkauns. After the Basant, Jogiya and Lalit, right up to the finale in Bhairavi.

"It must have been a four hour session!"

"And all sung with such vigour. Absolutely fullbodied."

I put on the tape and almost absentmindedly, we started drinking.

The doorbell rang. I opened the door and there was Lalita Honavar.

"Come in!"

"Sorry, I'm late."

She was wearing a purple silk sari with a green and turmeric yellow border. Her hair was tied up in a tight knot and she was wearing typical Maharashtrian eartops. Her fair, yellowish complexion was set off by the sari. She entered, bringing in with her a whiff of expensive French perfume. I introduced Antya.

"I have seen him in college."

Antya is an outspoken person. "How could you have seen the

likes of us," he said, "You never cared so much as to look at anyone. Besides, during the four years of college we rarely went to classes."

"Your crowd sat on the steps of Liberty Laundry every morning. Once one of you had said something and all of you had had a good laugh at my expense."

"That wasn't me. It was a chap called Oak."

"That forward chap with a flat nose and light eyes?"

"Exactly. You have a good memory."

"Anyone would have noticed your lot! You were in the college, yet went about as if you weren't. Of course, you weren't any trouble to anybody but you were universally known for the way you ogled at every girl and gave everyone – students and professors – the most peculiar nicknames."

"What will you drink?" I asked. "We're having gin but if gin doesn't suit you, there's Riesling wine or beer or fruit juice."

"I'd like some wine."

I gave her some.

"Cheers!"

"Well, carry on. I am an unwanted guest really. I couldn't help being curious about two college friends who keep meeting regularly even after they are past fifty. You probably know that I'm a student of Sociology. I have written a book on the loneliness of women. I propose to write a similar book on men."

"We agree that we are men," said Antya, "And we also agree that we cannot live without drinks. But how do you gather we are lonely?"

"He is a lawyer by profession," I said, "You must be careful."

"No wonder he began cross-examining me as if I had made an accusation. Now look, I haven't come here to study you. When I heard that the two of you have met regularly for the last thirty to thirty five years and still spend hours talking to each other, I was amazed. This man's a writer, you are a lawyer. You are so different in nature and by profession. And yet ..."

"You are making yet another assumption. My dear lady, even if Antya is a lawyer today there was a time when he wrote poetry. We are both equally fond of songs and films, besides enjoying each other's company. We used to take bhang, and smoke charas and ganja and wander all over the city. Now we only drink liquor. We have seen to it that our habits never cause anyone any trouble. What we really like is to listen to music and talk to each other when we are drunk."

No one said anything for some time. The tape was still playing. The Nand raag got over and the tappa in Kafi began, *Miya Janewale*, the most loved of the tappas that flash like swords in the arsenal of the Gwalior gharana. All the great exponents, from Krishnarao Shankar Pandit and Rajabhaiya Poonchwale, right up to Sharatchandra Arolkar and Jal Balaporia have sung it. The composition remains the same but every singer weaves into it his own colours. It has all the subtle tenderness of a maiden's plea to a lover leaving for distant lands. Panditji is basically a very masculine singer. His bass, sinewy and full of mingled notes like music played on the been, is his specialty. But when he sings this tappa ... the amazing range and wonderful abandon, the scintillating highlights, the cascades of mingled swaras, the persuasive returns to the dominant notes, the overpowering artistry makes you want to listen to it over and over again.

"*Allah ... di kasama ... twanoo ...* "

Antya had forgotten that Lalita Honavar existed. He had closed his eyes and was beating time and bursting into exclamations of delight whenever Panditji, making detours and feints, returned with a delicate modulation to the major beat.

"Who is the singer?" Lalita asked me in a low voice.

"Krishnarao Shankar Pandit of Gwalior. This classical stuff isn't boring you, I hope?"

"Oh no! It's not that. In fact, one of my sisters is a singer. But I do not understand Indian classical music, it sounds unfamiliar. I have listened more often to Western music. All my education was in English. We speak Konkani at home. I know Marathi because I've lived in Bombay, but I don't speak it fluently. My father was an ICS officer ... and he only spoke to us in English."

The tappa ended.

"Stop the tape for some time," said Antya, "It will be difficult to take it all in at one go."

I stopped the tape.

Being the host, I had to serve the drinks and pass the snacks around. Lalita's behaviour really astonished me. She had already consumed three quarters of the wine in the bottle, and she wasn't neglecting the food either. She was watching us closely, particularly Antya.

Antya however, was lost in his own world. At one point he brought up the subject of Madan Mohan, the music director, and I started telling them how Madan Mohan had used the single raag Bageshree for the composition of a number of very difficult tunes. I even sang out the sections. After that we talked about some other friends. It turned out that someone we knew at college had become a big time smuggler. Then we talked about someone else whose wife had come to Antya with her divorce case and how Antya had given her brief to another lawyer.

The chunk of society that we make up produces clerks, salesmen, doctors, engineers and lawyers. Some are poor or have become poor, some are rich, but most belong to the middle class. Some have gone abroad, others have scattered to various parts of the country, but most have remained in Bombay. Some have become famous cricketers, some have joined politics, some have become contractors or businessmen and some have even joined the theatre and cinema. Antya has all the latest information on everyone. Whenever and wherever he meets any of them, he invariably enquires after them. He carries in his head a prodigious file of information about his contemporaries. I am sure the latest information on Lalita Honavar had already gone into that file. If someone wanted to write a composite history of Ruia College, Antya could have easily written about the 1950s and 60s without a break. Even after he had received his degree, he and a few other friends continued to frequent the college for some years. Besides, some of our friends had become professors. Even as he quietly practised his own profession, Antya kept a close tab on the history of his own times.

I noticed that Lalita Honavar had become absolutely still as she listened to him.

"If you don't mind, you will give me a perfectly clear answer to a question I am about to ask you? Both of you."

"We've had so much to drink," said Antya, "That even a perfectly clear answer might not seem clear enough."

"Ask," I said.

"What exactly does The Full Moon in Winter mean?"

"Well, in Marathi we used to say the Pournima in winter."

"I am not asking you for that kind of an explanation. Why did you give a particular person that name? What did it mean when it was applied to me?"

"I shall try and explain," I said, "But after all these years, you mustn't read anything personal into it. Remember that we are speaking of boys who thirty five years ago were on the threshold of youth and who could not, very easily, have the company of young girls. Agreed?

"You were fair and good looking. You belonged to the upper caste and the upper crust. We came from Marathi medium schools and from the lower middle class. You spoke very good English ... you moved about with an air of self-importance ... you had a starched look ... behaved as if the rest of the world were inferior and of no consequence. We never saw you speak or smile freely with anyone. You kept a certain distance ... so, it was The Full Moon. And because you were beautiful and since you remained aloof and were difficult to understand, In Winter. What do you say, Antya?"

"Put it as you will. You are the poet."

"But you are the lawyer and this conversation is like a courtroom exchange. I think that this is really an accusation."

"She hasn't yet made a complaint."

"But tell me, did it never occur to you that the title you bestowed on her would have an effect on her mind?"

"Now look, we waited for four years for it to have an effect. You never even turned around to look. There were plenty of girls who would hit back, threaten us with their chappals, complain to the Principal. Their reaction was an acknowledgement of sorts, it showed that they had noticed us. Some of them even began to talk freely with us after that."

"Not a single girl ever spoke to me during the four years I was at college," said Antya. "Once to make fun of me, one of the girls from a group came up to me and innocently asked if a particular road went to Matunga station. I said, Yes, and the girls began laughing."

"How silly!"

"But at that age the silliness had quite a different meaning. They had found me alone and looking absentminded and must have decided to make a fool of me. It was their way of avenging the honour of the group, because usually every girl who passed by was sure to be rewarded with a verbal present."

"Shall I return to the subject? What if the label you attached to me, proclaiming me as an insensitive, unfeeling, hypocritical, vain, misanthropic girl, had an adverse effect? You are a lawyer, aren't you? Well, tell me, was this not defaming me? And what if this sobriquet you gave me inflicted a deep injury on my mind and ruined my future?"

"Miss Honavar, if I were stating your case as your lawyer, I would have to prove that you were defamed. I would also have to produce evidence of the harm done to your psyche. Perhaps the American law would have been more useful to you than ours."

"If you are a lawyer, you can also be a judge. Don't you think injustice has been done to me?"

"My God! Miss Honavar!"

"I am perfectly serious," Lalita Honavar said, extending her empty wine glass for a refill.

I filled it up and returned it to her. Antya said, "Excuse me," and went into the bathroom.

"I hope you aren't upset."

"I'm all right. I really shouldn't have brought this up. Our lawyer friend seems to be a trifle upset."

Antya, who was on his way back from the bathroom, overheard this last remark and like a character making his entry on the stage, said on cue, "My mind does not normally get upset. But my stomach sometimes does. Do we have a plain soda?"

I opened a bottle of soda for him.

"If an act of verbal aggression or indiscretion has been committed unknowingly, one can apologize and expect to receive a token punishment. Newspaper editors very often get away by tendering an apology."

"But is teasing a girl so different from a defamation in a newspaper? When editors make mistakes, it is considered to be an occupational hazard. After all one prints opinions or news for the common good of the people. Their intentions are never doubted. But passing remarks about a girl whom one does not even know is like slinging mud at random. There's no question of the common good in this sort of practice shooting."

"You're right in principle. But, in practice, such lighthearted teasing is part of the fun in school and college life. It is not good to ban fun."

"You will soon call ragging fun and rape fun."

"Certainly not. But do you have any objection to calling a joke a joke?"

"It all depends on what makes you laugh. Idi Amin used to find the atrocities he perpetrated on his prisoners very funny."

"What are you trying to say? Is calling you The Full Moon in Winter a moral offence, a heinous crime?"

"First let me ask *him* a question. He is a poet. What do the words suggest?"

"The Full Moon in Winter is like an image in a typical Chinese or Japanese poem. It can imply a number of things."

"In the context of a woman?"

"The full moon or pournima could be a figurative description of a beautiful face."

"And winter?"

"That would depend on the context."

"If the context isn't given, it would make the metaphor suggestive and mysterious."

"One must also consider the country," said Antya. "The winter of Siberia is different from the winter of our Karnataka."

"If the meaning is basically ambiguous it cannot be said that it is only defamatory."

So far Lalita Honavar had been speaking in a quiet restrained tone. Now suddenly she lost her poise. She was like an angry spitting cat as she said, "This is what I call male doubletalk. You can only think of a woman as a plaything whether in poetry or in real life! When you called me The Full Moon in Winter, you implied that I was cold blooded and frigid, a frozen girl. Some of you even called me Miss Iceberg. You were really taking revenge on me for ignoring your covetous male eyes. You ought to realize this at least now that you are past fifty. If I'd met your eyes with mine, replied to your questions, gone around with one of you, I would have been acceptable. You wanted to drag me into your fold at any cost."

The room had become very still. Her venomous outburst had made us tense. When she rose and went to the bathroom, Antya said to me in a low voice, "Hell! It's getting complicated. Beware of the woman. I'm off."

"No you're not. Please stay on. I can't handle this alone."

Miss Honavar returned from the bathroom and said, "I'm really enjoying this. I'm a stranger among you and yet I feel so free. It's as though we were friends at college."

"We didn't have a single girlfriend in college. I've never had one since. He may have – he's travelled all over the world. As for me, I am a simple man. I got married, brought my wife home and settled down right away."

"You didn't have any girlfriends in college?"

"Well, I wasn't swanky and I wasn't rich, I had lofty aims and I wasn't clever, nor was I a sportsman or an actor or a singer. It is not enough in our country to be just a man to be able to have girlfriends."

"I've read novels by that Nemade of yours. He speaks of a category of bachelor men – Kare lok."

"What do you think, is she right?" Antya asked me.

"I haven't read much of Nemade. I only remember his *Kosla*."

"But what about you?" Miss Honavar said, turning to me. "They say women are central to your writings. But I think you make a woman either an animal or a goddess."

"You are dragging me to court, aren't you?"

"Your best friend is a lawyer."

"My friend is unlikely to have read everything I've written. That is why we are friends. He'll defend me if it is anything else. But he will find it difficult to defend my writings. In other words I am defenceless."

"Shall I ask you a question?" said Miss Honavar. "But before that, give me a stiff drink."

I saw Antya grow serious. He looked worried. Nevertheless, I mustered up enough courage to ask, "Will gin do? There isn't much of a choice. Or would you rather have rum? Or brandy?"

"Brandy? I'd love some. Ple-ease."

Ple-ease? That was the limit. I poured out brandy for her in a fresh glass.

"Thanks." She took a small gulp. I gulped down all my gin.

"Ask your question."

"It is a delicate one."

"What can be more delicate than what we have already discussed?"

"You are both married ... You have children, I presume."

"I have a son. He has a son and a daughter."

"The children have come of age?"

"Well, yes. My son's married. I have a grandson who is four years old."

"Your wives have lived happily with you for several years?"

"This our wives alone can say," said Antya.

"Some thirty to thirty five years ago you teased and bestowed on me the title The Full Moon in Winter. But suppose I had at that time responded to one of you and then, as in Hindi films, the acquaintance had grown into a close friendship, would you have married me?"

"That would have been impossible in my case," said Antya,

because I am originally from Karnataka. After all my years in Bombay I speak Marathi like a Maharashtrian, but my English has never been good and I could never have coped with a wife who came from an English medium school."

"Why?"

"Well, I haven't been able to answer back my wife either in Kannada or Marathi. It would be out of the question in English!"

"And what do *you* say?"

"It is a tantalizing question, Miss Honavar," I said. "My English isn't bad. And at that time – I may say that even now you are very, very attractive."

"In the long run no wife is attractive."

"I still find my wife attractive."

"*Sare Jahan se achchaa Hindustan hamara!*"

When he heard this Antya burst out laughing. He too began to sing. "*Hum bulbule hai iske, ye gulsitan hamara ...*"

"You are very sexy, Miss Honavar," I said, "I don't think I could resist you!"

"That's all right in theory. But I am past my childbearing age and yet, not only am I unmarried, I am also a virgin."

The bell rang at this point. I opened the door.

"Hi, Dipi! Oh, Antya! What's on? Are you having a party?"

It was Damu. He was wearing a tie and carrying a bag full of medical samples. Then he saw Lalita Honavar and stopped short.

"Miss Honavar, meet my friend, Damu. He is not a college friend, we met later. Damu, this is Miss Honavar. She was with us at college."

"Hullo!"

"What will you drink, Damu? And what would you like to eat? Everything's on the table."

"Don't bother yourselves. I'll just go in for a wash."

And Damu made straight for the bathroom.

"This is Damu. He's a pharmaceutical salesman, playwright, short story writer, poet and lover of life."

"He's turned up so unexpectedly and so late?"

"All my friends come like that. Punctuality is for business matters."

"It's getting to be a crowd!"

"Damu's a fantastic man."

"And past fifty?"

"All fantastic men are past fifty, Miss Honavar. But what difference does that make?"

Damu returned. "Sorry friends, sorry Miss Honavar. Sorry for the interruption."

"Thank you for the interruption," said Antya, "It was desperately needed."

"Shall we go to the balcony?" Lalita Honavar asked.

We went to the balcony which overlooked the sea. A salty breeze blew in.

"On second thoughts," I said, "I too think I wouldn't have married you."

"Oh, how disappointing! But why?"

"I can't see even now how I could have controlled you."

"Does marriage mean having control over one another?"

"Yes, it is mutual control – a sensible rivalry to authority."

"And I'm not sensible?"

"Sensible people don't remain virgin till they are fifty."

"Why?"

"Virginity is related to the body. The body must age and with age there are changes in what the body means. After menopause a woman is no longer a woman. She doesn't become a man of course, but she becomes just a person."

"And this *person* has no sex life?"

"Of course she has. Human beings never cease to have a sex life. But towards the end it gradually becomes meaningless."

"Meaningless? Is being able to give birth to children the only meaning you attach to a sex life?"

"As I see it, sex can mean two things: One is orgasm or sexual gratification, the other is procreation. The first represents a desire to break free from nature, the second is an assimilation into it.

When it is not possible for you to have a child or when you don't want one, it means you want to be free from nature, be free of any obligation to human society. In the Indian tradition, sex for the sole purpose of self-gratification is regarded as asocial. The sexual union of Shiva and Shakti was responsible for the creation of human society, but Shiva and Shakti still remain absorbed in each other. Their separation will bring the deluge. The end of creation. The regeneration of man depends on the union of the two sexes. If a man and woman do not come together, the cycle of existence will stop as far as man is concerned. But even before we acquire the ability to reproduce, we have, even at a very young age, the rudiments of sexual desire. Even when the reproductive capability is inseparably linked with living. When a woman is past her reproductive age, the age of procreation, she does not lose her sexuality. Have you seen autumn in the colder countries? The leaves take on such vivid colours before they fall. And when they have fallen, the leafless trees continue to stand through the cold snowy winter. They do not die. In the spring they bring out new leaves."

"And you had called me The Full Moon in Winter," she said, "The pournima in winter, a moon shining on a barren landscape when life is ended."

"Sorry, Miss Honavar. But there is really no relation between that remark we made in our youth and what I have just said. Please do not allow the misunderstanding to grow."

"I have not misunderstood anything," said Miss Honavar.

Miss Honavar was seated in the armchair with her eyes closed. Antya had put on Panditji's tape again. He was singing a piece from the Basant raag, *Piya sang khelori.*

"Who is this woman, Dipi?" Damu asked in a confidential undertone, "She's a real peach! Haven't you laid her yet? I think she is up to something! It's just as in a story. Antya told me she was with you at college and that you didn't even know her then. And now she has suddenly turned up on some pretext and has stuck to you. Have fun, Dipi. Shall I take Antya away?"

"Why don't you and Antya escort her home instead? She has her car."

"In that case she can drop us where we can find a taxi."

There was a movement in the armchair. Miss Honavar emptied her glass and looking in our direction said, "Are you conspiring to get rid of me? I don't feel like going home. This is the first time I've been alone in the company of three men."

"Relax!" Damu said. "It's my first experience too, drinking with a single woman in the company of two men."

"Tell me," she said, "Why do you men always get together to have drinks?"

"Brotherhood," Damu said. "Solidarity."

Antya woke up. "Shall I tell you?" he asked, "There are many things that are not to be said in front of women."

"We talk about women among ourselves," Damu said. "That's not something women can understand. Because women never understand what they are from a man's point of view."

"Are you woman haters?"

"Not at all. As a matter of fact I love women."

"Love them or make love to them?" I asked.

"No, I am a bhokto as they say in Bengali, a devotee."

"You are a parambhakta," I said, "A super devotee."

"This party is turning into a fantasy."

"I've heard and also read that when there is a lone woman with several men, she is likely to be gang raped."

There was a glint in Damu's eyes. "Is that your fantasy?"

"Who said that only the body can be raped?" said Miss Honavar. "The mind can also be raped. When we were in college, these people used to call me The Full Moon in Winter. The whole college came to know of it. They used to call me Miss Iceberg!"

"I would have called you Miss Icefruit. You are so juicy."

"Careful Damu!" I muttered.

"But I don't find you cold at all," said Damu. "You look so lovely, so warm. These chaps did not really understand."

"You are flattering me."

"I am complimenting you because I can't help it," said Damu, going towards her. Antya looked very apprehensive. His straightforward, innocent mind could not approve of what was happening.

"You are pulling my leg!"

"I am being pulled into orbit around you," said Damu. And he actually spun round like a medieval knight in an English film and went down on one knee to kiss her hand. But when she started laughing hysterically he was completely bewildered.

"There's something of medieval chivalry still left then," said Miss Honavar.

"Damu was born in the fourteenth century," I said.

"I'm from the twenty second century," she said. "I see little difference between the fourteenth and the twentieth century. There used to be men, they say, in those times."

"You mean there won't be any men at all in the twenty second century?" Antya asked.

"But our remnants will certainly last," said Damu. "Why are you all so concerned about history? Good men are born at all times. Excuse me, I'd like to change into a lungi. I want to sit on the floor." And he picked up his black bag and went inside. When he returned he was wearing a bright red lungi and was carrying a snake charmer's pipe.

"What's this?" I said spotting the snake charmer's pipe in his hand.

"It's a new retailing aid our company has given us. There is a snake in the bag," he announced and opened the bag.

As soon as he started playing the pipe, a snake came out.

Miss Honavar shrieked and ran to me. Holding me in a frightened embrace, she shouted, "Please, ple-ase, put that creature back in the bag."

"This cobra has had its poison removed," said Damu. "He's just an earthworm in disguise. He only *looks* like a snake!"

"Where did you learn to play that thing, Damu?"

"A multinational company trains you well. We were taken to

Khajuraho for our course, and we were put up at the Chandela Hotel for eight days. There were lectures and discussions in the morning, followed by lunch, and then we had the pipe-playing sessions. After that, video shows, then drinks and finally, dinner. Occasionally, we had time off to go look at the erotic sculptures in the temples. It was fun. I put on eight kilos in a week."

And he began to play his pipe again.

"Take that horrible creature away!" Miss Honavar cried out again and again. "Take it away or I shall faint."

Miss Honavar had now been shifted to my bedroom. Bharat Patel who owned the place, had on the wall a print of Velazquez's The Toilette of Venus. A nude Venus is lying asleep on her side, her back to the viewers. She is looking at herself in the mirror. Of course, that was the only way one could have seen her face.

Lalita Honavar was also lying on her side. Though her sari was somewhat disarranged, she was certainly not nude. According to Damu, the drinks had gone to her head.

Antya, however, was of the opinion that I should call a doctor. We hardly knew her and she was over fifty, if anything happened to her, we'd find it difficult explaining the circumstances. Antya must have thought of this as a lawyer, but it was also what commonsense pointed to.

"Whose painting is this?"

"Diego Velazquez! A famous seventeenth century painter."

"Who's the woman?"

"Venus."

"What is it called?"

"The Toilette of Venus."

"The Full Moon in Winter," Miss Honavar mumbled. "The name of that painting is The Full Moon in Winter. Who's hung it there?"

"How are you feeling, Miss Honavar?"

"Fine! Fine! Never felt bet' in m' life, darling. Can I have some more wine?"

She sat up suddenly and looking at me with heavy eyes, said, "So you did bring me into your bedroom finally, didn't you? And there are three of you. There was only this bedroom scene left."

"You had too much drink. You passed out."

"That's what you think. I think I've not had enough. It was the snake that made me faint. Where's that snake gone?"

"He must have got to our head office at Worli. He slipped out of here in the confusion."

"What use is your pipe now?"

"The pipe, too, belongs to the Company. We use it instead of the medical samples nowadays."

"You are a tricky bastard," she said. "But I like you! Get me some wine. Let's all have another drink. Come, get the glasses, the glasses! This bed's very comfortable – we can all fit in quite easily!"

"You mean we should all sleep here?" Damu asked, feeling very happy at the thought.

"The joint family system is out," said Antya.

"Long ago, we little boys and girls used to sleep like that in a line. That's why we had no need for sex education later."

"We are all past fifty," Miss Honavar said. "Sexually speaking, a very different chapter in our life has begun."

"This is called a second adolescence. It is followed by a second childhood and then, a second infancy."

"Here's the wine! Where did these bottles come from?"

"They were kept in reserve. I had left them to be chilled. And here are some nuts."

Damu began to sing,

> Give me no "buts"
> Have cashew nuts –
> O Love, youth goes by ...

"Where did you get that song from?"

"It's a pada from my new play."

"A shwapada or animal rather, considering it's four footed."

"What's the new play called?"

"*Alibaag and the Forty Thieves.*"

"Alibaag?"

"Yes, Alibaag. That's a great place. You get good fish there, and the coastline is beautiful."

"But they say the builders from Bombay have spoilt it now."

"It's a great place I say. Witchcraft everywhere. I met a mantrik there. If you have an enemy, let me know. I'll arrange to give him hydrocele."

"Why hydrocele of all things?"

"He must be fond of playing marbles," said Antya.

"He gave me a couple of enchanted eggs once, this mantrik. Said I should make an omelette of them and give it to the woman I wished to seduce. I brought them home and they broke, and the cat in our building ate them. Now the cat always comes only to our house."

"And if the cat were to have kittens, you would say you are the natural father ..."

"Miss Honavar, do you believe in witchcraft?"

"I didn't. But from now on I'm not going to eat an omelette prepared by someone I don't know."

"My dear chap," Antya said, "It's almost morning. It's two thirty. I'll sleep outside on the settee, or do you have another bedroom?"

"There's one on the other side."

"Then I'm going there. I can't handle late nights any more. Goodnight!"

"Goodnight, Mr Lawyer."

When Antya had gone, Lalita Honavar pulled her legs up on to the bed to sit more comfortably. She took a gulp of wine, looked at Damu, took another gulp, looked at me, then stretched herself.

"Sorry to bother you," she said, "But can you give me something to wear for the night? I think your size will do. A kurta, perhaps? I can do without pyjamas."

I opened the cupboard that faced us. There were two muslin

kurtas and one silk kurta inside – three in all. I placed them before her and said, "Take your pick." She chose a muslin one.

"Come, Dipu, we'll sit outside in the living room.

"Dipu!" Damu whispered. "Go in and enjoy yourself. She has been signalling for some time now. I'll sleep here outside."

The telephone rang.

"Hello. Dilip Chitre here."

"Hello, is Lalita Honavar there?"

It was a woman's voice.

"Hello. Who are you?"

"Geeta Honavar."

"Please hold on."

I was about to go in to call Lalita when she came out herself, with nothing on except the muslin kurta. I was dumbfounded. I wouldn't have been as shocked if she had been completely naked.

"Phone ... There's a phone-call for you ..."

"Who's it?"

"Geeta."

"Geeta? My God! Phoned here? How did she find out?"

"What shall I tell her? Or Will you speak?"

"Tell her to mind her own business. She's always tailing me. Tell her she's made a mistake, that there's no Lalita Honavar here."

I picked up the receiver again.

"Hello."

"She won't take the phone. But let me warn you. She'll get you into trouble. Be careful. Get rid of her before it's too late." Click.

"What did she say?"

"Nothing. She put the receiver down when she heard my voice again."

"Bitch."

"Who was it?"

"Geeta. Geeta Honavar. My sister and my arch enemy!"

"I think she is worried about you."

"Worried! She's always watching me. This is the sister who I said sang classical songs and was culturally very Indian. I seem to be more Western, don't I? That's my father's influence. Geeta's taken after my mother."

"What does she do?"

"She is unmarried like me. There's no lack of money, so we don't have to worry about doing something for a living. Geeta sings occasionally on the radio or at public concerts. We live together. Tormenting me is her chief occupation. She's hated me since we were kids because she isn't good looking. That's why she makes such a fuss about the superiority of Indian culture. It's either yoga or spirituality or else, burning agarbatti – a dozen different fads. Even as she solemnly holds the tanpura, she keeps a close watch on where I go and what I do."

While Lalita spoke it was her body that I saw and was conscious of. She did not look a woman who had crossed fifty. She looked thirty or thirty five. A complexion like the golden kevda flower, clear skin, big eyes, an oval face. She was not very high breasted but tall and comely, with a flat stomach and below the waist, firm buttocks, well proportioned thighs, well moulded calves, only her feet were broad and large like a man's.

"Why are you looking at me like this? Haven't you ever seen a woman's body before?"

"I hadn't seen yours. You look very desirable, Miss Honavar."

"You're not the first man to tell me that. But what's next?"

"Let's see what next," I said in a gruff voice, as I pushed her in the direction of the bedroom.

Just then, Antya shouted from the adjoining bedroom, "Where's the light? Switch on the light, someone. Snake! Snake!"

There was a snake on the bed in the other bedroom, its hood raised and expanded, and Antya was standing against the wall with a pillow in his hand. Lalita, Damu and I stood at the door.

"It did not bite you, did it?"

"It was about to, when I woke up."

"This looks like Damu's snake."

"This doesn't seem to be our Company snake," Damu said, taking a close look. "A snake from our Company has a mark like the figure ten on its hood. It's the new logo of the Company. This one belongs to our competitors. But this one too is without poison. So don't worry."

"Play your pipe, Damu! Play it!"

"The pipe is useless. Snakes are deaf," said Damu. "Don't be afraid, Antya, this cobra belongs to an ayurvedic company."

"Ayurvedic, allopathic, or homeopathic," said Antya, "A cobra is a cobra. It is best to kill it."

"This is a female cobra, a nagin," said Damu, closely examining the snake.

"How do you know?" Miss Honavar asked.

Pinching her cheek and pulling it playfully, Damu said, "It's a female snake as surely as you are a woman. I have never made a mistake about sex so far. I can immediately recognize the female of any species. Even of plants."

"What shall we do now?"

"Well, fetch my bag. I shall lock her up in it – she will make a nice gift for our marketing manager."

As soon as I fetched Damu's bag for him, he caught hold of the snake and stuffed it into his bag.

Flinging away the pillow that he was holding against his chest, Antya said, "What's the time like? It will be impossible to get any sleep after all this."

"Three thirty," I replied. "It's Sunday tomorrow, sleep up to eleven if you like."

"It's going to be difficult to get any sleep, but I'll lie down at least. Sorry I disturbed all of you," he said.

"What's the sorry for? If a female cobra had turned up in our beds, we'd have been just as frightened," I said.

"If a female cobra had turned up in *my* bed, the night would have been most pleasurable," Damu said. "The female of the species is after all the female of the species!"

Shuddering, Miss Honavar said, "How is it you don't feel repelled, don't feel frightened?"

I placed my open palms against Miss Honavar's waist and said,

"Come Miss Honavar, we really need to sleep, all of us."

Damu actually winked at me and said, "Good morning, Dilip! Good night, Miss Honavar!"

Finally, like Velasequez's Venus, Lalita Honavar shed all her clothes. But as Antya, snoring away in the neighbouring bedroom, has a very thorough knowledge of the part of the Indian Penal Code which deals with pornography, and though it doesn't matter if I am punished for a crime I did not commit (my friend after all being my lawyer) I am, at least for the present, refraining from describing our boisterous lovemaking.

The story is neither a long short story nor a novel, it is only a prelude. The characters and situations of The Full Moon in Winter pass from truth to falsehood, from the art of love to poultry keeping, from poultry keeping to poetry, and manifest themselves in every field. To consider them purely imaginary would be an affront to Antya and Damu, but I am a law-abiding writer ...

The phone rang again.

Now who could it be so early in the morning? Annoyed, I left Lalita at the door of the bedroom and went to the phone. On the other side Damu lay snoring peacefully.

"Hello?"

"I am Geeta Honavar."

"Speak."

"What's the idea?"

"What about?"

"Don't pretend you don't know. I am talking about Lalita."

"Madam, I think you're making a mistake. Who is Lalita? What number do want?"

"I know your voice. I had dialled this very number sometime ago and you had answered. You went to call Lalita then and later the line was cut. I tried to ring up again but I kept getting a cross-connection."

"What exactly do you want?"

"Lalita has lost her mental balance and needs psychiatric help. She tried to commit suicide last week. She has developed an obsession for the company of men and she gets violent all of a sudden. Her moods change unexpectedly, so please send her back. It's best if you bring her back yourself. Let's avoid complications as far as possible. I am sure you have understood the gravity of the situation. Good-bye!" Click.

Lalita was standing behind me.

"It was Geeta again, wasn't it? I'll tell you what she must have said, Lalita is not in her senses. With men. Attempts suicide. Am I right?"

"How did you know?"

"I know my sister only too well. She's told our uncle the same thing. He did not believe her, of course, but I've felt a revulsion for her since then. Did *you* think I was mad?"

From the darkness Damu was heard: "Lali, Lali, my dear, you are mad, are you? What're you waiting for? He is a jolly good lay! He won't disappoint you. Have a good time. God will bring you together! Go, you have my blessings."

"Damu?"

"Don't worry Dipi, I've followed everything. This is all Jhaveri's doing."

"Jhaveri who?"

"The great grandson of Beelzebub."

"And who is Beelzebub?"

"Lucifer! Satan himself, Allah give him peace."

"But Damu, how does Jhaveri come in?"

"My dear chap, he's always watching us. He's our student, he studies us – he is trying to evolve into us!"

"Who are you talking about? I don't understand. The phone call was from my sister. How is she connected with Jhaveri?"

"You won't understand. Jhaveri is practising telepathy at the moment. But without their guru, those who are struggling to acquire extra sensory powers get very confused. Their experiments go haywire. Only the other day, this Jhaveri had sent a woman to me."

"Sent a woman to you?"

"It's all very complicated. Actually, Jhaveri had done an experiment to make her come to him. But the image he has of himself in his own mind is really that of us. He cannot recognize himself. And so there was a kind of telepathic cross connection and thanks to the experiment he performed to seduce her, the woman came to me."

"Who was the woman?"

"The daughter-in-law of a well-known goldsmith."

"What did you do then, Damu?"

"Well, what could I do? When I saw the state she was in, I knew that instead of going to Jhaveri she had come to me. I felt pity ..."

"For whom? For Jhaveri or for her?"

"For Satan, for Freud, for Mahatma Gandhi – for everybody. Because of their queer influence, Jhaveri's experiments in magic are always going wrong, yes, but they are never wasted because the two of us are deep down in his mind."

"But what has all this to do with Geeta Honavar?"

Damu laughed loudly. "Well, Jhaveri must have started off an experiment to seduce Geeta Honavar. But he missed his mark, and in two instances at that. Instead of Geeta it was Lalita who came to you. The telepathy traffic has grown enormously of late and seems to be quite cursed to be constantly getting hooked to the wrong frequency. However that may be, his experiment has harmed no one. Lalita's meeting with you has taken place in line with a deeper law of nature, or how could I have thought of coming here so unexpectedly? I'd been invited to a late party by some Gujarati friends and frankly, I had completely forgotten about it. But Dipi, I thought you might be in trouble. Something guided me here."

"What the hell!" I said, surprised.

"We are men who move in a wonderland," said Damu. "We must get used to it now. What use is realism after fifty?"

"Please!" Lalita Honavar said to me, "Let's go back to the bedroom. At least you can tell me a nice story!"

"Go to bed, children," said Damu.

Lying by my side, clinging to me, Lalita Honavar listened to my story. My voice had dissociated itself from the rest of me and sounded like a digital recording. I too was listening to my own story as I lay there by Lalita's side.

"It happened in the fourteenth century, a brahmin set out for Alandi on a pilgrimage to Dyaneshwar's samadhi ..."

Lalita began to run her finger over the hair on my chest. "What kind of story is this?" she asked, "I come from an English medium school."

Her French perfume was beginning to afflict me. My voice came to a halt.

"Gently ... it's the first time."

I began to fondle her body gently. She took off all her clothes. I began to satisfy the yearnings of her delicate body in various ways. While this quiet low key lovemaking was in progress, the doorbell rang.

Reluctantly, but hurriedly, I drew on my trousers and went out without my shirt. Lalita shut the bedroom door from the inside. I switched on the light and opened the door, and was shocked.

"I'm Geeta Honavar. May I come in?"

"Uhn? Of course! Come, come in."

Geeta Honavar had dark skin. She was short and somewhat stodgy, but her eyes were light and green in colour. She was wearing a sari of the purest white.

"Where is Lalita?"

"Lalita? She isn't here."

"I can smell her!" She said, sniffing hard. "Fragrance of *Opium* – that French perfume. It can only be her!"

Damu sat up. Looking intently at her, he said, "I've seen you somewhere, Miss Honavar. Do you recognize me?"

Geeta Honavar looked confused. She hadn't expected Damu or his question which was like a challenge.

"Ah, yes, I remember," Damu went, "Weren't you a patient last year at Dr Jeevanlal Patel's hospital? I think you were to go through some kind of operation. I was chatting with Dr Patel when you arrived."

Geeta's face turned white, she began to tremble.

"Dr Patel, Damu?"

"Ah there is one, the well-known abortionist!"

"You are making a mistake."

"I remember it distinctly," said Damu, "But never mind that. Will you have a drink? We've been drinking. One of us has retired. You see, we were arguing about what it means exactly when you say a woman has been raped. Our friend is a lawyer ..."

Geeta Honavar stood up and began to inch towards the door. Damu too got up and began to move towards her. She was terribly frightened.

"You are so luscious!" Damu said. "Miss Honavar, you look very sexy."

"Get away from me! Don't touch me!" she screamed, turning red and purple. "I'm warning you ... I'll complain to the police!"

"Easy, Miss Honavar, don't be nervous, Miss Honavar. See how uneasy you've made me!" Damu said as if he were reciting a poem. "Drone ... Drone ... Drone ... I'm a big male bee and you my lotus flower! I yearn to lie in the pollen bed of your pet'lous bower ..."

Geeta Honavar opened the door and stepping out, shut it with a bang.

"Shhh!" Damu said, hushing me up. "Dipi, I think Lalita's gone to Antya's room."

"Damn surprising!"

"What's so surprising about that? Antya must have her in his arms by now."

"Holding her? He'd much rather be holding a brief for lawful behaviour. Surely, you don't expect him to be kissing a woman other than his wife?"

"But after all he's only made of flesh and blood, a man like you and me. Won't he give a proper welcome to a woman who's come on her own to him? Dipi, I think we should have a little more liquor. Is there some fleshy stuff that I could eat?"

"Fleshy? You'll find a chicken leg and a piece of pomfret on the table."

Damu went off enthusiastically to the table. I sat on the sofa and emptied my glass, then lay on my side and fell asleep.

D amu shook me vigorously till I woke up. Antya was standing petrified by my side.

"Dipi! A ghastly thing has happened! Lalita has jumped down from the balcony! And she was naked!"

"O my God! How? When did it happen?"

"She was sleeping by my side – soundly. I was awake though. Then she woke up, stretched herself and said, I love all three of you, I shall become a man in my next life and you three can become women. And she promptly jumped down from the balcony!"

"It's going to be very difficult proving all this in court," said Antya in a low voice. "It's *finis* for the three of us."

First published in Marathi as "The Full Moon in Winter" (title of the original story) in *Gulmohar*, Diwali issue, 1989.

best of the
♨90s♨

**SUNDARA RAMASWAMY**

Reflowering

"Reflowering" is witty, engaging and enormously positive. A very humane story, that brings to mind the fact that while a machine may increase the efficiency it can be no match to the thinking, feeling, caring human being.  — **Adoor Gopalakrishnan**

Amma was lying on the cot and I was curled up on the floor right next to it. Amma and I were free to get up as late as we pleased. We had made it our habit over the years. We had to put up a battle of sorts to win it. Ours is a family that takes pride in the fact that we safeguard the dharma of the early riser – for generations now, we've all bathed before sunrise. But then, Amma and I were invalids. Amma had asthma and I suffered from joint pains. Both could create problems early in the morning.

Outside, there were sounds of the horse shaking its mane, of its bells jangling. The horse buggy was ready. This meant that Appa had picked up the bunch of keys for his shop. It also meant that the clock was inching towards eight thirty. He would now put on his slippers. Kweech. Kweech. Then, once downstairs, the abrupt impatient sound of the umbrella opening, closing. The daily umbrella-health-test, that.

The door opened slightly. A thin streak of sunlight pranced into the room, a shifting glass pipe of light, dust swirling inside it. Appa! I see him in profile – one eye, spectacles, half a forehead streaked with vibhuti and a dot of chandanam paste, golden yellow, topped by a vivid spot of red kumkumam.

"Boy! Ambi! Get up!" Appa said.

I closed my eyes. I did not move a limb. As if I were held captive by deep sleep.

"Ai! Get up. You good-for-nothing," Amma said. "Appa's calling."

On the sly I looked at Appa. He looked affectionate, even gentle. As if I were being roused from heavy slumber, I opened my eyes with pretended difficulty.

"Get ready, Ambi. Eat and then go to Aanaipaalam," said Appa. "Go and bring Rowther to the shop straightaway. I'll send the buggy back for you."

Sundara Ramaswamy won the Katha Award for Creative Fiction in 1991, for this story. India Today (Tamil) received the Journal Award for first publishing this story in Tamil. The Katha Translation Award went to S Krishnan.

This story first appeared in English translation in Katha Prize Stories 1, 1991.

We thank S Krishnan, our nominating editor, for choosing this story for us.

I looked at Appa, then at Amma. I had told her about the squabble between Appa and Rowther in the shop the previous day.

"Can you or can you not manage without him?" asked Amma. "This farce has gone on far too long," she said. "Making up one day and parting the next!"

Appa's face reddened. It seemed as if, if it grew any redder, blood might start dribbling from the tip of his nose.

"Onam is round the corner. *You* can come to the shop and make the bills," he screamed. Anger twisted his lips, slurred and flattened out the words.

"Is Rowther the only person in this whole world who knows how to make bills?" asked Amma.

"Shut your mouth!" yelled Appa. Abruptly he turned to me. "Get up, you!" he ordered.

I sprang up from my bed and stood taut as a strung bow.

"Go. Do what I told you to," he growled.

As if someone unseen had tugged at the wheels attached to my feet, I moved swiftly out of the room.

I heard the horse buggy leave the house.

I got ready in double quick time. What briskness! I wore – as I usually didn't – a veshti over my halfpants, and a full sleeved shirt, all in the hope that it would make me speak up with some confidence. I didn't feel my usual anger with Appa. I didn't feel sad either. It seemed as if even some little fondness seeped through. Poor thing! He had got himself into a fix. On an impulse, he'd spoken harshly to Rowther. He could have been more calm. Now, if a person is merely short tempered, one can talk of calmness. But if he is *anger personified?*

Excited by this paradox, I went and stood before Amma. I looked her straight in the face and said, "If he is anger personified where is the question of calmness?" Amma laughed. Almost at once, she made her face stern and, "Smart, aren't you?" she asked. "Now, if you are a clever boy, you'll go take Rowther to the shop." Placing her right hand over her heart she said, "Tell him whatever *he* may have said, I apologize for it."

I went and climbed into the buggy.

I too thought that we could not manage the Onam festival sales without Rowther. Who could do sums like him? He was lightning quick in mental arithmetic. Five people sitting in a row, with paper and pencils, would not be equal to one Rowther and his brain. Remarkable. Even regular buyers who flocked round him to have their bills tallied were amazed. "Is this a mere human brain?" many wondered aloud. "If the man can be this fast just by listening to the figures, what would he not do if he'd been granted sight?" And to think that Rowther has only studied up to the third class. That's two grades less than Gomathi who works in the shop, fetching and cleaning.

The dispute between Appa and Rowther had started mildly enough the previous evening. "Look here, Rowther, what are you going to do if you let your debts keep mounting like this?" Appa asked. Rowther had chosen all the clothes he wanted, piled them up by his side, before thinking of asking Appa for credit. It was quite clear that Appa did not like this.

"What can I do, ayya? My house is full of women. My sons are useless. My sons-in-law are useless. Four sons, four daughters-in-law, eight granddaughters, eight grandsons. How many is that? Just one piece of cloth each, and the cost goes up."

Appa was staring at Rowther, as if thinking, The man is getting out of hand. I must cut him to size. Right away.

"Kolappa, wrap up the clothes and give me the bill," said Rowther.

How dare he take the things before permission had been granted? Appa's face reddened. "It is not possible for me to give you credit this time," he said.

"So, you're saying you don't want our relationship to continue, no, ayya? All right. Girl, take me home."

Rowther stood up. Gomathi took his right arm and placed it on her left shoulder. They went down the steps. When the shop closed in the evening, he would usually look in the direction of my father and take permission to leave. That particular evening he did not take permission. That is, he had taken leave.

I thought I would first pick up Gomathi and take her with me to Rowther's house. That would perhaps lessen his hurt. But Gomathi was not at home. "Rowther had sent word that he was not coming. She's just left for the shop," her mother said.

I took a shortcut through the grove, and reached Rowther's house through a narrow lane. A tiled house, the roof low. In the front yard, there was a well on the right hand side, its parapet wall stark, unpainted, broken. Velvet moss sprang around it in bright patches. Stone steps led to the house. A strip of gunny bag hung from the main door.

"It's me, Ambi!" I announced my arrival loudly.

A little girl came out followed by another who was obviously her twin.

"Who is it, child?" came Rowther's voice from inside the house.

"It's me, Ambi," I said.

"Come! Come," said Rowther. His voice bubbled with happiness.

I pushed aside the sack curtain and went inside. The floor had been swabbed smooth with cowdung. Rowther was sitting cross-legged, like a lord. His arms reached out for me. "Come, come," his mouth kept saying.

I went and knelt in front of him. He put his arms around me. His eyes stared and stared, as if trying to recapture the vision they had lost long ago. He pressed me down by my shoulders, dragged me towards him and sat me down beside him. His emotions seemed to overwhelm him.

"Ah! You seem to be wearing a veshti today!" he said.

"Just felt like it."

"What's the border like?"

"Five striped."

"Just like Ayya, uhn? The boys in the shop tell me that you look just like your father, too. It is my misfortune that I can't see you."

He ran his fingers over my face, my nose, my mouth, my neck, my eyes, my ears, my forehead. "Everything in place, thank the Lord." He laughed.

I thought that this was the right moment to tell him why I had come. But the words stuck in my throat, as if held there by an unseen hand.

"Amma ..." I started to say, making a tentative start.

Rowther interrupted me. "How is amma's health now?"

"As usual."

"I have Thuthuvalai, Khandankattri leghiyam. No better medicine for asthma. Only, Ayya likes to see English labels on his medicine bottles. I don't have English here. Only medicine," he said, enjoying his own joke hugely.

This was the right moment to tackle him.

"Amma wants me to take you to the shop. She wants me to tell you that *she* is very sorry if Appa has said anything to hurt you. You are not to misunderstand him. She says please don't turn down her request."

Rowther's face visibly brightened. He raised his hands in salute. "Amma, you are a great woman," he called out. "Get up, let's go to the shop at once," he said.

That year the sales during Onam were very good. Rowther was in his element. With great elan he supervised the shop boys who constantly jostled around him. He looked like Abhimanyu in the Mahabharata fighting a whole battalion, single handedly. He would state the price as soon as the cost and quantity of the material were mentioned to him. Only the good Lord knew what spark it was in his brain, what genius that did not need even a minute to calculate? A brain that could multiply and total up the cost of sixteen different items in a trice to announce, "Items sixteen. Grand total – one thousand four hundred fourteen rupees twenty five paise," How could that be called an average brain? Even if the whole thing were written down on the blackboard, I would have easily taken half an hour to work it out. But for him, answers slipped forth like lightning. He had never till now made a single mistake. Amma has told me that in the early years of their association, Appa used to sit up half the night, checking Rowther's calculations. It seems he'd say, "That man is getting beside himself. I must find at least an error or two." But he never could. He just lost a good night's sleep.

One day, a cart drawn by a single bullock, heavily curtained on both sides, stopped in front of the shop. From inside came the wailing of women and children.

"Sounds like the females from my household," Rowther said.

Rowther's house had come up for public auction! Apparently the amina was taking all the household things and flinging them on to the street.

Rowther started crying like a child and called on god to help him out. Even as he was emoting, Kolappan came with a bill saying, "Forty five metres and seventy centimetres at thirteen rupees and forty five paise." Rowther stopped his keening for a moment and said to him, "Write this down, six hundred fourteen rupees and sixty six paise." He turned to my father who was at the cash counter and sobbed. "Ayya, I have to pay the court the loan and the interest on it, more than five thousand rupees. Where will I go for the money?"

Appa took Rowther in the horse buggy to see a lawyer.

Rowther did not show up for work the next day. The shop assistant Kolappan said he had with his own eyes seen Rowther, reciting the bills in Chettiar's cloth shop.

"What injustice! I have just come back after paying the court the entire amount for his debts. He's let me down, the ungrateful wretch!" Appa shouted.

Kolappan also whipped himself into a fury. "He knows how to calculate, but he's a senseless idiot. Wait, I'll go this minute and drag him here by his hair," he said as he jumped onto his bicycle.

Appa sat down on the floor, devastated. He started to mumble. "This is a wicked world," he said. "These days you can't even trust your own mother."

In a little while, Kolappan returned. Rowther was sitting behind him, on the carrier. He marched a stone-like Rowther to the cash counter.

"I lost my head, ayya," said Rowther as he stood before Appa, his hands folded in supplication.

"A time will come when you will be cut down to size," said Appa.

"Please don't say such things ayya," pleaded Rowther. "Come work for me and I'll pay your debts, the Chettiar said. And I lost my head."

Appa only repeated, "The time will come when you will be cut down to size."

And, surprise of surprises, things soon happened that made it look as if Appa was going to be right after all. When Appa returned from Bombay that year after seeing his wholesalers, he brought back a small machine and showed it to Amma. "This can do calculations," he said.

"A machine?"

"It can."

Amma made up sum. Appa pressed a few keys. The machine gave the answer.

I quickly worked it out on a piece of paper. "The answer is correct, Amma!" I shouted.

"Have they transformed Rowther's brain into a machine?" Amma asked.

That whole day I kept trying out the calculator. That night, I kept it by my side when I slept. I gave it the most difficult sums I could think of. Its every answer was right. I remembered something Gomathi had once told me. "Thatha! How can you do sums in a nimit?" she had asked Rowther, mixing up as she always did, the Tamil and the common English word. It seems Rowther had said, "Child, I have three extra nerves in my brain." Now, how did those extra nerves get inside this machine? I couldn't control my excitement.

I showed the calculator to Gomathi. She also worked out many many sums.

"Even I am getting it all right," she said, "This machine is more cunning than Thatha!"

One evening Rowther was totalling up for the day. Gomathi was sitting there, the calculator balanced on her lap, checking out his calculations. At one point, very impulsively she said, "You are correct, Thatha."

"Are you telling me I am right?" asked Rowther.

"I have worked it out," said Gomathi.

"Hmm," said Rowther. "I'll give you a sum. Answer."

Rowther gave her a sum. Gomathi gave the right answer. He tried sum after sum on her. She had the correct answer each time. Rowther turned pale. "Dear God. I am so dumb I cannot understand anything," he muttered.

"I'm not doing the sums, Thatha," said Gomathi. "It's the machine."

She stuffed the calculator into his hands.

Rowther's hands shook as he took the calculator. His fingers trembled. He touched the whole front portion of the calculator, the whole back.

"Is *this* doing the sums?" he asked again.

"Yes," said Gomathi.

"You keep it yourself," he said as he thrust it back at her.

After this, Rowther was a very quiet man indeed. Words failed him. He remained in a state of stupor, leaning against the wall. That day, Gomathi and I took care of all the billing. After a long time, Gomathi dug her finger into his thigh and asked, "Thatha, why don't you say something, Thatha?" But he said nothing even to that.

He kept coming to the shop regularly but he looked and acted like a walking corpse. It seemed as if all the laughter, happiness, backchat, teasing, sarcasm, had dropped off him. His voice was slow, hesitant. Even his body looked thinner.

Appa had stopped asking him to do the bills.

One afternoon, it was a busy time in the shop. Murugan had a pile of cut pieces with him. I was working out the cost. Suddenly, Rowther interrupted him, "What did you say was the price of poplin?"

Murugan stopped calling out and looked at Rowther's face, "Fifteen rupees and ten paise per metre."

"Wrong. Get the material out and look – it is sixteen rupees and ten paise per metre."

Appa got up. He came and stood next to Rowther.

Murugan's face fell as he checked the price. "You are right," he mumbled.

"You have sold ten metres. You could have lost ten rupees. Are you here to give away ayya's money to everyone who comes in from the street?"

"So, you know the price?" Appa asked Rowther.

"Only a memory, ayya."

"Do you remember all the prices?"

"It is god's will," said Rowther.

"What is the price of the smallest towel then?" asked Appa.

"Four rupees and ten paise."

"And the biggest one?"

"Thirty six rupees and forty paise."

Appa kept on asking. The answers kept coming.

Appa looked amazed. He could not believe his ears. He took a deep breath. He could not help doing so.

"If that's so, you do one thing. When bills are being made, please check the prices."

"I will do my best, ayya," said Rowther. Then he looked up and said, "Oh, by the way, have you paid your electricity bill, ayya? Today is the last date for payment."

"Oh, no!" said Appa, calling out to Kolappan.

Rowther said, "He hasn't come today, ayya."

"How do you know?" asked Appa.

"Everybody has a voice, a smell. Today I missed Kolappan's voice, his smell," said Rowther, and then he called out to Murugan.

"Yesterday he told a customer that we had no double veshtis. Please reprimand him," Rowther said.

"I don't understand," said Appa.

"Ayya, you put out ten double veshtis for sale. Weren't only seven sold? There should be three remaining, shouldn't there?"

Appa asked for the veshtis to be brought.

Sure enough there were three unsold.

Rowther let a sardonic smile play on his face. He said to Murugan, "Oh Lord Muruga, you merrily send customers away by telling them we don't have what we do actually have. Are we here for business or for charity?"

That evening Rowther moved away from the bill-making section and went and sat close to Appa.

"If I am by your side I will be more helpful, ayya," he said and without missing a beat, "And if you increase the speed of the fan a little, yours truly will also get some breeze."

Appa gave the appropriate order.

"It is time to pay advance income tax, ayya. Shouldn't you see your auditor?" asked Rowther.

"Yes, I must go see him," said Appa.

It was time to close the shop.

"Ayya, you had wanted to get some medicine for amma. Have you bought it, yet?"

"I'll buy it."

Appa was tugging at the locks to check if they had been locked properly.

"Ayya, you were saying that your mother's tithi was due soon. Why not ask Murugan to notify the priest on his way home?"

"Good idea," said Appa.

The employees left one by one.

Gomathi took Rowther's hand, placed it on her shoulder and started moving.

"Won't you be doing the bills any more, Thatha?"

"Ibrahim Hassan Rowther is no longer a mere adding machine. He is now the manager. It is god's will," Rowther replied.

First published in Tamil as "Vikasham" in the Tamil edition of *India Today*, January 31 – February 5, 1990.

best of the
90s

**M T VASUDEVAN NAIR**

Little Earthquakes

"Little Earthquakes" makes us believe in the supernatural in the most natural manner. The thin margin between the real and the unreal vanishes in this remarkably crafted story. Even ghosts keep their individual identity. The dream trips of a lonely child are so convincing that the reader tends to take it for real.

**– Adoor Gopalakrishnan**

L isten. I must tell you something. It is really interesting. How fearfully they talk about her, how scared they sound. I don't always understand what they say but ... even I believe them sometimes.

"She'll pierce you with her damshtra, that fierce canine tooth of hers and grrr ... she'll suck all your blood in one go. And your bones? She'll chew them up with her giant molars and spit them out."

And who is this she? Why, it is poor kunjathaal, the yakshi. They say she comes twice every day: At ucchakkaanam, and once again at midnight. They say, You can see her walking on the upper slope of the parambu.

Ucchakkaanam is that time of day which begins when Amma lies down in the kitchen for a nap after she's handed out the rice kanji to the servants and ends when Valiamma, my mother's elder sister, gets up to make the afternoon tea. It is called ucchakkaanam in our home. God knows what language that is!

It is at that time that Akkara Mutthashi – the grandmother who has come from the hamlet across the river to live with us in her old age – goes for a stroll in the parambu. She picks leaves and roots. Mutthashi alone knows which are medicinal. Before she dies she must pass on the secret to a little girl in the family, the kutty she likes best. Who else but me!

When Mutthashi became bedridden I started going alone to the parambu, when there was no one around to stop me. Amma and Valiamma say that it must have been then that some evil spirit possessed me. And there is this Thekkukaran Ravunni Nair to fan the flame. "All this trouble started when this cursed old hag came here," he says, putting the blame squarely on Mutthashi.

But when I go out I only see this other witch who walks stealthily

---

M T Vasudevan Nair won the Katha Award for Creative Fiction in 1992, for this story. *India Today* (Malayalam) received the Journal Award for first publishing this story in Malayalam.

The Katha Translation Award went to D Krishna Ayyar and Raji Subramaniam.

This story first appeared in English translation in *Katha Prize Stories 2*, 1992.

We thank Sujatha Devi, our nominating editor, for choosing this story for us.

through the parambu. No one knows about her, but me. She is none other than Valiamma's precious daughter. Sarojini Edathi. People don't know about her Celestial lover either, the gandharvan who waits for her on the steps of the Nambudiri's outer pond, fishing with line and tackle.

At ucchakkaanam every day I also see the one who stands at the wooden grille in the western wing of the house, all excited, gesticulating to Nanikutty who wanders into the parambu on the pretext of grazing her goats. It's my brother. If you ask me, Ettan is the one who's possessed. But who'll believe me?

And she who sits drying her hair in the inner courtyard ... She drives me away as soon as she sees me. She won't let me even peep into the large books filled with photographs of cinema stars that she devours every day. That woman thinks she's something great. She's just three years older than me, and my own sister too. But what's the use? She has no time for me.

One day, at ucchakkaanam, I was taking a stroll in the parambu. And ... There was someone under the mango tree. At once I knew this was the yakshi they'd been talking about.

I wanted to run but my feet wouldn't move. I wanted to scream but no sound would come out of me. I closed my eyes tight and chanted "Arjunan, Phalgunan, Arjunan, Phalgu ..."

I heard a soft voice.

"Janakikutty."

It had a strange fondness in it. I liked the way she called me by my full name. Others call me Jatti.

I opened my eyes slowly. Kunjathaal was standing next to me.

You've seen the Athemmar girl, haven't you, she who was married off to that Kunnamkulam boy? Well, Kunjathaal looked exactly like that. A white mundu with the traditional kara and kuri, a white blouse, a white cloth around her shoulder. She had a red

---

Except in towns, the pattern in Kerala is one of houses surrounded by groves and woods, ponds and, usually a serpent mound. This area is called **parambu**.

spot of chaandu on her forehead. Studs in her ears. A necklace of sovereigns around the neck.

"Why has Janakikutty come alone?" she asked.

I kept quiet.

"Why doesn't Janakikutty's Mutthashi come nowadays?"

I couldn't take my eyes off her mouth as she talked. I told myself that I should not show her that I'm frightened. So I asked her as if I was not at all scared, "Where is your damshtra?"

The Athemmarkutty burst into laughter. Ah, what pretty teeth! She said, "The damshtra grows big only when we have a prey. But it scared everyone away. That's why we have no one to play with."

In the rear slopes of the parambu there is a dilapidated outhouse. A servant used to stay there. Around it is a thicket of palm trees. Yakshi went and sat there, took out betel leaves and nuts from the folds of her mundu, tucked them between her molars and started chewing.

I looked longingly at her. Yakshi glanced at me as she said, "Small children shouldn't chew betel."

I collected seven small smooth pebbles. We sat there and played my favourite game, kothengkallu. You should see Yakshi playing! How easily she scooped up four, five stones at each throw. Naturally, it was Kunjathaal who won. That is what Yakshi likes me to call her.

"Tomorrow, Janakikutty, you win."

She smiled. What if I lose? At least I have someone to play with.

Yakshis are so true to their word. If my edathi says, "I'll give it to you tomorrow," it means she's putting me off. She won't give it to me. But yakshis are not like that. And the next day, it was I who won.

Every day at dusk, Mutthashi teaches me to say my prayers. This has started recently, after she heard my mother say, "At least this much good can come from this good-for-nothing hag."

I have not seen my real Mutthashi, that is, Amma's and Valiamma's mother. She died years ago. This Akkara Mutthashi is my real

Mutthashi's younger sister. Amma and Valiamma, when talking about this Mutthashi, always say, "It is due to this hag's character that her children didn't look after her. Etta!" Etta is their own language of abuse. And when this Mutthashi was laid up in bed Amma moaned, "What problems! Now I have to wait on this wretched old hag."

That evening I told Mutthashi about Yakshi and how I played kothengkallu with her.

"Shhh ... Don't tell this to anyone," Mutthashi warned. "I know these yakshis. None of them will harm you, kutty," she whispered in my ears.

When we got bored with kothengkallu, Yakshi and I would roam all over the parambu. It was then that I saw Karineeli. You know that parapoodam that comes dancing in the Velakali temple festival. And you must have seen Kali who comes to sweep our courtyard and collect the cowdung. Kali looks just like the parapoodam and this Karineeli is a younger version of our Kali. Karineeli wears no blouse, only necklaces made of stones and beads. Her teeth are black. That may be because she chews betel.

Karineeli was standing beneath the kanjira tree. I didn't know who she was. Kunjathaal was angry. She muttered, "Hmm ...! That Karineeli!"

Yakshi and Karineeli stood glaring at each other. I have seen Amma and Valiamma staring at each other like that. This was much more frightening. I feared war. But nothing happened.

"Why does thampuratti not let me join her game?" Neeli asked. My friend Kunjathaal grimaced, then nodded her head. "Okay. Come."

Karineeli drew a game board on the ground. She brought broken tiles. And the three of us sat there and played vattu.

When I told all this to Mutthashi that evening she patted me

---

There are many other-worldly characters who people Janakikutty's world. **Kunjathaal** and **Athemmar** are derivations from the word "Akathullaval," or the "lady inside," meaning a Nambudiri Brahmin woman. "Kunju" mean kutty or child. While, **brahmarakshas** is the spirit of a Brahmin, **Karineeli** and **parapoodam** are the spirits of lower caste persons. In temple festivals, a man wearing a dark mask plays the part of parapoodam.

**Thampuratti:** literally means queen. All upper caste women were addressed thus.

and said, "Nothing wrong with you, kutty. No evil will befall you."

One day when we were walking through the compound Kunjathaal showed me the brahmarakshas. It was standing on that dilapidated platform on which we had played kothengkallu. You've seen Kunju Nambudiri who died, haven't you? Imagine Kunju Nambudiri grown three times as tall. The brahmarakshas was exactly like that.

"If we don't go near it, not even for a friendly chat, it won't do us any harm," Kunjathaal said.

As a matter of fact it did not even look at us. Unlike those other friends of Neeli – Parakutty, Karikutty and Kallaadimutthan who always hid in the thicket and peeped at us. Sometimes they dared to inch towards us but one stare from Kunjathaal would make them scurry back into their holes!

One day, a poisonous thorn pierced my foot. The wound was deep. Neeli got angry and started abusing Kallaadimutthan. "If the wound turns septic and Kutty suffers ... I'll ... You ..."

Next day there was not even the pain of an ant bite. These people are so true to their word.

I used to sleep with my Mutthashi but now I sleep at the foot of Amma's bed, next to my sister. Edathi doesn't like this. She goes to sleep early, except on those days when Sarojini Edathi joins us. Then they jabber away till Amma comes.

I don't sleep well these nights. It's not a sickness like these people say. The reason is a secret. Shall I tell you why? It is jealousy. Envy of Kunjathaal and Neeli who could wander around and play even at night.

Once I saw them walking through the plantain grove munching something. I went to the window and called out softly. "Kunjathaal ... Neeli!" But they didn't hear me at all. What friends!

It was then that my mother woke up and what an earthquake there was! She lit the lamps. Everyone came running. Mutthashi also came, dragging her frail frame, grabbling the walls for support. Amma shrieked, "We have enough troubles, you old hag! Don't add to them. If you should fall down, collapse ... Maaranam."

Paniker was sent for. He was a clever man. He arranged cowries on the floor, studied the indications and told them all about my playing with Kunjathaal and Neeli – at least that's what they told me. But shall I tell you how they were fooled by him? When he said that Thekkanchovva was also with us, these people believed him at once. That's where Paniker made a mistake.

Paniker sent a hundred and one rupees through Ravunni Nair. An offering to the goddess Anakkara Bhagavathy. Good. May Bhagavathy enjoy the gift.

But, believe me, Thekkanchovva has never come to play with us. Or Vadakkanchovva. Even if they come, we shall not ask them to join us. How do we know what kind of people they are?

At times Amma would feel sad. Sometimes she'd be angry. I've heard her mutter so many times, "What if somebody falls ill? What if somebody dies? The father of my children, what does he care?"

But how can Achhan come here every now and then leaving his job in the tea estate at Valpara. Ettan has been there once. He says if they bring in even one basket of tea leaves that are not tender enough, Achhan rejects the whole lot. Even while processing the leaves Achhan has to be there. If Achhan doesn't supervise these things then complaints will pour in from shopkeepers – "Is this tea or is it dust?" and the customers will grumble, "This tea tastes like tamarind water."

It was when he recruited a woman on the pretext of needing an extra hand on the estate that Achhan lost his head. That is what Amma says. If this urvashi tries any of her tricks on Achhan, I will tell Kunjathaal. If I haven't done so yet it's because when she gets angry her damshtra comes out, and then it won't be this urvashi alone who'll get hurt. Achhan will too.

Even when I'm quiet, Edathi and Sarojini stare at me. I don't like it. When I stare back at them they run away. They are a little afraid of me. Aren't they?

Every day even now I go to Mutthashi after my head bath.

Mutthashi rubs rasnadi powder on my head. So vigorously that it hurts a little. Then she presses her finger, still smelling of the powder, to my nostril. To prevent my catching cold.

My school is about an hour's walk from home. It seems Achhan had written to say that I shouldn't walk down to school. Amma and Edathi seem to have agreed. If I go walking people will see me and what will happen to their prestige then!

If they'd asked me, I could have told them that there is a shortcut. How many times have Kunjathaal, Neeli and I walked or run through the western end of our grove to Asari's parambu near the bridge. I don't know why people foist fake diseases on me.

But now they are on the look out for someone to come and teach me at home. And they have clamped another restriction on me: No going to the parambu, noon or no noon.

I told Kunjathaal when she came near the deserted snake mound that day. So Kunjathaal and Neeli started coming into the house when everyone was asleep, during ucchakkaanam. We'd walk through all the rooms. We'd laugh at the funny postures of those sleeping. One day Ettan, who usually stood at the western window waving to Nanikutty, saw me and came at me with his hand raised. Kunjathaal's damshtra started lengthening dangerously. "Don't do anything!' I warned her. That's why she held back. Neeli starts spitting when someone makes her angry. And immediately that someone's body breaks out in bubble-like eruptions. If Neeli didn't spit now, it was only because *I* asked her not to.

We would always go to Mutthashi's room and play dice because Mutthashi never minded. Once Amma, or maybe it was Valiamma, saw us moving about in the house. At once ... another earthquake. And another astrological consultation.

This time they called not one Paniker but a set of two other Panikers. And it was not my horoscope alone that was studied. Everybody brought their horoscopes along. And why not? After all, the Panikers had come from so far away.

Amma wanted to know all about this urvashi who had administered the magic potion to Achhan. Hence the drawing of patterns on the floor, the arranging of cowries and the incantations that went on and on, for practically everyone in the house. And walking up and down, up and down in the southern wing, pricking up her ears to listen to what the Panikers had to say about the prospects of her getting married, was ... who else but Sarojini Edathi.

It was now decided that they would bring in a renowned sorcerer from Kallaadikottu or some such place. Thekkukaran Ravunni Nair went to meet this mantravadi and came back, having fixed an auspicious date for his visit. I overheard all that he said about that mantravadi.

Immediately I called Kunjathaal. She ought to know what they are going to do, no? A dagger would be made red hot on burning coals, nails would be driven into a log of the kanjira tree. The fire and the heat, the scalding and the piercing would drive the evil spirits away not merely from the humans but from the village itself.

Kunjathaal heard me out and pooh-poohed this with a giggle. So I told Mutthashi. Mutthashi also just laughed.

The mantravadi came from Kallaadikottu and started the elaborate ritual. A lot of lamps were lit and a round, sacred kolam was drawn on the floor.

In the beginning I was a little scared. When Kunjathaal and Neeli came and stood behind me, I felt better. Then Mutthashi came, dragging her aged frame. She sat down beside me and all my fears vanished.

The man drove nails into the kanjira wood.

I turned around and looked furtively at Kunjathaal. Kunjathaal was in a rage. But Neeli winked at her and grinned.

Then the wood was set on fire.

Oh, what heat! How much smoke! I fell backwards. Kunjathaal held me and I promptly fell fast asleep.

"The evil spirits have all left. Disappeared! Now there will be no trouble whatsoever." When the mantravadi said this, I was resting my head on Kunjathaal's lap.

I laughed.

Kunjathaal whispered in my ears, "Sleep Janakikutty, sleep." She smelt of sandal paste and new clothes.

Next day Valiachhan, that is Sarojini Edathi's father came. Mine didn't. Mutthashi sighed. "Mmm. Just two months leave. Within that time he has to get Sarojinikutty married. Luckily, the bridegroom has been found."

It was someone called Sankaranarayanan. He worked with Valiachhan.

Kunjathaal and Neeli crept quietly into the house that evening. Everyone believed that the mantravadi's ritual had banished them from the village.

"Will I be fortunate enough to see Janakikutty's marriage?" Mutthashi asked Kunjathaal. Kunjathaal seemed lost in thought.

Now the other story. When Edathi and I went to bathe, Bhaskaran who fishes there with line and tackle was shouting at Sarojini Edathi. Sarojini Edathi's eyes were filled with tears. When they saw us, they moved away, heads bent.

The wedding would be at the Bhagavathy temple, the feast at the house. How I wished Kunjathaal and Neeli and I could wear skirts and blouses of the same colour and style.

After Valiachhan came, the excitement started. People coming and going. Even on the day of the engagement ceremony there were about forty guests. Mutthashi was given Idichu Pizhinja Payasam, a delicacy made with lots of jaggery and coconut milk, besides the usual rice kanji. It was I who took it to her.

Mutthashi wanted to get up and get dressed. "Even if it gets dark I want to go to the temple to see the wedding," she said.

"No need," Amma said brusquely, "Two people would have to support you. Before she goes to the temple, Sarojini will come and do her namaskaram. You can bless her with rice and flowers."

That day, Mutthashi fell down on her way to the bathroom.

"Ah, and this person wanted to climb to the hilltop Bhagavathy temple," they sighed.

They lifted Mutthashi and put her on the cot in her room with Valiamma muttering all the time to Valiachhan, "This is just what we want, isn't it?"

"A fall at this age, and there's no getting up." Who else would say this but the all-knowing Ravunni Nair.

That night Mutthashi had high fever and vomiting. A doctor was brought from Padinjarangadi – a doctor with a large dot of sandalpaste on his forehead.

Mutthashi was restless.

I tiptoed into her room.

"Nothing serious. Don't worry," she said to me.

My friends Kunjathaal and Neeli also came to look Mutthashi up when nobody was around.

Pacing up and down the courtyard Valiachhan cursed and harangued. "This blasted woman! Sells and squanders everything, drives out her own children and when she has one foot in the grave she has to find this of all places to take refuge in."

"It's mahodara," Ravunni Nair said. "The doctor said we'd better get her into the hospital."

"Ha! Hospital! Even if it's a common cold, these doctors will say, Get into hospital. Must be getting a commission."

Every once in a while Valiamma would moan, "Oh God, what if she dies now ..."

"Well then, good riddance. She is not our direct mutthashi."

"Whether you like it or not, she is the eldest member of the Taravaadu. What difference does it make whether she is Mutthashi or Mutthashi's sister? If she dies there will be mourning," Ravunni Nair told Valiachhan. Living as he did in Bombay, Valiachhan was quite ignorant in these matters.

In the midst of all this, Valiamma and Valiachhan went all the way to Thrissur to buy the clothes, utensils, and ornaments for the

---

**Taravaadu:** is a joint family of Kerala, till recently, matriarchal.

wedding. Only these Thrissur people know the latest fashions. Edathi wore the new jewels and preened herself before the mirror in the room where all the purchases were displayed for everybody to see.

I prayed and prayed that Kunjathaal and Neeli would come now. They did come that night … just when I was praising the beauty of all the things. Kunjathaal wasn't impressed. After all, she is a yakshi. If she wants she can magic all sorts of beautiful jewels out of thin air. And, as for Neeli, she doesn't want gold either. She is happy with her necklaces of stones that jingle when she walks. "That's all we are allowed to wear," Neeli once told me. "Who said so?" And she merely said, "That is the rule."

The medicines prescribed by the doctor had arrived, but Mutthashi had not taken any of them. It was Ettan who found this out. Then Kunjan Vaidyar was brought in to treat Mutthashi.

Guests who came for the marriage would come to Mutthashi's door and peep in. A mother and daughter who'd come from Pattambi said to Mutthashi, "Why give these people so much trouble? Pray to God to take you away. Aren't these children looking after you as best as they can?"

I was standing at the door when they came out. The mother peered at me. "Isn't this Kunjukutty Amma's second daughter?"

The woman with them said, "Hmm."

"How is she now?"

"She's feeling better, they say."

I went and sat on the floor near Mutthashi's cot, winnow in hand. With so much to be done for the wedding, I've been given many responsibilities. I have to clean all the lamps in the attic. I have to clean the rice and lentils. One day when I was doing this Kunjathaal and Neeli came in. I didn't talk to them. How could I when I had so much to do?

Since Sarojini Edathi would have to live in Bombay after her marriage, my elder sister is teaching her basic Hindi. It is on me that Sarojini Edathi practises what she learns.

"Jatti, bahar jaao!"

"Jatti, idhar aao!"

I in turn practised this on Kunjathaal and Neeli. What fun!

"Kunjathaal, idhar aao!"

"Neeli, idhar aao!"

While at this one day I heard a sudden call. I turned. Ettan was standing there saying, "Edee! If you start all this nonsense again, watch out, I will tear you to pieces."

"What's the matter?" Amma came running. And, seeing me she started muttering, "Just in case anyone thinks we have money in this house, this cursed girl will see to it that it is exhausted! Go in," Amma ordered. "Don't you loiter outside at odd hours."

I secretly signalled to Kunjathaal – It's all right! – and went in.

Achhan was to come that night. But he didn't. That created a little tremor. Then, there was a letter from him. He had very little leave, he would come on the day of the wedding and go back the same day. An earthquake!

Guests started pouring in. They were received. Jewellery was displayed, saris and brocades too. Tall tales were exchanged.

Who had the time to see if Mutthashi or I had eaten? I was mad with rage. That night, when Kunjathaal was on her usual beat, she looked in through the wooden grille in the southern wing of the house. "Where is your damshtra?" I asked her. "You'd better suck the blood of all these wretched people."

"Really? You really want that?"

"Don't kill," I said. "Just frighten them."

She looked as if she was seriously considering my request as she shook out her hair, turned into a yakshi and looked at those who were sleeping. Then she laughed. They were all strangers. Folks who'd come three full days ahead of the marriage.

After Valiachhan came, Sarojini Edathi slept in Amma's room. My bed was shifted out. As if I cared. Let her practise her Hindi with Amma. If I want ... Hmm-hm, no. I won't do it.

That night, a sound woke me up. People were running all over the place. A real earthquake!

"Quick! Bring that pill of hers that will make her breathe more easily!" someone was ordering.

"May nothing happen before the marriage." This was Valiamma's prayer.

Mutthashi's condition was critical again.

So much noise and commotion and through it all some slept like logs.

I got up and rushed to Mutthashi's room. When I reached there, Amma saw me. "Get out! Go back to bed. Who asked you to come here?" she screamed.

Next day – the pandal was up in the courtyard. Alongside the kitchen a long, narrow shed had been erected for the cooks. Huge vessels and ladles were brought from the temple storeroom. Valiamma brought my new skirt and blouse back from the tailor. Not a colour that I liked. But the material was good. Silk.

"We have got all this for you. Do you know why? So that you'll be a good girl and behave. Don't make people say things about you. Understand?" Valiamma stroked my hair.

From now on, I'll not utter a word – that's for sure.

But I kept wondering what new games Kunjathaal and Neeli were playing without me. They were not to be seen around here. But then, looking at all the hustle and bustle, who'd want to come here?

Mutthashi's room reeks of urine. When Mutthashi breathes there is an awful sound. When she sees me she beckons me with her head and I go stand near her. Valiachhan and Ravunni Nair keep peeping in.

When the decoration of the pandal was over, two loudspeakers were mounted and they started playing recorded music. One loudspeaker was turned towards the fields. Another towards the hill. Let my yakshi too hear the music.

The bridegroom's party was to arrive in two buses and three cars. Ettan was to receive them. They would be taken straight to the temple. The nadaswaram players would be waiting under the banyan tree.

To the cooks Ravunni Nair said, "They will all be back here by nine thirty. By ten, the first batch of plantain leaves must be spread out for the feast. Will you be ready?"

The night resounded with the activities of the cooks. Inside, there was no space even to lie down.

It didn't look as if Mutthashi would attend the wedding.

"Touch her feet before you leave. After all, she has the status of a Mutthashi. Also place a new mundu at her feet. Not that it is going to bring any benefit. Still ... " Amma advised Sarojini Edathi, and Ravunni Nair said with a sarcastic chuckle, "Yes, shortly new clothes will be needed for the mourning."

I had planned to wake up early, bathe, wear my new skirt and go show it to Kunjathaal. But when I woke up, Ravunni Nair was shrieking to my mother. "She has wrecked everything, Kunjukutty Amma!"

Practically everyone was in Mutthashi's room. Valiachhan also came running.

"It's all over. All over!"

"Not a word. Not a soul other than us should know till the feast is over and the bridegroom's party has left. Understand?" When he looked up, it was at me. I was standing near the door. I could see Valiachhan was angry.

Valiamma called me to her. "Jatti, come here. Let me tell you something," she said. "Mutthashi's condition is very bad. You should not go into her room. Go. Have your bath and get ready. Achhan will be here any minute now. Um. Go."

"Thank God, the child knows nothing."

"Ravunni ... keep watch. Don't move an inch. If anyone else comes to know, there will be enough busybodies to say the wedding should be stopped. And they will quote the shastras. I hope you understand?"

I got dressed. Edathi plaited my hair with a beautiful blue ribbon.

Sarojini Edathi's makeup had started around midnight. Four people were needed just to decorate her hair. She was never beautiful.

But now, decked up in her loud sari and those glaring ornaments she looked worse.

"What are you waiting for, ladies? Hurry."

The women started to move.

"Sarojini Edathi, don't you have to go in and do namaskaram to Mutthashi?" I asked.

"Girl! Shut up and go!" Amma said to me. All the anger at Achhan not having come for the wedding was directed at me.

Nobody even paused at Mutthashi's door.

I stood in the corridor, hesitating.

"Edee, what are you hovering around there for? Come fast," Valiamma scolded me.

I went towards the kitchen, saying I wanted to drink some water. I got out from the rear and ran through the parambu.

The rustle of my new silk skirt was like music. Near the outhouse, Kunjathaal was sitting combing her hair. She was alone. "Do you know what Sarojini Edathi did?" I burst out. "She went to the temple without doing namaskaram to Mutthashi."

Kunjathaal said nothing. I became angry.

"You call yourself a great yakshi. What is the use? Can't you help Mutthashi? She wants to see the wedding."

Kunjathaal laughed.

"You said you could fly to the top of the pala tree. Is that also a bluff?"

Kunjathaal looked at me.

"Um. I'll come to the wedding too. You bring Mutthashi. Neeli and I will wait at the gate."

I wasn't sure if she was joking. I hesitated. Kunjathaal said, "I am serious. I am sure Mutthashi will come. You call her."

I ran back to the house. When I was entering Mutthashi's room, Ravunni Nair asked "Why is kutty here?"

"Mutthashi ..."

"You can't go in. Shouldn't you be at the temple?"

"Mutthashi should come too."

"Mutthashi is dead, kutty. We are not telling anybody until

the feast is over. Kutty should also not tom-tom it. Don't go in. You'll get scared ..."

I turned a deaf ear to him. I leaned on the door. It opened slightly. He looked at me in anger. "Go in, go in ... what does it matter to me?" he said.

I went in.

Mutthashi was still. She had covered herself up to her neck. She must be angry and so pretending to be dead. Sometimes when she has had a quarrel with Amma or Valiamma she'd lie thus, without even touching her food. Mutthashi always had such tricks up her sleeve.

Mutthashi shouldn't die without seeing the marriage. I won't allow it.

"Isn't Mutthashi coming? It is I ..."

Standing at the door, Ravunni Nair gave a sarcastic grin.

Mutthashi opened her eyes. Just as I expected.

"It is time for the muhurtham. Let's go. We have to rush."

Mutthashi sat up in the bed.

"Do you want to change your mundu?"

Mutthashi shook her mundu to take out the crinkles and wore it again. She draped a sheet over her head. In one quick movement she got off the bed, took my hand and started walking.

Looking triumphantly at Ravunni Nair who still wore his mocking expression, Mutthashi and I stepped out. Kunjathaal and Neeli were at the gate. Hand in hand, the four of us ran. Mutthashi was faster than us. In fact she was pulling us. When we had passed the lane and reached the foot of the banyan tree we could hear the nadaswaram.

We went through the outer courtyard of the temple. It was jammed with people. No one noticed us. We had arrived in time. The bride and bridegroom were about to garland each other.

A beaming Mutthashi sat through the whole wedding. When the ceremony was over all the elder relatives and friends came forward to shower rice and flowers on the bride and bridegroom. Mutthashi looked at me. I scooped up a handful of rice and flowers and gave it to her.

I asked Kunjathaal. "Do you want some?"

Kunjathaal was looking at the bridegroom. Her eyes spat fire. The damshtra slowly grew longer. And longer.

And when the bridegroom posed, bouquet in hand for a photo with Sarojini Edathi I noticed Kunjathaal jump towards him. I burst into a loud scream. What happened after that I don't know. Only when I saw Sarojini Edathi with the new Ettan who has become her husband did I feel relieved. So Kunjathaal didn't do any harm. They invited me to go to their house after I got well. "If you were not feeling well, why did you come running to the temple like this, alone?" they asked.

"Not alone. Mutthashi came with me."

"Bhagwané. Bhagwané!" Amma began chanting.

"Ask Ravunni Nair. He saw us."

"My kutty's having one hallucination after another!" Amma moaned. This has become their habit. They always invent something of their own.

To show them that I was saying the truth I described in detail how Mutthashi had come to the temple to shower rice and flowers on the married couple. All that they did was to look at each other and whisper.

After Sarojini Edathi and her husband's family left, they told everyone that Mutthashi was dead.

I said to myself, So what if she dies now. At least she saw the wedding.

If she didn't die till the marriage was over, it's because she was an old hag who loved her family," the maidservants who had come to sweep and clean the house were saying when Ravunni Nair came out of Mutthashi's room, screaming.

I could hear the commotion from where I lay.

"Was it not I who gave her her ceremonial bath? Who laid out the body? But, oh God, what do I see now. Rice and flowers in her hands!"

So! When I said so, they would not believe me.

"Mutthashi's spirit has entered kutty. Heard what she said?"

Nobody has entered or possessed anybody. The four of us did go to the temple. That is a fact.

"Even in death she won't leave us in peace."

Ravunni Nair began talking of sending for the mannaan to come perform the last rites. "If we don't, her spirit will hang around us forever."

I lay there with eyes closed. Kunjathaal and Neeli came into my room. I could sense that from their smell. I didn't speak to them. Frightening people with the damshtra at the wrong time!

"Don't come near me," I said. "Hereafter I am not going to play with you. Go away."

Even through shut eyes I could see them leave, heads bent in shame.

You know that a body has to be cremated only with logs of the mango tree. For Mutthashi, my relatives brought a tiny branch of a mango tree, saying there was a lot of the fuel left over from the wedding and that would serve.

From where I lay, I saw Mutthashi being carried out.

Mutthashi won't go. She'll stay. Isn't that what Ravunni Nair said?

I got up.

I could see the courtyard. Through the wooden grille of the front hall, beyond the cashewnut tree, I could see the funeral pyre. Four or five people lifted Mutthashi, laid her on the pyre and arranged pieces of wood on the sides and over her. The fire was lit.

Oh, how scorched Mutthashi must be feeling ... Don't, Ayyo ... Don't!

There's smoke all over the place. Nothing can be seen. But look! From out of the smoke, whom do I see coming ... yes! It is none other than Mutthashi!

Mutthashi will not die. Mutthashi will not leave this house. There's still much to be done. Mutthashi is still to show me what herbs and roots are to be gathered and how the paste is to be made and applied for eruptions, wounds, swellings.

The white cloth with which Mutthashi had covered her body turned into wings. Mutthashi came towards me, flying. Before I could turn my eyes from the courtyard, Mutthashi had landed on my bed. My happiness knew no bounds. I held Mutthashi in a tight embrace.

"You pretended you were dead and made a fool of all these people, no?" I asked.

Mutthashi laughed softly.

Do you know where Mutthashi is, Chechi? Chechi, you are a nurse, no? Then, why are you not wearing the white coat nurses always wear?

Let everyone go. So what? The one who came last has not gone. Do you know who it is? She sits right behind me, a little girl. She wears my skirt, her hair is cropped short.

Yes, it is Mutthashi.

Chechi, let's play.

Chechi! Why are you running away? Why are you shouting and calling people? Has an earthquake started here too?

Mutthashi? Has Mutthashi also gone?

No, Mutthashi sits on top of the window sill. How did she get there?

Yes. There, holding her hand, helping Mutthashi climb down – Yes that is *them.* So they have also come.

"Silly! You and your irritation. We hadn't gone anywhere," Kunjathaal whispered in my ear.

Now for kothengkallu and vattu and all my other games, there is a foursome. Mutthashikutty and I are partners. Kunjathaal and Neeli the other team. How well matched we are!

Ah! What more is there to wish for!

First published in Malayalam as "Cheriya Cheriya Bhookambangal" in the Malayalam edition of *India Today,* 22 August, 1990, Chennai.

best of the
90s

**MAITREYI PUSHPA**

The Verdict

Superbly told, it is the woman's eternal story. Maitreyi Pushpa is simply superb in crafting the tragic status of a woman in our society. It is modern, topical, and yet timeless.    **– Gulzar**

Respected Master Saheb,

      Pranaam!

You may have heard the news already, if you haven't you probably will before my letter reaches you three days from now. The results of the elections were announced today.

How did all this happen?

I feel as stunned today as I did that other day – the day I had won. I had never imagined that I could be elected to the post of the Pradhan. How had I managed to get so many votes? There had been groupism, party politics. And so much opposition. And yet ...?

I understood why only when I saw all the women of the village animated by the same sense of euphoria, the tumult of their inner hopes and aspirations reflected on their faces.

I had been told that, being the wife of the Block Pramukh, it was not proper for me to go to each household and thank my sisters. So I made for the pathanwara. This place stands witness to all our joys and sorrows, Massav.

Ranveer had warned me when he was made the Pradhan that I could not behave like the other women of the village any more, or carry pots on my head like them. And I was told that my presence at the pathanwara too, would no longer befit my position. After all I was the wife of the Pradhan. When he became the Pramukh, the restrictions had become more stringent. And then I was elected the Pradhan. Ranveer's status in the village rose further. He was now known to be a generous and progressive individual. Our village rose in the esteem of the neighbouring villages. And I found myself weighed down by the ever increasing restrictions. I had strict instructions to keep a distance from the women in the village. But I couldn't. Any excuse was good enough to lead me to their midst.

Maitreyi Pushpa won the Katha Award for Creative Fiction in 1993, for this story. *Hans* received the Journal Award for first publishing this story in Hindi.

The Katha Translation Award went to Meenakshi Sharma and Renuka Ramachandran.

This story first appeared in English translation in *Katha Prize Stories 3*, 1993.

We thank Rajendra Yadav, our nominating editor, for choosing this story for us.

Ranveer had remarked. "You're still inexperienced in the ways of the world. Someday you too are likely to be as particular about your dignity and status."

While I was in the pathanwara that day, Isuriya and her goats happened to pass by. I've mentioned her earlier. She is the blunt and outspoken one. I remember writing to you about her. She and I, we came to this village as brides on the same day. You were amused, Massav. "Of all the people, the goatherd's wife for your companion? Wah, Basumati!" you had said. But she's really sharp. I had barely lifted my veil and glanced around, while she was already familiar with every door and threshold. She'd even formed her own opinions about every villager. It is not in her nature to be diffident or shy. She would refer to the village elders by name. As if she were their great grandmother. Free from the paraphernalia of caste and family ties.

And that day she called out as soon as she reached the pathanwara. "O ... Basumati ... Bride of Ranveer! O ... Pirmukhani!"

The women burst out laughing, "Basumati, here comes everybody's grandmother. She's calling for you. Why don't you respond, Pradhanji?"

Isuriya pushed the goats forward in our direction and soon enough she was with us. She said complacently, "So, you are now the Pradhan. That can only be for the better."

Nobody paid her much attention.

Waving her stick wildly, she proclaimed, "Ai ... listen everybody. Listen carefully. Things will be different from now. We can demand our rights. Now if those spindly little men beat us, shout at us, don't let us visit home, if they force us to ask our parents for money or they harass us, then make straight for Basumati. Write it all down. Get them bastards jailed.

"O Basumatiya, you will not be unjust like Ranveer, will you? You would not destroy evidence, would you? That Saleega, he beat

---

**Pathanwara:** The place where the women meet and episodes from individual lives are frequently swapped while busy hands pat cowdung cakes into shape.

me black and blue. I made Leelo's son write this all down as evidence so I could get a hearing. I had gone and given it to Ranveer myself. That really scared Saleega. He was so scared he didn't even abuse me for a day or two. But Ranna, he didn't do a thing about the paper and Saleega turned into a lion overnight. So you were going to send me to jail, huh? Infernal woman, I made up my mind too. So what if I had to sell two goats to ... So much for your piece of paper ..."

Isuriya flung away her stick and held out her arms for all to see. She bared her welts and bruises. Nobody was smiling anymore, Massav. The mirth in the air suddenly seemed to freeze.

Gopi tried to lighten things up. Putting on a smile she said, "What are you blabbering about? What if somebody heard you? They'd go straight to the Pirmukhji."

Isuriya immediately changed her tone, "If somebody heard me? But that's precisely why I'm saying all this! Ranveer will get his due one day. He'll stay at home and slave over the fire. While our Basumati, she'll sign the papers. Give orders. She'll hold sway. Isn't that so, Basumati? Tell us truly, aren't you eleventh pass and Ranveer ninth fail? So, who is the intelligent one? No longer can women be herded along like so much cattle. These are the days of equality. After all, Basumati has become the Pirdhan, hasn't she? Indira Gandhi rules now. Long live Indira Gandhi!"

"Silly woman," scoffed Gopi. "Indira Gandhi's dead and gone. It's Rajiv Gandhi now."

"Dead? Still that doesn't change things. Mother, son what's the difference? It's the same thing. But tell me, when is the procession?" she asked, the thought suddenly striking her. "When Ranna became the Pirdhan, there was such a glorious procession. So many garlands and flags. They had carried him around the whole village on their shoulders."

Saroopi rebuked her again, "Mad woman, why do you keep going Ranna, Ranna? You'll be the first one that Pirmukhji will send to jail."

She shrugged nonchalantly, "Here, listen to her. Ranna? Why, even your father-in-law Gajaraj can't harm me. Not even your brother-in-law Panna. Can they, Basumati?"

One of the women said, "Why do you bother with this lunatic? O Isuriya, your goats are wandering off."

"O my god!"

Isuriya ran after her goats, brandishing her stick.

T he morning sun must have just touched the threshold. I had lit the stove and placed the tava on it. My hands were covered with flour.

A shadow fell lightly across the doorway.

Before I could see who it was, I heard her voice, "O Basumati! Basumatiya!"

It was Isuriya.

"The Daroga is sitting with the Panchayat. He's reading the papers. I swear Basumati, all the Panch are waiting for you." She could barely contain her excitement.

I called out to my sister-in-law, Kusuma. She said, "You go, Bhabhi, I'll make the rotis."

The women watched me go, from behind their windows. Maybe it was just to check whether my face was veiled or not.

We met Gopi on the way. "Basumati bhabhi is going to the meeting. Where do you think *you* are going?" she teased.

Isuriya flashed back, "Be off with you, Gopiya! Let me inform you I happen to be Basumati's sec'tary. We're headed for the meeting. You mustn't waylay the Panch."

"Where are your goats?"

"Saleega's taken them to graze. He's finally realized that the days of equality are here. He had better do his bit."

We had almost reached the chabutra when I spotted Ranveer. A few long strides and he stood in front of us. A look of surprise on his face. His mouth drawn in stern lines. "Where to?" he asked.

The answer came from Isuriya, "Pirmukhji, we're on our way to the Panchayat. Do let us pass, you are in our way."

He heard her out and then turned on me, "You'd better go home."

Isuriya was at a loss for words but she recovered soon enough to say, "Don't try to stop us pass, you are in our way."

His brow contracted and his eyes became balls of fire. "Basumati, didn't you hear what I said?"

I could feel my feet shrivel under his fiery gaze. But Isuriya still stood there. I signalled to her that we had best return home. She looked at me with strange eyes and helplessly followed me.

I returned to the kitchen chores. I did not have any answers to Kusuma's unuttered questions. There seemed to be no respite from this choking frustration that had taken hold of me.

Isuriya could be heard muttering in the courtyard, "Isn't this the limit? Basumati holds the post but Ranveer calls the shots. Arré! Why can't he mind his own business? He is the Pirmukh. Why should he interfere with the Pirdhan's work?"

Kusuma could not contain herself any longer. "Why should he not interfere? The money has to be extracted from Ramkisan the potter. Bhaiya must have given his word to Bani Singh. What if Bhabhi had gone and a wrong resolution had been passed?"

"Poor Ramkisan, he sold his bullock to Bani Singh so he could have a roof over his head. And that monster Bani Singh. He used the bullock to harvest his crop and once that was over he's returned it saying that the bullock is temperamental. Give my money back, he says. Now where is Ramkisan to get the money from? Sell his roof? Can roofs be sold? Who is to give him justice? The poor can't expect anything from Ranveer. Had you been there, the potter might have got a fair deal."

Isuriya dragged her feet homewards. And Massav, I could do nothing about the thorns that kept pricking at my soul.

On his return, Ranveer had done his best to make me understand. "Do you think your being on the Panchayat chabutra would have been in good taste? You must not lose your sense of propriety. Does our status, our standing, mean nothing to you any more? A woman is respected only as long as she keeps within her bounds. Besides, what would you know about the scheming people in the village?"

Since that day, there were constant summons for the Pradhan.

Although the village folk were aware of Ranveer's disapproval, they would still insist on coming to call me.

It was I that proved to be a coward. Or was it that Ranveer's image had become so much a part of me, a constant presence that reminded me every time I crossed the threshold, I'm here. Anyway, I've been handling this for a while. Why do you need to step out of the house?

My mind would heave violently in response, almost to the point of answering back. But being his wife, my anger remained mute, my words of protest subsiding like froth on boiled milk.

Massav, I had decided that I would not put my signature on anything. Let him do as he pleases.

So Ranveer sat with the register on the charpai. And I was tied up in the kitchen. There was always so much to do in the mornings. He had called for me. Perhaps many times. But I was still not free.

"I'm done with all the writing and you don't even have time for a single signature?"

I still didn't go.

Irritated he said, "How long am I expected to wait? I have to reach the Block. You've kept this hanging for a week."

I walked upto him, wiping my hands on my sari.

"Sign here."

He uncapped the pen.

"What are you waiting for? You could have signed some twenty thousand times by now."

I shut the pen.

Questions rose before me like a thick, dense forest. And I was lost in it. Couldn't Ranveer guide me out? Was I to be left defenceless amidst these thorns?

As Pradhan, Ranveer must have traversed the same paths. Or had his course been different? Shouldn't I make an effort to find out? Perhaps there was a way ...

"Ranveer? The labourers had come to me. They said they still haven't been paid."

A shocked look came over his face and he stood there staring at me.

I spoke on. "The women of the village jeer. Much good your being the Pradhan has done us. You've had your lane laid out with stones and levelled. What have we done to deserve this neglect, bahen? We are scared to send our children to school. The roof might cave in any day. You are the only one who can do anything about it. Who could believe that this was the Pirmukh's village? Potholes filled with water, breeding mosquitoes. Garbage everywhere. Fever and disease in every house.

"If only we had dispensaries and medicine," I said. "And, the roads ought to be repaired, like in Lalpur. Also, what about the money for the Jawahar Rozgar Yojana?"

Ranveer's gaze widened further. Anger simmering in his eyes. Darts of fire seemed to reduce me into ashes as I stood there, Massav. My words sizzled and died like drops of water on a hot tava.

"Did the women say this, or was it you? Since when have they begun to talk about their feelings? Who do you think you are? The Pradhan or the MLA?" Lines of ugly laughter distorted his face. "Tch ... Tch ... Tch. Nobody's ever asked me anything and you face so many questions!" His voice was dripping with sarcasm.

My hands shook as I silently wrote "Basumati Devi."

Signature!

The day I had signed and collected the JRY money, heaven had seemed a distinct possibility. I would constantly dream of shining, spotless schools and pukka roads. Of restoring houses ravished by the rain. Of supporting the unemployed through their bad times. Of providing relief and medical help to the ailing.

"Basumati Devi." These six syllables had put paid to my dreams.

An old woman knocked at the door.
"O, beta Basumati?"
By the time I placed the water pot on the stand, Devveer, my brother-in-law had reached the door.

"What is it, dadi?"

"Beta, would you send your bhabhi outside for a minute."

"Have you come here to call her to the Panchayat?"

"Why else would I call for her?"

"Go away dadi. Bhaiya is not at home. Bhabhi won't be able to go."

"Won't be able to go? Why? Isn't she the Pradhan? She has to go to the Panchayat."

"Why do you want to cause a scene at home?"

"Why should there be a scene? Anyway shouldn't you have thought of this earlier?"

I had reached the door by then. The old woman spotted me. She fell at my feet. "Beti Basumati, try and understand our plight. My son-in-law will not get any leave again for a long time. He's with the army, you see. Help us get a fair deal, bahu."

I stood there listening to her.

"Beti, I cannot bear to see my daughter Hardai's unhappiness anymore. Her father is a monster. We've never had the good fortune to lead a quiet life." Her eyes moistened. Tears streamed down her wrinkled face.

What could I do? I had no choice. Sympathy was all I had and that I gave her. "You'll get justice, amma. Have faith. Why should the Panchayat be unjust?"

I don't know how I made the decision then. But my feet suddenly fell in step with hers. Devveer was left standing, trying to stop me.

I had the verdict passed. My entire being felt drenched through with a strange sense of ecstasy, A decision taken with seamless compassion and loving uprightness. The chabutra seemed like sacred ground to me, the temple precincts from where I had released the stagnating water, cleared out all the filth with my own hands, prepared the ground as though for new seeds, a fresh garden.

That night Ranveer entered the house quietly. His stern face turned ugly. It seemed as though somebody was gouging away at my heart.

In the still and unnatural calm of the night, I could feel the poison in his voice flow all over me. "If you were so fond of playing lawyer, why didn't you ask your father and study law? Even when I had asked you so many times not to ...?"

I could not answer him.

"This daily drama, these scenes day and night! Tell me, when will there be an end to this?" Ranveer exploded into the silence of the house.

I was filled with dread. Waves of fear rose up in me.

Suddenly I spoke up, "I didn't go on my own. Amma and her daughter had come to call me. Who doesn't know about Hardai's woes?"

"And, you know all about it?"

"Hardai had begged me. She said Ranveer bhaiya won't understand my plight. Being a woman, bhabhi, you can feel my distress, give me justice. My husband works in the army. He won't get leave again for another two years. Seven years have already passed this way. My father thinks that the money orders will stop if I go with my husband. So he keeps me locked at home. I am not allowed to meet my husband. Whenever Amma managed to let me out there is an uproar at home. Dirty, filthy abuse. And ... I've been to the town three times for abortions. Have you ever seen such a father, bhabhi? Save me now, send me with my husband this time. I'll sing your praise all my life. Hardai wept uncontrollably. But still I was not able to recognize the extent of her anguish. All I could think of at that moment was, if only you had helped with the decision of her case."

His eyes bored into mine, "What kind of decision? Like the one you have just decreed? Do you think Hardai is living in a lawless society? She is staying in her father's house. She has to live by his rules. Besides, where will that soldier keep her?"

"Anywhere. If they love each other ..."

He rose violently, "You mean, I am in their way?"

I was deeply afraid, yet somehow uttered, "But I have heard that she had been taken to influential men ... to satisfy their lust ..."

"Really?" he spluttered. "And you haven't heard how her good-for-nothing brother got a job? Or under whose protection her father openly traffics in cement? Or how they came to build a pukka

house? Under whose patronage do you think they've been able to
live like this? What do I stand to gain from all this?"

"So you know all about Hardai's plight. Why don't you free her
from the clutches of her father?"

"Well, you've freed her. Against my judgement ... in this tasteless
manner."

"That was never my intention."

"O? And pray tell me what was your intention the day the police
arrested Ramsingh and were taking him away? Whatever possessed
you to run after the police van like that, as if you had taken leave
of your senses? What must the Darogaji have said? What would
the people have been thinking? That the Pramukhji's wife pulls
such cheap stunts! I have never been so embarrassed in my life. If
you ever try to create such scenes again ..."

"Look, Ramsingh was not guilty. Why punish the innocent?"

He trembled with rage. "Hear this once and for all. Have no
illusions about your position. I was forced to make you stand for
the elections. I can't hold two posts at the same time. I had believed
nobody would be more reliable than one's wife ..."

A poisonous smile passed over his face at the word "Reliable."

It was a cold winter night. Chilly and frigid. I remained sitting
outside. I tried to keep warm by drawing myself close. My hands
and feet were beginning to grow numb.

My mind was not at peace with itself. I felt that I should, at this
very moment, leave this house, this village, this earth, this sky. Go
somewhere far away.

I must have spent half the night sitting out there in the courtyard.

In that mist, I could feel a shadow approach me. I looked up, it
was Ranveer. He came and sat beside me. He stroked my hair and
tried to coax me, "Come inside. Let's sleep. It's cold out here. Do as
I say."

Straightening my sari, I sat upright, stiff as a statue. I had no
desire to protest. Nor did I feel close enough to him to complain. A
sense of alienation took hold of me and I dragged myself into the
room.

He kept trying to explain, "Is there any distinction between a husband and wife, silly woman. They live and die for each other. There's no reason why you should harbour such doubts on account of the village folk. They are all jealous of us, cannot bear to see the husband as the Pramukh with his wife as the Pradhan. They would like to see you roam around on the streets so that even the urchins can make fun of you. They're just waiting for an opportunity to comment on Ranveer's wife in the company of strange men ..."

You may remember. Massav, you had sent a note for me the day I had become the Pradhan. You had wished me a happy future and a life dedicated to my husband. But you had also urged me to seek new horizons for myself. Challenged me to overcome familial ties. You had written, "Basumati, your courtyard must have a roof of honesty built on pillars of truth, where the weak, the oppressed, the accursed and defeated will find shelter."

Surely you too must have been aware of the extent to which this could be possible. But your words certainly stirred me. And I forgot, Massav, that I was as much a part of the system as anyone else, a corrupt system that functions through the oppression of others.

If only I could have been Isuriya, outside the walls of propriety and decorum. Under the free sky. Beyond illusions fostered by the paralyzing customs and traditions of genteel society.

If only Ranveer did not hold the trump card of belonging to the aristocracy. Then I could have flown away from the cage that now confines my wings.

It was almost dawn. The chirping of the birds woke me up. Even though no trace of sleep or lethargy remained in me, the uncompromising way in which my wishes had been ignored had left me in low spirits.

I cleaned the stove and lit it.

Ranveer is in the habit of drinking tea before cleaning his teeth. The tea had been poured out. As I was carrying it to him, there came the sound of loud cries that resounded in the courtyard.

"O Ranna's bride! O Basumatiya ...! Why don't you come out? All your learning is useless. The hell with your education and so much for your Pirdhani."

It was Isuriya, carried away on the crest of her mourning, her voice quivering with emotion.

The cup and saucer I held in my hand rattled. God alone knew what had happened!

"Arré, come outside quickly! Hardai has taken her life by jumping into the well under the peepal tree!"

I turned to stone.

I ran in the other direction – towards Ranveer's room. My legs were shaking. Breathing was difficult. I could not believe it, but somewhere within me there seemed to be an invisible, intangible presence scraping away at my soul.

Ranveer was not on his bed.

My body felt heavier than stone. My legs couldn't move ... defenceless, I collapsed in the courtyard.

Who had overruled the judgment? How had things changed completely in one night? Who had annulled the verdict of the Panch? Who had stopped her from going with her husband?

Isuriya shook me violently by the shoulders. "Do you intend to keep sitting here? At least go see her face for the last time. Hardai had given you her vote. She had carried your banners in the procession."

Indeed, her image with its unusual dignity floated in front of my eyes. "Basumati Devi, zindabad! Long live, Basumati Bhabhi!"

Isuriya's dirge was not to be stemmed. "It would have been better if we had voted for a stick, a piece of lifeless wood. At least it would have risen on being lifted. Dealt blows on the enemy. Protested against excesses. But Ranveer's bride, you have only remained the bahu of a respectable family. The Pirmukhji's wife. Swaddled in your veil, you have been moving like a puppet, with your eyes shut."

We reached the peepal tree.

And, what happened there? What could have happened there? The Daroga, constables and Ranveer, the prominent people of the village. They were all there.

The official pen was recording Hardai's father's tearful statement. "There had been a quarrel with her wayward, dowry-seeking husband, during the night. We had never sent our daughter with him because of his wayward ways. But who can change the course of destiny, Darogaji, My Hardai has lost her life ... Her mother is lying unconscious at home."

Isuriya ran forward like a woman crazed, wailing loudly, "O Darogaji, the truth is ..."

Ranveer stopped her midway. "Where are you rushing to? Don't worry, you'll get justice. I will change my name if I don't get that butcher hanged. Go home. Take Basumati with you."

After getting the Panchnama written, Ranveer sat in Darogaji's jeep and they drove off in a blaze of glory.

Behind them the people were left in a cloud of dust. They returned to their homes lamenting the injustice.

Returning to my courtyard, I sat amongst the distressed women. I felt as if the funeral procession had set off from this house.

Numerous, unanswered questions seemed fixed in the still, stony eyes around me. Under the guise of holy matrimony, the association of a tormented bird and a powerful hunter ...

Did the women recognize this egotistical assertion of intimacy? Or else why had they risen and left like deaf and mute people?

No questions nor any counter questions!

Time passed. The elections for the post of the Pramukh were to be held.

Ranveer was once again in the fray.

Those days he was too busy even to breathe. I too was run off my feet, busy with all kinds of chores. The chulha would be burning all day. And there were the sleeping arrangements to be made too. A constant stream of visitors. It seemed as though a marriage were taking place.

Ranveer would say, "Villagers aren't as simple as they are believed to be. There are those who have mastered the intricacies of the political labyrinth. The adept ones can easily outsmart the slickest city politicians."

Ranveer had to indulge the whims of each of the Pradhans. I think all the Pradhans of the tehsil must have come to our house to pay their respects. People were even talking in terms of Ranveer contesting the MLA elections after the Pramukh's.

True enough, Ranveer was extremely clever. His campaign was not based on ordinary tactics like say, sponsoring liquor. He was the kind of person who was useful in moments of crisis. This was the reason why he still had a hold over the people of Dariyapur, even though his rival candidate was a relative of theirs. Like a messiah, he had delivered them from the clutches of the crocodile after a daughter-in-law of the village had stated that she had been burnt for not bringing two thousand rupees ... Father and son would have certainly been hanged, or at least sentenced for life. The pride and honour of their magnificent turbans had been preserved only by Ranveer's grace.

Popular opinion was such that three of the candidates conceded defeat even before the elections. There was only one rival left in the field. That too an ironmonger's son.

He must have been naive.

Ranveer left early in the morning. He sent a jeep for me in the evening.

The household chores seemed unending. I could barely make it there.

Anyway, even if I hadn't gone, what difference would it have made? I had said as much to Ranveer. He hadn't agreed. He said that the people would jeer that the Pramukhji's wife was the Pradhan, but still hadn't come to vote.

I returned after having cast my vote.

Ranveer returned at night.

As soon as they spotted the searchlight of the jeep, the villagers began to gather at our doorway.

Ranveer walked through straight to the dining area. He looked very tired, beads of perspiration glistened on his forehead.

I reached his side with a glass of water.

He was silent. The crowds dispersed slowly on seeing him unwell.

When we were alone, I smoothed my hand over his brow and he turned even more restless. His face took on a piteous aspect. In a little while, he began to tremble like a fish stranded on the sand.

There was nothing left to understand. Massav, I made an effort to console him over his loss. "Don't lose heart. Your job is to try. Defeat and victory are all part of the game."

The door was shut from inside. I caressed his hands, pressed his feet. I tried hard to console him but my being too was choked with emotion.

Massav, this is nothing to write about, but I did everything I could to comfort him. I prayed I could overcome his agitation by making my mind and body one with his.

He was lost in his thoughts, "Those promises, those pledges, the oaths on the Ganga, was all that an illusion, Basumati ...? Or a betrayal ...?"

Just at that intimate moment Devveer's voice caught my attention. He was talking to somebody outside the door, "Bhaiya would not have lost but for a single vote. At least then he would have been even with the ironmonger."

One single vote! I could not believe it!

Suddenly something within me gave way and everything seemed unsteady.

O God of fire! O great priest who had guided me through the seven steps to holy matrimony! O father, my creator! And Massav, you, my mentor ... you had made me his consort, companion and partner in all his joys and sorrows and bidden me farewell as Ranveer's wife.

But what could I have done?

I just couldn't kill the Isuriya in me!

Forgive me.

Yours,

Basumati

First published in Hindi as "Faisla" in *Hans*, April 1993, New Delhi.

best of the
~90s~

**NATARAJ HULIYAR**

The Magic Nymph

"The Magic Nymph" is about a non-achiever, his dreams, sexual urges, failures, frustrations, in short, about his being very ordinary. The twist in the end reaffirms the faith in the goodness of the common man. The simple narration is intimate and involving.

**– Adoor Gopalakrishnan**

He waited like he had never waited for any woman in all his thirty three years as a brahmachari. He carefully checked each one of the countless bodies that milled around him against the image that was impressed in his mind, afraid that he might miss her. She was a woman he had seen exactly twenty four hours ago.

Last evening he had been to see his friend, Ramayya, who worked as a clerk in the cash section of the Munsif's Court. It was a Thursday, the day the SITA cases came up for hearing. Ramayya's table was besieged by a pack of professional women, prostitutes who had been nabbed either while soliciting customers or during raids on lodges. They had been produced in the court and had now come to pay the fine. Achari had not been sure if he should visit Ramayya at such a time. He was worried about how he should react to these women – should he show sympathy or should he be disgusted? And since Achari had a history of misadventures with such women, he panicked at the thought of one of them recognizing him.

There was cause for such panic. He was the kind of person who once seen would be remembered. N Sheshamurthy Achari, who worked as a clerk in the Accountant General's Office, was a slightly odd looking fellow. In fact, he was scared of taking a good look at himself in the mirror. He was known to be a diligent worker, had a reputation of being somewhat of an intellectual. For no rhyme or reason whatsoever, he would throw long passages from the poems of Kuvempu and Ambikatanayadatta (poems he had memorized in school) at his superiors, confounding them. He was firmly convinced that it was this poetic soul of his that permitted him to rise above the trivial distractions of his earthly existence.

As the sole provider for six younger sisters and a bedridden father,

Nataraj Huliyar won the Katha Award for Creative Fiction in 1993 for this story. *Lankesh Patrike* received the Journal Award for first publishing this story in Kannada.

The Katha Translation Award went to Manu Shetty.

This story first appeared in English translation in *Katha Prize Stories 3*, 1993.

We thank D R Nagaraj, our nominating editor, for choosing this story for us.

Achari had all the reason in the world to don the role of a tragic hero in a progressive novel and wallow in misery. Most of the one thousand nine hundred and fifty rupees that came his way as salary was distributed among various claimants on the very first day of the month. And out of the hundred odd that remained, he'd spend twenty rupees downing a bottle of beer with his friend Ramayya. Forthwith guilt would well up in him. "Ayyo," he'd mourn. "My fourth sister Suma is ill. With this money I could have taken home some fruits!" This invariably led to his confiding in Ramayya the desires that tormented him in the dark loneliness of night. The next moment he'd decide to follow the path that his friend and mentor Chandre Gowda had shown him.

Chandre Gowda worked in Achari's office, on a table adjacent to his. He was a Casanova. By the age of twenty nine, he had seen all there was to be seen in this world – or so he claimed. As Chandre Gowda described in vivid detail his exploits with scores of women, Achari would listen silently, seething with envy. "Ché, all these must be lies!" he consoled himself. Chandre Gowda had decided that Achari was absolutely useless. "If you only keep counting your money, by the time you touch a woman, your balls would have withered away completely," he warned. Achari was terrified by the thought that this prophesy might come true. Whenever he was in the grip of that terror and resolved to do something about it, the memory of his failed adventures would haunt him.

It had happened when Achari was studying for his BCom. He lived in a rented room that overlooked an old park. Through the half-opened window of his room, he'd notice a woman who often came to sit on the stone bench in a corner of the park. She'd sit there swinging the end of her sari and rolling her heavily lined eyes to draw the attention of the whole world. The mere sight of her meagre blouse that clasped her heavy breasts revealing an expanse of belly and navel was sufficient to sustain both an arousal and a masturbation. Achari didn't have the guts to approach her directly. Money was another problem. One day, unable to contain himself he spilled his heart to Nair, the building watchman. Nair looked him in his face and asked him, "Saami, you want that one?" Achari said, "Hoon." Nair took thirty rupees from him, promising to bring her the next Saturday around seven in the evening, when the neighbours would be watching the television film.

At last it was Saturday. All through the day his limbs had trembled with nervous excitement in anticipation of the coming adventure. He racked his brain about what to say to her. Remembering an advice, he bought a packet of Kohinoor and kept it ready. He paced around in his room not knowing what to do. His watch showed quarter past seven. Darkness had descended all around. Then the door that was left unbolted opened. Nair stepped into the room, alone. Achari leapt to his feet. His eyes crossed beyond Nair to pierce the darkness outside. "Saami," said Nair. "Where?" asked Achari in an excited whisper. Nair had plonked a twenty rupee note that he held in his fist on Achari's palm and drawled, "Police took that one away. I'll return ten rupees on the first." Then he'd walked away as if nothing had happened, closing the door behind him.

A strange quietness enveloped Achari. He wasn't quite sure whether he was sad or happy at the turn of events. He told himself that at least he had saved the money. But soon a suspicion crept into his mind, Had Nair lied to him? No, he decided, maybe the police *had* taken her away. This thought made him rage at a system that browbeats someone who was merely trying to eke out a living. But then, maybe even this anger was really born out of his frustration? Finally, Achari had pulled the blanket over himself and gone to sleep.

Several years later, Achari made another attempt. This time it was under the guidance of Chandre Gowda. One day Achari got together enough courage to ask for tips on how to identify such women and how to go about the business. Chandre Gowda gave a neat little lecture on the kind of clothes they wore, their demeanour, the language they used, the places they haunted ... And finally instructed Achari, "The moment you have spotted her just start walking by her side. Ask in a soft voice, as if you are talking to yourself, some general questions like Where's the bank? or How far is the bus stand? If she is a professional, she'll smile coyly and give an indication. In case you've made a mistake, just remember to walk away." Achari followed these instructions diligently and went after a couple of women, but each time, at the crucial moment his nerves would fail him and he would jump into a bus and rush back home.

With such a history of misadventures, it was but natural that Achari panicked when he saw those women at the Court that day. Ramayya was lost in the swarm of women. But the moment he saw Achari he made him sit on a chair by his side saying, "Just a moment." He looked up from the receipt he was writing, turned to the woman next to him and said, "What's your name, amma?" "Kaveri," replied the woman. Achari ogled at the woman and noticed the bags under the eyes. Having spent the whole day hanging around the court her lips were dry, her face wilted. "Is that your real name or a duplicate?" taunted Ramayya. "Just write it down," she snapped and placed two fifty rupee notes on the table. "Take. One's for me, the other for Kamali. Give two separate receipts." She put her hand on the shoulders of the woman next to her.

After the two of them had left, a fair, well-endowed woman in a light blue sari placed a hundred rupee note on the table and said, "Chandrakala." Ramayya bent over his book and intoned as he wrote, "Chan ... dra ... ka ..." Chandrakala casually bent down, hitched her sari up to her knees, unhooked a gold chain that was tied around her left calf and wore it around her neck. Achari sat dumbstruck by the unexpected sight of her fair, shapely legs.

Then a hefty woman came, leading a group of some five or six women and paid all their fines. When they left, Ramayya closed the receipt book and sighed. "I've had enough of these whores!" Achari couldn't resist asking him why that woman Chandrakala had tied the gold chain around her calf. "Oh that," said Ramayya. "Well, the magistrate has a tendency to slap a big fine on any woman sporting an expensive sari or a chain around her neck or who has a watch. So these bitches play such games ..." As he was drawling along, looking at his watch every now and then, a woman in a green skirt with a yellow half-sari came in as if she were looking for someone. Although her face looked tired, Achari was struck by the sight of her firm breasts poking against the tight red blouse behind her flimsy sari.

She looked around and cursed her madam in a low voice. "That bitch didn't turn up!" Then, noticing Ramayya's knotted brows, she moved towards him hesitantly and placed a crumpled twenty rupee note on the table. "Anna, if you have some thirty rupees, could you please lend it to me? I'll return it tomorrow." Ramayya didn't even look up at her. He closed the ledger sharply, grumbling "Yes, yes. That's just what I want to do." Then, "Go see. There may be some fan of yours waiting outside," he said, winking at Achari. She started to whine. Ramayya growled. "You won't learn will you, unless you're kicked and locked up for two days."

But she kept on, like a child pestering her parents, as she stood there twirling the end of her sari. Achari suddenly pulled out a fifty rupee note and said, "Here. Take this." Ramayya was baffled by this unexpected gesture and tried to protest. The woman in the green skirt said, "Let annavaru give, anna. What's it to you?" She stood looking at Achari with adoring eyes. Achari seemed determined to help her. Grumbling, Ramayya wrote out the receipt. Noticing that Ramayya had no intention of returning her twenty rupees, Achari, forgetting that he too had once in a while pocketed ten or twenty rupees said, "Give her back the change, I say."

Ramayya's face fell. He contemptuously threw the crumpled note at her. She quietly tucked it into the folds of her sari at her waist and looking at Achari with deep adoration she said, "Tomorrow evening, come to the park in front of the court, anna. I'll return this," smiling coyly. Achari's heart that was overflowing with pity was suddenly smitten by an irrepressible desire. As she threw a smile and skipped out, Achari stood admiring her bouncing breasts. Ramayya stared at Achari, not knowing what to make of his action. Was Achari a fool or ...? Achari didn't like the look on Ramayya's face. He got up hastily. "I'll see you," he said. By then she had walked out of the main gate of the court.

All the way home he kept remembering the evening incident again and again. His sisters were surprised to see a spring in his gait. He took his bedridden father for a walk. For a change he ate happily, without complaining. He took out the harmonium he hadn't touched in ages, dusted it and started to play *Vara veena, mridu paani* ... It was a kriti that his father had taught him a long time ago. Although he had forgotten most of it, he sat there for quite some time repeating whatever he knew. Next day, at the office, he worked with great enthusiasm. Although he kept wondering if he should accept her invitation or not, by four thirty he had washed his face, styled his hair and started walking the kilometre and half to the meeting place. He reached the park at five sharp. He walked about, sat on the stone bench, looking around all the while. An hour went by. Clouds began to gather. I believed that cheap whore and she took me for a ride, he thought, thoroughly disgusted with himself.

She sat under a tree, in a corner of the General Hospital, a small mirror perched between her kneecaps, a hair pin between her teeth. She was trying to untangle the knots in her hair. Sharadakka sat beside her, threading flowers. "Hand me a rubber band," she said, turning to Sharadakka. "What, amma? Making yourself pretty, uhn?" Sharadakka pinched her cheek and pulled out one of the two rubber bands in her hair and passed it on. "If I were a man, I would have kept you permanently." Sharadakka's words brought some colour to her wilted face. "Sharadakka ..." she began. "Hoon, what is it?" There was impatience in her voice. Sharadakka had been home for the last three days, looking after a sick child. If she didn't get some money today, she'd be in serious trouble. She couldn't even ask this girl for help. During the raid on the lodge, two days ago, she'd been arrested and produced in the court and had come back empty handed.

But the girl wanted to say something. Sharadakka's curiosity grew. "Hoon, tell me," she murmured.

"Yesterday at the Court that anna who paid my fine ... well, I had told him that I'll return the loan today ..."

Sharadakka interrupted her. "Who says you have to return the loan only in cash, amma?" she asked, as she poked the girl's waist and laughed.

"Thoo, if you see that anna! He doesn't look that kind."

"Ayyo! Don't know the males of the species." Sharadakka's words sounded like a dialogue from a play. Long years ago, Sharadakka had been a member of the Basaveshwara Drama Company and had played bit roles in "Mother's Womb," "Tear-filled Eyes" and other such plays, and it was not uncommon for her words to sound like dialogues from those plays. Not knowing what to say, the girl stared at the mirror, her fingers busy curling her hair. Suddenly, she looked up, then spat out angrily. "Thoo, damn it!"

Surprised, Sharadakka also looked up and her eyes came to rest on the darkening clouds. She too was annoyed. The inky darkness of the clouds began to spread. They covered their heads with their sari pallu to protect their made-up faces and ran towards the water tank. What if this damn rain continues throughout the night ... If we don't get a customer ... As these questions rose in their minds, they noticed Chandraiah enter through the gate and walk briskly towards them, his dhoti tied up, a towel wrapped around his head like a turban. They felt happy just seeing him.

Chandraiah of Azad Nagar slum often brought them customers. And if one of the customers didn't pay up he talked about it all over town until, exasperated, they did. He saw to it that Sharadakka's and her interests were protected. Both of them looked at him expectantly. Surely he had a client for them? Chandraiah came scurrying on his spindly legs and, seeing Sharadakka after three days of absence, he smirked, "Oh! So we've reported for duty today, have we?" Seeing him go sit under the water tank in a relaxed manner and light a bidi, their faces fell. He was not going to be of use today.

Chandraiah sat inhaling deeply on his bidi. He looked up. The rain didn't show any signs of stopping. "Mother fucking rain," he muttered. The gods, who came in the way of poor people making a living, by bringing the rains, were blind, he contended, using the choicest of expletives.

Sharadakka was overcome by a sudden fear. If the rain continued all night, she would have to go home empty handed. In an attempt to suppress the fear, she pinched the girl's waist and asked, "What time did the man say?" Chandraiah grinned. "Oh, so it's already fixed!" Sharadakka, of course, had to tell him the whole story and he started to tease the girl for the principled stand she had taken.

Darkness poured down till they could hardly see one another's faces. Chandraiah muttered, "It's cold," and edged closer to Sharadakka who jabbed him with her elbow and shouted him right back to his place. The girl stood there, her mouth grim. "Poor thing! Will he be waiting?" She felt sorry for him and her gaze pierced through the darkness. But the damned rain showed no signs of stopping.

Maybe she was caught in the rain yesterday, Achari thought as he pored over his ledger and wondered if he should go wait for her again or not. The day passed by without the excitement or the anxiety of the previous day and he left his office ten minutes before closing time to go stand at the same spot in the park. Within minutes he was quite ashamed of himself for believing the words of a common whore. But, he decided, now that I've come let me see it through. He had already forgotten her face. It was half past five, and when nobody even remotely resembling her appeared, Achari started calling himself all sorts of names. He was terrified by the thought that someone might have noticed him hanging around here for the past two days. He decided that this episode too shall forever remain a secret. He stood there bringing up shards of memories feeling acutely embarrassed that each one of them, without exception, pertained to some sexual adventure or other.

The secret world of his sexual adventures came into being when he was in High School, with a homosexual encounter he had had with a kid from the neighbouring house. To this was added the episode when he had tried to embrace his uncle's daughter, Jalajakshi, one night while she was sleeping upstairs. She had created a ruckus and he had got away only by claiming to be a sleepwalker. Then there was a time when he had craved for his immediate sister, Rajeshwari. Since then, he'd never been able to face either of them. If ever he had to talk to them, he always pretended to be angry and irritated. He remembered all this now and laughed. Then it struck him that if someone saw him laughing by himself, they might think he was out of his mind. And as he looked around furtively, there she stood in front of him in a blue sari smiling at him as if at an old friend.

Achari was so flustered at seeing her that he could barely give her a smile of recognition. "Yesterday, it rained," she said. "Hoon." There was silence. Then, "If you have time, how about some coffee?" he murmured. Hearing his fumbled invitation, she looked at him as if at a strange creature. Achari not knowing what to make of that look said, "If you don't want to have coffee, then it's all right." There was more silence. He said, "If you have some time, can we sit and talk for a few minutes?" He pointed to the stone bench in the corner of the park. She frowned as if she found all these formalities tedious. Achari thought that she was embarrassed because he had used the respectful plural when addressing her. He started off once again, this time using the singular and ended up addressing her neither in the plural nor in the singular. She seemed perplexed. But when the clean shaven constable walked past them, leering at him as if he were a bungling impotent clown, it was Achari's turn to look embarrassed. Seeing him stand silently, she said. "You'll have to make arrangements for a room." Never in his life had he heard such a direct proposal. His mouth fell open.

She paused. Maybe this man had never had such intentions? "I couldn't arrange the money," she murmured, bending her head ashamedly. Achari was overcome by love and sympathy. "Ayyo, why do you worry about money?" Then he cleared his throat and said, "If you don't mind my asking ..." His words came in a rush. "... It's just ... someone like you ... doing this ..." Achari's voice faded into a small whisper and then into silence as her face turned stern.

Although by now she had a lurking suspicion that this man must be out of his mind, she tried her best to be polite. "Why do you say such things, anna?" she said in a soft voice as she sat down beside him on the stone bench. She had decided that this man who looked like a peon was a crackpot. But looking at his morose face, she felt sorry for him and not wanting to hurt him, she started working on how she could get away from him. He did look like he wouldn't hurt a fly, but she was afraid he'd ask all sorts of uncomfortable questions. Achari cast a shy look at her quiet, still face. He thought she must be crying within herself. Ah, if she were to start crying now so he could tenderly wipe her tears ... Such was the strange desire that blossomed in him.

Achari had never wiped the tears of a woman in his life and hence didn't know what a sense of fulfillment there could be in such an act. He sat waiting for her to cry. But he was disappointed when he realized that she had no intention of obliging him. She should pour out all the sorrows of her heart to me, then I will confide all my troubles to her, he thought. He looked at her face in anticipation. When she tried to avoid his gaze and bent down her head, Achari thought she'd break down any moment now. He decided that the moment the first tears rolled down her tender cheeks, he'd take her in his arms, wipe the tears and console her. "Don't cry, I am here."

But what did "I am here" mean? He didn't have an answer. He was nearing thirty four, his head was streaked with grey. A thought sprang to mind: What if I ask her to marry me? His heart began to pound. In all his life, this was the closest he had come to such a situation. The very next moment he chided himself. I must be out of my mind. Maybe these thoughts come to my mind because I've never had a woman in all my life. Or maybe because of the warmth of a woman sitting by my side. She was the first woman he had ever sat next to, talked to. All of a sudden he felt a strange intimacy towards her, felt that she was the one woman in this whole world in whom he could confide. As he sat musing, the following words slipped off his tongue, "Have you thought about marriage?"

"What do you mean?" she said taken aback by the question. Wrinkles formed on her forehead. All the excitement that was in him a moment ago vanished. And when he saw her straighten her sari and get ready to leave, he was filled with dismay. I must make her stay and talk to me, he thought desperately. He stammered, "Now, just say I ... if I were to ask you about your marriage ... what will you say?" The moment these words were out, he realized it was an awkward statement. She, who had stopped thinking of these things long ago, now gave a forced laugh. "Ayyo! Don't try to be funny, anna." She fussed again with her sari and made as if to get up. Achari didn't want her to go but when he tried to speak, words got stuck in his throat. Just then, a few feet away from their bench, by the barbed wire fence, an autorickshaw came puttering to a stop.

Achari saw a skinny fellow sitting in the rear seat thrust his head out and grin at her. Achari's whole body was aflame. She too seemed pleased to see him. A storm rose in Achari's heart. She jumped up from the bench saying, "Chandraiah, this is the anna who gave the money in court the other day."

Achari didn't know what to make of her relationship with this Chandraiah. He was skinnier than Achari, but didn't even bother to acknowledge Achari's existence. "Ready? There's a party. Waiting near Chanakya Hotel. Film people." He winked. The tone of his voice, his gestures, made Achari mad. Anger and confusion clashed with one another forcing him to stay glued to his bench, not knowing what to do. "Hmm, say yes," said Chandraiah, impatiently. She didn't know what to say, and through the corner of her eyes tried to read Achari's face, and then he heard her say, "No, anna. I'm booked."

Literally the whole of Chandraiah's body was hanging out of the autorickshaw by now. "Ai, don't joke avva. Good customers. They've brought Triplex Rum!" Chandraiah looked at Achari as if he were a worm and gave a scornful laugh.

Achari was furious. He stood up. At any moment now an event of great consequence will take place and I'll be playing an important role in it, he thought. A rare fervour rose within him.

Chandraiah was amused by the sight of this puny fellow. If he gave him one, he would fall reeling to the ground. Yet the man stood there, glaring at him. Chandraiah got down from the auto, lifted the barbed wire, crept under it with effortless ease and came towards them. Achari didn't know what to do or say. He looked at her.

She stood like a pillar with her feet planted apart. Chandraiah took a couple of steps towards them. "Ai, come. It's getting late." He pulled her by the hand, acting familiar. Achari felt as if someone had torn out one of his limbs. He, who never could raise his voice against even an attendant in his office, raged with anger. He looked at Chandraiah as if his look alone would bring Chandraiah to the ground and shouted, "Leave her alone!" Startled, Chandraiah let go of her hand and stepped back. But at the same time, it struck him that Achari had addressed her in the respectful plural and laughter burst out of him. She let her head drop, coyly. Seeing Chandraiah retreat, Achari, astounded by the sound of his own voice dared to grasp her hand.

He turned his back to Chandraiah and walked towards the park gate. She walked with him, hand in hand.

Chandraiah, who till then had treated the whole incident as a joke, suddenly turned serious. How dare they undermine his authority? He looked at the two of them walking away from him and in rising anger roared, "Stop right there. Your mother's ..."

As Chandraiah continued to fling abuses at her, she pulled her hand free from Achari's, turned and glared at him. Taken aback by the sight of her blazing eyes, Chandraiah smiled ingratiatingly. "You bastard! Do you see what's on my feet ... you pimp ..." Her voice was raised. Seeing her tuck the end of her sari at the waist and stand prepared to fight, Chandraiah slowly retreated with his head down. By then the rickshaw had left.

Achari had never seen a woman in fury before and was frightened by the sight of her ranting in the middle of the street. He worried about someone seeing him associated with the woman. Not knowing what to do, he stood still. She raved till Chandraiah looked around furtively, crept under the fence and disappeared. Then she turned to Achari who was standing there like a dimwit, firmly clasped his soft hand in hers and began to walk away dragging him along. Seeing the confidence and purpose in her gait all his fears, anxieties and difference melted away and Achari found himself striding along beside her with a freedom that he had never known before.

First published in Kannada as "Maya Kinnari" in *Lankesh Patrike*, March 15, 1992, Bangalore.

best of the
90s

## MANOJ KUMAR GOSWAMI

## The Return

A kaleidoscopic view of the social upheaval in Assam in recent times. The author displays a deep understanding of the true spirit of revolutionism and has tackled a difficult subject very sensitively, depicting how revolution is perceived as unimportant, even futile, by a wide crosssection of the society.　　　**– Rituparno Ghosh**

Barman lifted the receiver off its cradle. At the other end was DIG Har Datta – each of his words reverberating with tension.

"Yes *sir,*" said Barman, his voice properly respectful. "I have made all arrangements as per your directives, sir. Two Inspectors have been stationed at Saukidingi outpost. I myself am going on inspection. All the police thanas have already been put on alert. The latest IB report is with me ..."

More staccato instructions followed, terse and brief, the telephone cable trembling under their impact.

Barman knew the facts only too well. The man was a dangerous character, the leader of an insurgent group. He had been involved in a series of crimes. Seven years ago, he had been captured after much effort, but had soon slipped out of police custody. Despite the redoubled efforts of the police and the Intelligence, he had managed to escape their dragnet. Many of his associates had been arrested, others had negotiated terms with the government and surrendered. The backbone of the group had been broken. It was perhaps because of these developments that he was coming back. People said he had received training across the border in the latest and most sophisticated weaponry, that he was bringing across deadly ammunition.

"Yes, *sir,*" Barman replied in smart monosyllables. Ananta Barman had become an SP at a very young age, superseding many of his seniors. He knew the qualities that built careers, the devotion of a hound to its master, the swiftness of a hyena, the alertness of a hare, the hunting instinct of a wolf. His ambition knew no limits. But to rise any further, *this* man had to be caught. Even if it meant taking risks. It was an opportunity not to be missed ... Barman certainly had to think a lot about his career.

Manoj Kumar Goswami won the Katha Award for Creative Fiction in 1994, for this story. Journal Emporium received the Journal Award for first publishing this story in Asomiya.

The Katha Translation Award went to Jayeeta Sharma.

This story first appeared in English translation in *Katha Prize Stories 4*, 1994.

We thank Pankaj Thakur, our nominating editor, for choosing this story for us.

"Thank you, sir!" he said as he replaced the receiver.

Drops of sweat trickled down his face.

The layout of the first page seemed to be to the chief editor's liking. He took his glasses off, thought for a moment and said, "Yes, the headline is fine. It will sell. But we must have that man's photo. That's essential."

"But sir," remonstrated the staff reporter, "There is no way we could manage a photo. Goswami and Lahkar have tried their best. Even the police files don't have one."

The chief editor lit his cigarette, a new one from a fresh pack. "All right then. Goswami, you keep in touch with the police thana. Lahkar will have to do the rest on his own. Make daily box items of whatever information you get from our sources. If he is arrested, the first photograph should be in our paper. Our readers have to know everything about this case. Remember, this man's name sells."

The teleprinter was spewing out words in the next room – bits and pieces of news from various places. Muted sounds of traffic from the street below. A telephone rang in another room. The sub editor and Goswami bustled out.

Lahkar hitched his chair a little closer to the editor's table. He looked around carefully and then said, "We could do one thing, sir. As far as I can see, we don't have much chance of meeting him. The police haven't found any trace of him. How would it be if we ... set up a false interview?"

The editor reached out for an ashtray, his eyes glued to Lahkar. "You mean, one of us is taken blindfolded to a hideout used by these insurgents. There we meet our man, speak to him about his future plans, his experiences across the border, his views on the present government ..."

"We could have a blurred photo to go with the article," Lahkar finished enthusiastically.

The editor stubbed out his cigarette. "No," he said, his long years of experience coming to the fore. "That will cause trouble, Lahkar. Police interrogations, cross-examinations ... and if later it leaks out that it was all a cooked-up interview ... the paper's image will take a battering, all for nothing."

Neela was combing her hair, the huge dressing table mirror before her. It was a still afternoon. Music – a song by Cliff Richard – was playing softly in the background. The servant boy was out – for a matinee, he had said. There was no possibility of her husband, Neelam Mahanta, returning before half past four.

The emptiness of that enormous house was getting to her. From the window, she could see the afternoon street. Deserted, except for the rare vehicle that sped by. She got up abruptly and flung herself onto the bed. The wall clock relentlessly sloughed off the afternoon hours. The curtains rustled in the light breeze, Suddenly the harsh ring of the telephone made her jump. She was too frightened to even look towards it. What should she do? Pick up the receiver? Or not?

The telephone continued to ring. The house seemed to shake with the persistent ringing.

She approached the instrument hesitantly. What if she picked up the receiver and heard his voice at the other end? That grave, deep, well-remembered voice?

"Hello?" She could hardly recognize her own voice.

"What's up, Neela? Aren't you well?"

Oh! It was her husband. Even so, her heart continued to thud for a few more seconds.

"Neela? Is something wrong?"

"No, nothing. I had dozed off, that's all."

"Let's see a film today. There's a good one at the Spielberg. Get dressed. I'll be there in fifteen minutes. Don't we have to go to Bhatt's place this evening, for his son's birthday party?"

Neela shut her eyes. She tried to immerse herself in the

comforting tones of Neelam's voice. It seemed to be the only possible refuge. "Not today," she said. "This Anil has also gone off somewhere. See if you can come home a little early. I'm feeling quite lonely today."

Neela walked up and down the large room. The softly yielding carpet underfoot, the expensive furniture, the refrigerator in a corner, standing like a huge block of ice, the colour television reflecting off the Belgian mirror. Neela drew the curtain back. She could see the garage beyond the lush green lawn from where her husband, only a few hours ago, had driven their blood red Maruti to his company office. Her heart started racing again. She wondered, would she be able to give up all this without a pang? Would he allow her to continue the carefree life she led here, in the midst of all this abundance? One day, on one such afternoon perhaps, she would open the door to the insistent summons of the calling bell, and find him waiting there.

"How are you, Neelie?" he would ask, that cruel, slightly enigmatic smile on his face. Unruly hair, stubble on his chin, clothes dishevelled and hanging loosely on his frame, a vein throbbing blood-red on his arm. Perhaps he would slip into the room, to disgustedly survey the prosperity of her home. Perhaps he would look her straight in the face for a few moments, and say in his slow, calm voice, "Come back, Neelic. Come back to me."

Neela sighed. One day he would be back. That was certain. He would never forget her. Nothing would deter him – not even the prospect of death. And now, after having lived for seven years with wild beasts and wilder men, he must be that much more fearless.

She felt disgusted with herself. Ten years ago, she had been in love with him. Love ... the very word repulsed her now. But it would be because of that, that he would return to her. She had never been in love with Neelam, yet, surrounded by all his possessions – the fridge, the TV, the car, the house – she had lived a happy enough existence. All of it could disintegrate, now that he had returned.

Her cheek against a bar, Neela stared out of the window. Yes, he was on his way.

Someone had opened a fresh bottle of whisky, a glass dropped and rolled on the floor, there was the sound of liquid being poured, and a voice could be heard singing, *"It's been a hard day's night, I should be sleeping like a log ...,"* very offkey. The room was filled with cigarette smoke. In the dim light of the zero watt bulb could be seen a few scattered chairs, tables, a bed, and some young men, Bipul, Ajit, Dul, Bagen, Rafiul.

Ajit got up and opened the window, letting the night breeze into the stuffy room. Turning, he recited in a solemn voice,

> *We drink the whole night through*
> *A cocktail of darkness and wine ...*
> *for we are the ones who have to see*
> *the morning in*

Ajit was considered to be an upcoming poet.

"Shut up, fool!" said Bagen. *"This"* – an obscene gesture followed – "Is what I think of your poetry."

The room seemed to rock with Dul's laughter. "Why do you say that, comrade? It's through such poems that he makes such a name, has gamochas draped on him, gets mobbed by beautiful girls begging him to sign autographs. Remember, it's poetry that helps him lead so many of those girls on ..." Dul's words faded away into an indistinct mutter.

"What good does my poetry do?" Ajit asked sombrely. "Damn it, each word in my poems rises to mock me. The number of times I've taken them to interview boards, shown off magazines which had published them – I tried so hard for that job of a publicity officer. But what happened? Someone appeared from nowhere and just walked into the job."

A motorcycle stopped outside. They knew it was Ishwar. He had got a scholarship to an American University. He was treating them to drinks that day.

"Hello," said Ishwar as he entered.

"Are you leaving us, young man?" someone asked.

"Sure. I'm leaving you!" declared Ishwar, draining a peg. "You guys must come to the airport in the morning."

Rafiul walked unsteadily towards him. He put a hand on Ishwar's shoulder, "And what will you send us from America, bhai? Some good brand of liquor, pictures of sunbathing American blondes, some hot porn ..,"

"And real juicy stuff," finished Ajit.

"Promise, you bastard, promise," shouted Bipul.

"I promise," said Ishwar, solemnly.

"Go, saala. Go," Dul muttered. "And when you come back after five years, you'll find everything changed here. A quintal of rice for twenty bucks, a bottle of whisky for five, free fags, and girls queueing up to marry loafers like us, money blowing in the wind ... Our Ram Rajya. Because we have heard that ..."

"Achha, I'll be off," Ishwar announced briskly, "I have to drop in at a couple of more places. I haven't even been to Neelie's yet. I'll meet you guys at the airport in the morning."

"Goodbye, young man. Wish you all the best," someone said from a dark corner. "We've had some fun at your expense, but forget that, After all, you've had your share of amusement, too. Revolution, changing the entire system – we don't mind that you used to speak of all that. They should be shot, strung up the nearest telegraph post – that's what you'd say about all blackmarketeers, corrupt officials, MLAs, faithless mistresses ..."

Ishwar smiled thinly, "I have shut the door on yesterday, and thrown the key away. Good night."

He walked out. They could hear the motorcycle revving up and then its sound fading into the distance.

Bagen made his way unsteadily towards the open window, his hoarse voice raised in song, "Lying in someone's arms ..."

Suddenly, Dul shouted, "All right, saala. We'll shoot them. We'll hang them all ... blackmarketeers, ministers, MLAs, corrupt officials, unfaithful mistresses." He crawled on all four towards the centre of the room in his underpants. "Don't worry, brothers," he drawled out. "Everything will be fine. We'll take up sten guns and grenades ... Oh ... you want to know who'll give them to us? Don't worry. You know our Samiran Barua is on his way back. *He'll* lead us to heaven." Dul let out a cackle of laughter. He stopped abruptly and was sick all over the floor.

The flickering flame of the kerosene lamp failed to light up the veranda. The woman holding the lamp seemed even more emaciated in its light. The man opened the gate. He crossed the threshold and entered the house without uttering a word. The lamp followed his every movement. An extraordinarily calm face, framed by an untidy mass of hair. He unbuttoned his shirt and threw it on the bed. Then he sank onto the bed himself.

"It seems he's come back. Everyone says so."

The wick flickered – as did the shadow on the man's face. "Why has he come back?" he murmured, as if carrying on a monologue. "To me he was as good as dead. Did he ever send a single paisa to me, his old father? Now his three sisters have to be married off – will his being here bring that about?" His voice shook with suppressed emotion. "Why did he not die? So many wild beasts ... guns ... bombs ... how did he survive all that?"

The woman clutched the lamp. "All I know is that he's coming back," she said, speaking for the first time that night.

They were five people sitting around a huge, ornate table. Strewn across it were newspapers and magazines, an ashtray, a cigarette packet, plates of dry fruit, glasses of sherbet. A stocky man asked, tentatively, "So Phukanda, you should know Samiran Barua pretty well?"

"Certainly, I know him. I know him well," answered the old man. He was one of the most experienced of politicians. He sat ensconced in his chair, silver framed glasses upon his nose, two golden buttons glinting on his kurta, his walking stick propped against the table. "His father and I were in jail together. We were friends. After Independence, I became a Minister and we completely lost touch – I don't know where he went. He was a very self-sufficient person, very proud. He was just not meant for politics. After many years, I met him in a village where I was to address a meeting. He was the headmaster there. He hailed me cheerfully and introduced the small boy by his side as his son. The lad greeted me, calling me Khura. That evening, I had tea at their house. Yes. Of course I know him."

"Then why don't you tell him, Phukanda? Make him understand that our party will be the best platform from which to oppose the present government."

The old man's lips puckered into a faint smile.

"You must get hold of him. By whatever means possible. We'll get you all the information about him. Phukanda, you know that the only way for our party to make its political presence felt right now is through him. If we lose him, there's no hope left."

"All that I can manage. It will need some fast talking, some persuasion, but that I can do," the old man declared, fingering the tip of his stick, his voice dropping almost to a whisper. "I've reached such a position that I have left my own concerns far behind. I can't even hear my own voice any more. I no longer feel the need to look after my interests."

"The old fool must have tippled a bit too much."

"I will speak to him. I will put my hand on his shoulder, and in a voice glowing with pain and compassion, I will say, Sameer, you must return to a normal life. What will you get from all this? The path you have chosen is not fit for someone from our world. Give it up, son. Come with me. You can work with our party, for the people. Sameer, stay with me. You know how long your father and I have ..."

He had reached the cinema hall at the crossroads, a huge building, new paint still shining on its walls. Samiran remembered this spot. This was where Kusha Master's house used to be. But where were all the houses, the people? All that remained was this monstrous edifice of a cinema hall.

He had come into the city two days ago, after many years. There were changes everywhere, not a single familiar face on the streets, no one to recognize him. There used to be a huge banyan tree at this very corner ... it had probably been cut down. Now there were more shops, many more cars and buses, and hundreds of busy people on the streets. The shouts of the truck drivers and others, the blare of bus horns, all added up to a scene pulsating with incessant noise and motion. Samiran went into a nearby teashop. There were only a few people inside. He took an inconspicuous corner table and sat facing the door. He hadn't dared to spend the last couple of nights at any hotel. His own home was out of question. And he hadn't had the courage to seek shelter with any of his old friends. He realized that the police knew he was in the city. He had barely managed to escape the police cordon at Saukidingi. At the Lumding rail station too, there were several suspicious characters, possibly from the IB.

Two fire engines rushed past, their sirens wailing. He gave a start, looked all about him. No, there was only the clang of dishes, the manager's stentorian voice, a Hindi film song coming from a tape recorder. Everything else was drowned by those humdrum sounds.

So he had returned. Empty handed. The little money that he had was almost exhausted. He had managed some ammunition which was supposed to arrive within the next few months – but this hinged entirely on trust. And, increasingly, he was beginning to doubt whether he could depend on something so fragile. From what he had seen till now, most of his old comrades had drifted away. Pinaki Mahanta was in a cushy job, Dipen Phukan was a prosperous contractor, Ramen had become an MLA and he had seen, a couple of nights ago, a minister's car parked outside the home of his best friend, Dwigen. What was he to do now? Where could he go?

A marriage procession went past him – cars decorated with cascading flowers and bright lights, a hired band, clarinet and drum resounding, young men dancing – noise and lights filling the street. Samiran passed a group of young men aimlessly loitering outside a paan shop. They shouted obscene remarks at some girls who were walking past them. A crowd shuffled and strained to watch the television that was in the showcase outside a shop – a cricket match was on. A running commentary could be heard from the crowd, "*Another* wicket down! Ravi Shastri is bowling extremely well!"

Yes, thought Samiran Barua, he was definitely back in the city. People swarmed the street outside a cinema hall. A show must have just ended. On the wall in front of him were garishly coloured posters, a hero lifting the heroine off her feet, a musical nite sponsored by a cigarette company, a family planning advertisement, a hoarding extolling the undergarments in Ramlal Sevadutta's cloth shop. The city sprawled uncaringly before him, its inhabitants walking past him without even a second glance. A sudden gust of sound reached Samiran. It came from two buses with blaring loudspeakers, filled with youngsters. Perhaps a picnic party.

He trudged on wearily away from the uproar. Near a saloon was a man selling peanuts. He stopped and bought two rupees worth of the nuts. A furtive glance – no, there was nobody who had an eye on him – and then he stood there, shelling the peanuts, eating them one by one. From time to time, fragments of noise, light and dust from the road reached him. He caught sight of his face in the saloon's mirror – clean shaven cheeks, longish hair, spectacles. A gaunt, tired looking face, the cheek bones sticking out.

For whom had he returned? Why had he stayed away so long? What had forced him to give up his own youthful dreams? For whom had he done so? These people, didn't they want anything more? He had thought that people would be awaiting him, their saviour, like victims trapped in a rail carriage after an accident. But nobody seemed to need him here. Everything seemed to be running smoothly, effortlessly, with an abundance of money and happiness. Did he have any relevance in the midst of all this? If he was to stop and declare at that street corner – I am *Samiran Barua* – would anyone reach his side, apart from the police?

"Should I give you some more?" The old groundnut seller asked him, his trembling fingers raking the roasted nuts. His pushcart had a decrepit stove burning on it, the small heat from the quivering flame hardly making a difference to the cool air. The smell of fresh, roasted peanuts wafted in the breeze. Samiran bought some more. "Did you sell enough today?" he asked as he took the small paper bag from him.

The old man smiled, displaying toothless gums. "Just enough, just enough." he said, "It's the same every day."

Samiran continued to stand there. Should he go back to where he had come from? Or go to his mother? Should he surrender himself to the police? Or should he go to some distant city, begin once again, a law abiding, secure citizen?

Samiran walked slowly on. The city was still bustling with life, noise and light from numerous spotlighted advertisements. Under the steady yellow glow of a halogen streetlight, Samiran took the last nut out of the packet. He was about to throw the wrapping away when something on that scrap of newspaper caught his eye. Printed on it in bold letters was the headline – **SAMIRAN BARUA RETURNS!**

He stood there, clutching it tightly, growing cold inside. A stream of vehicles and people flowed past him. Laughter, gaiety, music. Young women walked by in their colourful dresses, some older women, a bunch of small children, a few elderly men. The gossipers at the paan shop had broken up, he could see the young men coming along the road.

He let go of the scrap of paper.

**SAMIRAN BARUA RETURNS** – this significant bit of news was picked up by the wind and blown along, to be trampled by the crowds of bustling feet in the city.

---

First published in Asomiya as "Samiran Barua Aahi Aase" by Journal Emporium, November 1993, Nalbari.

ф

best of the
~90s~

**VANDANA BIST**

The Weight
——~~~——

The story stuns with its sheer realism. Most Indian households experience the constant conflict for space, proximity and dominance. Like most people scrupulously trying to lead the "correct" life, as deemed by agencies outside of themselves, the characters too live, suffer and die under such a weight.　　　**– Sharmila Tagore**

From the top of her large pearl nose ring, Nima could see the louse crawling out of the cropped, but still matted, hair of the woman on the bed. Her eyes followed it along the entire length of the cot until it slid out of view, before she turned back to the rice she was cleaning. Her husband would be back soon and the rice had to be just the right temperature when he sat down to eat. She hoped he would be a little more cheerful today. The rich Thakurs in the neighbourhood had had a third son and, once again, Pandit Bhairon Dutt Joshi had been called upon to perform the naming ceremony.

A "long dhoti" pandit (claiming his descent from the region somewhere between Brahma's neck and head), he was pretty far up in the hierarchy of Kumaoni pandits, and fiercely proud of the fact that one of his clearly traceable ancestors had been a diwan in the court of the Chand rajas. Bhairon Dutt was known for his unrelenting belief in ceremonies. "Not a word short, or you can call another," he had often threatened his patrons. Even after fifteen years of marriage, Nima was still scared of her husband's piercing eyes. Every morning before his prayers, when he combed his hair back from his broad forehead, the face of a stranger would emerge, a stranger Nima was destined to spend her life with.

"Nima! Oh Nimuli!

The dry, rasping voice of the woman on the bed broke into Nima's thoughts. She hurriedly poured some water from the brass pot into the rice and began washing it, draining off the husk and the little black insects that floated to the top.

"Hurry up Nima! Take me out, quickly!"

"I'm coming Bubu! Just let me put the rice on for him! You know his temper, don't you?"

The woman on the bed became quiet.

Nima put the rice to boil, and wiping her forehead with her

Vandana Bist won the Katha Award for Creative Fiction in 1994, for this original unpublished English story. This story first appeared in *Katha Prize Stories 4*, 1994.
We thank Rukmini Bhaya Nair, our nominating editor, for choosing this story.

pallav hurried out of the kitchen. The woman on the bed was restless. Nima pulled back the smelly quilt. The woman's petticoat had risen above her legs, that she now held clenched together, and her wrinkled belly. Under the pale, tired skin, Nima could see the stark blue veins that sketched a frightening design. Nima brusquely pulled the woman's petticoat down.

"Come on now!" Nima helped her to her feet and supporting the old woman's arm on her shoulders, took her out into the aangan. The woman huddled inside the tiny urinal and the liquid gushed out sharply from within her, making a loud clatter as it fell into the tin kept there.

Each time Nima took the old woman out to ease herself, two words, sieved out from a secret her mother had told her, surfaced and frolicked in her ears, blocking out every other thought – virgin-whistle, virgin-whistle. Then, at other times, there were other words which hovered around this woman like obstinate flies. Nima listened silently whenever the woman spoke. She never questioned. And the woman talked on and on about her miserable childhood, a beleaguered youth and the endless suffering of old age. Her nephew, Bhairon Dutt, was the hero of many of these tales. But words, detached from these leaden tales, were all that remained in Nima's mind. Crisp dead words, like dry leaves fallen from trees, full-of-sound words – child-widow, cholera, vomiting, no dolls, no tomatoes, tamasik and chastity, moksha and karma and vaikuntha. Bubu talked only half as much as she did when Nima was newly married. Yet the words had been repeated so often that they were imprinted on Nima's mind, and every time the old woman opened her vacant mouth, Nima wished she would shut up.

Outside, the line of mountains was temporarily obliterated by a thin mist. Clouds covered the sun and a chill spread instantly.

---

**Long dhoti Pandits:** Pandits from Maharashtra and Jhusi (Uttar Pradesh) came and settled in Kumaon between the 9th and 11th centuries. Some of them managed to become priests of the Chand rajas. These pandits wore long dhotis and were considered to have a better knowledge of the vedas.

Nima hurried the woman across the cold stone aangan and pushed her into the bed roughly.

The woman pulled the quilt over herself, groaning loudly.

How did the naamkaran go?" Nima asked her husband that night, as she unrolled her mattress on the floor, next to her sons who were fast asleep. She sat down to massage the cracked soles of her feet with the tips of her fingers.

"Quite well," he replied, without turning towards her.

"And the horoscope? Must be good. A Thakur's son after all!"

Nima's husband covered himself with his blanket. "Ha! Thakur's son, indeed. A child cursed by Shani! They should be happy if he sees his sixteenth birthday."

Nima's hand instinctively reached out to caress her son. Stupid ominous things, horoscopes. Pronouncements that mesmerized you into proving them. *She will have a good husband and will bear him sons. A major obstacle will create unhappiness in the first few years of marriage.* Nima's horoscope had worried her father. But there were the rectifying ceremonies and after her marriage to a tree (the walnut tree in their field), Nima's marriage to Bhairon Dutt had taken place. Well, she had proved at least two of the predictions right – a good husband, sons ...

Nima looked at the man lying on the bed.

"Bubu had fever again today."

He turned and looked her. "Did you call the dakshaiv?"

The concern in his voice irked Nima but she also felt a certain satisfaction at having caught her husband's brief interest. It was only at times such as these that Nima felt she should be grateful for the old woman's presence in the house.

"Hari got the medicines, the same as before. The man at the shop wanted the money by tomorrow."

She revelled in the authority in her voice.

---

**Dakshaiv:** a corrupt form of "doctor saab"; the usual Kumaoni way of addressing a doctor.

"I'll give it to him tomorrow."

Her husband's back was turned to her again.

Nima was sure that if she measured the distance between her mattress and the bed, it would be exactly four steps even today ... Four steps ahead he had walked on the curving mountain path, the weight of an umbrella bending his back, and she, still in her bridal dress, her long, sequined ghaghar flapping heavily against her legs and slowing her down considerably. The unfettered rays of the mountain sun had beaten down on her. It had melted the raw colours of the magenta and yellow pichchaura that covered her, sending rivulets of orange perspiration trickling down her neck and between her breasts. On her head she had carried her belongings in a large aluminium trunk ... On just two nights in these fifteen years, that distance had disappeared for a few brief seconds, in a blur of frenzied hands, groping fingers, heaves and guttural sounds, before the room was engulfed in an embarrassed silence. Even through the opaque darkness, Nima had made out that he had risen and moved away from the bed, as quickly as he had come to it, to walk out of the room.

On that first night, Nima had lain awake for a long time and those muffled sounds had swirled around her in a ceaseless whirlpool, till her eyes had closed in sheer exhaustion. She didn't know when or whether her husband returned to the room that night.

The next morning, she had seen him sitting in a corner of the stone aangan, muttering to himself. He was scrubbing his dhoti with soap and beating it on the stone to rid it of its stains.

Now, Nima's gaze lingered on the man's sleeping body for a while. Then turning towards the products of those two nights, she closed her eyes.

Hai! I'm dying! Bhairon! Oh Nimuli! I'm dying! I don't want to die on a bed. Put me down, Nimuli."

"What happened, Bubu?"

Before Nima could get up, her husband hopped over her and the children to switch on the light in the old woman's room. Nima lay there, her eyes determinedly shut. This had happened three times in the past twenty days. Eyes rolled back, breath stuck in her throat, she had screamed. The same words – Hai Ram! I'm dying! Put me down!

The last time they had been so sure Bubu's end was near, that Nima had sent the boys away to her mother's house and her husband had waited by the doctor's side, ready with Gangajal and the Bhagavad Gita. But after three anxious, unsure days, the old woman had given the hopeful, waiting Yama, a solid kick on his rump and risen. Back to her smelly bed. Back into Nima's life ... The horoscope had been correct. Time would prove if these fifteen years were indeed "The first few years of her marriage."

Nima's eyes remained shut. The old woman had quietened down. Pacifying and cajoling sounds in her husband's warm voice floated out of the room and stung Nima's ears. Words began to rise within her. From the pit of her stomach. From somewhere even lower, Tough old hag ... lice-ridden parasite. More words rose wildly now, probably from the cracks and fissures within Nima, from those dark holes in her household where the old woman had made her home for years – hunger, sore feet, empty rice tins, school fees. Words now abandoned by their meanings surged upwards, horoscope ... good woman ... dharma ... patience ... fate ... future. They churned and convulsed inside her and banged their empty weights against Nima's temple. Hard, round words. Words she could hold with her fingers, like the lice she had picked from the clumps of grey matted hair, like the stones and husk she had weeded from the thali of rice every day for fifteen years.

Nima became hot and breathless. She felt her soft breasts shrivel, her teeth loosen, her throat going dry. Sweat formed on her forehead.

Nima's eyes flew open. Her husband was back in the room.

"Did something happen to Bubu?"

Her husband seemed to notice the innocence in her eyes. He nodded.

Nima got up and moved towards the door.

"It's all right now. She's sleeping."

Stupid things, horoscopes.


Eight days later, Bhairon Dutt's Bubu had a convulsion and lost consciousness. It was Mahashivratri and Bhairon Dutt had gone to the temple, to help the priest there with the surging crowds and their offerings.

It began as it usually did. Nima was in the aangan, scrubbing the large brass parat with ash and lime. It was one of the few utensils still with her, from the boxful that her father had given her when she got married.

"Hai! I'm dying! Oh Nimuli!"

Nima scrubbed harder. The two dekchis had been given away for her first sister-in-law's marriage and the younger one took away the three thalis. All this on the old woman's orders. Nima had cursed her through clenched teeth as her husband had looked on helplessly.

"Hai! Today I won't survive! Call Bhairon! Oh Nimuli! Come here woman!"

The parat shone like gold as Nima washed it slowly. And her anger ebbed just as slowly. She carried the pile of utensils into the kitchen. The groans and wails continued. Then there was an unexpected silence. When Nima saw the old woman, fallen half out of the bed with her arms dangling to the ground, and the white of her eyes bulging, she screamed.

The neighbours rushed out. "She's dead! Bubu's dead!" somebody shrieked. "No! No! She's still breathing!"

"Hurry up and call him!" Nima yelled to Kishna, her husband's cousin who lived across the courtyard.

Nima's husband brought Mahesh Pant with him, the doctor's slow steps in complete contrast to Bhairon's agitated strides. Mahesh Pant's narrow topi, balanced at a precarious angle, the oblong, vermilion pitha on his forehead and the elbow-patched tweed coat that had lived on him for years made a curious combination. Anyone who knew Mahesh Pant knew that it was as inseparable from him as was the incident that led to this prize acquisition. That was the day he had excised a painful boil from the armpit of an Irish member of the local seminary. And the coat was the priest's grateful gift to the "Doctor." That was the day Mahesh Pant had happily traded the antiquity of his existing title of Vaid-ju for a more suave Dakshaiv.

And it was Pant Dakshaiv who sat next to the unconscious woman now. From the depths of an ancient leather bag he pulled out a worn-out stethoscope, pressed it to the woman's chest. Poking her with a careless finger, he rolled his eyeballs under closed lids. Lines formed on his forehead, breaking the vermilion pitha into several smaller segments. Then he pursed his lips and said, "Can't do much Bhairon-da, it all depends on Him now," pointing the same careless finger to the heavens above.

The old woman was put back on the bed. There was an awkward, unearthly quiet in the house after that. As wobbly and unsure as the thread on which hung the old woman's life. Every time Nima looked at the inert form in the corner, she felt an uncomfortable tightness inside her as if something was trying to push itself out. It was a feeling Nima couldn't identify. Sorrow? The woman wasn't dead yet. Anger? Irritation? She hadn't heard those demanding tones for three days now, though she still picked lice from the old woman's head, still wiped and changed her, and washed her soiled and stinking bed clothes. No, it wasn't guilt. Maybe it was something Nima did not feel at all. The ambiguity of the disquiet confused Nima as the tightness inside her grew. She was waiting for release as probably the old woman was, too.

Two days later, when the old woman's breathing became perceptibly irregular, the fear and panic that had lain dormant in the household, surged into a storm. Neighbours rushed in again. But Mahesh Pant had shaken his head and refused to come.

Bhairon Dutt sat with his head in his hands, as the old woman on the bed hovered between two worlds.

"Don't just sit there Bhairon, do something!" Kakhi, Kishna's mother, urged. She had been sitting in the room since the previous night.

"What should I do?"

"Put her down on the floor and put some weight on her chest. Her time has come, son. Stop that breathing!"

There was a sudden silence among the neighbours who had gathered there.

Bhairon jerked his head up and looked at Kakhi.

"Help her to get deliverance from this damned world!"

Bhairon Dutt knew that somewhere inside one of his innumerable yellowing books, there lurked a wayward paragraph which did permit him such benevolence. But he still sat motionless.

Kakhi turned towards Nima.

"Go get some rice from your kitchen."

Nima went into the kitchen. Her husband followed her. And, as she stretched up to bring down the rice tin, his voice stilled her.

"Nima!"

It pierced her, a sharp needle on soft flesh. Alien, yet exciting, full of promise. She stood frozen for a second. But then, as though with rehearsed ease, Nima replied, "Mm?"

Her husband stood close. "Should I do as Kakhi says?"

Everything around her suddenly seemed so different. Totally vincible. On another plane of existence, Nima had lived this moment innumerable times ... The tiny rice tin in her large palms, those dwarfed men and women gathered around the semi-corpse, whispering to each other ... She had explored this moment over and over again in all its dimensions of time and space and now Nima's limbs moved with the ease of practice, like a performer in his moment of triumph before a thousand eyes.

And the words came, moulded and flawless. "Bubu is suffering, but of course, you know best." Nima did not stay the light, gliding movement of her hand as she handed him a brass bowl, with the last two measures of rice from the tin.

Bhairon Dutt walked out with the bowl.

With the help of the other men, he carried his still unconscious Bubu and laid her down on the cold, stone courtyard.

Nima sat down on the kitchen floor. Waiting.

Words began to rise within her. Murderess ... hell ... Nima pushed them back, back deep into their pit. She didn't want their weight to fill the pleasant emptiness of this moment.

Outside, the weight of the two measures of rice on that frail chest did its work in a short time.

"Hai! Bubu's gone!"

The wails emanated one at a time, then streamed out in a torrent, searing across the aangan to rise to the rubescent evening sky.

Nima rushed out.

It was a curious sight. Her husband sat with his head bent. On the ground beside him lay the lifeless body of his Bubu, the child-widow, his aunt, she who had lived in that corner of the room ever since he could remember. And balanced on her inert chest was the brass bowl, brimming with rice grains.

Nima sat down beside her husband. The same hand that had handed him the last two measures of rice, touched his taut, bare arm. "What was to happen, has happened. It was her fate."

Perfectly moulded words again. Pristine and unblemished.

Pandit Bhairon Dutt looked at his wife. Nima did not remove her hand from the warm flesh of his arm. This pulsating moment, in complete isolation from the rest of time was hers. This fragment of infinity belonged only to her. Like those two vagrant nights in fifteen years.

"Go in and light a diya."

On the thirteenth day after his Bubu's death, the aangan of Bhairon Dutt's house filled up again. The pandit served the rice, repaying his debt to all those who had borne the burden of the dead woman. And in the kitchen Nima rolled out the puris.

The words rose again. Only this time it was from the mouths of those men and women in the aangan. Full and pregnant words, precious and pure. They fell, like the petals of delicate flowers and floated on a gentle wind towards her, caressing her sweat-flushed skin lovingly: patience ... good wife ... moksha ... dharma ... vaikuntha.

After everybody left, Nima picked up the brass bowl kept under the tulsi plant and, with a carefree swing of her hands, scattered the rice grains for the waiting birds.

best of the
90s

**SURENDRA PRAKASH**

Aaghori

The dream images of "Aaghori" are mystic and epic like. Superb.
Abstract.                                          **– Gulzar**

My father had a weakness for amruti, besan laddu and chitriwala kela. Once we – my father, Bawaji and I – were walking past Chelaram Halwai's shop when his feet suddenly stopped. The sweets were tastefully decorated and arranged in huge trays. Chelaram, dressed in clean, neat clothes, was being his usual attentive self, deftly weighing the sweets for his customers. On his left, his assistant was frying the amruti in a shallow frying pan.

My father's nostrils began to twitch. Without uttering a single word, he went and stood in front of Chelaram.

"Come bauji," Chelaram said, a faint smile on his lips, "What can I serve you?"

"Give me one quarter seer of steaming hot amruti," my father said, and looking at us he added, "And yes, one quarter seer of besan laddu. Now, what will you have, Bawaji?"

But Bawaji was not paying attention. "And you Bawaji?" My father asked again. "Nazar Suwalli," murmured Bawaji. "No, nothing, I don't care much for these things." He was pushing an exploratory finger into his right nostril.

"But still ... something?" You could see from his face that my father's mouth had begun to water.

"All right then, get me a quarter seer of raw bhindi, Nazar Suwalli," Bawaji answered with utmost indifference.

Chelaram placed the packet of amruti and besan laddu in my father's hands. We paid him and started walking towards the vegetable shop. There were all kinds of vegetables there, freshly sprinkled with water and glistening. At my father's request, the vendor chose small, tender bhindi, weighed them and gave them to Bawaji. He tied them up in one corner of the chadar that was wrapped around his shoulders. We started on the laddu and amruti

Surendra Prakash won the Katha Award for Creative Fiction in 1993, for this story. *Zahn-e-Jadeed* received the Journal Award for first publishing this story in Urdu.

The Katha Translation Award went to C Revathi.

This story first appeared in English translation in *Katha Prize Stories 4*, 1994.

We thank Anisur Rahman, our nominating editor, for choosing this story for us.

while Bawaji ate the raw bhindi as we walked towards the graveyard.

The graveyard had many small and big graves. Grass had grown wildly on some, some had raised platforms, while a few others had headstones. We stopped near one which was bigger than most and had a plastered platform. On the headstone was engraved,

BABA FAKIR SHAH, SON OF ...

DATE OF BIRTH ...

DATE OF DEATH: 15 AUGUST, 1947.

The three of us fell silent for a moment, our eyes fixed on the grave. Taking a deep breath, Bawaji spoke, his voice so strange that the hair on my body bristled.

"Arré Kirpa Ram, ask for whatever you want. You are in Baba Khizr Shah's durbar."

My father had always wanted enough money that would buy him certain conveniences – a two or three storeyed house with six rooms, which, no doubt, would have a municipal water connection but there would also be a hand pump, in case of an emergency. In one corner of the large courtyard in front, there would be two or three plantain trees with huge bunches of long chitriwala plantains which, on plucking, would become speckled and have just the right sweetness. There would be a guest house just off the courtyard – always filled with guests – and a huge veranda with comfortable cane chairs. During summer, the courtyard would be sprinkled with water and charpais would be brought out. Sitting on these charpais, everyone would feast on piping hot amrutis, washing them down with cold lassi. The safe would be stacked with money and the keys to it would hang at my mother's waist.

I thank Shri Dhian Singh Chawla for his help in editing this translation – GD.

**Aaghori:** A group of sants who reject society and any identity bestowed on them by society. **Amruti:** Also known as imarti and as jangri. **Chitriwala kela:** Special plaintains that are speckled when ripe and very sweet. **Nazar suwalli:** May the benevolent eye be on you!

My father looked at Bawaji, amazement flooding his face. "Baba Khizr Shah is dead?" he asked. "But I thought he was immortal. How can such a man die?"

"Nazar Suwalli," said Bawaji, kindly. "This is not that Khizr, child. This Khizr was my fellow disciple. We were followers of the same saint. He is dead. And I am about to die. He was older than me and attained eminence in his life. He now stands in the presence of the Holy Cherisher. I have seen him in my dreams several times, sweeping the durbar. Go ahead, don't hesitate, your wishes are sure to be fulfilled."

My father removed his footwear and fell to his knees. He spread out both his hands and started muttering something. Presumably, he was praying for his dreams to come true.

On our way back, a thought suddenly struck me. The year was 1945. The month, April. I was still a fifteen year old. Why did the tombstone on Baba Khizr Shah's grave show 1947 as the date of his death?

When I asked my father, the look on his face changed as if an unexpected tragedy had befallen him. He remained dumbstruck for a minute and then he asked, "Now Bawaji, what is all this?"

Bawaji looked evasive. "Nazar Suwalli," he murmured again. "What does this slave know about the ways of the Invisible?"

Where was the time for my father's wishes to be fulfilled? In just two years the Partition took place and we moved over to this side. My father died a few years later.

When we returned after performing his last rites, I saw my brother open his diary. He put his right hand over his eyes. Tears flowed down his cheeks and into his beard, as he picked up his pen.

"What are you writing, Bhapaji?" The words tumbled out of my mouth before I could stop them.

"Bauji's date of death." The words choked in his throat.

"Then write, Kirpa Ram, son of Attar Singh. Date of death: 15 August, 1947."

My brother just stared at me with tear filled eyes.

B ut then these are matters about days that are no more. What's the use of remembering them, I asked myself. Except that ... Bawaji was still on my mind.

Bawaji (whose name was Dayal Das), belonged to the town of Jhang where the grave of Waris Shah, the well-known poet of Punjab, is situated. The grave has neither fence nor roof. Yet, it is said that, during the monsoons, not a drop of rain falls on it. Some say that the grave is Mai Heer's. Maybe Waris Shah, Heer and Ranjha, all lie buried in the same grave, though there's no headstone declaring that – but such things are of no consequence, really.

Bawaji. The man with a shaven head, a broad forehead, large eyes, a round, lustrous face and a short, stocky body. Whenever we asked him, "Bawaji, who are you? Where do you come from? What is your caste?" He would reply with a smile, "Me? Oh, I'm a mad, mixed-up man, neither a Hindu nor a Mussalman. I am a native of Jhang."

The astonishing thing about him was that, when he was in deep thought, his face had a striking resemblance to a hooded snake. He had lost both his parents when he was a child. He had joined a group of Aaghori sadhus and had later become a disciple of a Sufi saint. Thus was his life spent ... but was this how his life was spent?

I asked him once, "Bawaji, who are the Aaghori?"

"Nazar Suwalli," he said, after a long, meditative moment. "You are a child, just a child, and you wish to plumb the depths of the sea by jumping into it?"

All I could gather was that these people wish to live with only one identity, that of an Aaghori, casting aside every other identity bestowed upon them by society. But it is a lifelong struggle.

---

**Waris Shah (1730 – 1790):** One of the greatest poets of Punjab. No Punjabi poet has translated its deepest desires and dreams into verse as well as he has. The story of the legendary lovers, Heer and Ranjha, had already acquired fame by the time Waris Shah wrote his famous poem in 1766. He became so possessed by the characters, especially Heer, that he wrote very little else.

I am seated in my room when someone suddenly emerges from within me and sits down on the sofa by my side.

"Who are you?" I ask.

He says he does not yet have an answer to that question. He's still trying to understand himself. And at that moment, he's in the process of effacing the identity bestowed on him by society.

I don't know him, don't recognize his voice. There's a strangeness about him that fills me with dread. My heart is thumping as I get up and quickly walk out, leaving him behind.

The lane from my house leads to the main road with its continuous stream of scooters and cars and trucks. These things are mightier than man, they are made of metal that is much stronger, and the speed at which they run can smash a human to smithereens if he gets in their way. The one lesson I have learnt in my life is, Follow all the rules of the road conscientiously, otherwise ...

I turn right. There is the huge forensic laboratory that belongs to the government – a place where tools used in crimes and the fingerprints of criminals are identified. It has a compound wall behind which everything lies hidden. Huge gates open out onto a bridge that spans a dirty drain. One or two people are always sitting on the broad parapets on either side of the bridge. When I walk past, I see a man whose face resembles a hooded serpent. His large eyes seem to bore into me. The man I thought I had left behind in my room is here. He becomes one with the crowd and loses his strange identity.

I feel a tingling in my feet. My heart beats louder, my mind seems possessed as I walk on. The road I'm travelling on dissolves into another, which merges into a third and that in turn into another ... endlessly.

What is your destination? I ask myself.

But then, no one has a true destination. At some point in time, we all start on our life's journey but later lose ourselves in something or other. The identity bestowed on us by society disappears, I now understand the meaning of Baba Dayal Das's words of long ago: Every human being's struggle throughout his life is to establish an identity for himself which will continue to live even after his death.

The road which I have taken is coming to an end. I have reached the main road. Darkness has set in. Street lamps glow on either side.

I n spite of the darkness, our flight continued. Was the first flight the one made from Canaan to Egypt? Or was it the one from Mathura to Dwaraka? Or the one from Mecca to Medina?

No, people have been fleeing for countless years, but those who fled during those early days had no special identity of their own. Their stomachs were empty and their throats parched. They all lie buried in graves around Baba Khizr Shah's tomb. And once a year when the moon is full, they rise from their graves, to narrate the story of their flight to each other. They relate the hardships they faced before they acquired an identity and the oppression that was their lot afterwards.

N ow I understand it all. When Baba Dayal Das and my father returned after praying at Baba Khizr's grave, one half of me had stayed behind while the other had walked with them. While the former self witnessed the narration of the corpses, and later became one with the dead in their graves, the latter self witnessed the untimely death of my father's wishes.

It was a time when gods and goddesses were not born and we were a group with no identity. What was our strength then? I have no idea. I only know that thunder, rain and storm filled us with terror, our hair was matted, our beards unkempt. There were some amongst us who did not have hair on their faces, whose bodies were soft and exuded a strange warmth and they carried our children in their arms ...

When I return home after the long journey, I see that he's still there in my room. He raises his head and asks, "Is it raining outside?"

I am puzzled. "What makes you think so?" I ask.

"You are thoroughly drenched."

Arré, what is this? I am drenched to the skin. When did it rain? And where?

I feel very foolish. I have been unaware of a significant reality in my life. There I have been, out in the rain, I have got wet and yet, I am totally unaware of it.

To hide my embarrassment, I say the first thing that comes to mind. "Did you have tea?"

"No, I was waiting for you."

He speaks as if we are well acquainted. But why, why is he acting so familiar? Who is he? Why is he here? In what way is he related to me? These and other questions jostle for attention within me. Time itself seems to come to a standstill while I'm waiting for answers.

But nothing, nothing comes to my rescue. My wife comes in with tea.

What is this? When did I ask for tea?

"Will you have something to eat?" my wife asks.

"Yes, yes please – something light," he says, then turning to me, he asks, with the familiarity he had adopted earlier, "What would you prefer? Sweet or salted?"

I'm taken aback. Who's the master of the house, he or I? "Who the hell are you?" I demand.

"Arré, don't you recognize me? I am the master of the house," he says, chuckling.

"Then who am I?" I shout, pounding my chest with both my fists, each word dripping poison.

"You are the self I left behind when Baba Dayal Das took us to visit Baba Khizr Shah's grave," he explains patiently.

I am stupefied. I suddenly remember words once heard from Baba Dayal Das. Such experiences are inevitable when one is in the process of moving from a state of identity to one of non-identity.

I have to accept the fact that I am that self which had stayed behind in the graveyard. And now after a long journey, had reached here in search of its other half.

We have tea and snacks together and then he says, "Tell me, what brings you here?"

"I have come all the way to narrate the story of my flight."

"What do you mean?"

"I mean this: Once upon a time I had an identity which was bestowed on me by Him. Then there came a day when He could not tolerate that identity of mine. He ordered all of us, that is, all those who had that identity, to flee – and I ..."

"Mmm ..." He slips into deep thought and for sometime keeps staring at the empty teacups. Then all of a sudden, he says, "Listen!"

I look at him, all attention.

"Was the tomb really Baba Khizr Shah's?"

"That's what we were told by Bawaji."

"Was there not someone called Hazrat Khizr who showed the way to misguided travellers?"

"Yes, I remember! Bauji had also asked the same question that night when we were at Baba Khizr's tomb, How can death have any effect on him?"

"Where was he, then? When you were forced to flee, did you not ask Hazrat Khizr, Where should we go?"

"Such a thought never occurred to us. All of us gathered on a full moon night around Baba Khizr Shah's grave and prayed and lamented for a long time."

"Did Baba Khizr listen? Were your prayers accepted?"

"How can one know the ways of the Invisible?"

"No. But how long can such things remain concealed? When God's creatures are in peril, when people of one identity compel those of another to flee, then it becomes the duty of Khizr – whether he is Hazrat Khizr or Baba Khizr – to tear the veil of duality and show the right path to misguided travellers. Allah has made this task obligatory on him."

"Perhaps you are right. We belong to the race which has been guided by Khizr."

"Then come, let us pray and plead for guidance."

We embrace each other and weep bitterly for long, till the moon disappears from the sky and the Universe envelopes itself in darkness.

A nd in the stillness of the night, all of us who were bound together by a common identity, lay fast asleep. We had left our houses and gathered in an open place, waiting for Hazrat Khizr ..."

Who had started the narration? He or I? I experience a moment which is drowned in silence. I look around me with a great sense of uncertainty. The room has a cot, a centre table, and shelves filled with books. Standing next to the books is a statue of a half-naked black woman, holding a small black child in her arms.

I've seen the statue several times before. The black woman has always looked sorrowful, while the child's face is devoid of any expression. But, but what is this! Today, her face wears that curious expression which appears just before laughter bursts out. Already the whole place echoes with her laughter.

Once I had imagined that she was the Holy Virgin and that the little child was Christ. Why can't this be so? Can't the Messiah be black? But then, with blacks all over the world awaiting their sacrifice on the altar of identity, wasn't it a time for great sorrow rather than for mirth?

The sound of her laughter fills me with dread and a scream dies within me. For God's sake, revert to your sorrowful state, the look of a mother is what befits you ...

Suddenly he, who is my other half, speaks softly.

"Where have your thoughts strayed? Why have you stopped the story of your flight?"

"Yes, yes," I say, shaken out of my reverie. "It's a story. But remember there is a story within a story and that in turn leads to another story. Grasping the identity of the story, finding the essence of that which is a figment of the imagination, is your business. This story is such that it cannot be put into words."

The words I speak come out as if from a void. I start narrating the events of the night once again.

"When the sky was moonless and the world was in complete darkness, those of us who had been bestowed the same identity, awaited Hazrat Khizr. We spotted in the distance, the dim flare of a torch moving towards us. Those of us who were not asleep, woke the rest. We looked towards the approaching light. There was not just one torch out there, but many,"

Someone asked, "Do these lights which brighten the Universe herald the arrival of Hazrat Khizr?"

"Maybe," someone else said, "Though our forefathers have been guided by this light, it is the first time this has happened in our lives."

And then the sound of slogans rent the air – there seemed to be many voices.

Was Hazrat Khizr accompanied by his army?

"Yes," said a voice. "They are for our protection. Now rest assured that our long wait has ended and we shall soon begin our journey towards our destination."

The last words of the speaker were drowned in the deafening sound of slogans. Then we heard screaming and shouting from one side.

Perhaps, perhaps it's Hazrat Khizr? Ha, Ha, Ha! Sounds of hysterical laughing, The voices reached a crescendo.

I was startled. The smile on the face of the Black Virgin vanished abruptly. I looked around. There were many people there, confronting us with guns in their hands. They wore huge turbans, one end of the cloth covering their faces, We could not make out whether they were laughing or crying. Then all of a sudden their guns started spitting fire, and one by one our people fell to the ground.

But we were saved! My black mother had shielded me.

"We are safe, aren't we Mother?" I asked.

"Yes, my son," she said, softly. "Because we are idols of clay."

At this moment, a man appeared in front of us with a gun in his hand. He asked, "Who are you people?"

Looking towards me, my mother replied.

"We," she said in her soft voice, "Do not have an identity."

"All right then, we will grant you one," he said and rituals were performed which bestowed us with an identity.

We were thrilled. They started dancing with joy. Then, suddenly they stopped and turned to us.

"We know who you are!" one of them said, "You belong to the same group of people whose corpses lie scattered all around!"

"Maybe," my black mother murmured.

But this mild answer only provoked a volley of shots. We stood there, amazed.

"Why don't you fall down and die?" they asked in unison.

"We don't know. Perhaps because our identity is self-made," my mother replied.

They stared at each other in silence and spoke to each other in gestures. The fire they had lit had spread and was about to reach the place where we stood. They seemed to be in some sort of a hurry.

One of them removed a sword from the cloth tied around his waist and moved towards my mother.

Everyone watched him with bated breath.

Grabbing the left breast of my mother, the man swung his sword. The next moment, my mother's breast was in his hand.

Now, he attacked the other breast.

My mother's chest was soaked with blood.

She stood there in silence, watching, while I struggled to find the meaning behind this madness. The black child's eyes continued to be expressionless.

We stared at each other, astonishment growing on our faces. The man stood up. He snatched the child from its mother and started walking away.

"Stop" I shouted. "What is your intention? Why are you separating a child from its mother?"

"I do not know the reason behind the commands of the Invisible. I am merely following an order to separate the child from the black mother after her breasts are severed."

"But where are you taking the child?" I asked.

"To Baba Khizr Shah's tomb. He accepts everyone's prayers," he said. "I want this child to give up that identity which can be killed."

Tongue-tied, I watched him as he disappeared from sight.

I turned round and saw the black woman. She still stood on the book shelf, bleeding profusely. She no longer held the black child with the expressionless face. But the face of the black woman now reflected a myriad emotions.

First published in Urdu as "Aaghori" in *Zahn-e-Jadeed*, February 1993, New Delhi.

best of the
90s

## YASHODHARA MISHRA

Purana Katha

A bold story on an issue which is sensitive and relevant even today.
Peppered with earthy humour, it has a very clear feminist dimension.
The pace, the constant moving between times, and the rural–urban
connectivity are represented beautifully through vivid imagery.

**– Rituparno Ghosh**

The jatra troupe opened its performance with a few notes of music. Almost at once, the guests lost interest in the wedding feast and the children scampered away towards the jatra ground, leaving their food half-eaten. An elderly woman from one of the villages, called out to them, saying, "Fill your stomachs first. The jatra will go on all night. But how often do you get to attend a feast like this one?"

I may not get to watch another jatra, I thought to myself. Once, when I was very small, a troupe had staged *Ushabati Harana*, a jatra about the abduction of Ushabati, for my youngest aunt's marriage. They had barely started when I fell asleep ... Who knows when I shall be in a village again. That too when a play is being staged! I gulped down my food and made my way to the jatra ground.

The players had started enacting *Karnabadha*, the story of the slaying of Karna. The place was filling up. Women were finding safe places for their children before calling out to friends to settle down together. I was about to sit when someone pulled at me, saying, "Don't sit there. These people will just keep chatting and getting up every now and then. Come, we will sit out there!" Some of us girls had become friends in the course of the last two days, and we sat in a group. Sati Bahu, a relative from one of the villages followed us to where we sat, saying, "I will sit here with you, yes?" Her eyes smiled at Neera.

Neera and I exchanged a look. Everyone knew Sati Bahu!

Sati Bahu sat right next to us and, putting an arm around me, said, "Come. I will explain everything to you. I have read the *Mahabharata* eight times, cover to cover." The girl on my right was leaning forward so she could overhear our conversation. Suppressing giggles, she whispered into the ears of her two friends.

Yashodhara Mishra won the Katha Award for Creative Fiction in 1996, for this story. *Jhankara* received the Journal Award for first publishing this story in Oriya.

The Katha Translation Award went to Mahasweta Baxipatra.

This story first appeared in English translation in *Katha Prize Stories 6*, 1997.

We thank Pratibha Ray, our nominating editor, for choosing this story for us.

This was how it always was. Hushed whispers followed Sati Bahu wherever she went. Variously addressed as Sati Kaki, Sati Bahu and Sati Piusi, Satyabhama was also called – behind her back, that is – Sati the dimwit, Sati the derelict, and Sati the deserted.

Suddenly Shanti nudged me, "Look, look! Rajkumari Kunti and her companions!"

My eagerness burst like a bubble when I saw the princess and her retinue on the stage. To think of all the fuss they made about this play! I giggled. "The Rajkumari and her companions? I can see stubble on their faces!"

Neera and Shanti looked hurt. "You people can watch the cinema in your town. We can't. We are happy with our jatra," they said. No matter how very cautious I was, I kept making such mistakes. Anyway, I tried to forget the comparison with the cinema and concentrated on the play.

I remember distinctly that it was in such a play that I had been first introduced to the character of Kunti, though I can no longer recall the details such as who wrote the script, who directed the play or for that matter, where the troupe came from. I knew the many stories of the *Mahabharata*, with different episodes gathered from diverse sources converging in my mind. However, the character of Kunti had never caught my attention till that day.

Now, I watched on as Sage Durvasa, pleased with Kunti's service, granted her a boon. Such was its power that the moment Kunti thought of Surya, the sun god appeared before her in all his resplendent glory. The background singers sang of the beauty and splendour of Surya. This was followed by a lengthy scene in which the god insistently pleaded with Kunti with the latter refusing. The music reached a crescendo even as the drama drew to its climax. The crowd watched, all movement suspended, as the noise of the

---

The title of the story can be interpreted both as "A tale from the Puranas" and "An old tale."

**Aai:** Grandmother. **Bahu:** Sister-in-law. **Nani:** Elder sister.

world was drowned by the ascending beats.

Neera shook me out of my total absorption with the play. "Will you come with us?" she asked.

"Where?"

"We are going back to our villages."

"Now? But the jatra will go on all night!"

"We have to go in bullock carts, so we have to start now. You, of course, can leave in the morning in your jeep."

At a distance I could see the vaulted roofs of a train of carts with lanterns hanging between their giant wheels. The bullocks were distinctly visible under the moonlit sky. I sighed. Why do so many things happen at the same time? Under the blaze of powerful lights, Kunti and Surya were still dancing in a circle, to the beat of drums and cymbals.

"I asked because your grandmother is travelling with us. I thought it would be nice to chat on our way. I wonder when we shall meet again. But, why should you suffer a night-long, bumpy cart ride if you can speed away in your jeep?"

Thirteen of us had crammed into a jeep on our way here. My grandmother was evidently reluctant to undergo the torture all over again. Barely interested in the jatra, she was probably already ensconced in one of the carts.

"Will I find some space in your cart?" I asked.

Neera grinned. "Ask if you can travel with us. I will have to go and help," she said, walking away.

But she came back to add, "I can also tell you the story of *Karnabadha* on the way. We saw this jatra during Dashhera last year. Shanti even knows some of the songs. She can sing them for you."

When I cajoled Badamaa to allow me to go with the other girls, she declared in a tone mixed with pride and anxiety, "Look at our citybred girl. Wants to travel in a cart! But what will your parents say when they get to know?" She seemed to think that urban life was only about distancing oneself from one's rural roots as much as possible.

I waited near the carts and, while they loaded the luggage and made place for everyone, I continued to watch the jatra. Kunti was setting afloat her newborn child, Karna, down the river.

A string of bullock carts, about eight or ten of them, dawdled down the road, one behind the other. It was well into the night. People from different villages enroute sat in groups. They were mostly women and children, but for the men who drove the carts. Six of us – Neera, Sati Bahu, an aai from Jhikarpur, two aunts and I fitted into a cart somewhere in the middle of the file. My grandmother, and Hema Nani's two children sat in another. People kept calling out to each other, across the carts, to ensure that their luggage was secure.

I could feel my enthusiasm waning, just the way it had at the start of the jatra. The blaring of a transistor reverberated across the moon-blanched fields that stretched as far as the eye could see. A child was howling in a cart behind us while the bells around the bullocks jangled in wild cacophony. And then the many conversations ... "Wonder how far they have gone with the play. I wish we could have stayed on!" ... "O! I put my gamuchha out to dry and I have forgotten to bring it!" ... "It was much better during the last Dashhera. Durvasa was good. Even Kunti was better." ... "How could I forget my gamuchha, Hema?" ... "I agree. But last time, Kunti was fat. This Kunti looked very pretty. No, Neera?" ... "Don't worry. These things keep happening in such gatherings." ... "But, whatever you say, the khata that they served tasted *awful*. So watery and bland!"

Every time, even before we approached a village, I could see its lamps twinkling at a distance. Slowly the houses would appear on both sides of the road and, as our file of bullock carts came to a halt, the village would be wide awake. The wedding guests who belonged to that village would unload their bedding as if they had all the time in the world, say their farewells, convey good wishes through people in the carts to their various relatives in other villages, send blessings to youngsters, pranams to older people. Every one of us would get down from the carts and gather on the village road – except Sati Bahu, as Neera pointed out to me. Sati Bahu sat, all alone inside the cart, mumbling to herself.

"Which village is she from? You had promised to tell me more about her, remember?" I whispered to Neera.

"How could I? She came and sat right next to us! But I'll tell you in a little while."

I had heard a lot about this enigmatic woman in the past two days, Yet, I was curious to know more. But, with so many people talking around us, one could neither chat as one wished nor sleep.

The bullock carts resumed their onward journey. People had moved from one cart to another. Hema Nani and Maya Nani were in our cart now. The roads were completely deserted, and not a soul could be seen for miles on end. It had grown more peaceful inside the cart as well. The transistor had been switched off quite some time ago. The topic of the marriage ceremony had been exhausted. People were now talking about a certain Lakshmi, the youngest daughter of so-and-so, who had suddenly died two months ago. No, she had not committed suicide. Her own people had poisoned her! The case was hushed up by giving heavy bribes to the police. Even this yarn lost its edge after several recountings. Sati Bahu continued to sit silently, staring out into the dark. Hema Nani and Maya Nani sat whispering and giggling together. Our aai from Jhikarpur was dozing. Neera said, "I wonder where the jatra would have reached by now. The sons of Kunti must have all been born."

"We should have stayed at least till that point."

"Our poor Lakshmi had to suffer so much just because she had a child. And look at Kunti. How easily one escaped in those days!" said Hema Nani.

"Imagine! Kunti, being a princess, how *could* she make such a wish? And how did that old fool of a sage grant it to her? And *what* a boon! You just had to think of a man and he would instantly appear before you!"

"What do you mean by Think? Durvasa said *desire*. Didn't you hear that?"

"What fun it would be to get such a boon, what do you say Jhili? Even to meet such a sage!"

"But Nani, what annoys me is the boon. The sage could have blessed her saying, May you get a good husband, a virtuous husband. Instead, he says, Any man you want!"

"No, not want, but *desire*."

"It all means the same."

"And she goes and calls the first person she sees!"

"She must have desired him."

Jhikarpur Aai moved restlessly, her sleep disturbed. "What nonsense you people talk!" she said, irritated. "Is this all that you learned from the Puranas?"

"But tell me, Kaki, can you think of a princess, a virtuous one at that, desiring so many men, one after another. Even her husband allowed her ..."

"So, that is how your feel! Tell me, who are all the men you would have desired, if your husband did allow you?" demanded Maya Nani.

"Why, your husband would be the first!" Wild giggles followed.

"Shame on you, Hema! And you the mother of two children!" Aai lost her temper now.

"And whom would you desire? That schoolmaster, Rabi for sure!" More laughter and teasing followed.

"Why did I sit with you girls?" Aai mumbled. "Such unholy things you say! Just wait. I am going to report each one of you to your mothers-in-law."

"But Aai, it would have been a sin only if we had made it all up. We are only discussing what we saw in the jatra, a Purana Katha!"

"They are all stories of gods, from the sacred ages of Satya and Tretaya. It's a sin to make fun of them."

Neera, who had said nothing till then, quipped, mimicking an elderly woman, "True. We who live in this heinous Kaliyuga, how can we even think of getting such boons?"

"You can. I know. I had a boon."

Astounded heads jerked towards the back of the cart. Some of us peered into the dark, to make sure it was indeed Sati Bahu who had spoken. Most of us had forgotten all about her.

"What did you say? What boon did you have?" Maya Nani asked.

"It is possible for you to have a boon that draws towards you any man you want. You only have to look at him and he will be there before you," Sati Bahu said.

"And you had that boon?"

"Shut up, Sati Bahu! Don't babble like a madwoman."

Sati Bahu turned silent like an obedient child. Maya Nani and Hema Nani went back to whispering amongst themselves. Neera came close and tried to say something into my ear. "I already know that!" I said.

Earlier that afternoon, Sati Bahu had been the subject of fervid discussion in the marriage crowd. After their midday meal, the guests lay down here and there in the hall, and soon were talking about all sorts of things. In one corner of the room, Sati Bahu was giving a sympathetic ear to a sad-looking woman, apparently a poor relation, who had come to attend the wedding.

On seeing me with Sati Bahu that morning, Badamaa had taken me aside to say, "She is a sister-in-law and you have touched her feet. Now, keep away from her. Your mother will be angry if she hears you've been talking to her." That was enough to make me find the tall, reedy woman even more intriguing. I don't usually get an opportunity to come to the village, except occasionally during the holidays. And whenever I get a chance to slip out of the bounds of parental control, my eyes and ears flare open in search of new wonders. Now, in this alien place, in a barely familiar crowd, where even the days had lost all recognizable routine, I saw possibilities of mystery and romance everywhere.

In our corner of the room, they had made Sati Bahu the subject of their gossip. The prime narrator plonked herself on a trunk, leaned against the wall and recounted Satyabhama's past. Sprawled all over the floor, the audience listened and added grist to the rumour mill. The group consisted of women of all ages, ranging from eight year old girls to women well past their middle age. This was one of the rare occasions where I could get a taste of freedom – the freedom from feeling small and worthless because I was a child. On such occasions there was no age bar, except that, when the narrative took a very sensitive turn, someone or the other would say, "Shhh! Children are present." Or they would say, "Out, children! Go play!" No one really bothered to see whether we children kept sitting a little way off or returned after a quick stroll around the house to join the group again. Besides, as their bodies began to fill out, girls were easily admitted into the category of women.

I turned to look at Sati Bahu. But she was oblivious to all this discussion about her. She sat there, quiet and motionless like a figurine, listening in rapt attention to god-knows-what tales, her face now puckering in sympathy, the next moment breaking into a childlike smile.

The prime narrator said, We are doubly related. I could call her kaki as well as mausi. Indeed, Satyabhama is much older than she appears. One could never tell her age because of her figure. Born in a well-to-do family, she was married into a rich house at a very young age. No one who was there at the marriage can ever forget its pomp, the gaiety. Nor can one forget the bridegroom, Pitambara, who was as handsome as the celestial Kandarpa.

Satyabhama had four children, one after another. One has to be very fortunate to acquire such a noble household. Do you remember how pretty she used to be? Like a delicate reed of gold. And then came that incident. Her eldest daughter was already fourteen. A Gountia family of a neighbouring village came to ask for the girl's hand in marriage, with a necklace worth six tolas of gold and a sari for the engagement.

And that was when disaster struck. A sadhu had come to the village from Rishikesh. Wandering from one village to another, talking on the holy scriptures, he stayed in the homes of the rich. People visited him with offerings of food as well as gifts as dakshina. Many were given the Karnamantra for their spiritual initiation. He also came to stay at Satyabhama's in-law's house. And then, something strange happened. They found their enlightened Baba had absconded one fine morning. With Sati Bahu!

It was an evil hour for that house. The family was plunged into grief and misery. The marriage alliance for Satyabhama's daughter broke and the engagement gifts were returned. Satyabhama's husband went to her parents and declared, "As far as I am concerned, your daughter is dead. She has disgraced me beyond any measure."

She had four accomplished brothers, all feared in the ten neighbouring villages. They said, "How dare you say such things to us! What did we do? You couldn't keep your own wife in check. One wretch of a mendicant walked away with her from your house, right under your nose! Why don't you hang yourself?"

Our poor Pitambara Kakai could no longer contain himself and broke into a wail. Such a respected man. He had studied in college and even had an MA or a BA degree. He had turned down a government job to look after the family's vast agricultural property. And now, what a fate! "I admit," he said, "It's all my fault. But now what should I do? Should I go to look for her or should I report this to the police? Tell me, what do I do?"

Satyabhama's brothers said, "Don't go to the police. Everyone will get to know about it and we will lose face before the whole world. We take the responsibility of bringing her back to you."

"But how can I accept an unchaste wife? Can you imagine the problems that my children will face? You will be like my own brothers always. And your parents are no less to me than my parents. But I cannot take your sister back. If she returns, she will have to stay with you."

The brothers held their peace. What could they say? Then they disappeared from the village for a while. It seems they went towards Vishakapatnam or maybe Raipur ... No one knows what different villages they went to, what enquiries they made, but they managed to bring Sati Bahu with them when they returned.

For a moment, there was silence among the listeners. Then the narrator leaned forward and continued in a whisper, I don't know whether it is true or false but I heard from people from various villages that the Sadhu was nabbed with Satyabhama on the way to Waltair. Her brothers hired some goons and set him right.

Someone else added that the Sadhu was sent to jail. Others maintained that the brothers returned only after they had killed and buried the Sadhu. The narrator finished, I went to their village only a few days after the brothers returned with Sati Bahu. They told me that Sati was never seen outside the house. She had locked herself in a room, they said. Sati had gone mad!

Obviously, the entire story was not narrated too smoothly. Nor could it be given an uncontroversial ending, but a variety of opinions were put forth that afternoon ...

"No that is not true. I have known her ever since she was a child. Even then she was soft in the head. Often, when we bathed in the nearby pond, we would all finish on time, but Sati, oblivious of everything, would take hours to finish."

"Everyone knows she had one of her usual bouts of madness while the Sadhu was in the village."

"We never heard of such a thing! When she was a child, they called her Softhead, but that was only an endearment. She was such a lovely girl. What an efficient housekeeper she used to be!"

"Believe it! Sati ran away with that Sadhu, that is nothing but the plain truth. Go and ask the people of her village. As eye witnesses, they will recount all that they have seen."

At some distance, an elderly woman lay on the floor, warding off flies with the pallav of her sari. Now she yawned and sat up to join the discussion. "I have been listening to you all for quite some time. Well, it isn't your fault. People tend to make mountains out of molehills. Parasu Panda of the same village started the rumours about Sati – the two families were involved in some land dispute. The Sadhu had come to the village, but he left alone. Soon after his visit, Sati fell ill. Her brothers came and took her to Waltair for treatment. But then, some fellows in the village also had a bone to pick with the Sadhu. We all know how rumours spread."

The original narrator bristled. "Now, Aai, don't blame me! I was only putting into words what the whole world has seen and heard. Why else did Sati Kaki's daughter's first engagement break? Why do you think Pitambara Kakai married again?"

"She was always a little strange. I don't deny that. But that Pitambara is no saint! He made all this an excuse to marry again."

The narrator flared at this. "How dare you say that! Who can point a finger at Pitambara Kakai?"

Some of the others quickly managed to make peace between the two. And that was also the cue for the group to break for the evening tiffin.

Sati Bahu and her friend got up from the other side of the room. Nothing showed on her countenance, neither her past experiences, nor any knowledge of this afternoon's conference on her. "I know a lot more about her. I will tell you later," Neera confided. However, who could know the truth better than Sati Bahu herself?

W ho would have thought I would be so lucky as to travel with Sati Bahu that very night? And now, there she was, sitting in the same swaying cart as me, saying that she had once possessed that powerful boon!

By now, our aai from Jhikarpur had had enough of this nonsense. "You young girls," she said severely, "What do you gain by poking fun at our sacred books? As it is, we hardly understand the significance of those ages, born that we are in this Kaliyuga!" She would have continued her diatribe, but her intervention suddenly strengthened the desire among the yawning travellers to sleep.

Suddenly, we jolted to a halt. There was some commotion at the head of the line. It seems a wild animal had lumbered across the path of the first cart. Panic-stricken, the bullocks had reared and the cart had overturned. Luckily, there were only two young men inside it, and hardly any luggage. No one was hurt but people got down from their carts. Someone jangled a bell loudly – it seems wild animals run away in fear of loud noise. Not that there was any possibility of wild animals with nothing but endless stretches of paddy fields and a few shrubs here and there. But we were all wide awake again. And the halt became the topic for heated discussion, for the next half-hour.

It was well past midnight. We had stopped for quite some time at the village we had just crossed. Apart from exchanging greetings and drinking water, the recent accident had to be discussed afresh with one's relatives there. A couple of carts had stayed behind when we moved on, as they had reached their destination. Now there were hardly five or six carts left in the file, with fewer people in each of them. The bullocks were weary and the carts moved much slower now.

The bumpy ride had tired me. Sleep did not come easily, and I longed to return home and jump into bed. Hema Nani had gone over to sit with her mother-in-law, and held her two sleeping children against her. Maya Nani had got off at her village. Aai had nimbly moved into some other cart at one of the stops.

Three of us continued to sit in the same cart – Neera, Sati Bahu and I. A strange feeling of loneliness, of melancholy had crept in, the festive spirit of the previous hour suddenly vanishing. It had been such a wonderful experience; how we had all cuddled up to each other, people calling out from one cart to another. The almost continuous refrain of the cart drivers' songs had also stilled. It seemed as if everything had come to an abrupt halt, as if nothing was left save the dark night and the humming of the cicadas. Rocking, as if in a cradle, I felt I had entered some strange, unreal land. Sati Bahu had returned to her figurine posture. I shook Neera awake. "You can't sleep now. You have a story to tell me."

She mumbled sleepily, "Do you know what it was? The creature that came across our path?"

"Most people thought it was a fox or bear," I said. "But, we shouldn't be discussing it. Remember what Aai said? Thinking of bad things will only provoke the evil elements."

"Keep chanting her words. Let me sleep," Neera mumbled sleepily as she tried to make more place for herself. Shaken from her thoughts, Sati Bahu shifted a little and said to Neera, "Stretch out your legs here." Then she looked at me and asked, "Can't go to sleep in a cart, citybred girl? Come here and see how the world looks in moonlight."

I moved near her, to the front of the cart. One could almost see every leaf of the trees on either side of the path. Within the dark thicket, a thousand fireflies twinkled incessantly, as if the sky had come visiting the earth. The cartman was dozing. But, there was no trace of sleep in Sati Bahu's eyes. Sitting silently, she let her body sway with every movement of the cart. I was scared. I felt as if I had only a few threadlike links with reality to cling to. If Sati Bahu did not stay awake, unless I knew definitely that she was awake, I felt I might slip into some unknown land, never to return again. Why did she sit so still? After some time, I summoned courage and slowly called out to her, "Sati Bahu, could you tell me a story, please?" When she looked up at me, I could feel a chill run down my spine. Perhaps I was not too sure she was really there.

She smiled, "Are you scared, child?" I was trying to compose myself when she said, "You're an educated girl. What are you afraid of? There are so many of us here. Come closer and try to sleep."

"No, I am not scared. I don't feel sleepy. You too are wide awake. So why don't you tell me a story?"

"Why don't you? Tell me about your town shops, your school, studies ..."

I tried to think of something interesting to say. The only pictures that came to my mind were distant, dull, greyish images. "I go to school everyday, study there, come back and get down to studying again. There is no story there. You tell me a story, Sati Bahu."

"What kind of story?"

"You said you had a boon. Were you joking?"

"No, I actually had a boon. Don't you have one too? We all do when we are young."

"What boon?" I could feel my heart beating wildly.

Her eyes searched my face. "Don't you know if you have already got your boon or not?"

"I was talking about a real boon, like the one given by gods and sages," I said, fumbling for words.

She nodded and was silent. I was scared that she would revert to being a statue again. Bracing myself, I asked, "The Sadhu who stayed in your house ... Did he grant you the boon?"

She shook her head, as though to banish some thoughts. "It was too late by then. I had forgotten I had the boon."

"Did he curse you?" I asked, impatient again to break her silence.

"Who?"

"That Sadhu who ..." I swallowed.

I was afraid she would be annoyed. Instead, she smiled fondly. "So, our learned girl is curious! I shall tell you everything. But, is there any difference between a curse and a blessing? When Surya appeared before Kunti, was it a blessing or a curse?"

"I don't know," I said, disappointed.

She kept looking at me, the light of the moon falling on her, but I could not see her face clearly. As if gauging the extent of my anxiety, she began to laugh. It was a girlish laughter, like what I had shared with Hema Nani and the others earlier that night. "Who does not have this boon, tell me. In their youth, all girls have it. I am sure you tell yourself, I just have to call the man I want and he will come on his own. Isn't that true?"

I smiled helplessly, but shook my head to say No.

She closed her eyes in recollection, rocking to and fro all the while – "Well, listen to my story." she began. "When I was a small girl like you or even smaller, I would fast on Mondays. I offered prayers at the Shiva temple to attain a good husband. My mother had taught me to pray and fast. But, I knew that the one I wanted would be magically drawn towards me, like iron filings to a magnet. Which is why I had to live in constant fear. If any man looked at me, I lowered my eyes instantly. You probably do the same thing now."

"Then?"

"Kunti is a character from the Puranas. An ordinary girl is ruined if she doesn't keep her boon. The man who comes is free to leave the scene, wiping his hands and mouth clean.What has he got to lose? That is why dear, a girl has to bury her boon or hide it in some dark corner and forget all about it."

"Hmm ..."

"As a young girl, I was pretty and loved to dress up. I remember I used to massage my body with oil and turmeric every day before my bath. I believed that the one who would marry me would be truly fortunate. I would desire him and him alone and no one else. And thus my blessings would bear fruit, I thought."

"What happened then?"

"Then? Nothing. Do you think the right man really comes?"

"Didn't you marry into a rich family? They say your husband looked like a celestial being ..."

"Nonsense!" she said, before lapsing into silence.

"Wasn't he a nice person, Sati Bahu?" I asked finally.

"He was a good man. My father married me into a rich family. People of at least ten neighbouring villages were invited to the feast."

"You were supposed to tell me about the boon that you were granted."

"I had one. In due course, I forgot all about it. I bore children. I was so preoccupied with the duties of a daughter-in-law that I could no longer remember anything about the boon."

"Didn't it work on your husband?"

"I never looked up at my husband's face. His eyes had never met mine to be drawn to me. We met only in the darkness of the night when we went to sleep."

Silence. A few minutes passed like an aeon.

"Sati Bahu, tell me about the Sadhu. I swear by God, I won't tell anyone."

"What can I say? I told you I hadn't looked at the face of any man. By the time the Sadhu came, I was no longer aware of my body, or the boon. I wore gold and other jewellery but I had no mind to apply turmeric on my body. My daughter was engaged to be married and the elder boy had grown tall like a man."

"So the Sadhu came to your village?"

"What do I tell you about the Sadhu, my girl! He was giving a discourse on the Bhagavad Gita. The entire village savoured his stories like nectar. When he narrated Krishna's leela with the gopis one could see the scenes clearly before one's eyes – on his face and eyes. Everyone would slip into a trance. People would fall at his feet. Women of all ages used to get food for him by turns. Men would sweep the floor of his room and carry water. They vied with one another to massage his legs."

"And then?"

"He stayed in our house, in a room next to the outside hall. I too took food for him, massaged his legs, cleaned his plate after he finished his lunch and fanned him ... One day he read my palm and said, Your daughters shall marry into good families. Your sons will do well in life. You have nothing to worry about."

I was listening to Sati Bahu with bated breath, fearing she might get distracted.

She resumed her story, "I looked into a man's eyes, the first time ever in my life, as he held my hand and read my face ..." Suddenly, Sati Bahu hid her face in her pallav and suppressed a sob. I did not have the heart to pester her any more, but she started again on her own. "That moment I could clearly see in his eyes that my boon was coming true. It was taking shape with all its power. I don't know where it had been hiding, but it caught me at an unguarded moment and engulfed my entire self. As if I had nothing to hold back, not a worry in the world, I was only aware of the fact that my god was there before me that minute, in all his magnificence."

"Then?"

She was silent. The bullocks plodded on and the cart swayed as if to an unheard song. I summoned courage and asked again, "Did you actually run away from home?"

Sati Bahu was lost in her own world again. Then, she said, "Do you see how the night looks, how different the universe seems now? When you contrast this with the hustle and bustle of the marriage, doesn't all that seem unreal? And, when dawn breaks, all this will be gone, like a figment of the imagination. Can you perceive that now?"

I did not say anything, just waited patiently. The only sounds one could hear were the crickets and the sharp repetitive noise from the cart's left wheel.

Finally, unable to wait any longer, I said, "But did you really walk out on your children, your home?"

"If Surya had asked Kunti to forget everything else and come away with him, what would Kunti have done – woman of flesh and blood that she was?"

After a while, I ventured again. "So what happened, Bahu?"

She was so silent!

"How did you come back? Where did the Sadhu go?"

There was no answer. Her body swayed as she sat looking at the distant sky. Perhaps dawn was about to break. The moonlight looked pale. Another question escaped my lips, "Tell me, Sati Bahu, do you feel sad when you think about it now? Do you have any regrets?"

She turned towards me, I could feel her clear eyes on me. Outside, a new landscape was emerging with the break of dawn. "That's my village. There! The next one is yours," she said. Then, as she collected her things, she asked, "Will you ever get another chance to travel in a cart like this, my city girl? Will you regret you had to suffer such a journey, sitting up all night?"

First published in Oriya as "Purana Katha" in *Jhankara*, October 1995, Cuttack.

best of the
90s

**NAZIR MANSURI**

The Whale

Intense passion held on a leash ... searing heat and salty air scorching the skin in tactile prose ... "The Whale" is a robust yet extremely sensitively observed story of interplay between sexual desire and elements of nature.    **– Govind Nihalani**

Evenings the tide began to swell, the waters silently moving in from the port's inlet to the creek, the cold and frost of the dark month of Kartak growing intense. At dusk, a fog would form, thicken and hang till late. The siren of the lighthouse on the shoal blared incessantly.

The Kotada village lay like an anchored vessel opposite the village of Vanakbara. And, across the wide gulf between them, that yawned like the jaws of a mammoth whale, came the fishing boats from the open sea.

Lakham Patari's large whaler entered the inlet, laden with fresh catch, slow as a pregnant woman, lugging a monstrous blue whale behind it. A hundred tonner at least, the nylon ropes fastened to the spears in its belly and side were taut and twisted. Its black and blue body glistened with white spots. Fish traders on the open dunes near the storage huts stared at it, slanting sly eyes into the descending dark.

By now the inlet was in a ferment. Lakham, at the rudder, shouted instructions to Atham Hendiwalo, the khallasi at the engine below. Dropping a huge anchor, the whaler came to rest opposite the huts, the ragged thrum of the machine skimming the water behind. The whale struck the shore, pushing sand and foam further in.

Beyond a stretch of wet sand, on the western strip of the inlet, lay the dunes. On them, fish of all shapes and sizes dangled from kathi ropes. Behind the huts, bladders, fins and tails of whales had been left to dry on raised platforms. Lakham's crew and some willing fishermen hauled the whale into the knee-deep waters with great effort. The whale lay on its side, bleeding from the jaw. The clear waters of the rising tide turned crimson with the blood of the convulsing animal.

Nazir Mansuri won the Katha Award for Creative Fiction in 1997, for this story. *Gadyaparva* received the Journal Award for first publishing this story in Gujarati.

The Katha Translation Award went to Nikhil Khandekar.

This story first appeared in English translation in *Katha Prize Stories 7*, 1998.

We thank Ganesh Devy, our nominating editor, for choosing this story for us.

Labourers came crowding to see the giant whale. Lakham Patari sat on a wooden barrel on the whaler, his crew, exhausted and weary, were still to get off the vessel. In the fading light, silhouettes of the traders clustered around the whale, trying to estimate how much it would fetch at the auction, even as the labourers began transferring the ravas, the dara, the chhapra-chapri, the ghurkas, the large pomfrets, the jew fish and the eels lying in the thick net into broad iron buckets.

Meghji Bhandari selected some jew fish, large black pomfrets, palvas, a couple of rajratads, some shark younglings and lobsters which he put into a nylon bag.

Tall and robust, his face marked by small pox, Lakham stared at the whale's back, his eyes shot with a brute murderous strength. He undid the strip of cloth that tied together his blonde unruly hair and shook it out. As he stepped ashore, lighting the bidi that he pulled out of his khaki shorts, he suddenly turned gloomy.

The inlet meandered into muddy ground at the end of the village. There, at a higher level, were coconut and palm groves. Dragging his feet through a narrow, sandy path, somehow managing to lift the bag over the cactus hedges, Meghji Bhandari reached Lakham's house. Rani had already made the rotlas but was waiting for the whaler to bring in the fish. The moment she saw Meghji Bhandari, she got up from the cot with a scowl, grumbling, La, Meghji, how come you are so early, you wicked pimp, you swindler.

Meghji Bhandari was exhausted, at the end of his tether. He flared up. La! That captain of ours, that accursed, possessed man,

---

We gratefully acknowledge the assistance rendered by Sarala Jag Mohan in editing this translation – Eds.

**Patari:** Shark. Lakham's nickname, on account of his passion for killing them.
**Khallasi:** The ship's navigator.
**Portugis:** Portuguese.
**La:** Informal address; equivalent to "O."

he brought us in this early. If that portugis fellow finds a whale near Navabandar, can he let it alone? Along with the whale, he laid the rest of us flat! Who wants to work on his whaler?

O, so he has caught a whale? asked Rani, as she delved deep into the nylon bag. How big is it?

La, Rani Maasi, once he sees a whale, he is as one possessed. He cannot resist a whale, and we others are unable to kill one. We tremble at the very sight of the whale, and this accursed Lakham takes his spear and starts prancing upon the whaler, delighted. The bastard.

Hearing Lakham's name, Rani turned away as though she hadn't heard Meghji and went into the kitchen with the nylon bag. Meghji, still babbling, went off, down the narrow path.

After her husband's untimely death, Rani had become the owner of the whaler. She took good care of her brother-in-law Lakham's crew. Lakham Patari was considered a master at killing mammoth cetaceans – ber, hammerheads, malar, blue whales and sharks. He would give away the young ones and the mantas at the traders' huts, but got the whales, sharks, hammerheads and the huge sawfish properly auctioned. In fact, he had been nicknamed The Possessed One because of his passion for killing those monstrous creatures of the sea. But Rani found these stories about her brother-in-law difficult to believe.

Lakham's crew often turned against him. Killing the great whales was a highly risky job, requiring frenzy and passion. Only last year, Meghji Bhandari had lost an eye. But it seemed Lakham was so obsessed that the moment he spotted a whale with its glittering black-and-blue-speckled back peeking out of the waters, he could not help but rush for it. Picking up his spear and ropes, he would climb on to the bow of the whaler and thrust the spear into the whale's heart and let loose the rope attached to it. If the wounded cetacean wasn't entangled in the thick net, it would flee, befuddled by intense pain. But before it could get out of sight, Lakham would have tied the rope to the bow. The exhausted dying creature would flounder, beleaguered by its own massive body as well as the weight of the whaling boat, whereupon Lakham would jump into the water, reach its hindquarters, and stick another spear into its mouth. He could do all this in the time it would take another to merely decide to kill the whale. Many a time, owing to his impatience, he had been wounded by these creatures. But his colossal frame was still lusty and full-blooded, except for a slight limp which happened once when, while killing a finback, his leg had scraped through its jaws. It was risks such as this that made his crew curse him all the time. The glistening back of the whale seemed to hold a fatal attraction for Lakham. As though he found some unknown relief in the anger, sorrow and frustration of the chase.

Rani brought out two black pomfrets from the nylon bag and took them into the backyard for cleaning. The yard was surrounded by a hedge of columnar cacti. Behind the side wall of the house there were five or six barrels of caulking paste on top of a chulah made of several craggy rocks. The strong stench from the blackened chulah and the vapour of the caulking paste bubbling on it would fill the air till it was taken off the chulah. At the year's end there was usually enough for the whaler, and Lakham sold the extra paste to fishermen.

As she cut and cleaned the black pomfrets Rani was lost in her own thoughts. The boils take him, the eunuch! How he dances while hunting the whales ... how he rejoices. But the moment he sees a woman, he cowers like a green crab, this vile panderer, son of a portugis. Kills whales. How could he, an effeminate clown, kill a whale? Tell him to marry, and he acts as if he knows nothing. What does one do with this poisonsucker? He makes me so angry!

Rani was fed up. Lakham had killed a blue whale once again. So Meghji had said, though Rani was not sure. Deep in her heart lay a doubt, almost a pang of fear. Her husband, Punjo Bhadelo, used to be the captain of a cargo vessel from Navabandar. He carried lime,

**Bhadelo:** Punjo's nickname, the name of a Muslim community of this region among whose men traits like neglecting their homes, and travelling all year are commonly found. .

dates, onions and garlic to Basra, Iran and Africa. He would return at the end of every season, in the month of Jeth. But he had been gone for five years now. Two years ago a khallasi returning at the end of the season had said, That bastard has kept a Negro woman in Africa. Has children from her. Look here, I'm only telling you the truth. Such a shrew that woman, she doesn't let him come back. She has cast such evil spells that Punjo stays on. Have you seen the spirits of the Negroes? Baap re baap! Other khallasis spoke of other things. Some said he died in a storm, and that his vessel had just narrowly escaped sinking. Some, even from the same vessel, would give confusingly different information. Be it as it may, everyone at Punjo's house had given up hope of his returning, except Rani. Her longing would swell and recede like the tide. Punjo's aunt, Ladudakni, had accepted Punjo's death after five years of waiting. My poor Punjo, she would wail, how can he keep a Negro when he's gone into the lap of the saint of the sea? These no-good sailors will say seventy things. The old woman got Punjo's putalvel rites performed. And she wanted to get Rani's dervatu done with Lakham.

Not sure if she should say Yes, Rani simmered all the time, like a barrel of caulking paste. It was her yearning for Lakham that made her wait for Punjo. As for Lakham, he did not mention marriage at all. Finally the old woman had got tired of waiting. She consulted a tantrik, who declared, Rani has cast an evil spell on Lakham, that is why he will not have her. Ladudakni, tired and unwilling, accepted it, and Rani was totally isolated now. No one could hear the scream that resounded from the depths of her mind – I will wait forever for Punjo! Sometimes sailors return even after five to seven years. Perhaps Punjo too would return.

The thirty eight year old Rani had a full figure, and a dark ebony complexion with sharp features. Her thick hair embellished her broad, sturdy back, like the rudder of a boat. Tied into a knot,

---

**Putalvel:** A ceremony performed when a fisherman is believed to be dead and his body is not found. An image is made with pulses and the last rites performed.
**Dervatu:** Another local ceremony, for marrying a widow to her brother-in-law.

NAZIR MANSURI • 179

it was larger than her head, like a jet black, ripened toddy fruit. Full lips on a chiselled face attracted attention. Colourful satin petticoats she wore, and short tight blouses, her full body swelling out in them.

It grew colder as the dark fog spread. Lighting an oil lamp in the kitchen, Rani squatted on a wooden plank to prepare the black pomfrets, fuming at the old woman. That Ladudakni, how she speaks! *I* cast an evil spell on Lakham! Why would *I* do that? Let those who do so suffer tumours. She listens to banter and then how she screams. Sharp tears trickled from Rani's angry eyes. If that bastard himself refuses, what can anyone do?

The aroma of cooking food swirled around the house. A wintry air blew in through the thin wire net tied across the kitchen window.

The whale had been auctioned off. Lakham received good money. Besides, the whale's liver was his. Lakham sat drinking with his crew on the deck of the whaler. The inlet was ablaze with lanterns and lamps. Lights began to twinkle in the village. Flaring petromax lamps hissed in the traders' huts. There was great activity ashore as more fishing boats returned and the first thing the returning fishermen saw was the great whale. A petrified buzz of comment and discussion rose amongst them. La, it's gigantic! That possessed man will surely leave us one day, while killing whales, to go press his ancestors' feet, they said, even as they sat down with titbits of roasted fish to drink liquor on the bobbing whaler. A dour Lakham sat in the dark, staring at the whale, feeling sad and bitter.

Among the crew, Atham Hendiwalo and Ramo Moto, both elderly, started scolding Lakham. Son of a portugis, said Atham in gruff tones, Didn't you stop to think? What blasted thing could you have done if the treacherous whale had overturned the boat? You shameless fellow, I was so annoyed, you idiot, I could have made you weep with a single tight slap.

And Ramo Moto bawled, Did you see the whale? It was not even harpooned and this bastard Lakham dove into the water like a bloody whale himself. Up against the whale, you would have been murdered for sure and what could we old men have done? Where could we have gone?

Said Atham Hendiwalo, puffing on his bidi, Remember the sawfish that last time? Had I not pulled you away, it would have ripped open your stomach.

Son of a portugis, la! Ramo Moto said, crunching away at the fish. He has become so vain that he goes around jingling the magic beads. I have told him so often to stop ... Lakham, let it be. But it is all water over an upturned pot. Who listens to us?

Meghji Bhandari's squint eye careened as he turned his face away, grumbling.

As soon as a finback was caught, Lakham promptly killed it. He would dive into the water, climb its back and severe its fins and tails, and the waters would heave and rage in mid-ocean. Large-bodied finbacks, soaked in blood, with the fins and tails severed, would be thrown back into the sea – only their fins and tails were of use.

After every hunt, the crew blamed him in a similar fashion. Lakham chewed silently on the roasted bombay duck, staring at the whale all the time.

La, Moto, hear this. I went now to give the fish to Rani Maasi. On hearing of the whale, she started screaming, Poisonsuckers, may you suffer boils, you effeminates, nothing but hijras ... going to hunt whales. Brazen men, indeed!

Hearing Meghji Bhandari, all except Lakham fell to laughing. Lakham continued to look sullen. He grew agitated at the very mention of Rani.

Atham instinctively understood this. La, come on now, bhai Lakham, he said, The drinks are beginning to affect us. Let's leave you now. It is night already. And tomorrow is the eleventh day after the full moon. Soon we'll go to serve our ancestors, hunting whales once again!

And so they left, in the barge of the whaler.

Lakham kept staring from the deck of the whaler. As soon as the fishermen had reached shore, clambered over the whale and left, he pulled up the barge with the rope.

The tide was rising now. It was time for the night's meal. From the wide inlet creek the flood waters surged into the muddy ground of the coastal village. Foxes set out in search of dead fish and crabs. The nets from the creek lay haphazardly entangled on the saline land. Flamingos and Siberian cranes settled down in the shallow water for the night. Lakham felt irritated. His urge to go home had died. How she speaks, the shameless woman. So we are effeminate. How come she wants to embrace us then, this whale of a woman? Ladudakni understands. She says, Marry again, marry, even the eunuchs fare better than you ... Lakham was lost in the smouldering past.

L akham had been a mere sixteen years then. That bleak, joyless winter noon, he had come home with crabs from the creek. Sidi Moto was sewing nets on the shore. Punjo was at sea. Rani was alone at home.

Lakham had a bath in his loincloth and came into the house, his body muscular and burnished. Rani had dragged him into her little chamber, desperate, blind with passion. Though physically strong enough, Lakham was stunned by Rani Bhabhi's assault and started wailing. Rani had seethed, lashing at him with a stingray cane till, whimpering, Lakham had fled towards the haunted place in the palm grove.

Some distance away, under the palm trees, a group of hijras squatted around a bonfire. On seeing a robust, fair complexioned boy, they started to cheer. When they left, they took him with them. This troupe of hijras used to come to the village every year, but was not seen after that.

In the four years Lakham spent among the hijras, he was forcibly stripped, and had many sexual antics performed on him. His tender mind was torn asunder, it blazed at the very reference to sex. One day he got the chance to flee and after two, three days of wandering, he managed to reach the Mandvi port. The captain of a vessel at the Malabar coast took him in and put the sturdy youth to work as a khallasi under the storekeeper. The great freight ship plied all the year round between Calicut, Cochin, Mangalore and Basra, Iran. Whenever Lakham had some time to himself, he would remember the hijras' antics ... Rani Bhabhi's lusty embrace one bleak afternoon ... he understood it a little now.

About six years later, the vessel anchored at Diu. Only then, after ten years of wandering, did he come back to the village. Sidi Moto was on his deathbed and Punjo had not come home for five years. Like the flood tide at the end of the fishing season, Ladudakni could not contain herself. She sat cross-legged and cried to her heart's content. My portugis has come ... O Bhagwan!

And now, sitting alone on the deck, Lakham suddenly felt something within him flare up. He got into the barge and went ashore. Securing the barge to the whale's tail he left for home.

Her cooking over, Rani sat in the front yard on a cot, taut as a bowstring, thinking of Lakham and the whale. In the courtyard, a lantern hung on the stump of a half-dried branch of the huge saragwa tree. Seeing Lakham enter the house in a bad mood, she went still.

Lakham bathed, standing on the smooth stone slab in the backyard, taking water and an earthen pot from behind the house. Rani Bhabhi ... the hijras ... his mind's sky was luminescent with memories. He cleared his throat and bathed somehow, watching Rani's back as he washed himself. She got up abruptly, took the lantern down from the saragwa branch and went into the kitchen. Keeping the lantern in the middle room, she lit a bright lamp. When Lakham felt an urge to turn and look, he found her gazing at him with gleaming eyes. Her eyes looked like those of whales and sharks in the unfathomable waters of the sea. They filled him with repulsion.

Rani swiftly shifted her gaze. Stoking a couple of dung cakes in the hearth, she started roasting bombay duck, tura, and anchovy. The smell of roasting, sizzling fish spread through the house. Her gaze returned to Lakham's body. He was drying his blonde hair. That body with a bit of cloth around the waist annoyed her. Enraged, she drew the hot roasted bombay duck from the hearth and vigorously rubbed the pieces. The fish scalded her palms, but, unmindful in her rage, she started cutting it into pieces.

Lakham put on fresh khaki shorts and sat down to eat. The copper bowl contained a large arab pomfret in a red spicy gravy. The millet rotlas were like the green crab's convex back. And there were slices of roasted bombay duck. Rani sat on her haunches, her legs wide apart, as she ate. The hearth was behind her. Its heat struck her ebony back. Between them lay a silence, like a dead whale. Lakham's fair form had taken over Rani's mind. She was vexed to see that he kept eating, his face long and sullen. The crust had puffed up on the tava. She took the tava down, and thrusting a finger through the crust she said without raising her head, La was it a huge whale? How much did you get?

Impudent woman, is there ever a small whale? That wretched man gave a hundred rupees, Lakham almost screamed. I got this much only because it was large.

Why do you lose your temper if I ask?

Drops of sweat clung to Rani's face. Lakham was mesmerized by the fleshy calf of her leg. She sensed his eye. Both kept eating, their faces wooden, still sitting on their haunches.

Lakham began to be afraid of Rani. Somehow he finished the meal and, putting a cot under the saragwa, lay down outside. In the empty kitchen, Rani continued to eat, as one famished. The rotten man, just speak to him and how he jumps up, like a sawfish. Though he seems fine in Ladudakni's lap, he gets meaner by the day.

Winding up her work in the kitchen, Rani came out, saying, La Lakham, are you making your bed here? Not going to sleep at the whaler tonight?

He was silent. Without waiting for his reply, Rani picked her cot up from the front yard, hung the lantern on a peg and thumped into the house.

Lakham kept staring at the dark back in the tight blouse without the overcloth, as though he were gazing at the glistening back of a whale or a shark swimming far into the sea. Just that afternoon the back of the whale that had been trapped in the nets had seemed to shine at him in just this way. His veins started pounding. Dhak, dhak. Enraged, he clenched his fists. The veins grew taut and in his eyes welled up a terrible sadness.

Rani slanted a glance at Lakham and bolted the door. The clatter of the bolt rose like a scream and then all was quiet.

Was there a difference between Rani ten years back and now? Lakham was immersed in thought, comparing the length of her back with that of the cetacean.

In the rear room, Rani tossed and turned, gazing at the glowing lantern. In her eyes remained the great fleshy male in the loincloth. His body so tall and sturdy – in just ten years? Rani became restive. That winter noon Lakham had taken the lashing from the stingray cane … from the depths of Rani's mind, lust for Lakham, like a scream, like an uproar, had continued to swell and then cease and swell again. He was barely sixteen then, but had looked a lusty youth of twenty five. Now he was twenty six but looked like a mature thirty five. The poisonsucker had started crying then, otherwise … She had a burning itch to embrace Lakham again.

She swiftly got up and extinguished the lantern, filled with hatred for its steady flame. In the dark her sensual thoughts began wandering like nocturnal creatures.

A howl rose from Dadmadada's temple end, accompanied by plaintive groans. In a short while howls could be heard from the salty stretch of land behind the house. It seemed as if jackals had surrounded the village. There was a chill in the air, and late in the night the frost set in. Rani became suspicious. She had sensed at times how Lakham's eyes roved over her body like a seahawk. How was Lakham, who slept at the whaler even at the end of the fishing season, home today? The thought stayed embedded at the bottom of her mind like a small, pink oyster, and would not come off. Eeyaa ... eeyaa. The howling drifted in from the distance, now sounding like a queer shriek.

It must be the jackals chasing the hyenas. The silly creatures must be cold, that is why they cry. Distracted by the howls, Rani began to worry for the cocks and chickens cooped inside the farm.

But Lakham wasn't concerned. Tired, he set out for the whaler, to sleep there. Watching the backs of the cetaceans in the deep sea made him feel a hovering absence. Irritation. Gloom. He felt a strong urge to kill those creatures.

He lit a bidi near the lane in Waghra. Just then, a jingling laugh rang in the air. Lakham started. His feet turned towards the yard of the house at the back. The bamboo window panes were ajar. There was a screen of net on it. He looked in. Startled, he thought, Don't these people rest even at night?

As Lakham stomped his way through the cold sandy path, the jackals that had come to gnaw at the body of the whale escaped towards the wooden platforms built in the dunes. He untied the barge from the whale's tail and jumped over the whale's back into it. It seemed as if the howling of the jackals was chasing him.

He spread the mattress on the deck, wiped his sweat, lit another bidi ... The hijras used·to strip him naked and play with him, embrace him, an odd one would lick and even bite his fair body wherever he pleased. Lakham would scream, but could not escape from their clutches. The scene he had witnessed in the lane in Waghra mingled with the antics of the hijras in his mind. Spitting hard in frustration, Lakham stared at the sky. Why the hell had she been laughing? In the dim light of the lantern ... an adult fisherwoman with her man.

Then it struck him that ten years ago Rani had embraced him that way. His body tingled strangely. The jackals hadn't yet started howling. As the tide rose, the whaler kept bobbing in the lapping waters.

That night, the jackals struck without warning, sneaking into the farmyard to drag away the chicken. Very softly opening the bolt, Rani peered out through the partly-open door, then took a bright lamp to the yard, closing the palm leaf door carefully behind her. She placed a few stones there. She stared far into the dark as she came back into the house. Lakham's bed – empty? La, la, the deathstricken man, where has he gone now? Back to the whaler? She was quite relieved that Lakham was not sleeping there. She banged the door shut and bolting it, came to her little room with a bright lamp. Had he been there ... A storm raged in Rani's mind. She felt lonely. Then furious. With Lakham. Her full lips twisted with pain. She cursed Punjo who had been missing for five years. May he get boils all over. Who knows if he stays with a Negro? May he fall to pieces. I'll thrust the grain sampling rod up his buttocks the moment he gets back. Rani pushed away thoughts of Punjo. The bastard portugis, could he not have slept here? Going off to the whaler. The insult hit hard. What difference was there between Punjo and Lakham?

She suddenly felt it was growing colder. She took the mattress lying on the trunk. Then, on impulse, she threw open the trunk. In the bright light of the lamp she saw Punjo's thick waistband decorated with faint pink oysters. Rani's mother had given it to Punjo at their marriage.

Not thinking clearly, she pulled the waistband out and kept it on the trunk. Then she put out the lamp and lay down. She rarely opened the trunk. Why had she opened it today, why had she looked into it? Dragging her gaze away from the trunk, she looked up. The main beam of the roof was black with soot. The tiles of the roof had not been cleaned at the end of the last year. It would have to be done this year. A thought flashed in her mind. Her gaze returned to the top of the trunk. In a rage, Rani turned her back to it.

D awn broke. The tide began to ebb. Having been awake till late in the night, Lakham had barely fallen asleep when the labourers brought knives, blades and whetstones and began tearing up the whale near the inlet in front of the traders' huts. The commotion woke him up. As eight or ten workers tore up the whale, Lakham looked on, sullen. At ebb tide he freed the barge and got down into the water, just behind the whale. La, you bastards, keep aside the liver. I'll take it later. He spat hard and set out for home.

He was already hungry at daybreak. After devouring last night's pomfret curry with cold rotlas, he went to the shore, stuffed the whale's liver into a barrel and brought it back. Behind the side wall, he put the chopped liver into the caulking paste barrels with carbonate, and set it to boil. He sat against the raffia palm in his underclothes, smelling of the blood and secretion of the whale's liver, and lit a bidi.

Rani had been up since first crow. The servant she employed had delivered some bags of neera. As the sun rose, she filled the glass bottles in the nylon bag with vinegar and got busy in the kitchen, making maikulal with jew fish. Rani could not help looking out now and then, beyond the side wall, outside the door. The terrible stench of the boiling caulk paste came in with the smoke, pervading the kitchen. She came out to put liquor and roasted bombay duck before a glum looking Lakham.

In a short while, Lakham's crew arrived. Atham said, La, why are you sitting with the face of a nursing mother so early in the morning? Are you ill? Why are you looking like a dead whale?

Lakham stalked up to the chulah and stirred the mixture forcefully with a thin bamboo, without meeting anyone's eyes.

It was getting hotter. At the yard's end, near the well behind the cactus hedge, Rani sat down for a bath. She remembered that earlier that morning she had been excited on seeing the almost naked Lakham and had felt a sudden urge to marry him.

His crew drank liquor for a while, and then went off dragging their feet in the sand. Lakham, stinking of blood from the liver, took a rope and the leather bucket that hung from a cactus branch and went to the waterwheel well. At the edge of the well lay a couple of broad buckets full of washed clothes, a large pot and a rope. He stood there, not seeing anyone around. A stream of falling water attracted Lakham's attention to the cactus hedge.

Oonaa ... aa ... Rani was startled.

Lakham tautened like a bowstring, something snapping inside him. His heartbeats hammered. He stomped away to go sit in the front yard. He was perspiring, as if he had suddenly sighted a whale. The brazen one! Who asked her to bathe naked? Lakham trembled. Not knowing what to do, he went behind the side wall, covered the barrels of cooling caulking paste, placed the bamboo sticks against the cactus before coming back to the front yard.

She came in noisily after her quick bath, swinging her wet tresses, carrying the water pot upon the bucket. And there was Lakham sitting in the front yard like an owl. Irritated, she banged the pot down in the front yard, made a face and stamped into the house.

Lakham watched her long face. What do I tell her now? La, did I come to look?

She was drying her hair in her little room. Agony reddened her eyes. So what if he happened to see her naked? Why had he come running to where a woman was bathing? He must have done it deliberately.

The winter gust made the afternoon even more dull. Lakham lay sleeping in the middle room. He had eaten a lot, drunk a lot, and now snored heavily. Outside in the yard, Rani sat on a small stool, weaving a net hung from a post. Through the open door, she could see Lakham's back. Her gaze stuck there, unmindful of the net she was weaving. Abruptly she got up, went to the kitchen and gulped down a pitcherful of water. She then came noiselessly into the middle room. Stopped near Lakham. Gave him a close look. In the silence that made breathing audible, Rani's face shrank. Was her gaze searching for something on his back? She shuddered, veins taut. Then she moved away with difficulty, and went to her own room on shaky legs.

Behind the side wall a sterile hen had dug up the earth and sat squawking in a long pitch which reverberated in the afternoon.

Somewhere far beyond the lighthouse, the whaler moved. On the deck, the crew were separating a host of nets. As he sat at the steering, Lakham's mind wandered emptily and far. The old men would gossip, That bastard Lakham is of Portuguese blood.

Near Diu in Dholawadi, the crewman of the farm, Bhikho Jharakh had lived with Lakham's ma, Lakhmi. So too had the Portuguese army officer, Marcus da Cunha. Lakhmi, in love with the Portuguese, was as firmly stuck as an oyster is to the bottom of a ship. This angered Bhikho Jharakh. One day, in a drunken state ... within the Diu fort, in a dark corner, Lakhmi and Bhikho were tortured and ... no one knows whether the Portuguese was annoyed or angry. Soon after, the Portuguese lost both his mind and his fortune. He left Diu and went away, leaving behind the five or seven year old Lakham.

The old folk talked, but Lakham could not make head or tail of it. He bore a terrible rancour against his Portuguese father. Though his mother's misfortune upset him, he would often feel a passionate urge to lash her with a cane. He had heard something else from Ladudakni. She said, Your ma was just like Rani. Wouldn't fit even into a large bed when she slept. Was as lovely too. But that bastard Portugis, your father, the poisonsucker, he was a crafty man. The old woman would leave it at that.

Since then, the very word Portuguese angered Lakham. He addressed the whales and sharks, the finbacks and sawfish as Portugis. And he never let by a single opportunity to kill a cetacean.

They had by now reached the spot where the net was to be spread. Lakham's eagle eye saw a glistening black back upon the surface in the light of the setting sun. He immediately got the speed of the whaler reduced. The crew stood stunned to see the back of a whale.

Lakham recognized that it wasn't really a whale, but a gigantic ber. Floating like a corpse. Almost dead. Lakham gazed in silent concentration, La, you can spread the net later ... I'll ... Lakham dangled the wooden stick of the spear, holding it powerfully through the attached skein. Atham babbled, La Lakham, it is a ber. Where can we possibly drag it? The crew started muttering angrily among themselves, This bastard Lakham, did he want to overturn the whaler?

Lakham tucked a sharp knife at his waist and dived deep. The ber had a splinter stuck in its white belly. Ah! Lakham thought and he climbed its back, cut off its fin. The ber, breathing its last, crashed into the water and the crew started yelling. Lakham again climbed the back of the ber. Severing both the back fins as well as the tail, he put them into the nylon bag at his waist and swiftly boarded the whaler. The blood-soaked finback was left floating as the whaler went on its way.

The tide quickened at evening. The whaler anchored after the nets were set. Meghji Bhandari sat down to make rotlas. Lakham went to sit at the steering handle, his whole being suffocated. Meghji was talking to Atham as he made rotlas, Why should one prance about without confirming if the whale is dead or alive? Can you trust the portugis? Remember how the sawfish ... Meghji had lost an eye in an attack by a sawfish.

It was the twelfth day of a lunar fortnight. In the pitch dark, bright lights twinkled in the fishing boats. The great beam from the lighthouse began whirling. Spreading mattresses on both sides of the deck, the crew curled up to sleep. Lakham put a burning light at the bow, and slept uneasily, images of Rani tugging at his mind – Rani bathing, screened by the cactus, pulling a face when he sat down to eat at noon ... Suddenly, there was a frantic movement in the nets which had been set up. Lakham peered into the dark waters. Was a portugis trapped there? Sitting on his haunches on the bow, he glowered into the depths. The surface of the water splashed sporadically and everything froze again.

The next day, the whaler cast anchor in the inlet. There were whales, sharks and rays trapped in the thick net. Younglings too. There was a heavy catch of bombay duck and anchovy. Lakham took home the ghurkas and gulaliyas in a nylon bag. Two soles floundered in the nylon bag. Rani was very fond of soles.

As expected, she was delighted to see them and immediately started to cook the sole. Lakham went to the waterwheel well with a leather bucket and a rope for his bath. More fishing was to follow after the meal.

Wiping his body, Lakham took a small lamp and went to the dingy room at the back. The nets lay here. He put down the lamp and groped for the fine nets – a whole new bundle had been kept separate. From the window, where some bamboo strips had broken off, a blast of cold wind rushed in, blowing out the lamp. Lakham shouted, La Rani, bring the lantern, but he mumbled to himself, Now she'll not hurry.

But Rani did hurry, leaving the fermented liver of palva she had wrapped in an old wet cloth and put on the tava along with a few turas and bombay duck. Then her foot got caught in a net in the dark room and she lurched towards Lakham, making him lose his balance too. Her touch sent tremors through Lakham, as if he were touching a whale's back. Rani's lantern toppled over on the cold floor. The chimney broke. The spilt kerosene caught fire.

Behind the farm in the salty patch, Siberian cranes and flamingos, who had settled for the night, suddenly raised a din, maybe sighting jackals. In the kitchen, inside the broad bucket, the soles flapped as though they would slough off their skins.

One and a half months later in the bright fortnight of Poush, fishing was discontinued on account of the winter blasts. The whole inlet was full. Boats lay inactive. Lakham made nets and baits. Then when the full moon rose high and there was a thin layer of ice on the surface of the sea the fishing resumed.

The whaler had been out fishing since dawn. The crew were busy collecting the catch. Lakham sat behind the bow to smoke a bidi. A couple of gigantic whales had been circling in the same area for a long time now, and he wondered which way he should guide the whaler.

Seeing Lakham look far into the distance and tremble, everyone fell quiet. Will this man go after them? If he does, he'll carry on till morning. Will he ever let alone a whale? Meghji Bhandari looked at Lakham with utter disgust. Standing in the heap of baited fish, the crew began guessing the direction the whaler would take. But no one had the courage to ask Lakham. A whale sucked fish in its monstrous jaws and rose high, out of the water, spraying some around.

The whaler set off at a slow pace. But surprisingly, the whales were soon left far behind. The crew heaved a sigh of relief, Isn't he going to kill the whales? The crew gossiped among themselves. The gyration of the machine increased. Something glowed in Lakham's expression ... At daybreak when the whaler set out for fishing under the dew, Lakham had seen a whale splash and the sight had saddened him. The crew too had seen the whale in the fog, but had gone back to sleep, rather than tell Lakham.

The whaler entered the inlet once again. Lakham said, La Mota, the whale we saw in the morning, wasn't it fierce? It's liver would have been excellent, it would have made barrels of paste.

Atham Moto was stunned; the rest of the crew grew uneasy. With both hands, Lakham heaved the great anchor overboard. There was a splash in the creek ... the crew was silent.

Ashore, the fishermen talked, What a mighty whale! Lakham is so possessed, he might go and bring it now.

But tossing his blonde locks, Lakham picked the nylon bag and sat on the dunes. He lit a bidi and looked at the lobster in the bag. On the belly of the female stuck a thick, orange fold. Eggs. Are there hatchlings too? wondered Lakham.

At nine that night, Rani thought worriedly, Why hasn't the whaler returned yet? It will be nice if he hasn't stayed to kill a whale. Today, after a long time, Rani had donned a dark blue skintight satin blouse. The blouse had been made a long time ago. Her figure was now fuller. In the tight blouse and overcloth, her body burgeoned, like her intense desire to marry Lakham. Ladudakni could not be told anything about it yet.

Rani put a chain across the door and came on to the road. She got to know from some passing fishermen that the whaler had anchored. She walked on, swinging her full figure confidently. The food is yet to be warmed, the poor ones must be exhausted after fishing, she thought. In the cactus lane there was a strong fragrance of arani flowers.

That evening she prepared the young sharks and boiled kati in the black earthen pot. When made in a new pot, the shark and kati are so tasty. And these days the younglings of sharks are at their best. Late that night the lantern burned bright in Rani's room.

Rani stood combing her hair. Lakham sat on the broad bed, smoking a bidi. Rani flung her overcloth on to the trunk. Her back made Lakham's eyes ache. She looked even sturdier in the bright glow of the lantern. When she had embraced Lakham ten years ago, had she been in the same dress then? A slow shriek rose from Lakham's mind. Grumbling silently he went to the front room.

Having combed her hair, Rani lowered the flame to a minimum. She lay on the mattress. Bolting the front door, Lakham came into the house. As she lay on her side, Rani's back tugged at him desperately, like the back of a whale.

Lakham blew out the lantern. Rani's bewitching laughter resounded in the dark, her eyes flashed like a whale's – at Lakham's waist was Punjo Bhadelo's waistband, decorated with pink oysters. Lakham felt it prick, so he undid it and placed it on the trunk that contained Punjo Bhadelo's old clothes.

The jackals howled on and on ...

Overcome by ardour, Lakham felt as though he was about to climb a whale's back to cut its fins off.

First published in Gujarati as "Bhuthar" in *Gadyaparva*, September 1996, Panchmahals.

best of the
90s

**PREM PARKASH**

Mohdi

I liked Mohdi for its very sensitive narration and a study of human bondage with the past. For the way it lingers on like dust of the Journey! For the very well orchestrated characters. **– Gulzar**

Sitting in the speeding train which will take me from Delhi to Punjab, I feel as if I am going to Shahpur, my ancestral village, under the influence of some evil spell. Right from childhood I have often experienced this sense of being in a spell-induced state. Whenever I am trapped in such a state, I behave as one possessed. I find that these spells have increased since I retired.

In the thirty eight years that I have lived in Delhi, I have visited all its old buildings. Yet, when that wave of anxiety engulfs me, I go and sit in some deserted ruin and I just keep looking at the worn centuries old bricks, the peeling plaster, the puffs of dust accompanying a bird's sudden flight, the ants residing inside the cracks ... Before my eyes the courts of kings assemble in splendour, armies march past, battles are fought, bhikshus sit silently in their viharas, or preach in towns, someone ploughs land, corpses lie within a hand's reach of each other. I see ash from hearth fires, broken vessels ...

This morning, at a merry gathering of retired men, Sehgal Amritsari had announced, "I am leaving for Sharifpur soon. The soil of Amritsar is calling out to me."

"Wah! All the crooks of Delhi want to die in Sharifpur!" Mohan Lahoriye laughed out loud.

And Sharma, the postmaster, trying hard to hold back his laughter, said, "Sehgal, remember there will be no one to mourn your death there. It is here that baraats are taken out."

D K Pathak had broken into a loud song, "*Kabran udhikdian, jyon putranoo maanwa.*" ... Graves wait, like mothers do for sons.

Everyone cursed him loudly.

A journalist, whose name I keep forgetting, pointed to a dead

Prem Parkash won the Katha Award for Creative Fiction in 1997, for this story. *Aarsee* received the Journal Award for first publishing this story in Punjabi.

The Katha Translation Award went to Reema Anand.

This story first appeared in English translation in *Katha Prize Stories* 7, 1998.

We thank Kartar Singh Duggal, our nominating editor, for choosing this story for us.

dog lying on the road and said, "No ... like roads do for dogs ..."

As soon as I reached home, I don't know why but I was gripped by that possessed feeling again. I started packing to leave for the village. My daughter-in-law prepared a tiffin for me. She put my medicines in the pocket, just like her mother-in-law had done when she was alive. Her younger son helped me board the train.

The medicine, which I took after lunch, has made me drowsy. Things which I have seen or thought about earlier, keep coming back to me in my dreams – a small railway station, a two kilometre stretch, shrines of pirs, samadhis, bus terminals, the village shivala, Delhi Gate, our ancestral house where my taya's son Mukundi Shah and his family live ... all these images merge into one another, blur, then scatter ... Suddenly a shot is fired. Many people, sitting and smoking a hookah under Teju's neem tree, are killed. Those who are left behind prepare for a mass funeral ... There's a loud thud as my arm and leg hit the wooden wall of the compartment. My co-travellers stare at me as if I am having an epileptic fit. Embarrassed, I start drinking water from my bottle.

Now there isn't so much to fear while travelling to our village. Earlier, a terrorist's bullet could kill one anywhere – in a train, in a bus, on the road, or in the house. My taya's youngest son Shankar was killed in a shivala. A simpleton, Shankar had immense faith in Shiva's protective powers. Early one morning, he went to make an offering of water to the shivalinga. A blood offering was made instead.

T he sun is about to set. I get down at the small station. Tangawalas who know me call out to me, but I walk on with the bag slung on my shoulder. Midway I relieve myself in the shadows cast by sarkarian, the tall elephant grass. I like this freedom. I walk along in the company of the tahli and kikar

---

We gratefully acknowledge the editorial assistance rendered by Manjeet Kaur in editing this story. – Eds.

**Sharifpur:** The name of a place. There is a play on the word "Sharif" here, which means "Honourable/upright."

trees. The village boys had killed Shankar as if he was a dog from another village. When Pakistan was created, people from the village had killed each other in this same way ... But why did I keep coming back even in those dark times? When the end draws near, why does one want to return to one's ancestral village? Why does one desire that his arthi should pass through the same lanes where he had once played? That one should be put to rest at that very place where his ancestors had been cremated?

Near the bus terminal small shops have sprung up close to each other. Only when I reach the village will I get to know how many of those who had locked their doors and run away have returned, or how many have sold their land and house and got permanently uprooted. My heart beats nervously. I draw water from the well in the shivala and gulp my medicine ... Have I also come here to die? Didn't Byo Mata say so this morning?

Once home, after a cup of tea, I go to look at the spot marking the mohdi – the place where our forefathers, at the time of setting the village, had laid the foundation stone, to the accompanying chants of the purohit's mantras. People had gathered there to seek blessings and happiness for the entire village. It is a lime-washed mound of small bricks and above it is a heavy roof. As I climb the stairs, the bricks and the gathered dust emanate a smell similar to the musty air hanging over the ruins of Delhi. Standing on the last step, I peep inside through the broken door. There is a sudden flurry as a flight of pigeons takes off just above my head. In the darkness inside, the big pans hanging from heavy chains jangle. The pigeons must have settled themselves on the pegs further inside.

Back home, I open the room on the first floor, drag my grandfather's easy chair out into the balcony near the grill and, after dusting it, sit on it. Looking around idly and smoking a cigarette, I feel now a ripple of pleasure and contentment rise within me, then sorrow that makes my heart heavy. I could not bear to see the terrible state Mukundi is lying in, downstairs.

Some years ago, terrorists had whisked him off in a jeep. He was sixty then. After the payment of ransom, when Mukundi was brought back from captivity he found that this experience had reduced him to the mental age of an adolescent. His powers of reasoning are not more than that of a fourteen or fifteen year old. His brain is half-dead. Now his body too is dying. He cannot get up by himself, he walks very slowly, the eyes have a vacant stare and he can't speak except in broken words.

When I started climbing the stairs he had struggled to get up and ask, "Kishu, can I come with you?" His drunkard son, Maddi Shah, had caught hold of him and made him sit on the charpai. But he had got entangled in its loosened strings. Like an animal in the throes of death, he had thrashed his hands and feet and screamed. And then, in sheer helplessness, he had grown quiet. I have come to know that Maddi does not let his father stir out. He was known to be Mukundi's pampered son, but now he does not want to be called Mad Mukundi's son ...

Why have I come back to see all this?

Before me is Teju's neem where we used to play. There is a lock on Teju's pukka house. Once he would come every five years from abroad to clean and whitewash the house. Now he is not well enough to visit and his son does not feel the need to do so.

Later, during dinner at my younger brother's house, Nikka and his wife tell me about the families which are half here and half in Haryana. Maakhan Halwai's family had suffered losses, he has not come back. They also tell me in great detail about those sons of Jats who had either been caught or killed. But I am sick of all this. I steer the conversation to the demolition of Delhi Gate. "You'll see the tamasha tomorrow when the lathis clash," Nikka says.

"One fifth of this common land belongs to our family," I say.

"Who is bothered? The shallow Panch Tirthi pond has been forcibly taken over by the Jats. Shops have been built there."

This news should not be immensely saddening – isn't it enough that we are alive, I think, but do not feel like saying it, for I know that I will have to bear the brunt of my statement. So I talk instead of Banta Sialkotia, of Rahian Vehre. "Hasn't he gone to Pakistan to look up his house yet?"

"No. Banta first said, I will get my eyes treated in Amritsar, and only then will I go and see my house. But, when he heard that the committee is getting it demolished he said, If I am not going to Sialkot, why should I get my eyes treated? Do I have to thread a needle?" Nikka laughs as he recounts this.

Today Delhi Gate will be demolished. It is eight in the morning. I am sitting in an easy chair at my taya's house, in the balcony on the upper floor, smoking a cigarette. It was beneath this gate that we would play cards or games with marbles and walnuts. The elders would sit gossiping and smoking hookah. Mukundi and I studied under the light of a lantern in this room on the first floor. The big almirah was Mukundi's, the smaller one was mine. We would climb the neem tree in front of the house for the sole pleasure of listening to Teju chacha's scolding. The lock on his door bothers me ... He had served my grandfather with great loyalty. There were times when my grandfather would abandon his game of cards or his hookah, rise abruptly, get his horse saddled and start for the well named Pilkankhoo. Sometimes I followed him. He would pass his hand through his white beard gently and stare at the standing crops in the fields, or at the trees. And he would say, "Cremate me here. Put four bricks where the pilkan will give its shade at the end of the day." I remember being surprised, remember thinking, How does it matter to a person who is dead and gone as to where he is cremated? What comfort will the cool shade falling on the four bricks piled atop his ashes give him? What joy or pain?

The magistrate and the police guard are here. People have climbed on to their roofs to watch the drama. The demolition of the Gate has begun. The rubble is being loaded on to a trailer and emptied into the pit behind the shivala. The pradhan keeps giving instructions and, finally, the eight feet broad wall falls, exposing a peepal tree with a diameter of six handspans. There were hardly any leaves or branches to be seen on the tree. Yet it has been evolving inside the wall just like that mythical Ashtavakar who had a twisted figure but possessed enough knowledge to answer any wise man. The bricks and the roots are tightly coiled together. The kuccha mud plaster falling to the ground raises a cloud of dust which reaches me. It carries a musty smell.

The duty magistrate has departed and with him the rest of the government staff. Standing inside the intact portion of the Gate, the pradhan throws out the utensils and rags of the beggars. They curse him, take their belongings and move towards the bus terminal.

A man has been discovered among the rags, we are told. Fair, with a stubble several days old, and wearing spectacles. Awaiting an early death, he had refused to drink water ...

The work stops. My bhabhi layers the platform with fresh cow dung. The menfolk remove the dead man's dirty clothes and lay him on a clean place. They light the diya. Vishnu Purohit is reciting from the Gita, and people try to identify the man. Sadhu Ram Hakim, who lives in Billa's shanty, announces, "That is Jagat Ram. He used to grind and strain my medicines. Two of his sons are lawyers in Ludhiana. He used to say that he would never live on the earnings of his sons and daughters-in-law. He wasn't even willing to die in their house." Baba Jog identifies him as the son of Sud, who had left before the 1947 riots. I keep thinking I have seen him somewhere. Maybe in school?

Soon the chanting ends. Bhabhi puts a shroud over the dead man. There is no one to claim him. But a bier is being made. The brahmin priest has arrived. All the necessary things have been put together as if automatically. The elders talk of the fate of such anonymous deaths. Women are crying and laughing and teasing each other. They keep instructing the men on what to do – wash the corpse, take it now for cremation. The day is about to end.

The pradhan too is keen to finish the demolition of the Gate. He glares at the labourers in an effort to make them get on with their work. After some time four youngsters lift the bier. There are so many people walking behind it, it seems as if we are all going to a mela at Jarg. Even the pradhan's father's bier did not have so many people accompanying it.

The bier is first taken to the gurudwara, then to the mandir. As we leave the village behind, my brother comes near me and asks in low tones, "Veerji, if you agree, should we sell that barren piece of land? I am getting a good price for it."

"I will think about it," I say. I place my arm across the shoulders of my classmate Tilku and ask him, "What are you doing these days?"

"I'm at the Patiala Palmistry Institute. Tell me, have you come here to sell land, or have the planets dragged you here?" He smiles and signals towards the dead man being carried by the four youngsters. "This man did not come here of his own will. This outhouse was built here centuries ago so that he could breathe his last here. We will also have to come here when our time comes." He laughs, "Happiness of the atma, the soul, is to unite with the parmatma ... but what do you know about all this, you khatri, son of a warrior! Just like human beings have horoscopes, so do houses, places, villages, and cities. One never knows which planet will get a person to which place. The earth pulls a little, the rest is done by the planets which push."

There is a big crowd at the cremation ground. Everything is ready. Lakha, the sweeper, cuts the ropes of the arthi. Raghu Pandha performs the rites. The brahmachari of the orphanage, who has never seen his father, lights the pyre. After the kapal kirya rite of breaking the skull of the dead man, he throws the bamboo pole away from the corpse. And the soul, Jagat Ram of nameless varna, nameless gotra, nameless father and nameless place, is released from its worldly bearings.

Raghu Pandha is about to announce the date for the kirya when suddenly three, four cars arrive – they are the sons, grandsons and other relatives of the dead man. The women, who were sitting quietly till now, start screaming. As if they are mourning the descendants and not the dead man. All the newcomers are quiet, standing there with folded hands even as the eldest son wanders around with a bundle of notes to give to anyone who will accept it. Raghu Pandha, who has taken a vow that he will help perform the last rites of the stranger without taking a paisa for it, is most at ease. He walks with an easy gait, doesn't sit in anyone's car.

It is a moonlit night. The pradhan has completed the demolition of the Gate. Snakes were found in the rubble, and I know Mukundi is yearning to come up and talk of all those snakes seen in our school days. But he cannot climb the stairs. My younger brother comes with news of an increase in the offer for the house. I hear him out, but when he asks in the end, "Well, Veerji, what about the land?" I say, "I will tell you in the morning before I leave," making an excuse of feeling sleepy. "Kishu, Kishu, Kishu," Mukundi calls out to me constantly.

I feel as if the sounds are coming from the roof above the mohdi, from the stairs, from the pegs where the pigeons are perched, and from the fallen Delhi Gate. I know that this gate would have fallen by itself one day. And many people would have been crushed under the rubble. Still I feel like telling the sarpanch, Leave at least one thing in memory of our ancestors.

In the morning Nikka comes to see me off at the station. Standing on the platform he asks me the same question in a hesitant manner. From the train I tell him, "This village was settled by our forefathers. Now I don't have any land here, nor any roof. What will I gain by holding on to this barren land? You take care of it. I will send you the power of attorney, but I will not *sell* this land."

As I talked the train started moving. It seems to me as if I have let go of all the attachments – that with this village, with the houses, with the streets, with the earth and the farms, and even that bond that goes by the name of blood ties. But, why did I still say, Don't sell that barren land?

First published in Punjabi as "Mohdi" in *Aarsee*, September 1996, Delhi.

# क

best of the
~90s~

## RAM SWAROOP KISAN

## The Broker

A simple story about a complex dilemma ... of interplay between greed and poverty, commerce and compassion. **– Govind Nihalani**

I am a well-known broker in the cattle business. A load of lies on my head and nectar on my tongue, I assist cattle traders in their deals, and as a result those of this area have a lot of regard for me. As soon as people spot me, they take me to the teashop and say, "Dhabewala, make tea for two." Seeing me, the owner of the teashop eagerly asks, "What's on these days, Tansukh?" to show that he knows me well. It's a different matter that sometimes I am unable to place that man.

I keep moving from one cattle fair to another. What else does a cattle broker do? Fairs are held somewhere or the other all year round and they are the source of my income. I have already told you, I tell a lot of lies. It quite suits my lips. I can get the most useless cattle sold in broad daylight, or keep even a gem of an animal tethered to its stake. It takes me no time to turn a pearl to a pebble or the other way round. I know such tricks that the buyer mistakes the iron lying in front of him to be gold. It's not that I fool the buyer alone, I hoodwink the seller too. I cast such a spell that the animal is unable to move from the tether. Some owners sit through fairs, rubbing their eyes and yawning. To them I make buyers as scarce as the new moon. My account can make the owner of a sterling she-calf, reared with his own hands, feel that his animal is full of defects. He finds himself saying, "How do you find such things, Tansukh? Is the wretched one worth anything at all? I'll reduce the price if you say so ..." What I mean is that I do know how to manipulate people. After all I am Tansukh, the broker.

I know well that mine is not a good job. All day one has to cheat the innocent. I do realize that a lie is the lowest form of sin but I have to resort to it for the sake of my livelihood. There is no other way I can earn my living. Neither land nor property have I. So, what else can I do? All I understand is Commission. I know that

Ram Swaroop Kisan won the Katha Award for Creative Fiction in 1997, for this story. *Jagati Jot* received the Journal Award for first publishing this story in Rajasthani.

The Katha Translation Award went to Shyam Mathur.

This story first appeared in English translation in *Katha Prize Stories 7*, 1998.

We thank Vijayadan Detha, our nominating editor, for choosing this story for us.

the word Broker evokes contempt, that a broker gets no respect in society. But I'm helpless. And, I was not boasting of my cleverness earlier, merely describing how skilled I am in my brutality.

This incident took place one summer evening. I had just returned home and was lying on a charpai beside the entrance to my house. I couldn't get a wink of sleep as some sparrows were creating a racket above my head. Just then I noticed that the plaster on the ceiling had worn out and the peelings, flapping loosely, seemed to be vying with one another to suddenly descend on me.

The decayed thatch of the roof was a reminder of approaching old age. The holes made by the birds all over the ceiling spoke of the emptiness of my life. My mind turned to taking account of how much I had lied and sinned, how many sick cattle I had got sold in exchange for hard earned money, and how many good ones for next to nothing. How many, many sins had I committed for the sake of this stomach which, even after all that, was empty!

I was still thinking of the past when I was abruptly pulled back into the present by a visitor.

"Ram-Ram, saa!"

"Ram-Ram, bhai!" I said.

"You are Tansukh, aren't you?"

"Yes."

"I need to buy a buffalo," he said as he sat on the charpai, near my feet.

He was old – sixty or so. That he was a broken man was evident from his face. It immediately struck me that here was a wonderful opportunity to wash off all my sins. I could do that by getting a good animal for this needy, troubled person.

He drank some water. "Did you hear what I said?" he began again.

"Yes, I did. Have you seen one that you want?"

"Yes. If only you could get it settled ..."

"Where is it?"

"Actually, it's just here. There is this Kashi Regar who lives in your neighbourhood."

On hearing the name of Kashi, a poverty stricken house and an innocent face flashed before my eyes. I saw his wife languishing with cancer, her infant children staring into her face. Kashi had wanted to sell his buffalo to pay for his wife's medical care. He had often said to me, "Tansukh, get my animal sold, friend! My wife's treatment depends solely on this. The doctors have advised surgery and I don't have a single paisa with me. You are a broker. Just get this little bit done for me! You can even take your commission, friend."

Even that wasn't too bad. But the name brought yet another picture to my mind. That of Kashi's sick buffalo. She had had four miscarriages. The vet had treated her, but he had warned that another miscarriage would surely kill her.

I was greatly distressed. I could not say a word, but just kept brooding.

After a long while the old man broke the silence.

"So, what are you thinking? Have you decided to overlook my request?"

"No, I haven't. Did you say Kashi's buffalo?"

"Yes. What makes you look so worried? Is there a defect in the animal? Don't get me into trouble. I'm a poor man. I need it for my son."

"For your son?"

"Yes, my son is sick. He was in hospital for two long years and was discharged just yesterday. The doctor says that he should drink milk. So I thought I should buy a buffalo. It would be a source of income for the family as well as nourishment for the boy."

"Oh!"

"Yes. Tansukh, please see that I am not ruined. Don't add to my woes."

I heaved a sigh and sat motionless. The sky seemed to be

whirling around me. My heart shuddered. Never had I been trapped like this in my twenty long years as a broker. With a single stroke the old man had invoked the punishment for my sins.

There stood before me two hungry figures with their arms stretched out, two diseased bodies breathing their last. Who shall I not save? Who should I cheat, Kashi or the old man?

These questions stared at me, taunted me. What should I say to the old man – Yes or No? A Yes would mean the murder of the old man while a No would mean the end of Kashi.

"Tansukhji, shall we go to Kashi's house?" the old man said again.

"I am not a broker, you old man!" I heard myself shriek. "Do whatever pleases you."

I saw the old man rise with the support of his stick and hobble out on trembling feet. I sat alone on my charpai. Finally, I lay down again and looked at the roof as I had done earlier. The sparrows were quarrelling, as always.

---

First published in Rajasthani as "Dalal" in *Jagati Jot*, Bikaner.

best of the
90s

**AMAR MITRA**

Swadeshyatra

A powerful story raising questions about identity, country and most of all, human bondages, in terms of the relationships between the powerful and the powerless, the employer and the employee and the perpetrator and the victim. The description of the fish as a sensual presence in the story is very important. – **Rituparno Ghosh**

Jogen Sadhu, the cashier of a branch office of the Municipal Corporation, is returning home with a whole hilsa. It is the first of the season and a fairly large one. The papers had mentioned that fish was not being brought in from Bangladesh that year. But Noni, the fisherman, swore that *his* had actually come from the Padma. After all, if one could not sell hilsas from the Padma in the rainy season, why bother being a fishseller at all? Jogen likes the fish very much. Narrow headed, broad bellied, the silver of its body is tinged red. It weighs about a kilo and a half. The fish, Noni vouches, is without eggs. The maachwala had offered to carve it, but Jogen will have none of that. To get back home with a whole hilsa puts him in a happy mood. This way he can watch it being carved as he sips a hot cup of tea.

Jogen's wife, Anima, cuts fish very well, especially the hilsa. She does not like her fish to be brought into the house cut and dressed. In her opinion, fish loses its flavour if you don't cut it yourself. The real pleasure is in that moment when the belly of the hilsa is poised against the sharp bonti and thrust forward. Deftly, suddenly, it is in two pieces, filling the room with the raw, wild smell of fat and blood. Anima always exults, "Everything about the hilsa is good, even its scales." And how fond she is of scraping off the scales. Every once in a while the fifty-something Jogen tells his forty-something wife, "You must have been a fishwife in your previous birth and never stopped being one." Anima, his mechuni wife, is not offended. She laughs and says, "Hanh! But tell me, do you think such fisherwomen still exist, the kind the babus were always crowding and buzzing around? You know the kind don't you, those dark skinned, buxom, pan-chewing mashis with their nosedrops and silver anklets. Wonder when they disappeared from this city!" She is right. Jogen hardly

Amar Mitra won the Katha Award for Creative Fiction in 1998, for this story. *Desh* received the Journal Award for first publishing this story in Bangla.

The Katha Translation Award went to Dilip Kumar Ganguli.

This story first appeared in English translation in *Katha Prize Stories 8*, 1998.

We thank Debes Ray, our nominating editor, for choosing this story for us.

sees such fisherwomen in the market these days.

But on his way back home, the pleasant image of his mechuni wife is jerked out of his imagination. Jogen stops abruptly, calling out, "Aei, Lachman, Lachmanram!" not knowing why he has called out so suddenly.

There he is, Lachmanram of Bhojpur, loading his wheelbarrow with rubbish. He will push it to the dustbin and from there to the dhapa. The rubbish – cabbage and cauliflower, greens, maize and drumstick – will be spread over the low, marshy landfill area and burnt, the flames crackling and leaping skywards. Lachman is still at work. Perhaps, the man has not heard the call? Look at Lachmanram's brilliant white dhoti and vest! Jogen thinks he wears extra clean clothes precisely because he deals with dirt. Jogen calls out again. This time, turning his head and seeing him, Lachman tosses his broom to one side and walks up to Jogen.

But what is Jogen going to say? After calling out to Lachman, he wishes he hadn't. Lachman would hear the news himself soon enough, so why should Jogen be the one to tell him? He should have simply avoided him. Anyway, is this something that can be discussed? Jogen shudders just thinking of it.

His eyes soften as he sees Lachman. The elderly looking man is standing before Jogen, his head bent, an expression of respect on his face. That's just like him, he's an extremely timid fellow. Moreover, Jogen is the cashier Lachman gets his salary from. He will not say a word till Jogen speaks. If Jogen were to start walking homeward without a word, Lachman wouldn't even ask him why he was called. He would simply return to work. He will not wonder why Jogen Sadhu walked away abruptly after calling out to him. In fact, Jogen can easily leave now and return home, holding the hilsa in his hand. Or, he may even ask Lachman what he thinks of the hilsa. Jogen knows Lachman will smile, bend his head and barely manage to whisper, Hujoor! For him it is sufficient that

---

**Bonti:** A sharp, curved knife attached to a base of wood; **Mechuni:** Fisherwoman.
**Dhapa:** A low, usually marshy, land where rubbish is deposited.

Jogen has asked for his opinion. Who is he to give it?

Jogen considers moving on. But, he must talk about it. Only Lachman can give him more news about Bhojpur, after all he belongs to the place. It is unthinkable that a Bhojpuria will have no news about Bhojpur! Jogen is curious about everything. He loves to talk, to get to know about things, to investigate matters. This morning, before starting out for the market, he had scrutinized the newspaper for details about the disturbances in Bathaniatola village in Bhojpur, caused by the Ranvir Sena – a private army of gangsters of the local bhumihar landlords. Shouldn't he give Lachman the news, even if he is bound to learn of it sooner or later, and if that be the case, why should he mind if Jogen tells him now? Perhaps he can get some more information, Jogen tells himself, and there's still plenty of time before he has to leave for office. He usually goes late to office. But so does everyone else. And what can Jogen Sadhu do there if he does report on time? Probably just suffocate from the boredom of having no one to talk to for an hour and a half.

Lachman is standing before him, waiting. Jogen looks this way and that and says, "Water is collecting again in my dirt lane. I wonder where the water is getting clogged. Check the line, Lachman. Has the drain been cleaned?"

Lachman's head is bent submissively. "Not yet, Sadhuji."

"But that's not important. What was it I wanted to tell you?" Jogen hesitates. He wants Lachman to ask him why he has called him. But Lachman is never curious enough. Jogen clears his throat noisily and mumbles, "I say, when will you go to your native place?"

"On the twenty fifth, for cultivation, hujoor."

"Cultivation? Is your son coming over?"

"Hujoor."

"Have you got any news from your place?"

"Hujoor."

Jogen Sadhu realizes that the news about Bhojpur has not reached Lachman yet. And such important news! His tongue begins to itch. Looking around conspiratorially, he whispers, "Don't go to your village now. There has been a lot of trouble in the villages of Bhojpur. Have you heard the news?"

Lachman's glassy eyes are bewildered and frightened. He stares at Jogen, waiting for more. Whether afraid or dismayed, he is not in the habit of saying anything. Nobody expects him to, and now he has forgotten how to. He will listen as long as Jogen Sadhu talks, but as far as possible, he will not react. Lachman is looking at the sky – after all, one can hardly keep staring at Babu Jogen Sadhu. And you can't catch every word if you keep your head bent.

Jogen too gazes at the sky. The sky is clouding over. It has turned dark with gathering clouds. This year the monsoon has arrived early. Monsoon clouds floating in from the Bay of Bengal mean crops and seeds. The clouds from the south have drifted as they should against the Himalayas and flooded the north of Bengal and Assam. Then, unable to cross the hills these north flowing clouds have turned west, advancing along the Gangetic plain, to rain over the Bihar plateau. People have begun work on either side of the river. The sowing season is about to start. The monsoon clouds have finally reached Bhojpur after their journey through Rajmahal, Bhagalpur, Moonger, Nalanda, Vaishali and Patna. From there they have continued further northwest. Is Lachman thinking about his rain flooded land, about whether to advance or postpone his visit there?

Lachman has to return to his village when it is time to plough the fields. And at harvest time, too. If Lachman is away from Calcutta it means that either it is the tilling season or the crops are ready. Then Mahender, Lachman's son, comes to town. He works in place of Lachman. This is not legal but then this is how it has always happened. Sarkar, Lachman's supervisor, has accepted this. In exchange, he gets a monthly return from Lachman. And Lachman has no cause to worry. He will go home in the beginning of Shravan, will return at the end of Bhadra after cultivation, and go back again in the middle of Aghran, when he gets news that the crop is ripe. In fact, Lachman knows instinctively when he will leave. It will be the end of Magh or the beginning of Falgun before he returns once again. And so it goes. Cashier Jogen Sadhu continues to give Lachman's salary to his son. That's why Lachman is grateful to

Jogen. If Jogen wants, he can hold back Lachman's salary, or even dismiss him from work. But Jogen doesn't do that, neither does he take any commission in return. Jogen reasons, Our family is one of the oldest in Calcutta. We have been in business for a long time. I may have joined the corporation when I failed at the business but that doesn't mean my family has lost class. Take money from a labourer! Can I stoop so low?

The previous cashier used to take a cut. But because Jogen doesn't, Lachman is afraid of him. Jogen understands this. Lachman knows that Jogen can withhold his wages, or even dismiss him. Many a times, when Lachman has to go back to his village, he mumbles, "Hujoor ... Sadhuji, I am off to Bhojpur, there's work on the land ..." and Jogen listens, but doesn't comment. "Sadhuji, Mahender, my work ..." And then Jogen will spy a face behind Lachman's – Mahender, fresh from Bhojpur, a touch of Bhojpur's air and dust still lingering on his face. A month in this city and all that will disappear. Jogen invariably asks about his part of the world. "Aei! Mahender, is the news good?" Mahender grins, "Good, hujoor." Jogen asks, "Is the Bhumihar Raj getting on?" And Mahender smiles again, "Hanh, Sadhuji."

Mahender is twenty five years old and already a father of three. But not as shy as his father, when asked a question. When Jogen asks him why he doesn't remain at home during the reaping season, why he comes to Calcutta instead and sends his old father back there, Mahender's face darkens. His constant questioning has helped Jogen understand that if Lachman is not at home at the time of the harvesting no work gets done. If Mahender remains at home, no crops are brought in. And now Jogen Sadhu asks, "When is Mahender coming?"

Turning his eyes away from the sky, Lachman says, "On the twenty first."

"Go, go back to work,"

Jogen starts to move – he can't keep standing there holding a hilsa! He has given him the news. Now Lachman can do whatever he likes with it. Jogen walks away at a rapid pace.

J ogen's mechuni wife is delighted to cut the hilsa. She calls out to him, "Look here, so much blood, and eggs too!" Sitting on a bed with a cup of tea, in the room facing the road, Jogen is looking through the newspaper once again. The news of Bathaniatola in Bhojpur has been printed in detail. These journalists are everywhere – they have reached Bhojpur as well, reporting on the subdued wailing in Bathaniatola, replete with photographs of rows of dead bodies laid out on the ground. But Anima's call disturbs his reading. He says, "There should have been no eggs."

"There are! Come and see! The hilsa's full of eggs. Ishh! What aroma." The raw smell of the hilsa makes Jogen's wife restless. Jogen has helped his daughter into the school bus early in the morning. Now he and Anima are alone at home. Her call can still intoxicate him, send him reeling even today. He is suddenly aroused. Setting the newspaper aside and carrying his cup of tea, Jogen goes to Anima at the water tap.

Her hand wet with blood, Anima is laughing, "Have you seen the eggs?"

"Noni has cheated us."

"How? What a beautiful fish, dripping with fat."

"A fish full of eggs is tasteless." Jogen is startled by his words. He can't explain the eerie sensation that sends a shudder through his body. He can only think of the Bathaniatola news. Should he tell Anima? Many women have been murdered. A pregnant woman was raped, beheaded. Na, na, why should Anima hear of that? Anima is laughing at his words, bent over the fish. Blood drips from the sharp bonti, staining the area around the tap. Gouging out the eggs with three fingers, Anima says, "You don't even spare fish eggs, I know you very well, you little rogue!"

Jogen bites his lip. He has been itching to talk about it ever since he read the newspaper. He can't do without talking, but he is afraid of telling Anima about it. It's a strange feeling. Why did he buy the hilsa today? But when he saw the fresh hilsa ... chhee! Why is he thinking of all this, what has happened to him? After all, the news in the newspapers is simply news. It is always like that. If Anima hears of it, she will be angry once again, Have you nothing else to say early in the morning? If you do nothing but dole out salaries to sweepers and scavengers, what can you notice except garbage.

"There is no kochushak in the market as yet, or else I would have cooked it with the hilsa head." Anima is holding the fish head and chopping it in two, marvelling, "What fat!"

Jogen, teacup still in hand, wants to get back to his room. The newspaper report on Bathaniatola pulls him but he senses someone standing outside his window. Is that why the room has darkened slightly? Or have the clouds thickened? Once inside the room Jogen sees a troubled face appear on the other side of the window. Lachman. Jogen has guessed right. Perching himself on the cot and sipping his tea, Jogen smiles, "What's happened?"

"Hujoor, Sadhuji."

It is up to Jogen to try and understand what Lachman wants to say. Having become a man of few words he cannot even think up things to say. His son Mahender is not like him. That's why he can't remain at home during the harvest – if you talk, no work ever gets done. Silence protects a harijan. Every year there is some trouble or the other during the tilling.

Lachman and Mahender have two bighas of land to grow rice on. The remaining land, donated to them during Mahatma Vinoba Bhave's bhudan movement forty years ago, is rocky and arid. Even grass does not grow there. Vinobaji acquired the land for the poor by requesting the bhumihar and rajput landlords for it with folded hands. Makkhan Singhji, Bhumihar Raj Dasrath Singhji's grandfather, had given two bighas of land to Mahender's grandfather, Chitaram. That land was a gift, a chakran, like food given to a servant in lieu of wages, the property of the servant. A rent free piece of land. The government charged a revenue on it. The landlord didn't, but the holder had to donate hard labour. It is as it was in

---

**Kochushak:** An edible root.

the past. You can begin to till your own land only after toiling for the Bhumihar Raj. Let the law be what it may, this is the law in Bhojpur. Jogen Sadhu is always amazed as he listens to the tales of the chakran land. Nothing seems to have changed there.

Now Lachman says, "Hujoor, Sadhuji ..."

"What is it, Lachman?"

"Bhojpur." Lachman says in his laconic way.

Yes, Bhojpur's Ranvir Sena! Now he must tell it all. Lachman's eyes are moist. He has understood. As he is able to divine when the rains will descend on his native place, just by looking at the Calcutta skies, so he does now. Perhaps he has guessed everything.

Jogen assures him, "Nothing much has happened, Lachman. The naxalites have had a fight with the Ranvir Sena. What a place, your Bhojpur! Landlords maintaining armies which wander around with rifles and stenguns, spoiling for a kill? No such thing as law there, right?"

Lachman stands outside the window, trembling. "What happened, hujoor?"

He is afraid of asking for details. Maybe not from fear. Even after living in the city Lachman hasn't changed from being a villager. "Bhojpur is not a small, unknown place," Jogen says, reassuringly, "Why are you frightened?"

"Hujoor!"

"The wages had been fixed at twenty rupees, but the landlords are not agreeable to that. This is all that's given in the papers. Lachman, have *you* heard of Bathaniatola village at all?"

Lachman's grip tightens on the window bars. And right under Jogen's nose, the Lachmanram who stands there, gripping the bars of the window, has become a caged prisoner, with everything – the stained light of an overcast sky, the expanse of the heavens, the lush, unending vegetation – behind him. But Jogen still cannot believe his eyes. He rises and switches on the lights in his room. Lachman stands at the window, his face pressed against the bars.

Jogen is suddenly confused. "Go," he says, "Nothing has

happened. Go, start your work. Take a look at the dirt lane behind my house, will you?"

"Have they killed people?"

"Lachman, that's how it always is. People kill."

"Hujoor, what happened to the village?" Slowly, Lachmanram's questions become words.

"Bathaniatola?" Jogen stutters, trying his best to smile, "Look Lachman, Bhojpur is such a big place. In Calcutta when there is trouble in Ballygunj, do you hear anything about it here in Talla?"

Lachmanram's tears start rolling. "My daughter's father-in-law's house ..."

What is Lachman saying? Can such a ghastly coincidence happen? Jogen has never known it to. So there has been a massacre in Bhojpur. But Lachmanram will not be affected by it. It is always that way, Jogen's experience has proved it time and again. So many incidents take place in Calcutta but Jogen is never involved in them. People die in bus accidents, in police firing, in bomb blasts, in scuffles between political parties. They die in and around the suburbs. But has anyone known to Jogen or related to him ever been killed in such cases? Never. There have been so many train accidents, plane crashes, boats capsizing, disasters by fire, but has Jogen ever been affected by them? The closest he comes to a disaster is through the newspaper. A few feverish days of horror and excitement with the newspaper and there the matter ends. Yes, there was one early morning, some twenty five years ago, during the naxal regime, when the lifeless bodies of two of his classmates had been found, lying by the side of a road in Beliaghata. The police had picked them up from their homes the previous night. In those times there used to be so many murders everyday and Calcutta was littered with dead bodies, thanks to the police. That was the first time people known to Jogen had died like that. But that was such a long while ago. And he had even forgotten what they looked like. Anyway, the two boys who died had been extremely proud. Jogen had never understood them. And, as they were not close friends, Jogen had managed to live on.

Now, Jogen stares at Lachmanram in amazement. Bhojpur is so large and Bathaniatola village like a speck of dust in it, and that it should contain Lachman's daughter's father-in-law's house! Slowly, things seem to add up. It seems to Jogen as if one of his dead classmates has come to stand by his window. A shiver runs down Jogen's spine. It seems as if someone has set fire to those very newspapers that have always fuelled his excitement, and now, his whole body is burning with it.

Lachman is banging his head against the bars, "Is it true, hujoor?"

So Lachman's daughter had gone to Bathaniatola to set up house. But is there only one Bathaniatola in Bhojpur? He is about to ask, when he hears Lachman say, "I got news of my daughter, hujoor. Mahender sent a letter last month."

"What letter?" But Jogen doesn't have to ask. He knows what news Lachman has received about his married daughter. What else can it be? Lachman's daughter is expecting a child in the month of Kartik. Lachman has plans to go to Bathaniatola, twenty miles west of his village, to bring her home for a few days. After the tilling is over, he will take his daughter back to her sasurghar and return to Calcutta as early as possible. He will return to his village before the harvest and, during his daughter's confinement, he will take his wife to her, and he too will stay back. He adores his daughter. He has planned everything, down to the last detail.

Jogen Sadhu is still dumbfounded. It is Lachman who is doing all the talking! His son had written that a lot of trouble was brewing because of wages. In his village, Surajpur ...

"Your son-in-law is not a naxalite, is he?" Jogen asks.

Lachman is silent. Jogen stares at him. Lachman starts crying.

Outside, it has started to drizzle. Jogen gets up. Can this be true? The private armies of the landlords obviously don't differentiate between the naxalite and the non-naxalite when they kill. Just to vent their rage, they will slaughter ordinary, innocent people whose only crime is that they don't want to live as they have in the past. They are no longer willing to grovel before their

"Hujoor Mai Baap" and work gratis for them. And the Ranvir Sena suspects that the naxals are instigating the people.

When the trouble started in Bathaniatola, the men were away at work. The Sena had slaughtered the women, set fire to houses, thrown babies into the fire and killed the old. They butchered all those who came in their way and raped pregnant women. Then they had returned jubilantly. Every newspaper is full of the news. Jogen's mind refuses to go any further. He doesn't want to face Lachmanram anymore.

"I must bathe. Can't not go to office, hanh?" he says as he walks out of the room.

The entire house, every single room, is filled with fragrant smoke bearing the smell of fried hilsa. The heady aroma wafts out through the window. Breathing deeply, Jogen turns back and sees Lachman standing, still clutching the bars of the window. The smell seems to have enchanted him too. Jogen picks up his shaving set, towel, shampoo and soap and gets ready to bathe.

"Whom were you talking to?" Anima asks him.

"Lachman."

"Jamadar! Call him, call him, ask him to clean the lane, it is clogged up with water for the past few days."

"Not today."

"Why not, can't you see how it has been pouring? Maa! How filthy it is outside!" Anima rushes out of the kitchen, calling out to Lachman, "Aei, Jamadar, arré, where is he?"

Jogen looks out of the window. Perhaps, Lachman left as soon as he heard Anima call. Or, perhaps he left earlier. Anima is furious. "He has run away, the sly fellow. Pretends to be as innocent as a newborn babe! He hasn't even cleaned the bathroom today."

Jogen says, "He may come later."

"As if he'll come again," Anima grumbles, "Now I have to do all his work, the bathroom is so slippery. How much work can I do?"

Jogen walks towards the bathroom. One has to step carefully, that's all. He will take half an hour to shave and bathe, may be more, but not less. He is a man who loves his bath. He uses up six soaps a month.

When he leaves for office, the taste of hilsa on his tongue, he takes the newspaper along with him. There isn't much work today. It is not payment day. On these days he completes the cashbook in his cash payment counter that is like a cage enclosed by a mesh. Jogen sits there with the large ledger, restless. He spreads his newspaper over the ledger, reading the same news over and over again, filled with a strange restlessness. He lights cigarette after cigarette, folds and unfolds the newspaper incessantly. He belches once. The taste of hilsa, the smell as well.

Incredible! Can such things really happen? Jogen cannot even begin to imagine how someone slaughtered in distant Bhojpur can be so closely related to someone he knows so well, a man he speaks to everyday, standing across his window. Lachman's daughter is married in Bathaniatola village. She is pregnant, excitedly awaiting the special day. Even the month of Kartik is as pleasant as the season of Basant to Lachman and his daughter. And then he suddenly thinks, Is Lachman's daughter's name Phulmotia Devi, the one who was murdered by the army of the bhumihar landlord?

Jogen is once again amazed at how he has always subconsciously supposed that those killed in freak accidents cannot be anyone's dear ones, nobody's son, daughter, father or mother. They are, he has always argued, as if self-created. Only the newspaper reporters know them. Such people are born only to die in mass murders, riots, and floods, to be raped, to be scorched to death in fires. Like insects. Their faces all look the same. It seems as if they come to this earth from other planets to suffer such insulting, undignified deaths. This is their profession. Then why should they be so intimately related to Lachmanram, whom Jogen knows so well?

At office, Jogen tries to discuss the matter but nobody is interested. Or, if they are, they have nothing to say. Jogen's colleagues do not want to stray from the arena of the latest juicy gossip. Stories about the latest movie stars and their various scandals abound, television serials, cricket – who cares about Bhojpur? What will they do, even if they knew about it? What will they talk of? They don't know a thing about Bhojpur. If Jogen tells them that the daughter of their ward sweeper is married and lives in Bhojpur, they will not be disturbed. They will simply say that it was destined to happen. After all, the naxals were driven out of one place and simply gathered in another.

Jogen feels all alone. Sometimes he feels that Lachmanram hasn't told him the truth. But it just can't be. Why should Lachman lie? Jogen Sadhu tries to remember everything he has ever heard about Bhojpur from Mahender. He knows why Lachman must return home at the time of cultivation and again when the crop is to be harvested. When the city was flooded after the first rains, and Mahender, newly arrived from Bhojpur, stood in the manholes trying to clean them up, he told Jogen that his father could return to Calcutta only after he had offered a hundred rupee note at the feet of the Bhumihar Raj Dasrath Singh, and had obtained his permission to till the land. The land is bonded property, permission must be asked for. Lachman's father had become a servant of Makkhan Singh. He used to run errands for him, clean his house, work on his land for free, follow the bhumihar landlord around, keep vigil outside the door with a stick in hand when the Babu enjoyed a new girl – and that was why the land was granted. Makkhan Singh has gifted land to many – the shoemaker who made his shoes, the man who looked after his elephants and horses. Now, there was no more land to give, it had all become private property. But so what if the land is owned by Lachman, he has to work all the same, as a servant without wages. All laws in Bhojpur are for the Bhumihar Raj. The government and the police go by the laws laid down by the Bhumihar Raj.

Jogen has heard all this from Mahender in bits and pieces. Mahender said that he does not obey Dasrath Singh's orders. He does not want to work without a salary, and that is why his father must go back home. If Mahender stays back, Dasrathji will not allow his family to work in the field. Dasrath Singh calls him a naxalite. Mahender does not know the naxalites, but he has heard of them from here and there. The naxalites have infiltrated into a number of villages close to Arrah town. At times, Mahender wishes to somehow get the Naxal Party into his village. Dasrath Singh had once handed him over to the police declaring him a naxalite and the police had beaten him up mercilessly. In the end, his father Lachmanram had returned home on hearing the news and got him released after falling at the feet of Dasrathji. Once Dasrathji had beaten his father Lachman with a shoe. Mahender was very young then. But he remembered the incident. He has heard that, ever since, Lachman has done the cultivation and harvesting only after begging permission at Dasrathji's feet. This is chakran land, so one is forced to remain a servant, said Mahender. If one doesn't behave like a servant, Singhji will destroy the crops by letting loose ten buffaloes at harvest time. If need be, he will shoot down the whole family. Who can dare say anything? If it so pleases him, he can drag a girl from Lachman's house to his bungalow. Who can object? Only if he agrees to work for free can a harijan till his land, only then can his wife and daughters feel at peace.

Jogen repeats Mahender's words to Anima, pretending that he is relating an item from the newspaper. Anima yawns. "What a pack of lies! Nothing can be like this. Mahender is too clever, this is a trick not to do work," she says. "You must tell him to clean the lane, the drains, the bathroom and the toilet everyday. Tell him tomorrow itself to see why the safety tank is leaking."

Jogen too used to think that Mahender's tales were exaggerated, fanciful stuff of the sort one finds in the movies. How can zamindari still exist? Is this such a completely lawless country? Mahender is a shameless fellow. He doesn't want to do any extra work. It is only because Jogen Sadhu pays him his salary that Mahender does his work silently, with his head bent. No matter that Lachman always maintains that after his death the land will be taken away and given to somebody else. It is chakran land of the Bhumihar Raj.

adhuji, hujoor!"

Jogen looks up in surprise to see old Lachmanram on the other side of the mesh. "Hujoor, Sadhuji!"

Jogen stands up. He walks quickly out of his cage, agitated in the anticipation of fresh news. One never knows when one's hair can be made to bristle.

"Lachman, is your son Mahender a naxalite?"

Lachman is stunned. He shakes his head, "No, hujoor, he is not a naxalite, it is all a lie."

"Come, come out," Jogen beckons Lachman with his hand, and walks out of the office compound with him. "Have you got any news? Oi Lachman, did anyone say anything?"

Lachman grins. "Hujoor, everything is fine."

"Fine?" Jogen is surprised, "What is fine?"

"There has been no disturbance in our Bathaniatola, Sadhuji. Sugribji told me."

"Who Sugribji?"

"Sugrib Singh is the son of Bhumihar Raj Chandeshwar Singhji of village Andharpur, which is next to Bathaniatola, my son-in-law's village. He is a bhumihar, but with the Calcutta Police, in the Salt Lake Police line. I went to see him, he told me so. He says there are three Bathaniatolas in our Bhojpur, hujoor."

Strange! Jogen Sadhu's personal experience, his view, nursed over such a long time, is being upheld again. It had to be so. It has always been so.

Jogen Sadhu believes what Lachman says. There is a Belgachia next to Talla and another Belgachia in Howrah. The mouja in which Jogen Sadhu owns land on the Canning line is called Sitakund, and he has found a village of the same name beyond Bantola. Jogen lights a cigarette and draws on it with relish. Lachman is saying, "If there's trouble in my son-in-law's village, Bathaniatola, Sugrib Singh will not be found in Calcutta, hujoor. For who do you think commits these murders? Who sets fire to

---

**Mouja:** A block of villages.

houses, who are they? None other than the police posted in various places, the BSF, the CRP. When the bhumihars, rajputs, kurmis, decide to set fire to the villages of the harijans, the chamars, the dusads, letters reach Punjab, UP, Bengal, Orissa, Gujarat, Maharashtra. Setting their uniforms aside these policemen return on leave to their villages – as bhumihars, rajputs, kurmis, jadavs. They rejoin their senas – the Ranvir Sena, Brahmarshi Sena, Kunwar Sena, Lorik Sena. Since Sugrib Singhji hasn't returned, there has been no trouble in my son-in-law's village, hujoor! But ..."

"But what?"

"Sugrib Singhji says there will be trouble soon, hujoor. As soon as he receives the letter, he will apply for leave and return home."

"But why?"

"Many naxalites have become active, hujoor. My son-in-law does not work for free, he does not clean the Bhumihar Raj's bungalow, or fall at his feet. Everyone there is becoming like that. Bhumihar Raj will teach them a lesson. Sugribji also told me about my son."

"Mahender?"

"Hanh, hujoor, Mahender never works without wages, Sugribji knows that. Even from a distance of twenty miles, he knows that Mahender does not prostrate himself before the Bhumihar Raj. All bhumihars keep tabs on other bhumihars. Sugribji said, Mahender will be killed if he continues to do this. Women, children will all be wiped out if they talk about wages, nobody can save them."

Jogen Sadhu knows what kind of people are killed in riots, and mass killings. And because he knows, Lachman's words do not affect him. He had been thrown into needless confusion, thinking his theory was wrong. Now he needs a cup of tea. Leaving the office compound he heads for BT road. The clouds are travelling upstream along the river Ganga to the rest of India. Moving northwest, they will burst open on drought-afflicted, rain-dependent, sky-gazing earth. The tiller, seeds in hand, waits.

Jogen looks at the sky and then back at the earth. Lachman is standing there, his body slightly bent, talking away. Jogen knows that Lachman's fear is baseless. Jogen believes this wholeheartedly.

Just an hour ago he had lost faith in himself. Now he understands that if there is a carnage in Surajpur, that must be another Surajpur somewhere, as happened with Bathaniatola. Anyway, villages that are witnesses to mass slaughter are not a part of this world, he tells himself again, they do not belong to the map of India. Jogen Sadhu, a citizen of modern India, can never ever build up a relationship with such persons and these villages. There is no need. Just as he has no links with Bhagalpur, Arowal, Jahanabad, Surat, Latur, Mumbai, just as Bathaniatola and Bhojpur will remain unknown to him, so too the Surajpurs, Andharpurs and the other Bathaniatolas of the future.

"Hujoor, Sadhuji, what do I do? Go to Bhojpur?"

"You can go only after Mahender is here."

"No, hujoor, I must go today."

"When?"

"There is a night train, hujoor. Once there, I will get Mahender to work in the Bhumihar Raj land without wages, make him fall at the master's feet, I will ask my son-in-law not to talk about wages, they must both work free."

"What? You really want to leave today?"

"Hanh, hujoor, I will go to Bhojpur, just for a few days I will not be here, nor Mahender. Will I get my full salary for the month?"

"And your duties?"

"Ramu will do my duty. I did his when his father died and he had to go back home. The superintendent knows, hujoor, I got his permission but he could not say anything about the salary. You give our pay. Hujoor, will I get the full salary, hujoor, Mahender will come next week?"

"You mean, neither of you will be there?"

"Hujoor! Sugrib Singhji said, I will go back to the village as soon as I get a letter. Many naxalites have become active, hujoor, Sadhuji."

Jogen cannot decide what to say. Things like this do happen. Such incidents are routine when one has to work with people from many states. Yet, fancy going home whenever one likes! When the whim gets you, whenever you think of your native village, your children, the face of your wife – and it comes like a sudden gust of wind – just jump on to the first train. No need to take a bath or think of food, simply push off to Howrah Station with a bundle tucked under your armpit. Jogen's maternal cousin, Adrish, lives in Sambalpur. Works for the Railways. He too comes over suddenly, saying, "I'm fine, everything's fine, just that I suddenly felt I must come home and who can stop me? Think of Calcutta and be there!"

Jogen lets out a hilsa-smelling belch. And, with it, Anima's face floats back into his mind. What time is it, three o'clock? Lachman must soon start his walk to Howrah Station to buy the ticket. But has he finished his work?

"Have you checked the drain? And the dirt lane behind my house?"

"No, hujoor," Lachman says, blinking his eyes, "There was no time to do it since morning."

"So I have to live in dirt?"

"Hujoor, Sadhuji."

"Before you go, clean the drain and the lane, Lachman. None of your lame excuses, or else I will send the whole salary back to the head office. Clever, aren't you? You will take your salary and go and sleep back in the village. You didn't do a spot of my work the last few days."

"Hujoor, Sadhuji!"

"If you go home without doing the work, I can't guarantee that your salary will be paid. Your master cannot save you. Aren't you ashamed? I have been telling you repeatedly."

"Hujoor!" Lachmanram folds his hands. He has no more words. Jogen Sadhu is the only one who is talking. Jogen never takes a cut from Lachman's salary. Only gets his bathroom and dirt lane cleaned, once in a while. If Lachman ever asks for money, he will pay.

"Hujoor!" Lachmanram starts walking away with his head bent. It begins to rain. Lachmanram sets off in the falling rain. In the direction of Jogen Sadhu's house.

First published in Bangla as "Swadeshyatra" in *Desh*, February 1997, Calcutta.

best of the
90s

**VIBHA RANI**

The Witness

This story gives a symbolic insight into the new emerging literature in Maithili short story and the potential of promising writers. A simple theme with an appealing straightforward style.

— **Rituparno Ghosh**

*Rau Baap, Rau Baap! There has been a dacoity in Bhola and Ramchannar's house, Ha Daib!, even one's enemies should not see such a day!*

*Barely ten days ago, the whole family had turned out at the Chhat Ghat for the riverbank puja, a celebration the family attended every year – Bhola and Ramchannar, their wives, Gauri and Gayatri. And the lovely Munia, how she had shone like a moon among the brothers' starlike children, draped as she was in a red banarasi sari and loaded with jewellery – tika, nosestud, a seetahar necklace, cummerbund and anklets, her lustrous hair in an elaborate red cloth braid. Munia, just barely in her teens, had looked like a winsome child bride, soft and smooth like the new leaves on a mango tree, and even as one looked, she had seemed unusually grown up. And today the entire village is scurrying to their place, filling the frontyard and the inner courtyard. And what are Bhola and Ramchannar up to? Fainting, that's what, one after the other. For the brief moments when they regain consciousness they flay their chests with both their hands and with a cry of "Ha Daib!" fall into a dead faint again, now one, now the other. Bhola's wife is pulling out her hair and beating her breasts and abusing her God – "Rau Mudai, Rau Mudai! You could not bear to see even a single day of our happiness, Mudaia ... If I don't brand you with a burning wood, I am not my father's daughter." Ramchannar's wife sits in the other room, surrounded by women, dangerously quiet till she totters up once in every sudden while, looks around wildly, screams, "Baap re baap! Let me go, l-et me go, let ..." then just as suddenly her shoulders droop, and she lapses back into a stupor – Oh, such misfortune!*

As children, Bhola and Ramchannar helped their father sell balloons, toys and whistles pegged on to a bamboo stick. They

Vibha Rani won the Katha Award for Creative Fiction in 1999, for this story. *Sandhan* received the Journal Award for first publishing this story in Maithili.

The Katha Translation Award went to Vidyanand Jha and the Editors.

This story first appeared in English translation in *Katha Prize Stories 9*, 2000.

We thank Udaya Narayana Singh, our nominating editor, for choosing this story for us.

roamed the city, their usual haunt being the rickshaw stand outside
the railway station. There were four trains which crossed the station
every day – the up trains came in at seven in the morning and six
in the evening, and the down ones at nine in the morning, and
eleven in the night. Bauji never waited for the eleven o'clock train
because, one, it was quite late in the night, two, people were in a
hurry to grab a rickshaw or tanga as soon as they got off the train,
and three, all the children were asleep. When it was festival time, be
it Jhoolan, Janmashtami or other festivals, Bauji would land up
at the melas without fail. They did brisk business there, Bhola and
Ramchannar had to work harder too, inflating more balloons and
making more toys. And come the kite flying season, father and
sons were into making kites, grinding glass to make the manjha,
applying this bristling paste on to the kite string – better to cut
other kites with!

Mai had a goat. Both brothers grazed it by turns, wishing
desperately they were in school instead, studying. The teacher of
the school, Ramnath Babu, used to let them in sometimes but how
much can one study, without a slate, a pencil or books? Bauji
wanted them to study but could not afford to educate them. He sat
them at home and taught them how to count up to a hundred, to
multiply up to twenty times twenty, to calculate fractions and
multiply sawaiya and adhaiya – just some basic math, really. This
little knowledge held them in good stead. Then Mai's goat gave
birth to three kids, clean and small chagaris, and Mai made a pact
with God, Settle my sons, O Bhagawati, and I will offer one chagari
to you. At the festival of Chhat that year, she made another
maanata to Chhat Maiya, I'll offer bamboo baskets to you Chhat
Maiya, but please settle my sons. So ten days before the festival,
Bhola and Ramchannar went out early in the morning and placed
a red ekranga cloth in a bamboo basket and then religiously offered
to Chhat Maiya, the alms collected.

Human beings do their calculations while bidhna does its own.
If the two match it's god's will, if not ... Luckily Fate smiled on
Bhola and Ramchannar. In time, Bhola started helping out in

Ramasra Babu's grocery store. Ramchannar worked in Baldev Babu's Mithila Cloth Store. Baldev Babu was a Marwari and had quite a range of fabrics of different colours. His clientele ranged from the very poor to the wife and daughter of the town's chairman saheb. Ramchannar displayed the rich fabrics to them, dreaming all the time of owning his own cloth shop.

Mai's household however continued to run on the money Bauji brought in. The brothers gave half their salaries to Bauji and Mai immediately appropriated them from him. With this she got made two nose studs for her future daughters-in-law. And a pair of tikas from the money earned from the sale of the chagaris – Mai had sold two on her own, the brothers insisted on selling the third as well, saying, "Mai, by the time we are well-settled in life, it will be too old. Then nobody will give you the proper price for it. Let another chagari come. Then you can fulfil your maanata to the Bhagawati."

Both brothers dreamed of starting a business with the portion of their salaries that they saved each month. Bhola wanted a grocery shop. But Ramchannar had his heart set on a cloth store. Bhola was just three years older than Ramchannar, but a great deal wiser.

He said with a laugh, "Ram Bhai, with the kind of money we have, we won't get more than ten thaans of cloth and it is only a big and well stocked shop that attracts customers. People look at twenty five thaans before they buy half a gaj. A cloth store is for people with a large capital. If you sit with ten thaans like a pauper, nobody will even come to your shop. Also, cloth is not bought everyday. Unlike groceries, a daily necessity. Somebody needs salt, somebody else turmeric. The business will not collapse even with less capital. Let's open a grocery store. We'll not spend the profit. And with the increased capital we'll expand our shop. Once this shop is expanded, we may even be able to open a cloth store. But, not just yet."

*Munia sits silently in the room. She cannot understand the terror that fills the house. Why is everyone crying? On one side, Barka Bauji and Chhotka Bauji are having fainting fits and on the other both the mais ... Everybody says that there's been a dacoity, but no thief or dacoit has entered the house. Everything is as before. Then what dacoity are they talking about, and who's the dacoit?*

Time befriended Bhola and Ramchannar. The grocery shop prospered. Mai ordered two sets of silver hansuli necklaces and cummerbunds for her future daughters-in-law. Bhagawati's maanata had been fulfilled, so too the one to Chhat Maiya. Now all she waited for was her daughters-in-law. Mai wished both brothers would wed on the same day, even if the ceremony had to be performed in a mandir. And then a bride came for Bhola. The bride's father said, "If you think it appropriate, my chhotki beti, Gayatri, is also of marriageable age. If along with Gauri for Bhola Babu, you accept Gayatri for Ramchannar Babu, then, my responsibilities will be over and I'll be able to go bathe in the Ganga."

Such marriages were not common in their family, but both Bauji and Mai agreed to it. If both brothers were married to sisters, they would be fond of each other and there would be no rifts over property and inheritance later. Anyway, some dowry was necessary for them to make their capital grow.

*Munia comes out of her room and goes into Barki Mai's. The womenfolk stare solemnly at her, each experiencing a wetness in the eyes and a shooting pain in the heart. A sigh escapes every lip. Munia goes and sits near Barki Mai and holds her hand. Barki Mai looks up and seeing Munia, hugs her tight and starts howling again. Munia also begins to cry. But while Barki Mai cries from the pain of knowing it all, Munia cries, in imitation, without understanding why.*

Gauri and Gayatri were wed to Bhola and Ramchannar respectively. They shimmered resplendent in all the ornaments Mai had got made for them. And soon Gauri and Gayatri worked inside the house as hard as Bhola and Ramchannar worked in the shop. The house became nicer and more inviting. Mai oversaw the work of both the daughters-in-law at home and Bauji sat at the shop. But, most of all, Mai and Bauji spent time in puja path and dan dakshina. Mai continued observing Chhat. Bhola and Ramchannar still went and collected alms, only now it was no more than a token ritual. They bathed in the evening of the penultimate day of the puja and collected alms from five houses each just as, on the day of the parana, they collected prasad from five ghats.

*Munia is still in Barki Mai's embrace. The women seated around are openly shedding tears. One woman starts to break the lac bangles on Munia's hands. The red and yellow bangles crack with a soft chat-chat sound. The lahathi, which she first wore five months ago, breaks free of her arms and falls to the ground in pieces.*

What an arduous wait it had been. For fourteen long years no doctor was spared, from Madhubani-Darbhanga to Patna, Mai did not overlook any healer, vaid, ojha, guni, or peer-maajar, and for their part, Gauri and Gayatri kept all the fasts recommended by all and sundry. The doctors said, There's no problem medically. The sants said, Have patience. But Mai was impatient. Bhola and Ramchannar also were. What was the use of toiling so hard at this business they had built up with their sweat and blood if they had no children to pass it on to?

Time passed. Mai, completely drained of all energy, handed over the Chhat fast to Gauri. Bhola stood waistdeep in water, doing penance each day. And every year, the same plea to Chhat Maiya. Bhola and Gauri wept and wept, Gayatri and Ramchannar pleaded silently. Till at last Chhat Maiya came to their rescue.

Gauri and Gayatri both became pregnant at the same time and gave birth to a son each. Then, one after the other, both had sons again, with remarkable similarities. The third time round, along with the sons and their wives, Mai also said, "Chhat Maiya should give us a daughter this time. Without one, how do we do kanyadaan, how do we amass the punya of bathing in the Ganga?" Bhola and Ramchannar begged Gauri and Gayatri, "We want a girl this time, we want a girl." And the two sisters giggled in unison, hiding their faces in their ghunghats, "Is this in our hands?"

Gauri gave birth to a son. But Gayatri, she fulfilled everyone's long cherished desire with the adorable Munia. Everyone forgot Gauri's newborn, Gauri too.

"She's my daughter."

"No, she's mine."

Both the brothers wrangled as Gayatri smiled benignly, and Gauri too smiled. In the end Gauri said, "Don't strangle the child in your fights. Is there anything in this house which is exclusively mine or anyone's, then how can Munia belong only to any one of us? She belongs to us all."

Munia turned and Munia crawled, Munia grew, day by delightful day. Every year, people saw her on Chhat Ghat, Munia at her mother's waist, Munia running, the tinkle of pajebs around her small ankles, Munia twirling in a red dacron frock, her hair in two long chotis, standing up.

Then one day, Bauji collapsed as he sat at the shop. Mai too left for baikunth while offering water to Tulsiji. Alas, they both died without seeing Munia married.

The seed of this desire was taking root inside Bhola and Ramchannar, Gauri and Gayatri. They were impatient for Munia to grow up. If it were in their hands, Munia would have crossed each year in a second. Every year, throughout the month of Katik, Gauri and Gayatri made Munia light the lamp to Tulsi.

*Oh, say the people gathered around, What sin did poor Munia commit, that far from protecting her through all her seven lives Tulsi Mai has wrecked even this one, snuffing out her marriage at such a tender age?*

Years passed like seconds indeed and people started seeing Munia wearing a tika and nose stud. She was still in a frock and pajamis but oh, she looked such a doll! People only had to see her, glowing and radiant, and they would break into smiles.

The whole town gathered for the bariat. The arrangements were top class. Snacks and dinner were arranged for all the guests. There were eleven types of mithais and puris and bunia in unlimited quantities. One could eat as much as one liked. The son-in-law was handsome too. About sixteen or seventeen with just a hint of a moustache. A widowed mother and another brother in the family. And rich. Even if the brothers did not study or work, and just frittered away their inheritance, it would last them seven generations.

Bhola and Ramchannar had made their intentions very clear. "We will fill your whole house with things. The bride is young right now. We will not send her to you immediately. The bidagari will be only after five years."

The mother-in-law was adamant and said, "How can this be? Will the bariati go back empty handed? You have to follow the dharma."

"All right. Please send her back after the chauthari," Ramchannar and Bhola, Gayatri and Gauri requested. "This way you won't lose face. We told you, we got our young daughter married only because we wanted to see her future secure. But we are responsible for her still."

And so, with her aanchal full of rice and paddy, in a sari trimmed with yellow gota and an oversized blouse, Munia reached her husband's home, like a beautiful gift, warm, delicate and soft like an unbaked diya. The groom was taken aback. He was around sixteen or seventeen, and understood the special relationship between a bride and a groom, and the importance of the first night. But he could not muster enough courage to touch this fragile unbaked diya. He felt as if she would crumble if he touched her. So he drank in her face, talked a bit, and fell asleep.

On the day of the chauthari, the fourth day of the marriage on which it should have been consummated, the brothers reached Munia's new home with the puchhari. The bidagari was done the next day. Little Munia flew like a bird from its cage, prancing around in a red and yellow sari, nakhi, lahathi filling her arms, two chotis and peepa sindoor in her parting. Whoever looked at Munia, radiant in the morning light, could not take their eyes off her.

And now, the whole Chhat Ghat was numb with grief. Gauri was offering the arghya – with a soop in her hands and tears in her eyes. Bhola stood in the waters of the pond with his head downcast. People came by, on some pretext or the other, stole a glance at Munia and went back. When they saw Munia, a deep sigh escaped their lips, Ha Daib! People were so used to seeing her in her tika, nose stud and dacron frock. And just last year she had charmed them all in her red banarasi sari, her body adorned with ornaments, the parting in her hair filled with sindoor. Newly wed Munia had not known the meaning of marriage but the unforgettable picture she made, as a sweet and charming baalvadhu, was in everyone's mind. It was quite natural to sigh seeing Munia now.

Munia was in a stark white sari, with arms devoid of bangles, and the parting in her hair without sindoor. No bangles, no large bindi on the forehead, no smile on her lips. It seemed as if she had aged thirty years.

When her mother-in-law had been widowed at a very young age, she had had her strapping sons, Ramkumar and Ramprakash, by her side. She had yearned for a daughter-in-law as deeply as Bhola and Ramchannar wanted to marry off their little daughter. There was no pressing need on either side, both sides were tied with just the thread of longing.

How the groom and his brother had opposed the wedding. "Neither are we adults nor is she. What is the point when she would be in her father's house for five years after marriage?" But the mother reasoned, "I know, but just the marriage will take place for now. Your father is no more. If I were to die suddenly who will arrange the marriage of two orphans? If you are already married, then even if I die, Ramprakash will not be called an orphan. The hand of his Bhai and Bhaujai will be on his head." But the person meant to extend his hand had disappeared himself. The doctors said his heart failed. Such an ailment at such a young age?

Who has ever understood the games of bidhna?

Bhola and Ramchannar approached Munia's mother-in-law. "How will she live a life of widowhood from such a young age? Though it's not done amongst us, we are willing to take on society for the sake of our daughter. But before that we want your permission ..."

"Permission, I give you agreement. You want me to agree, no? I agree. Who understands the travails of widowhood better than I? I had my two sons to help me live. I passed my time watching them grow. She, poor child, has not even seen her husband's face. I know, traditions and norms are made by us. If we break them, they are made afresh, in a more logical, more rational manner. You want to get her remarried. If you ask me, I too want the same. But now that she is the daughter-in-law of this house, how can I let her go to some other? She'll have to live with me."

"But, how is this possible?" Ramchannar had no idea what she was saying.

"Why? Why is it not possible? Only Ramkumar has gone away from us. Ramprakash is standing right here. May he live long. May my remaining years go to him. I am only concerned about my daughter-in-law. I need her."

Bhola and Ramchannar were speechless. They had thought that the sasu would not have much sympathy for them, her heart filled with bitterness after the death of her young son. They and their Munia would get nothing but the choicest of abuses and curses, that, though it was no fault of theirs, they would be branded dishonest and Munia declared an evil, inauspicious being, a dayan, a churail, a saikhauki. But here, instead of seething hate, was the gentle balm of chandan, fragrant, soothing and cool. Their wounded souls were anointed with affection, trust and adhikar.

This time round too, the Chhat Ghat bore witness. All the women there made a special detour to see Munia, who stood again, entrancingly innocent in her finery, a red banarasi sari, sindoor in her maang, tika, nose stud and lac bangles. She was at a becoming age, her beauty was like the sun dancing on the water. It was a year after Ramkumar's death. The anniversary had been observed. Bhola and Ramchannar had reached Ramkumar's place with all the saris and ornaments which Munia had received in the marriage. A year ago Ramkumar's mother told them, "Wait a year. After that I will get Ramprakash married to your daughter. But there would not be any bariati this time. The wedding will be a subdued affair in some mandir." And true to her word, Ramprakash and Munia entered a new life together, with the blessings of Lord Shiva and Parvati Ma in the famous Garibsthan temple of Muzaffarpur. And people said, If there were more people like her on this earth, no bride would ever be tormented by her in-laws again.

No, the Chhat Ghat's story does not end here. The next year the people saw a Munia who could barely walk. Her face was pale. Each woman's eyes lit up with expectation as she placed the lamps on the arghya.

And then, the following year, Munia came again, not in her banarasi sari with the bridal tika on her forehead and nathia in her nose, but with a bag of baby clothes! Ramchannar walked in with a six month old infant and handed him to Munia. Eyes glazed. Memories came of the dacron frock, the red banarasi sari, then the white sari, and then the red banarasi again. Whether time is a witness or not I can't say but the Chhat Ghat was. The women lit the lamp and sang,

*Aihen ge sugani chhati mai*
*Hoinhen unhin sahai*

The baby looked in fascination at the swaying flame – clapping his chubby hands and gurgling. And so evening came once more, time for people to offer arghya. A small smile played on the corners of Gauri and Gayatri's lips. Munia's baby clapped baby hands.

First published in Maithili as "Rahtu Sakshi Chhat Ghat" in *Sandhan*, October 1998, Patna.

𝕯

best of the
~90s~

## V CHANDRA SEKHAR RAO

The Story of the Firebird, Red Rabbit
and the Endangered Tribes

Very modern and contemporary in its concerns as well as its treatment. I liked the way it talks about the urban mindscape of the intellectual middle class. It is specific and at once universal in its reach and relevance. **– Adoor Gopalakrishnan**

On the table before us is a brain afloat in thick, brick coloured curry, soft, tender, puckered. Gazing at it for a long time before she tucked into it, Mohini said, "Sea caverns, gruesome forts, nights fraught with dreams ..." then she paused a space, and continued, "I eat this for the sake of nostalgia! When I eat this I am reminded of that scene in which the fellow rips open the ram's head and deftly pulls out its brain." Mohini slipped into a Kafkaesque state. "It is a painful feeling, chewing the forgotten memories of childhood. But, of course, it's just protein, mere animal protein that gets finely ground under my teeth. But the grinding vengefully wakes up a flashback ..."

That was Hotel Alpha. We were seated on the first floor in a corner that overlooked the Railway Station. The jostling and the pushing was like a scene from an old English war movie. The screen jostled with people in interminable movement. As if there was nothing else to life except journeying.

Next to the table where we sat was an iron mesh. On it sat the cooing pigeons that Mohini loved. "They look like mothers blessing their children ... I like the sight of them," she said. All of a sudden, as if they had remembered something, a couple of the pigeons spread out their wings and swooped down to another wall. The others, too lazy to open their wings, moved their bodies as if suspended in midair. "What creativity there is even in laziness! There is creativity in the very air of this city," chuckled Mohini delightedly.

Taking out a pocket radio from her bag, Mohini tuned to the first audible crackle as if trying her luck in a lottery, and then put the radio on the table before her, as if to create the aura of another human being tossing words and phrases across the table at us.

Abruptly leaving the rotté that she was eating, on her plate,

V Chandra Sekhar Rao won the Katha Award for Creative Fiction in 2000, for this story. *Andhra Jyothi* received the Journal Award for first publishing this story in Telugu.

The Katha Translation Award went to N Pranava Manjari.

This story first appeared in English translation in *Katha Prize Stories 10*, 2000.

We thank Amarendra Dasari, our nominating editor, for choosing this story for us.

Mohini pulled out a leather folder from her bag and fished out a research report from it, which she then flung at me.

"What arrogance! What malice! What bigotry pervades your Y chromosomes!" she said, suddenly declaring war.

It was a sociological survey report. One of those reports that details how, because of the feminist movement and women being in high positions, sensitivity and tenderness among women was on the wane, and how women with beauty, love and compassion were fast becoming an endangered species.

I grinned. I like to sit before Mohini and watch this anger, this impatience, this play of emotions that shifts with every shifting second. Mohini is not just a friend to me. She is a metaphor. Her friendship is both a hard fact of life and a dream – as necessary as oxygen to survive this city.

A boy brought another hot rotté and put it on the table. The rotté, thick as it was, seemed to dare our hunger. Dividing it, Mohini threw one half on my plate. In the manner of someone who had just remembered something, I chewed the rotté thoughtfully and, with a slight smile playing around my lips, said,

"I had a strange dream last night. It seems celebrations were afoot for the new millennium. It was a large auditorium and I was making a speech from the stage. Whatever I said was turning into music!"

"Interesting! What kind of music?"

Racking my brains a little, I said, "Classical ... maybe ragas from a violin or flute."

"Lucky you!" said Mohini. "Music and such beautiful things have long ceased to appear in my dreams! What I see in my dreams are deserts, inexorable oceans and people dying. For a long time now I have been waiting for a dream where dead people come back to life."

"Today is the last day of this century and millennium," I reminded Mohini. There was a quiver in my voice when I said this.

"Sure you want to celebrate?" she asked in a detached manner. And then, after a moment's pause, continued, "I'll agree, but on one condition. Not in a congested room in a lodge or a quickie next to a toilet somewhere. Positively no! Find a place that's a little pleasant and inspiring."

"You remember Kukkatapalli Pragatinagar – where the Reddys live? The huge lake, and the marvellous rocks on the banks of the lake? Will that be okay?" I asked.

"Mmm."

Death has lost the power to terrorize. What frightens people now is the destruction of human relations. What terrorizes more than death and disease are the deserts within man. Mohini was a psychologist in an NGO set up to further the cause of street children. She had extensively researched their psychological makeup. "It frightens me to see the deserts growing in these children. Will we be able to nurture at least a small patch of green in their hearts? Although they pay me only two thousand rupees, the job is absolutely essential. I feel so compensated when I spend time with these children. That's when I realize that there is a desert inside me too, a desert that is impervious to pain, love or sex. We, the desert people!" said Mohini, and her eyes unexpectedly welled up with tears.

The wetness is enough. Mohini will be able to conquer the desert.

Kamala, Mohini's eighteen year old sister, committed suicide recently – hanged herself from a fan. There was no real reason for it. Somehow, Kamala was gripped by the fear that she might never marry. When she saw her feminist sister, she felt marriage was an absolute necessity. Convinced that a girl like her – without a job or the capacity to pay a dowry – would never be able to marry, she surrendered to death. Mohini called the university at ten in the morning.

Hurrying to her place, I found Mohini on the doorstep looking completely detached. Before her lay the corpse. Kamala used to have a pet dog. Don't know whether it was male or female but she called it Mruthyunjaya. The dog was now whining desolately and circling the dead girl. "Why don't you throw this dog into the crematorium too?" asked Mohini. Her face gave nothing away. To this day, I can recollect Mohini's expression with a certain sense of horror. "My mother, who is blind, has to come from a distance of six hundred kilometres. I don't want to tell her to come. I will tell

her that her stupid daughter eloped with some half-baked sorcerer."
I thought she was joking, but that is actually what she told her
mother. Luckily she didn't chuck the dog into the crematorium but
took it to Blue Cross.

We left the hotel and got on to the road, walking along its edge,
talking of this and that. People on all sides. It was as if we were
walking on the bank of a river. The sweat, the odour, the eatables
on the roadside, the gossip of the tea stalls, the heady fragrance of
sweet smelling flowers – all these fused to form the strange new
smell that is Hyderabad. We covered a great distance, walking in
crowded places. Motors and cars brushed past us. It felt as if we
were in the centre of a battlefield. Here, in this city, travelling is a
war tactic.

"That's it. Let's take a bus," said Mohini, plonking herself down
at the bus stop.

We had reached Paradise Centre in Secunderabad. Before us
stood Paradise Hotel. There was a crowd of at least five hundred
people in front of the hotel, enjoying their tea. "Patanga, Patanga,"
shouted two boys selling kites. There were at least ten or fifteen
kites fluttering in the wind and the road was a dream of colours.
Mohini stopped them and bought one for five rupees. Holding the
string and flying the kite about her, Mohini became she who has a
rainbow stuck to her shoulders.

We walked on. A few minutes later, the spectacular surroundings
vanished, and the road took on the look of a silent, lonely mourner.
A group of fifteen or twenty people wearing badges and carrying
banners with the words, Human Rights Movement Committee,
marched silently by.

"Come on," said Mohini, forcing me to my feet and walking me
towards the procession.

For a long time then we walked with them. Somebody handed
us black ribbons to wear. As we neared Tank Bund, we tore away
from the procession and resurfaced on the road again. Saying, "Let's
take a bus. Come on, let's go to my office. There is an interesting
seminar on there!" Mohini pulled me into Bus No 5 and we landed

up at the seminar organized by ROPE – Research and Orientation of Psychological Environment – an NGO. They had set up a shamiana. The members were busy arranging chairs and hoisting banners. When Mohini opened the door of her room a marvellous fragrance enveloped us. On the table were beautiful garlands and bouquets.

"This is a seminar of an unusual kind. On Meditation, but not just meditation. It's all about bringing the mind to a stillness, exorcizing painful memories. It's like a lobotomy which erases all memory from the brain. Nothing exists but the present. That is the state the seminar hopes to achieve – minus surgery, of course. The misery of death, painful childhood memories, pain, anxiety, the worry of the future – all these are going to be wiped out. The mind is going to be rendered fresh and blemishless like the mind of a month old infant. They have invited two Professors of Psychology from Japan for the seminar."

Noises at the gate. One by one, the delegates began to come in. Most were about forty or fifty years of age. A few were teenagers. Bouquets were being carried out of the room. The fragrance, however, did not diminish, it filled the room just as strongly as it had earlier. Is it possible to wipe out memories either?

The Minister arrived. More commotion.

"Come on, let's go in." Mohini led the way.

"Mohini, why don't *you* take part in the proceedings?"

"There is then the danger of forgetting even you," she said, laughing. Two minutes into the meeting, she abruptly said, "I don't want to lose my memories – this death, suffering, anxiety, fear, desire, struggle. I would like to live like a soldier. I am a product of my times! I want to be with the times!"

She was serious.

To part with memories, especially those associated with Mohini! A shiver ran momentarily through my body. At some point in the old, anarchic days, when I roamed aimlessly around, Mohini transformed from stranger to friend. And the friendship gradually developed into a necessity. Samosas in Bluemoon, kababs in

Paradise and scooter rides at ten in the night. We would stop at Paramet or near Chaurastha and gaze in delight at a sky not besmirched by pollution. When a policeman shouted at us, we would set off on our scooter again, towards Charminar or Chadarghat, have a bracing cup at some teastall on the way, and at about two in the night, I'd drop her at Vidyasagar and reach the University myself. Once in a month or two, when the sexual urge was upon me, she would chide me saying, "Rascal," while at the same time adding, "Think of where we can go." And we would find some place beside the Odeon or in the overcrowded bylanes of Afzalganj.

Once, in the Threecastle Rest House, the room was oppressively hot and humid. There was no tubelight, only a dim bulb burned, bathing the room in yellow. It looked surreal, as if painted with dreams. A bird trilled just above the window. Mohini forgot all about me and the room as she gazed at it. "Birds are symbolic of rebirth and renewal!" she said. There she sat, next to the window, gazing at the bird for two hours. I did not have the heart to disturb her. Darkness outside the window. The sheen of the bird's feathers. Mohini gazing at it. A wonderful sight indeed!

Mohini lay back on the cot, tired. A short while later, I saw the bird silently treading Mohini's naked body. Its wings were pale red. They signified an experience, deep and intense. It walked up and down Mohini, without making any noise, for some twenty minutes. Mohini was lost to the world around her. After sometime, the bird, shook itself, opened its wings and flew out of the window and, "That was my alter ego!" Mohini said, dreamily, "When I am happy, really happy, it issues forth like this!"

Yes, how can I part from these memories!

"Hello."

I was startled to hear the familiar voice. Mohanasundaram. With his thick beard, khadi kurta and pyjamas, he looked like a prophet. He flopped down into the chair next to mine. He was carrying a red baby rabbit. It looked strange. Seated in his lap, with Mohanasundaram caressing its head and back, the rabbit looked mysterious, baffling, not unlike Mohanasundaram himself.

As if reading my thoughts, Mohanasundaram explained. "This is no strange animal. It is a red rabbit. Of a species that is almost extinct. Perhaps this one is the last of its tribe! I found it in the burial ground in Venkatapuram.

"In the outskirts of the city, in the shmashana in Venkatapuram, live over fifty Begaree families. They earn their livelihood cremating the dead. Their houses are adjacent to the cremation ground. A week ago, when these people woke up from their sleep, their houses were not to be seen. The cement sheets, the palm leaves, right down to the very foundations – everything had gone.

"In their place appeared one hundred crushing machines, cement bags and lorries loaded with sand. The foundation of a new apartment block was being laid. For a people who eke out a living cremating the dead and relating their own stories to the skeletal remains of the dead, this plight became another tale. But where could they live? We won't burn your dead. To hell with you, they said, and disappeared overnight with their families.

"We went there," continued Mohanasundaram, "On behalf of the Committee for Struggle Against the Extermination of Ethnic Communities. We could have sat in dharna for four days and halted the construction of the apartment block, but we failed to locate the Begarees. Searching for them, we came upon this red rabbit instead."

My heart beat wildly. A certain uneasiness pervaded my entire being. This Mohanasundaram always has only such news to tell! Sighing heavily, I said, "Mohana! To talk to you is to listen to a relentless tale of woe and misery. When will that day come when you will relate a happy story?"

Fixing me with a sharp look, he said, "Daggers are drawn all around us, musical instruments that produce wonderful music are all broken. Everywhere, there is only agony and despair! But no, we will not fear, we are inveterate optimists!" A little later, as if suddenly remembering something, he pulled me to my feet, saying, "Come on! We will go towards Lakdi ka Pul. I will show you a strange spectacle there!"

Mohini accompanied us, stroking the red rabbit.

It was afternoon. The traffic lights weren't working. The cars moved on interminably. Some fifteen minutes passed. Mohanasundaram dashed recklessly, like a man possessed, into the speeding cars. The cars screeched to a halt one behind the other.

Mohanasundaram, like Moses, had ripped the sea apart and now crossed over to the other end of the road. Some twenty others crossed the road with us. Mohini brought up the rear end. The cars started once again. At that very moment, the red rabbit jumped out of Mohini's hands and a Maruti car ran over it. All that remained was the sound of its strange moan that lingered in the air and a road splattered with blood.

Mohanasundaram stood, his face dark with rage, seething like an ocean of fire. Sinking down on his knees, he picked up the mangled rabbit and said, "This one committed suicide of its own free will." Then, turning to us, he said, "You go on. I will join you after cremating it somewhere," and disappeared into the crowd. From a distance, he looked like the Prophet carrying Death in his hands.

We walked on, in the direction of Lakdi ka Pul, till I stopped abruptly, horrified by a sudden spectacle that met our eyes. On the pavement was a huge pile of human torsos. Next to the pile, as if they had been only recently dug out of their graves, were severed legs, arms and heads. My legs trembled with fear. Mohini giggled. I turned to look at her.

"So you got taken in by their magical illusion? Just like human beings, aren't they? But they are only terracotta figures. I have been seeing them for a week now. I come here, straight after office everyday and sit beside the pile of human figures for a long time. Great craftsmanship! They have been made by a family of six who have no intention of selling their work. People come, admire their work and try to buy it. I have tried to question them so many times, Why do you make these dead figures? Nobody's going to buy them, are they? But I get no answers. The woman of the family just keeps wiping her tears. That fiery eyed old man must be her father.

Or father-in-law. His eyes bespeak a deep injury. But, they won't tell anybody why they make these images of the dead. The old man is an unending mystery to me. Only yesterday, the woman broke the practice, and spread a cloth in front of the figures. There was a good collection of coins and five and ten rupee notes. The old man, however, was there looking like a maharshi muttering curses!"

Mohini and I stood riveted to the spot. Here was creativity of an exceptional kind. Mohini was right. The old man seemed in great anger. He was kneading the clay with single minded concentration. Perhaps another human figure was on the way?

Picking up tea from a restaurant nearby, we returned to our places with our cups. This was truly a magic show. From the red clay sprang a living form. A man of great energy and spirit. Broad shouldered. The image of a rustic peasant, a dhoti hugging his loins. It was indeed a great piece of work. Shabash! I was silently lauding him, when, all of a sudden, the old man slit the throat and began reworking the face, rubbing in the look of death. The sight wrung my heart. For a second, I was even angry with the old man.

Pressing my hand tight, Mohini pulled me away and we walked on, along the edge of the road, not saying anything to each other. Finally, "The old fellow seems to have put a curse of silence upon us! We seem to have lost our power of speech!" I said.

"The curse of ordinary people," she said, with a little laugh. Then, "Let's stop worrying and catch a bus!" said Mohini, heading towards the bus stop. "Didn't you say we will go to Pragatinagar? Let's. We are approaching a historic moment! We are entering the new millennium! Let us set aside these Kafkaesque anxieties and curses. Let's get some good biryani, cakes and some Coke! We will welcome the new millennium in our own way!"

The night was quiet and lonely, like a forest simmering. Kukkatapalli is a long stretch of kutcha road just beyond the Housing Board Chaurastha. To go here one has to break off the main road and enter into an enigmatic world free from the din of the city, the fiendish cacophony of motor vehicles and the blinding neon bulbs.

The place looked innocent and full of compassion. There was hardly any activity on the road. A little distance away, the road magically became a magnificent lake. No one could have imagined such a wonderful lake. Cutting through the middle of the lake was a small bridge with a longish stone bench. I sat down on the stone bench, feeling a tremendous sense of bliss and contentment. Across the lake were small stone mounds and rocks standing like beautiful sculptures.

The ecstasy in Mohini's eyes was unmistakable. We began humming a tune that soon took on the dimensions of a full throated song. "*Enki evvarante?*" sang Mohini. Her eyes were moist. Somewhere a bird could be heard. Was it a signal that the bird recognized Mohini? A firebird fluttered down to where we sat. "My alter ego again," Mohini said with a small happy laugh. In the faint moonlight, its soft red wings shone brilliantly. "*Panchi banu, udti phirun, mast gagan mein,*" the Lata Mangeshkar song rang out in Mohini's sweet voice, breaking the silence of the lake.

I took out the biryani and Coke bottles from my bag. The night was racing by. One by one, the lights in the colony houses were put out. Darkness was gathering. And a secret desire slowly opened its wings within us. Walking along the bank, we headed to a spot where the hill seemed to lean forward to kiss the lake. Birds twittered. Occasionally, a splash could be heard in the waters. A slight breeze wafted by, barely touching our bodies. As Adam, as Eve, as Satan, as God, Mohini's bare breasts were all these as they shone in the ripeness of the moonlight! I bent forward to drown myself in their bounteous beauty. Somewhere the bird called.

All of a sudden, a flash of brightness dazzled our eyes. "What was that? What happened?" asked Mohini beginning to cover herself with the sari. The lake was filled with light, like a hundred thousand lamps burning. Then, the sound of someone running, the thumping of rough boots. Slipping into our clothes, we emerged apprehensively from behind the stone mound. Police jeeps everywhere. A shot was fired ... and then another!

A death cry rent the air and immediately chup! It was choked into silence. But the struggle against the violence of death lasted a long time. A couple of minutes later, all at once, the lights went out! The sound of jeeps moving. Like a film scene, the brightness and the brutality faded into stillness and oblivion.

Once again it was only the lake, the hills, the moonlight that enveloped everything like a magic curtain, and us. We walked apprehensively towards the bank. The body of a woman lay sprawled on the edge of the lake. A pregnant woman. Floating gently.

Mohini slumped to the ground and wept inconsolably. The red winged bird came out of nowhere and paced around the dead woman on the bank. I can still hear the sound it made.

I lifted Mohini to her feet and holding her against my shoulder, walked her towards the road. From the distant city came happy voices. Happy New Year! Welcome to the new Millennium! We walked towards the shouts and the familiar ocean of people.

First published in Telugu as "Nippu Pitta Erra Kundelu Mariyu Adrusyamavuttuna Jaatula Katha" in *Andhra Jyothi*, May 2, 1999, Hyderabad.

# ✒CONTRIBUTORS' NOTES✑

## ASOMIYA

**Pankaj Thakur** writes in Asomiya and is known mainly for his satires. His collection of short stories, *Apuni Kiba Kaboneki* has been translated into Hindi. He has translated works of Ibsen, Strindberg, Sartre and Wole Soyinka into Asomiya. A former Associate Editor of *Ajir Asom*, he is an honorary editor of *Paryatak*, a magazine on culture and tourism. He has edited works on developmental studies as well. Currently, he is based in Kolkata working with TISCO.

- The short story became a recognizable form in Asomiya around 1892 with "Seuti," written by the doyen of modern Asomiya literature, L N Bezbarua. There was a fresh burst of creativity in the 1970s with the Natun Prithivi Movement. Today, amongst the most promising writers of the new generation are those born after Independence.

    Manoj Kumar Goswami is aware of the reality that is Assam and the role of the true revolutionary. He has put them together to come up with **Samiran Barua Aahi Aase**, which looks dispassionately at the north eastern part of our country. Assam is in dire need of social change, but we find that most people are unable to accept that such change is a long and painful process. This story deals with a difficult and sensitive subject of contemporary relevance, courageously and skillfully.

**Manoj Kumar Goswami**'s first short story was published in 1979, followed by several collections of short stories – *Iswarhinata, Samiran Barua Aahi Aase, Moi Rajen Borak Samarthan Karon*. A postgraduate from Guwahati University, he taught Physics for three years before he took up journalism as a profession.

- The unrest in Assam and the resultant deterioration of values in politics, academia and in all other aspects of society disturbs me. The rise of extremism purportedly to wipe out social evils or to bring change in society, has no relevance for the middle class.

---

This section is organized language-wise. It contains the biographical details of the Nominating Editor, the state of the short story in that language and the Editor's reasons for nominating the chosen story. This is followed by the biographical details of the Writer and her/his notes on the story, then the notes on and by the Translator.

**Jayeeta Sharma** has lived in Assam, Delhi and Cambridge and is a historian by training. Her special interest is the history and politics of the north eastern part of India. She has just completed a PhD at the University of Cambridge.

- Some of the pithiness of the original comes from the very effective use of English slang words – I haven't been able to find a suitable mimetic device for this.

### BANGLA

**Debes Ray**, eminent fiction writer, has about twenty six books to his credit – of which about thirteen are novels – and nearly a hundred short stories. He received the Sahitya Akademi Award in 1990. He resides in Kolkata and is currently researching a book on pre-British Bangla Prose. Reticent by nature, he has refused to speak much about himself.

- The short story has developed into a very powerful genre in Bangla literature over the last one hundred years and has faced social crises and political upheavals. This genre has always excited authors to innovate and experiment, and there are few writers in Bengal who have not written at least one very good short story.

  **Swadeshyatra** is a complex narrative with manifold layers, raising questions about the identity of the individual and what he considers to be his "country" or "home" and how these identities collide and coalesce with each other. The metropolis and the Bihar countryside, where a massacre of peasants has taken place, are, in a sense, two sides of the same coin. A significant story in which the present has been critically and ironically connected with history.

**Amar Mitra** has five published short story collections, ten novels and a book for children to his credit. He writes regularly for the dailies. His short stories have been translated into English, Hindi, Malayalam and Tamil. He has won a number of prestigious awards including the Katha Award for Creative Fiction, the Samaresh Basu Award, the Samatat Award and the Nikhil Bharat Banga Sahitya Sammelan Award.

- The mass killing of landless peasants in Bathaniatola, Bhojpur district, Bihar, in August 1996, forms the root of this story. The incident shocked me deeply. But there was nothing I could have done about it. I had to find an outlet for my sorrows and tears. As a writer all I can do is write and, therefore, I have written. The story speaks about the land, the people, clouds, rain, cultivation and the great middle class. People may not always see eye to eye, but I believe the clouds join West Bengal to Bihar, and Bihar to Uttar Pradesh, and so on.

**Dilip Kumar Ganguli** worked as Under Secretary in the Ministry of Commerce and lives in Delhi. His writings are published regularly in *The Statesman, The Times of India, The Hindustan Times* and *Maharashtra Herald*. He has travelled extensively in India and Europe.

- The story is topical and metaphorical at the same time. Vividly described and above all, in the way it ends – keeping the readers in suspense – it is well worth the award. The Bangla spoken by Lachman and Mahender seems to be a blend of Bangla and Bhojpuri, a touch of Magahi and Bihari Hindi. Though my mother tongue is Bangla, I faced a slight problem in translating certain colloquial expressions, perhaps due to differences in dialect and corruption in the language, or because popular variants have been used in this story that are now obsolete.

**ENGLISH**

**Rukmini Bhaya Nair** was educated in Calcutta and Cambridge, where she obtained her PhD in Linguistics. A number of journals in India and abroad have included both her creative and academic writings. She has two volumes of poems to her credit, *The Hyoid Bone* and *Ayodhya Cantos*. She has taught at Jawaharlal Nehru University, the National University of Singapore and the University of Washington and has been a visiting professor at the Indian Institute of Advanced Studies, Shimla. Currently she is a Professor in the Department of Humanities and Social Sciences, IIT, Delhi.

- I chose Vandana Bist's **The Weight** because the story was full of gravities, rich in local specifications and gendered description. To me, this story was intriguing because its moral "weight" appears to derive not in the least from the fact of death itself, but from the intense effects of dark and light produced by the play of tradition, language, sexual desire and apprehension within the interior landscape of a woman's mind. Finally, as a writer in the English language, I have to say that I was deeply impressed by the unselfconscious confidence with which Bist manages to keep at bay the spectres of both linguistic and political correctness. This seems to me to be a hopeful indication of English having now become a wholly Indian tongue.

**Vandana Bist** has a degree in Fine Arts from the Delhi College of Art and has specialized in illustration. She was awarded the Chitrakala Award by Katha for her illustrations in *The Princess with the Longest Hair*, a Tamasha Picture Book for children, the encouragement prize in the Children's Picture Book Competition organized by the Noma Concours Foundation, Japan and the Katha Award for Creative Fiction for this story. Starting with her first book, *A Ticket to Home and Other Stories*, a collection for children, her works have been exhibited in Japan and Bratislava. Her writings and drawings have been published in various children's magazines and books.

- The characters and situations woven into this story are inspired by accounts of the lives of people who belonged to the households my mother was born and married into. It is especially about women. The story has its origin in my resentment of the fact, that behind all facades of social progress, a cause and effect relationship persists in all dimensions.

### GUJARATI

**Ganesh Devy** is an activist working with denotified tribals. He has written several articles on mainstream and tribal literature, culture, languages and oral traditions. He has held distinguished fellowships including the Commonwealth Academic Staff Fellowship and the Fulbright Fellowship. He translates from Gujarati and Marathi into English and has received the Katha Award for Translation and the Sahitya Akademi Award.

- As this story may indicate, the Gujarati short story today is innovative in technique as well as sophisticated in its fictional disclosure. It has been exploring various new realms of social reality which have so far remained outside the bounds of literary rendering. What is really a welcome change in the field of recent Gujarati short fiction is that writers from a variety of social classes and linguistic margins have started contributing to it. This is a rich harvest.

In Gujarati, **Bhuthar** is an extremely powerful narrative. Its metaphoric depth is immense. It has brought to Gujarati fiction an experience of social life that had not been presented before. The transformation of the complex emotional relationship between the protagonist and his sister-in-law, in terms of a narrative structure, is amazingly complete.

**Nazir Mansuri** published his first story "Dhaalkachbo" in *Gadyaparva* in May 1996. **Bhuthar** is his second story. He has a number of published short story collections. Apart from this, many of his short stories have been published in literary magazines. Three of his novels are currently under print. He has written about the fishing community, their society and lives, in these pioneering works. He has been the recipient of the Katha Award for Creative Fiction and is the first Gujarati writer to win the Sanskriti Award for Literature awarded by the Sanskriti Pratishthan. He is a lecturer in the Department of Gujarati Literature at SB Garda College of Arts, Navsari.

- Having been born and brought up in the very locale of the present story, I have always been able to empathize with the members of the coastal community. They lead solitary lives, and are very different from other village communities in Gujarat. I have immense respect for them. Their ways of living are worthy of attention and contemplation. **Bhuthar** revolves around the polemical relationship between the individual and his/her society. The focus is on what results from respecting social order, the conflicts caused by it. It took me approximately three months and eight drafts to complete the story.

**Nikhil Khandekar** is working on a Sahitya Akademi project on tribal literaure and oral tradition at Vadodara under Dr Ganesh Devy. He has translated Kanji Patel's novella, *Dahelu*, published as *Rear Verandah* and was the editor of *A Journal of New Creative Writing*. He teaches English to students from poor families on a voluntary basis.

- **Bhuthar** is about roots, roots that are depicted as being entangled. It is these complications that make it a story with a modern sensibility. A part of coastal literature, this story captures an ethos that is novel. I prefer to stay faithful to the original, as far as possible, and to earn the author's trust. Translating has been an educating discovery for me, but often a thankless job!

## HINDI

**Rajendra Yadav,** an eminent writer of the Nai Kahani movement in post Independence Hindi fiction, is also a critic and translator. His stories and novels have been translated into Indian languages and have been made into films, telefilms and plays. He is currently the editor of *Hans*, a Hindi literary magazine renowned for discovering, nurturing and promoting emerging writers with freshness of approach and creativity.

■ **Faisla** entwines the traditional husband-wife relationship with the corrupt political processes in today's rural India. Basumati is an ordinary woman and yet she is not. Ordinary because she remains bound to the traditional role of a wife and strives emotionally and physically to do what she is expected to. Not only has she gone through more formal education than her husband, she has also acquired sensibilities of fairness and social justice – sensibilities which daily confront her with the corrupt bureaucratic political tie-up in the countryside, at the centre of which is located the man she is married to ... Torn between being a wife and the political responsibility of administering justice, Basumati manages, albeit silently, to put at least a temporary stop to her husband's anti-people regime.

**Maitreyi Pushpa** is known for breaking conventions, setting rules. She is the voice of Bundelkhand and its people – especially the women, strong-willed despite all attempts to suppress their individuality. She brings these women alive depicting the truth of their lives in a simple and compassionate way. Their struggles are artistically woven into stories that describe the rustic beauty of Bundelkhand and grip the reader with their powerful rendition. The short story collection, *Chinhar*, won her the Hindi Academy Award. She has a number of novels to her credit including *Alma Kabutari, Idannumam, Chak, Betwa Bahti Rahi, Jhula Nat, Aganpakhi, Vision* and *Kasturi Kundal*. She has been honoured with numerous awards, the latest being the SAARC Writers' Award.

■ What inspired **Faisla**? Maybe it all began with the visit to the Block Pramukh of my village. I mentioned to him how pleased I was to hear the news that his wife had been elected Pradhan ... "She has no need to go to the Panchayat," he replied. "I take care of all the work ... things are just as they were when I was the Pradhan." This one sentence was the catalyst to all the seething contradictions within me. The latent fear of men in women and the limits defining a woman's existence as laid down in the *Manusmriti* – in spite of all these my instinctive responses were those of rebellion and these gave shape to the character of Basumati. Isuriya's character, free from all the oppressive customs and traditions, is my ideal of the liberated woman.

**Meenakshi Sharma** and **Renuka Ramachandran** have been associated with Katha since their days as students at Lady Shri Ram College, Delhi. They now live in the United States where Meenakshi is the Publications Manager at a software firm and Renuka freelances as a Communications Editor in the IT sector.

■ Our main effort has been to capture the terse, staccato tone of the first person narrative, especially the significant silences. The plurality of reporting voices led to some confusion in the translation. Added to this was the problem of a highly fragmented structure. So we have been forced to do away with the ambiguity at certain points so as to keep the character of the narrative voice constant and the sequence of events clear. The dialectal corruptions in the forms of address have been retained, whereas the dialect has been rendered in normal English.

## KANNADA

**D R Nagaraj,** a noted writer and critic, has two books of critical essays and has co-edited a book on Urdu literature. He was awarded the Karnataka Sahitya Akademi Award posthumously for his work *Sahitya Kathana*. He was also a recipient of the Vardhamana Award for Literature for his *Amrutha Mattu Garuda*. He was deeply involved with the dalit cause as part of his study of literary and culture criticism. He was a visiting professor in Dravidian Studies at the University of Chicago. He had also taught at the Centre for Kannada Studies, Bangalore University. His other interests were rural development work and people's movements.

■ Nataraj Huliyar belongs to writers of the "Mode of the bee." These are the writers who are shy and reluctant to take on ambitious themes. But the way they treat "minor" themes eventually brings a profound kind of seriousness to their writing. **The Magic Nymph** can be read as an ironical comment on the nature of human relations in a society of caste and gender segregations. The sexually hungry hero of the story finds his glorious moments of love in the company of a prostitute. The author narrowly escapes the charge of sharing the value system of a casteist society which ridicules and condemns the age old profession. What saves the story is the lyrical humanism of the narrative viewpoint which invests the street girl with a touching dignity. For her, too, it is a glorious moment of love, quite genuine at that.

**Nataraj Huliyar**, eminent fiction writer, has won the Sivarama Karanth Award for Creative Writing for his collection of short stories, *Mattobba Sarvadhikari* and is the recipient of the Karnataka Sahitya Akademi Award. He has been the editor of *Aniketana*, a literary magazine since 1995 and has translated stories and poems from several languages into Kannada. He has a doctoral degree from Bangalore University and teaches English at NMKRV College, Bangalore.

- The seeds of the story **Maya Kinnari** were probably sown on a late winter night when I witnessed a fight between a prostitute and a customer who had underpaid her ... When I came to the city, I happened to share a room with some friends. One day they brought home a woman. Though nervous, I spoke to her for a long time after my friends had left her exhausted. When I started writing the story, I happened to see a young prostitute standing under a water tank and combing her hair. This sight caught my imagination. But I was puzzled at the shape the story took later, for it turned out to be a story not about a prostitute but about a shy, nervous youth.

**Manu Shetty** is with the South Asian Studies Centre, University of Chicago. He has earlier worked with the University's Committee on Social Thought on Tulu oral narratives and has also collaborated with A K Ramanujan in translating works in Kannada. While in India, he was on the faculty of the Department of Philosophy, University of Mysore.

- This sensitive story about a young office-worker's unintended encounter with a prostitute explores the inner sexual-psychological travails of a young man in the context of his social set up. The language of the story, which is trained carefully to delineate both the inner troubles of the man, as also his interaction with the world outside, had to be translated with extreme care. Further, the language of the narration which employs comic-hyperbole, is in an urban middle class dialect with a generous mixture of adapted English and Urdu words which function as specific social registers. This aspect, which contributes significantly to the value of the story, is unfortunately lost in translation.

## MAITHILI

**Udaya Narayana Singh** is a playwright and poet in Maithili, as well as a poet and critic in Bangla with numerous books and papers to his credit. He is the Director of the Central Institute of Indian Languages, Mysore. A gold medallist from Delhi University and a Jubilee Awardee of Calcutta University, he has been a visiting professor at the Indian Institute of Advanced Studies, Shimla. A Fellow of the Linguistic Society of America in 1978, he has taught Linguistics, English, Anthropology and Comparative Literature in leading universities across the country.

- Maithili short story emerged prominently only after 1947, and along with poetry and essays, is one of the strongest genres. Prior to that, there were only four writers with anthologies to their credit. Stories, however, appeared in literary magazines right from Kali Kumar Das's "Bhishan Anyay" (1913). Among writers like "Suman," "Kiran" Yoganand Jha, Umanath Jha and Upendra Nath Jha "Vyas," the ones who made their mark then and continued to do so in the post-independence period were Harimohan Jha and "Yatri." Maithili writers have always represented different trends. Some like Manmohan and Sudhanshu Sekhar Choudhury tilting towards emotional, some like Manipadma, Mayanand or "Kiran" showing a preference for the realistic and others like Lalit and Dhirendra leaning towards socially relevant themes. There was yet another group continuing with the tradition of humour set up by Harimohan Jha. The best known writers of today, like Somdev, Prabhas Kumar Choudhury, Dhoomketu and Rajmohan Jha, have shown preferences for psychoanalytical, political, symbolic and realistic topics. Amongst the youngest generation, Sukant Som, Shivsankar Srinivas, Vibha Rani and others have shown a lot of variety and freshness in their treatment of characters, style and choice of themes.

The sheer simplicity of the plot and superb use of the female register of speech to write the story tilted the scale in favour of **Rahtu Sakshi Chhat Ghat**. Here, the context is highlighted, which is, the Chhat Ghat, a silent witness to the joy, sorrow, trials and tribulations of a community. And as time heals their wounds, as men and women bring in revolutionary changes in their attitudes and practices, the Chhat Ghat too lights up with earthen lamps floating on the water.

**Vibha Rani** regularly contributes short stories, poems, features, and reviews in leading Maithili and Hindi dailies and magazines like *Navbharat Times, Jansatta, Hans, Mithila Mihir* and *Aarambh*. She has also written scripts for Films Division and Zee TV. Her book, *Band Kamre ka Koras* won the Ghanshyam Das Saraf Sahitya Samman. Her translated works have been published by Vani Prakashan and Bhartiya Jnanpith among others. She is a post graduate in Hindi and works for the Indian Oil Corporation, Mumbai. She presents programmes on All India Radio and Vividh Bharti, Mumbai. She has previously been a radio announcer, drama artist, compere and folk singer on All India Radio, Darbhanga and Calcutta.

- I come from Mithila, a small town in the northern part of Bihar where women, in my opinion, are like sealed envelopes, not allowed to express themselves and live their lives the way they want to. Their destiny is in the hands of their family members. A real incident inspired this story.

**Vidyanand Jha**'s poems have been published in Maithili magazines and have also been translated into Hindi, Bangla, English and Telugu. He translates from Maithili into Hindi and English and from English into Maithili. He had also been a political activist with an underground communist party for a few years. With a doctorate in management from the Institute of Rural Management, Anand, he now teaches Organizational Behaviour at the Indian Institute of Management, Calcutta. He likes listening to nirgun bhajans, Indian classical and jazz music, loves watching movies and going on long walks.

- It is a tough story to translate as it is replete with a whole lot of words associated with rituals and ornaments, some of them long out of fashion. This required that the reader be given some exposure to the ceremonies associated with chhat and marriage. But bringing all these details into the story would have made it an anthropological treatise. Footnotes too, after a point, hinder the smooth flow of the narrative.

## MALAYALAM

**Sujatha Devi,** a retired English teacher, writes poetry and articles in Malayalam. She is a committed environmentalist and has authored an award winning travelogue on the Himalayan forests, titled, *In Search of the Rhythm of the Forests.*

- **Little Earthquakes** is an indepth study of a mind in transition from childhood to adolescence. The mind of the budding teenager Janakikutty is an amalgam of childhood fears and playful mischief spiced with an occasional dash of the intense emotions of the adolescent world. This psychological complexity is portrayed with admirable dexterity by M T Vasudevan Nair, the master craftsman. The approach of adolescence, especially in an insecure loner, can develop undercurrents of turbulence capable of producing minor earthquakes within and without. It is with deep understanding and keen observation that MT records them and unveils the colourful flashes of imagination, as well as the destructive squirts involved in such a process. Born and brought up in an atmosphere of village myths, like her author, Janakikutty's mind moulds and unwinds spirits and ghosts and inexplicable mysteries. Without dissecting them in the gleam of reason, the author retains the magical charm of that twilight world.

  In its original version **Little Earthquakes** can claim all the typical charms of MT's language. The familiar atmosphere of his more famous works – the cracking up homes of feudal North Kerala – is also preserved intact in this short story.

  In every trembling of **Little Earthquakes** we can see the essence of MT's art,

**M T Vasudevan Nair** is acknowledged as one of the outstanding living writers of India. His publications include several volumes of short stories, novels, plays, critical writings, stories for children and travelogues. He has received all the prestigious awards for fiction in Malayalam, among them, the Katha Award for Creative Fiction, and the Kerala Sahitya Akademi Award thrice – for his novel, *Nalukettu*, his play *Gopuranadayil*, and also for his short story collection, *Swargam Thurakkunna Samayam*, as also the Sahitya Akademi Award for *Kaalam*, and the Bharatiya Jnanpith Award. He has also won the President's Gold Medal for the film *Nirmalyam*, written, produced and directed by

him. He joined the Malayalam journal, *Mathrubhoomi* in 1956, and is
presently its editor. He lives in Calicut.

- As children, we were familiar with a number of spirits, good and
  evil. We had heard so many stories about them from our elders. In
  the vast backyards of our ancestral house, there were two tribal
  spirits, Karimkutty and Parakkutty. Annual pujas were conducted
  to please them. The sacrifice of a fowl was a must. The mango
  grove was supposed to be the playground of a yakshi. Some claimed
  to have seen her in late afternoons or moonlit nights. Clad in
  spotless white, she wandered around with her dark, loose tresses,
  fluttering in the wind. Yakshis are supposed to be the reincarnations
  of young Namboodiri women who die unnatural deaths. There were
  cruel yakshis and benevolent yakshis. From the stories we knew,
  our yakshi was a very sweet person. Leave her alone and she
  would not harm you. Against the orders of the elders, I wandered
  in the prohibited areas in the afternoons hoping to see her from a
  distance. Peering into the plantain groves from my window, I tried
  to spot her moving figure on moonlit nights. I was not lucky. My
  younger cousin once had a severe hysterical fit. The astrologer
  proclaimed that it was due to her encounter with the yakshi. The
  mantravaadi conducted the necessary rituals and she was free
  from hysteria. But I found her always talking to an invisible person
  when she was alone. (This habit was there till she got married.) I
  envied her because she was seeing the yakshi and was even
  chatting with her! One day I suddenly remembered this, and that
  whole period of childhood came alive. That is how I started to
  work on this story.

**D Krishna Ayyar** has, for the past decade and a half, been devoting time
exclusively to the study of Advaita Vedanta under a traditional preceptor,
after an active career with the central government. During the freedom
struggle he was inspired by the nationalist spirit and throughout his life
by leftist and Gandhian ideologies.

- Was it difficult to translate **Little Earthquakes**? Yes and no. When
  the author himself warned us that it was an untranslatable story,
  he was evidently referring to its deeply regional flavour and its
  many colloquial expressions. The style of the narrative is oral, going
  back and forth a little and sentences beginning with significant
  words. This style and the rhythm of the original language have

been retained in the translation. The beauty of the story lies in the juxtaposition of attitudes, in the ambivalence and the style of the narrative. Care was taken to see that, in the translation, this ambivalence was not erased and the style and rhythm of the narrative was matched as much as possible.

Coming to colloquial expressions, in conformity with the practice followed, the terms of relationships have been borrowed from the original. To retain the flavour of the original story certain other expressions have also been borrowed from the original. The way of addressing elders by the term of relationship, and equals and the young by name instead of the second person singular You has been retained, so that the implication of respect et cetera are not lost.

Sleepless nights were spent debating over whether the original Malayalam term should be retained for the female spirit. "Ghost" was ruled out because the connotation would have been that of a frightful apparition, which would not suit the relationship with the little girl. "Spirit" or "elf" seemed anaemic; either would not fit in with the person in flesh and blood as the girl perceives her. And above all, besides a benign connotation, there was a certain euphonic attraction in the word Yakshi. So, Yakshi it was. On similar considerations, was the word Damshtra retained, because it is not just canine teeth but something more terrifying and lethal. Care has been taken to see that where literal translation would not convey the meaning intended in the original, the implied meaning is given.

With all this, the question that lingers is whether a non Malayalee or a Westerner would understand and enjoy the story, in translation. Let those readers give the answer.

**Raji Subramaniam** is a freelance journalist. Her articles have appeared in *Malayala Manorama*.

## MARATHI

**Vilas Sarang**, apart from his short fiction, has published collections of poems in Marathi as well as in English and a novel in Marathi set in pre-Saddam Iraq titled *In the Land of Enki*. Sarang's short fiction has appeared in leading journals both in India and abroad. A collection of his stories have been published in French and he has many scholarly works to his credit. After his postgraduation he went to do further research at Indiana University in the US. He has taught at the University of Basra in Iraq, was the Head of the Department of English at Mumbai University and is presently teaching English at Kuwait University. Around 1990, he edited a short-lived but highly acclaimed journal, *The Bombay Literary Review*, for the University of Bombay. He is now starting a new journal named *The Post-Post Review*. Simultaneously, he is editing an annual journal for new, innovative writing in Marathi.

**Dilip Chitre** is a bilingual writer with over twenty five publications in different literary genres including poetry, fiction, plays, screenplays, essays, and criticism to his credit. A winner of the Katha Award for Creative Fiction, the Sahitya Akademi Award for *Ekoon Kavita-1* and the Sahitya Akademi Translation Prize for *Says Tuka*, he has won an award for his film *Godam* at the Festival des Trois Continents, Nantes, France. He is a practising painter and lives in Pune.

- Much of the author's poetry and fiction is preoccupied with what used to be his "home" city, Mumbai. **The Full Moon in Winter** is the author's own fictional world of "reality without frontiers." It depicts the contemporary urban "hell, purgatory, and heaven" where a set of menopausal men and women meet and interact in a comic dream that turns into a subtly terrifying nightmare where their desires turn out to be their fears of life and its unpredictable possibilities.

**Suhas Gole** teaches English at Patkar College, Mumbai. His translations of the poems of Dalit poet Namdeo Dhasal have appeared in *The Bombay Literary Review*.

## ORIYA

**Pratibha Ray** is an eminent novelist in Oriya. She has a PhD in Educational Psychology and has been teaching in different colleges around Orissa for about thirty years. After taking voluntary retirement, she is now a Member of the Orissa Public Service Commission. Her novel *Yajnaseni*, received the Moorti Devi Award by the Bharatiya Jnanpith. The Orissa Sahitya Akademi Award was conferred on her novel, *Shilapadma*. The film based on her novel *Aparichita*, won the Best Film Story Award from the Culture Department, Government of Orissa.

- In Oriya literature postmodernist impressions are visible more in short fiction than in other genres. Recent fiction has been multidimensional and challenges conventional concepts of fiction and tradition. Though written in the realistic mode, it provides a newer vision of reality. Conscious artistic experimentation in short fiction, with fine narrative art, modern technique, use of myth to express the complexities of reality, has given the Oriya short story the strength to cross the boundaries of regionality to universality. Some women writers are brilliant and have proved their excellence beyond doubt.

In **Purana Katha** Yashodhara has used her creative pen to disturb the slumber of society on a sensitive issue. A bold story about the psyche of a not-so-young woman, it has been crafted in such a fine manner that the canvas of the story expands to that of a novel even within the limited framework of the short story. One can clearly visualize all the aspects of rural life in the remote district of Kalahandi. The truth that is communicated with uninhibited frankness by Sati Bahu in the story fills the hypocritical modern mind with anxiety at crucial moments. From a controversial character she rises to being a mythical one. As agreed by many, the history of humanity is a history of systematic attempts to silence the female. Wrapped carefully in artistic brilliance, there is a creative feminist dimension to **Purana Katha**.

**Yashodhara Mishra**'s published works include short story collections and novels in Oriya, two collections of short stories and two novels translated from Hindi and English. Some of her poems and articles have appeared in journals. Her works have been translated into English and other Indian languages. Her writing also features in *In Their Own Voice*, a collection of poems by Indian women. She is a recipient of the Orissa Sahitya Akademi Award, the Orissa Book Fair Award and the Jhankara Award. She is currently the Professor and Head of English Department at the Sarojini Naidu College, Bhopal.

- The story was brewing in my mind for a very long time. I do not know which recent incident made it take off. It must have been drawn from impressions and experiences spread over my whole life: a bullock-cart ride in childhood, a neighbourhood scandal, flashes of unexpected facets in familiar faces, some living memories of growing up, human relationships which are based on terms and conditions and look firmly fixed in intricate networks, and yet are so brittle at times. And then there are the bonds that spring up defying all social dictates, even in the most unsuspecting men and women. All these must have gone to make the story.

**Mahasweta Baxipatra** teaches English at Delhi University. For her MPhil degree from JNU, she had researched on the fiction of three women writers of Orissa. She enjoys translating fiction and nonfiction from Oriya into English.

- Two strands of narratives of two women – one mythical and distanced in time, the other physically participating in the immediate plot – are woven into a neat and distinct pattern. While the mythical Kunti is constantly struggling to hide the repercussions of the boon granted to her, Sati has no qualms in declaring that the boon was given to her naturally and simultaneously with youth and beauty. The writer questions the credibility and sanctity of Kunti while Sati emerges as a more genuine and sympathetic character. While translating **Purana Katha** I realized that the original did not seem to have been carefully edited, at least in the construction of paragraphs and in maintaining a consistent sequence in the storyline. This added to the "eternal" problems of finding equivalences of language-situations.

## PUNJABI

**K S Duggal**, a leading writer in Punjabi, has written about five hundred short stories (in twenty two collections), ten novels, two collections of verse, seven plays, over fifty short plays, an autobiography in two volumes and several works of literary criticism. He has been honoured with the Padma Bhushan and the Soviet Land Nehru Award for his contribution to Indian literature, as well as the Sahitya Akademi Award for his short fiction, the Ghalib Award for drama, the Bhasha Parishad Award for fiction, the Bhai Mohan Singh Award for autobiography and the Sarvasreshta Sahitkar Award. He has served as the Director of both All India Radio and the National Book Trust and as Advisor (Information) to the Planning Commission.

- **Mohdi** is a reflection on urbanization in India today. Prem Parkash has handled the theme skilfully.

**Prem Parkash,** has short story collections and a novel to his credit. A postgraduate in Urdu from Punjab University, he has been awarded the Punjab Sahitya Akademi Award twice and also the Sahitya Akademi Award among others. He has worked as a farmer, teacher and then as a sub editor with two Urdu dailies. He currently publishes a literary bimonthly called *Lakeer.*

- I belong to a small town, Khanna, and now live in Jalandhar. Though I feel no attachment towards my ancestral home or agricultural land, there is a mysterious attraction or whim to have my last rites performed on the same land where my forefathers were cremated. In this story, I try to look for the reason behind the feeling of love for the place of one's birth. While writing **Mohdi** I had in mind the migration of Punjabis to Pakistan and other countries. The process of writing this story has taken several years but I am not satisfied with it. It is too simple as it stands to contain such complex thoughts.

**Reema Anand** is a poet, journalist and film maker. Among her published works is *His Sacred Burden*, a biography of Bhagat Puran Singh. She lives in Delhi.

- Probably many in Punjab have experienced the angst expressed in **Mohdi**. But to transmit such thoughts through a story requires a forceful way with words. The writer has portrayed the political temper, as well as the typical village culture with great sensitivity.

## RAJASTHANI

**Vijayadan Detha** is a pioneer of modern writing in Rajasthani. He began writing in Hindi and Rajasthani while he was still a student. He has edited numerous journals, magazines and anthologies in Hindi as well as in Rajasthani. His short story anthologies include *Batan Ri Phulwari, Dvandh, Duvidha* and *Alekhoon Hitler* and his novels include *Pratishodh and Mahamilan*. He has also written stories for children. His works have been translated into English and many regional languages of India. He is the recipient of several awards and honours that include the first Sahitya Akademi Award for Rajasthani literature in 1947, the Rajasthan Shree and the Bharatiya Bhasha Parishad Award. He is actively associated with "Rupayan," an organization devoted to the culture and literature of Rajasthan, of which he is a founder.

- Writing in Rajasthani has traditionally been dominated by poetry while storytelling was often verbal. However, modern story writing began in late 1940s. Vijayadan Detha provided a new dimension to Rajasthani short story writing by adapting tales from the rich folklore to give them contemporary connotations. Annaram "Sudama" came down heavily on the evils in our society, making an effective use of symbolism in many of his stories. Narsingh Rajpurohit has brought alive the rural scene and successfully depicted human emotions and relationships in his writings. Other writers have followed and the works of Yadavendra Sharma, Malchand Tiwari, Ram Kumar Ojha, Kamla Bhadani, to name a few, have been read and appreciated widely. Although there had not been a movement like the Nai Kahani in Hindi, the works of the contemporary writers in Rajasthani are no less modern in their subjects and treatment. Human beings and the world around them have been portrayed with sensibility.

**Dalal** is a story that appeals at once. The writer has presented an episode in the day of a· dalal in a simple and straight narrative which leaves the reader astounded.

**Ram Swaroop Kisan** is a farmer by profession and writes in both Rajasthani and Hindi. His poems have been translated into Hindi and other languages. His collection of poems and stories in Hindi are *Gaon ki Gali-Gali*, and *Bapu and Other Stories*, respectively. Many of his works have appeared on Akashvaani and Doordarshan. He received the Choudhary Ranbir Singh Memorial Award and has been honoured by the Rajasthani Bhasha Prasar Sansthan and the Rajasthani Language, Literature and Culture Academy among others.

- **Dalal** is a milestone in Rajasthani literary world. It is a story about the victory of a poor man over evil. The end takes a predictable turn when he is forced to abandon his wicked way of life.

**Shyam Mathur** writes stories, poems, one-act plays and mathematics puzzles in Hindi for children. He works for Children's Theatre and has directed a five week theatre camp for children at Udaipur organized by the West Zone Cultural Centre. He also translates works of Rajasthani into English. His awards include two Sahitya Akademi Awards for his translations of anthologies of Rajasthani poetry. He serves as Head of the Mathematics Department and as Director of Cultural Activities at Mayo College, Ajmer.

- **Dalal** is a direct and simple narrative, the author's use of Rajasthani phrases and idioms being immaculate.

### TAMIL

**S Krishnan**, translator and journalist, served as Cultural Advisor to the United States Information Service for several years. He was a regular contributor to a number of Indian and foreign journals. A book reviewer and occasional poet, Krishnan was a senior editor of *Sruti*, a Chennai-based magazine of music and dance. He lives in Chennai.

- I liked the ambience and the setting of the story in a small town in South India and the strong regional flavour that is prominent throughout. What also intrigued me was the touchingly close relationship the blind Muslim cashier has with the Brahmin family, the insight and concern he has about their little needs, apart from being an honest, excellent worker.

    I liked **Reflowering** so much that I simply enjoyed translating it and faced no particular problems while doing so.

**Sundara Ramaswamy** is one of the finest contemporary Tamil writers. Despite a writing career spanning some fifty years, the volume of his writings is relatively small though it cuts across genres – short stories, novels, poems, essays, criticism, translation and polemic. His stories are marked by conscious experiments with form. All his three novels are watersheds in the history of the Tamil literary scene. *Oru Puliamarathin Kathai*, is the first dialect novel in Tamil. He is known for his stylistic prose, the scalpel-like precision of his diction and the metaphorical use of language. He is the recipient of the Kumaran Asan Memorial Award for poetry from the University of Toronto and the Tamil Literature Garden of Canada. His works have been translated into Indian and European languages and he has travelled abroad extensively for literary talks and discussions.

- In my youth I used to see a blind, wandering Muslim fakir in my hometown, Nagercoil. He was well versed in Muslim religious songs written in Tamil. He used to sing these songs in busy streets, especially on market days, in a loud melodious voice, with an emphasis on selected words, according to the meaning they carry in those songs.

    Later I came to know that he had extraordinary capabilities with numbers. In his early days he had worked in many shops for textile dealers. He had the ability to add up a bill containing many items within a split second. Hence, he was a highly sought after commodity by all local merchants who could use this skill. But this fakir never cared about his job and took decisions impulsively to quit any given job, even for petty squabbles. The idiosyncrasy of this character attracted me very much in my younger days. **Reflowering** can be looked at from two different angles. Despite the fact that both master and servant represented different religious faiths, they were able to come together on issues that concerned them. This level of understanding and cooperation of people of various faiths have been questioned in recent years. The other point of interest is the discussion by great scientists on the pivotal question of whether it is possible to substitute human brain using artificial intelligence. My story tries to throw some light on these issues.

## TELUGU

**Amarendra Dasari** is a writer, translator and literary enthusiast and has two travelogues to his credit besides a number of short stories, book reviews and literary essays published in various magazines. He translates with felicity from Telugu to English, English to Telugu and Hindi to Telugu. He is presently working for Bharat Electronics Limited and is stationed at Bangalore.

- The Telugu short story is passing through both an interesting and a disturbing phase. It has always been reflective of society. Transition of the politico-economic scenario from a pseudo socialistic pattern to an unabashed capitalistic pattern has been affecting the lives of the middle and lower classes. Added to this, factors such as subregional imbalances, an emerging Dalit consciousness, exploitation of women and tribals are coming to the forefront. During 1999, a wide spectrum of short stories dealing with varied subjects appeared. A recent development is the disappearance of outlets for serious short stories.

    **Nippu Pitta Erra Kundelu Mariyu Adrusyamavutunna Jaatula Katha** erases the dividing line between the subject and the form, having the form itself as the subject. It employs a unique, powerful and gripping narrative technique which leaves the reader disturbed. It also touches upon the failure of feminism and communism – their failure to get to grips with social reality. This story opens a new dimension in Telugu short fiction!

**V Chandra Sekhar Rao** started as a poet but the short story slowly intruded and encircled the entire literary space. He has written around fifty short stories and one novel and has published two anthologies of short stories *Jeevani* and *Lenin Place*. Both of these have won many literary awards. Some of his stories have been translated into Kannada,

Hindi and English. A medical graduate, he opted for the civil services and is presently working with the Indian Railways.

- **Nippu Pitta Erra Kundelu Mariyu Adrusyamavutunna Jaatula Katha** was originally born on a footpath in a metropolis. Under the shadows of claustrophobic chambers, I found a group of rural peasants sleeping. The peasants were from a Dalit community and had been thrown out of their village for reasons they refused to reveal. They slept like hunted animals, in silent protest. They were a mystery to me for more than a week or two. These strangers on the footpath had disturbed me for so many nights that the disturbance transformed itself into a story.

**N Pranava Manjari** translates from Kannada and Telugu into English. She has co-translated Dr Chandrasekhar Kambar's Kannada novel *Chakori* into English. She holds a doctorate in Russian literature from Bangalore University. After teaching in a post graduate centre in Bangalore, she now teaches in an Engineering college in Noida. She also reviews books for *Indian Literature*, a Sahitya Akademi journal.

- The story is a bold attempt at evoking the decadence and rot of a world on the threshold of a new year and a new millennium. The *perfect* bifurcation and alienation of a part of the world that goes on shouting celebratory slogans of "Welcome to the New Millennium" while being completely impervious and oblivious to poverty, hunger, struggle, violent death, is brought out in telling detail. Using the leit-motif of *red* through a host of images, the writer conveys the violence we unleash even as we welcome the new millennium. But then, as birds signify hope and renewal, so *red* in **Nippu Pitta Erra Kundelu Mariyu Adrusyamavutunna Jaatula Katha** becomes symbolic of a new life.

## URDU

**Anisur Rahman**, Professor of English at Jamia Millia Islamia University, New Delhi, works in the areas of post-colonial literature and translation. He translates both from Urdu to English and English to Urdu. Amongst his publications are two monographs, *Nissim Ezekiel* and *Kamala Das*, *New Literatures in English* and *Anthology of Modern Urdu Poetry in English Translation*.

- The Urdu short story scene is not very encouraging. Only a few remarkable stories appear within any given year. The ratio of pulp fiction as compared to serious fiction is frightening. Maybe this is a time of transition for the Urdu short story which is in search of real authors who will help it emerge with greater resilience.

**Aaghori** has been selected for its immense readability, for its effortless narrative brilliance and its linguistic ease, and above all for its effective use of symbols to recreate a difficult time in India's history.

**Surendra Prakash**, pen name of Surendra Kumar Oberoi. is a Sahitya Akademi Award winner. Born in Lyallpur, Pakistan, he migrated to Delhi after the Partition and made his living as hawker, rickshaw puller, flower seller and travelling salesman. His works include *Doosre Aadmi Ka Drawing Room, Baraf Par Makalma* and the award-winning anthology, *Baz Goyi*. He now lives in Mumbai and writes scripts for films and television plays.

- Partition brought about the death of a composite culture. This story, as I have said in **Aaghori**, is "a story ... but remember there is a story within a story and that in turn leads to another story.

   Grasping the identity of the story, finding the essence of that which is a figment of the imagination, is your business. This story is such that it cannot be put into words."

**C Revathi** has an MPhil degree from JNU in Latin American Studies and a masters in public affairs from the University of Texas where she has worked as an intern and research assistant on several social work and community projects. While in India she was an assistant editor with Orient Longman. She is fluent in English, Hindi, Tamil, Telugu and Urdu.

- A word-to-word translation seems to rob the life of the story while enhancing the danger of misinterpretation of the original. Translating speech or customs peculiar to this region into a language like English proved difficult at times.

Filmmaker par excellence, **Adoor Gopalakrishnan**'s movies have inspired a whole new generation of filmmaking in Indian cinema. Born in Kerala in a family of Kathakali patrons and actively involved with theatre since a very young age, Adoor displays a mastery of craft, conveying through his path breaking films the crisis of the middle class, struggle of man against institutions and crumbling feudal structures.

Through a succession of award winning films – starting with his first film *Swayamvaram* which won the President's gold medal in several categories, followed by *Elipattayam*, *Mukha Mukham* and *Mathilukal* – Adoor has helped place Malayalam cinema on the world map. Adoor has also produced a number of documentaries, a national award winning book on films, *Cinemayude Lokam* and three other books on plays and playwrights. He has set up the Chitralekha Film Society in Thiruvananthapuram to promote, produce and distribute non commercial art films.

- "The Magic Nymph," "Little Earthquakes," "Reflowering" and "The Story of the Firebird, Red Rabbit and the Endangered Tribes" are his choices for this volume.

Well known filmmaker **Govind Nihalani** started off his career as a cinematographer with *Shantata! Court Chalu Aahe!*, based on Vijay Tendulkar's play. Nihalani went on to work with Shyam Benegal on several documentaries and about ten films, notable among them being *Junoon* for which he received the national award for best cinematography in 1979. Then came *Aakrosh*, his first film as a director–cinematographer which won the Golden Peacock at the International Film Festival of India, 1981. The same year he assisted Richard Attenborough in the Oscar winning film, *Gandhi*.

Thereafter followed *Ardh Satya*, *Party*, *Aaghat*, *Tamas* and *Drishti*, all of which received national as well as international honours and acclaim and established him as a top league director. Nihalani's more recent film *Hazaar Chaurasi Ki Maa*, based on Mahasweta Devi's novel, won the national award for best Hindi film in 1997. Along with films, he has made a number of documentaries and has also served on the jury of International Film Festivals.

- "The Whale," "The Full Moon in Winter" and "The Broker" have been chosen by him for this volume.

Writer, poet, lyricist and filmmaker **Gulzar** started his film career as assistant to Bimal Roy and gradually went on to work with stalwarts like Hemant Kumar, Hrishikesh Mukherjee and Kishore Kumar. He soon gained recognition as an evocative lyricist with *Bandini, Kabuliwala* and *Khamoshi.* With the release of *Mere Apne* in 1971, he turned to film direction. He has written scripts for about sixty films and has directed some seventeen films, including *Anand, Bawarchi, Gharonda, Mausam, Koshish, Ijaazat, Masoom* and *Maachis.*

Gulzar is renowned for his understanding of solitude and pain and his sensitivity to human conditions amidst blatant materialism. And for his simple, beautiful lyrics and play of words. For him, "Words are not solid blocks of meaning. They say much more than their apparent shapes." He is unique in his exploration of human relationships both in his writings and his films. With a deep love for literature, especially children's literature, filmmaking for him is a medium for sharing his views on life.

Gulzar is a recipient of several awards and honours, including seven national awards for his films and documentaries and the Filmfare Lifetime Achievement Award for his contribution to Hindi cinema.

- "The Verdict," "Mohdi" and "Aaghori" have been chosen by him for this volume.

Acclaimed Bangla film director, **Rituparno Ghosh** is known for his sensitive portrayals of women protagonists. But few know that he switched from the world of advertisements to the world of motion pictures with a children's film, *Hirer Angti* in 1993. However, it was with *Unishe April* in 1995 that he experienced box office and critical success. This film and the others after that – *Dahan, Bariwali, Asukh* and *Utsab* – have all won awards at the national and regional levels. *Bariwali* has also received international awards at the Berlin and the San Francisco film festivals. Rituparno Ghosh has been felicitated by the Bimal Roy Memorial Committee for his contribution to Indian cinema.

Critics and film watchers have attributed his success to polished execution, to strong themes dealing with issues and sentiments of concern to the middle class and to an ability to extract the best out of his star-actors. He contends, "It's just that I feel I understand the inner feelings of women, their passion, agony and suffering."

A multifaceted personality, Rituparno Ghosh along with directing films is the editor of a film magazine, *Anandlok*. He has hosted talk shows on television channels featuring celebrities and has also been on the panels of beauty pageants. Among his forthcoming films are *Shubho Muhurto* and *Chokher Bali.*

- "The Return," "Swadeshyatra," "The Witness" and "Purana Katha" have been chosen by him.

**Sharmila Tagore,** a member of the illustrious family of Rabindranath Tagore, was a Satyajit Ray discovery. After a successful stint in Bangla films, she made an entry into the Mumbai film industry with *Kashmir Ki Kali* opposite Shammi Kapoor. She went on to do many more hit films, acting with some of the biggest stars of the time like Rajesh Khanna, Dharmendra and Sanjeev Kumar in a host of films including *Amar Prem, Anupama, Aradhana, Mausam, Chupke Chupke,* to name a few.

Apart from being recognized as a good actress, she was an embodiment of beauty, glamour and unconventionality, setting quite a few trends in her time. "Looking back," she says, "I realize I was very different from the actresses of my time." She also earned critical acclaim for her roles in offbeat films like *Aavishkaar, Dooriyaan, Grihapravesh* and *Satyakam.* Married to former Indian cricket captain Mansoor Ali Khan Pataudi, Sharmila currently devotes time between family, causes close to her heart and an occasional film.

- "The Weight" is her choice from amongst the English stories featured in the *Katha Prize Stories* volumes.

# A SELECT LIST OF REGIONAL MAGAZINES

## Stories in this volume are from

*Goriyoshi* (Asomiya)
Assam Tribune Building, Silpukhri, Guwahati 781 003

*Desh* (Bangla)
6 & 9 Prafulla Sarkar Street, Kolkata 700 001

*Gadyaparva* (Gujarati)
12 Gayatri Society, Veri Road, Lunawada, Panchmahal

*Hans* (Hindi)
2/36 Ansari Road, Daryaganj, New Delhi 110 002

*Lankesh Patrike* (Kannada)
9 E A T St, PB 416, Basavanagudi, Bangalore 560 004

*Sandhan* (Maithili)
2/36 Ansari Road, Daryaganj, New Delhi 110 002

*India Today* (Malayalam)
98-A Dr Radhakrishna Salai, Chennai 600 004

*Gulmohar* (Marathi)
S K Belwalker Publishing Co, 1347, Sadashiv Pet, Kamalabai Bhat Marg,
Pune 411 030

*Jhankara* (Oriya)
Prajatantra Buildings, Beharibag, Cuttack, Orissa 753 002

*Aarsee* (Punjabi)
K24 Hauz Khas, New Delhi 110 016

*Jagati Jot* (Rajasthani)
Sahitya Evam Sanskriti Akademi, Bikaner

*India Today* (Tamil)
98-A Dr Radhakrishna Salai, Chennai 600 004

*Andhra Jyothi* (Telugu)
Road no 8, Banjara Hills, Hyderabad 500 034

*Zahn-e-Jadeed* (Urdu)
Flat No 7, Fourth Floor, 137-B Lane, 12th Zakir Nagar, New Delhi 110 025

# Other Journals

## ASOMIYA

*Ajir Asom*, Omega Publishers, G S Rd, Ulubari, Guwahati 7
*Anvesha*, Konwarpur, Sibsagar 785667
*Asam Bani*, Tribune Bldg, G N Bordoloi Rd, Guwahati 3
*Budhbar*, Shahid Sukleshwar Konwar Path, Guwahati 21
*Goriyoshi*, Assam Tribune Building, Silpukhri, Guwahati 3
*Prakash*, Publication Board of Assam, Bamunimaidan, Guwahati 24
*Prantik*, Navagiri Rd, Chandmari, PO Silpukhuri, Guwahati 3
*Pratidhwani*, Bani Mandir, Panbazaar, Guwahati 1
*Sadin*, Sadin Karyalaya, Maniram Dewan Path, Chandmari, Guwahati 3
*Sreemoyee*, Agradut Bhawan, Dispur, Guwahati 6
*Sutradhar*, Manjeera House, Motilal Nehru Path, Panbazaar, Guwahati 1

## BANGLA

*Aajkaal*, 96 Raja Ram Mohan Roy Sarani,Kolkata 9
*Amrita Lok*, Binalay, Dak Bungalow Rd, PO Midnapore 721101
*Ananda Bazar Patrika*, 6 Prafulla Sarkar St, Kolkata 1
*Anustup*, P 55 B, C I T Rd, Kolkata 10
*Bartaman*, 76 A Acharya Bose Rd, Kolkata 15
*Baromas*, 63/C Mahanirban Road, Kolkata 29
*Bartika*, 18 A Ballygunge Station Rd, Kolkata 19
*Basumati*, 166 Bepin Behari Ganguli St, Kolkata 12
*Chaturanga*, 54 Ganesh Chandra Avenue, Kolkata 13
*Dainik Pratidin*, 20 Prafulla Sarkar Street, Kolkata 29
*Galpapatra*, C E 137 Salt Lake, Kolkata 64
*Galpa Sarani*, Debuvuti Bhavan, Birbhum, West Bengal 731101
*Ganashakti*, 31 Alimuddin St, Kolkata 16
*Hawa*, 49 Brahmapur, Bansdroni, Kolkata 70
*Kuthar*, Canara Bank, 25 Princep St,Kolkata 72
*Madhuparni*, Sitbali Complex, Balurghat, South Binajpur 733101
*Manorama*, 281 Muthiganj, Allahabad 3
*Nandan*, 31 Alimuddin St,Kolkata 16
*Parichaya*, 30/6 Chautala Rd, Kolkata 17
*Pratidin*, 14 Radhanath Choudhuri Rd, Kolkata 15
*Pratikshana*, 7 Jawaharlal Nehru Rd,Kolkata 13
*Proma*, 5 West Range, Kolkata 17
*Raktakarabee*, 10/2 Ramnath Majumdar St, Kolkata 9
*Yogasutra*, TG 2/29 Teghoria, Kolkata 59
*Yuba Manas*, 32/1 B B D Bag (South), Kolkata 1

## DOGRI

*Sheeraza*, J & K Academy of Art, Culture & Languages, Canal Road, 181 Paharian Street, Jammu Tawi, Jammu-180001

## GUJARATI

*Abhiyan*, Shakti House, Ashok Road, Kandiwali East, Mumbai 1
*Buddhiprakash*, Gujarat Vidya Sabha, Ashram Road, Ahmedabad 9
*Dasmo Dayako*, Sardar Patel University, Vallabh Vidyanagar 388120
*Etad*, 233 Rajlaxmi, Old Padra Road, Vadodara 15
*Kankavati*, 24 River Bank Society, Adajan Water Tank, Surat 9
*Khevana*, 9 Mukund, Manorama Complex, Himatlal Park, Ahmedabad 15
*Navchetan*, Narayanagar, Sarkhej Road, Ahmedabad
*Navneet Samarpana*, Bharatiya Vidya Bhavan, K M Road, Mumbai 7
*Parab*, Govardhan Bhavan, Ashram Road, Ahmedabad 9
*Shabdashrushti*, Gujarat Sahitya Akademi, Sector II, Gandhinagar
*Sanskriti*, Sandesh Bldg, Gheekanta, Ahmedabad 9
*Uddesh*, 2 Achalayatan Society, Navarangpura, Ahmedabad 9
*Vi*, 6 Vishwamitra, Bakrol Rd, Vallabh Vidyanagar 388 120

## HINDI

*Dastavej*, Vishwanath Tiwari, Dethia Hatha, Gorakhpur
*India Today*, F 14/15 Connaught Place, New Delhi 1
*Indraprastha Bharati*, Samudaya Bhavan, Padam Nagar, Delhi
*Kathya Roop*, 224 Tularam Bagh, Allahabad 6
*Pal-Pratipal*, 372 Sector 17, Panchkula, Haryana
*Pahal*, 101 Ramnagar Adhartal, Jabalpur, M P
*Pratipaksh*, 6/105 Kaushalya Park, Hauz Khas, New Delhi 16
*Sakshatkar*, Sanskriti Bhavan, Vaan Ganga Chauraha, Bhopal
*Samaas*, 2/38 Ansari Road, Daryaganj, Delhi 2
*Samkaleen Bharatiya Sahitya*, Sahitya Akademi, Rabindra Bhavan, New Delhi 1
*Vartaman Sahitya*, 109 Ricchpalpuri, PB 13, Ghaziabad 1

## KANNADA

*Karmaveera*, Samyukta Karnataka Press, 2 Field Marshal Road, Bangalore 560025
*Mayura*, 16 M G Rd, PB 331, Bangalore 1
*Prajavani*, 66 M G Rd, Bangalore 1
*Rujuvathu*, Kavi Kavya Trust, Heggodu, Sagar 577 417
*Samvada*, Samvada Prakashana, Malladihalli 577 531
*Shubra*, Shubra Srinivas, No 824, 7th Main, ISRO Layout, Bangalore 78
*Tushara*, Press Corner, Manipal 19
*Udayavani*, Manipal Printers and Publishers, Manipal 19

## KONKANI

*Chitrangi*, Apurbai Prakashan, Volvoi Ponda, Goa
*Kullagar*, PO Box 109, Margao Goa 1
*Rashtramat*, Margao, Goa 1
*Sunaparant*, BPS Club, Margao, Goa 1

## MAITHILI

*Antikaa*, 2/36 Ansari Road, Daryaganj, New Delhi 2
*Vaidehi*, Samiti Talbagh, Darbhanga
*Mithila Chetna*, 1/C Kakeshwar Lane, Post Bali Howrah 1
*Janaki*, Similtil, Damodarpur Road, Dhanbad
*Pravasi*, Mithila Sanskritik Sangam, Kendranchal, Allahabad
*Pallak*, Shri Mahal Pul Chowk, Lalitpur, Nepal

## MALAYALAM

*Desabhimani Weekly*, PB 1130, Kozhikode 32
*India Today*, (Malayalam), 98A Radhakrishnan Salai, Chennai 4
*Kala Kaumudi*, Kaumudi Buildings, Pettah, Thiruvananthapuram 24
*Katha*, Kaumudi Bldg, Pettah, Thiruvananthapuram 24
*Kerala Kaumudi*, PB 77, Thiruvananthapuram 24
*Kumkumam*, Lakshminanda, Kollam
*Malayala Manorama*, Malayala Manorama Building, PB No 26 Kottayam, Kerala 679001
*Madhyam*, Silver Hills, Kozhikode 12
*Manorajyam*, Manorajyam Press, T B Junction, Kottayam
*Mathrubhumi Weekly*, Cherooty Road, Kozhikode 1

## MARATHI

*Abhiruchi*, 69 Pandurang Wadi, Goregaon East, Mumbai 36
*Anushtubh*, Anandashram, Near D'Souza Maidan, Manmad 423 104
*Asmitadarsha*, 37 Laxmi Co Chawani, Aurangabad
*Dhanurdhari*, Ramakrishna Printing Press, 31 Tribhuvan Road, Mumbai 4
*Dipavali*, 316 Prasad Chambers, Girgaon, Mumbai 4
*Grihalaxmi*, 21 Dr D D Sathe Road, Girgaon Mumbai 4
*Huns*, 4 Bhardwaj Apts, Near Krishna Hospital, Paud Road, Kothrud, Pune 29
*Jatra*, 2117 Sadashiv Peth, Vijayanagar Cly, Pune 30
*Kathasagar*, Akashdeep, Milan Subway Marg, Santa Cruz East, Mumbai 55
*Kavitarati*, Vijay Police Vashat, Wadibhikar Rasta, Dhule
*Lokaprabha*, Express Tower, Ist Floor, Nariman Point, Mumbai
*Lokarajya*, New Admn Bldg, 17th Floor, Opp Secretariat, Mumbai 2
*Loksatta*, Express Towers, Nariman Point, Mumbai
*Miloon Saryajani*, 33/225 Erandwan Prabhat Road Lane 4, Pune 4
*Vipulshree*, Shreevasta Prakashan, 67 Shailesh Society, Karve Nagar, Pune 52

284

## MANIPURI

*Ritu*, The Cultural Forum, Manipur, B T Road, Imphal
*Sāhitya*, Manipur Sahitya Parishad, Paona Bazar, Imphal
*Wakhal*, Naharol Sahitya Premee Samiti, Keishmapat Madhu Bhawan, Aheibam Leirak, Imphal 795001

## ORIYA

*Anisha Sahitya Patra*, Chandikhol Chhak, PO Sunguda 754 024
*Jiban Ranga*, Stoney Road, Cuttack 2
*Nabalipi*, Vidyapuri, Balu Bazar, Cuttack 2
*Pratibeshi*, 236 Acharya J C Bose Road, Nizam Palace (17th flr), Kolkata 20
*Sahakar*, Balkrishna Marg, Cuttack 1
*Samay*, Badambadi, Ananta Aloka, Sankarpur, Cuttack 12

## PUNJABI

*Kahani Punjab*, Kuccha Punjab, College Road, Barnala, Punjab 148 101
*Nagmani*, K 25, Hauz Khas, New Delhi 16
*Preet Lari*, Preet Nagar, Punjab
*Samdarshi*, Punjabi Academy, New Delhi
*Samkali Sahithya*, Punjab Sahit Sabha, 10 Rouse Avenue, New Delhi

## RAJASTHANI

*Binjaro*, Pilani, Rajasthan
*Manale*, Jalori Gate, Jodhpur
*Mansi*, Ambu Sharma, Kolkata.
*Rajasthali*, Rajasthani Bhasha Parishad, Shri Dungarpur, Bikaner

## SINDHI

*Sipoon*, 13B/3 Jethi Bahen Society, Mori Road, Mahim, Bombay 16

## TAMIL

*Arumbu*, 22 A Tailors Road, Chennai 10
*Dinamani Kadir*, Anna Salai, Chennai 2
*Kalachuvadu*, 669 K P Road Nagercoil Tamilnadu 629001
*Kalki*, 84/1-6 Race Course Road, Guindy, Chennai 2
*Kal Kudhirai*, 6/162 Indira Nagar, Kovilpatti 2
*Kanaiazhi*, 245 T T K Salai, Chennai 18
*Kanavu*, MIG 189 Phase II, TNHB, Thiruppatur 635602
*Kappiar*, Kaliyakkavilai, K K District, Tamil Nadu 629153
*Kavithaasaran*, 31 T K S Nagar, Chennai 19
*Pudia Paarvai*, Tamil Arasi Maligai, 84 T T K Road, Chennai
*Puthiya Nambikai*, 13 Vanniyar II Street, Chennai 93

*Sathangai*, 53/2 Pandian St, Kavimani Nagar, Nagercoil 629002
*Semmalar*, 6/16 Bypass Road, Madurai 18
*Unnatham*, Alathur PO, Kavindapady 638455

## TELUGU

*Aahwanam*, Gandhi Nagar, Vijayawada 3
*Andhra Patrika*, 1-2-528 Lower Tank Bund Road, Domalguda, Hyderabad 29
*Andhra Prabha*, Express Centre, Domalguda, Hyderabad 29
*Chatura*, *Eenadu* Publications, Somajiguda, Hyderabad 4
*India Today* (Telugu), 98-A Dr Radhakrishnan Salai, Mylapore, Chennai 4
*Jyothi*, 1-8-519/11 Chikadapally, PB 1824, Hyderabad 20
*Mayuri*, 5-8-55/A Nampally, Station Road, Hyderabad 1
*Maabhoomi*, 36 S D Road Hyderabad
*Rachana*, PB 33, Visakhapatanam 1
*Srijana*, 203 Laxmi Apts, Malakpet, Hyderabad 36
*Swati*, Prakashan Rd, Governorpet, Vijayawada
*Vipula*, *Eenadu* Compound, Somajiguda, Hyderabad 4

## URDU

*Aajkal*, Publication Division, Patiala House, New Delhi 1
*Asri Adab*, D 7 Model Town, Delhi 9
*Gulban*, 9 Shah Alam Society, 12 Chandola Lok, Davilipada, Ahmedabad 28
*Kitab Numa*, Maktaba Jamia, New Delhi 25
*Naya Daur*, PB 146, Lucknow
*Shabkhoon*, 313 Rani Mandi, Allahabad
*Shair*, Maktaba Qasruladab, PB 4526, Mumbai 8
*Soughat*, 84 III Main, Defence Colony, Indiranagar, Bangalore 38
*Tanazur*, C 117 A G Colony, Yousufguda Post, Hyderabad 45

NB: This is by no means an exhaustive list of all the contemporary journals, periodicals, newspapers (the magazine sections), little magazines and anthologies which give space to the short story. But, for the most part, these names represent the range of publications consulted by the Nominating Editors in their respective languages. However, since the compilation of a more detailed list of publications is one of Katha Vilasam's objectives, the editor would welcome any additional information on the subject, particularly with respect to languages not covered in this list.

# INDEX OF NOMINATING EDITORS, AWARD WINNING WRITERS, TRANSLATORS AND JOURNALS OF KPS VOLUMES 1 TO 10

LOOKING FOR KATHA BOOKS?
FIND US IN THE BOOKSHOP CLOSEST TO YOU!

**AGRA**
**Modern Book Depot**
4, Taj Rd, Sadar Bazar
Agra

**AHMEDABAD**
**Art Book Centre**
Ellis Bridge
Ahmedabad 3800 06
**Book Self**
16 City Centre, Near
Swastik Char Rasta,
Navarangpura
Ahmedabad 3800 09
**Kitab Kendra**
Gujarat College
Cross Road
Ahmedabad

**BANGALORE**
**Books for Change**
28, Castle Street
Ashok Ngr
Bangalore 566025
Vinayaka Book Dist
No 13 K Kamaraja Rd
Bangalore 560042

**BARODA**
**Acharya Book Sellers**
R C Dutt Road
Alkapuri
Baroda 390005
**Baroda Book centre**
20 Step- N- Shop Plaza
Offtel Tower Premises
Alka Puri Rd
Baroda 390005
**Chirag Book Dist**
Raopura
Baroda 390001

**Manish Book Shop**
7&63 Payal Complex
Opp M S University
Baroda 390005

**BHUBHANESHWAR**
**The Modern Book**
Unit III Station square
Bhubhaneshwar

**BIKANER**
**Sugan Nivas**
Chandan Sagar
Bikaner

**KOLKATA**
**Book Line**
7, Tottee Lane
Kolkata – 700016
**Classis Books**
Middleton Street
Kolkata – 7000 71
**Ekushe**
Bankim Chatterjee Street
Kolkata – 7000 73
**Indiana Distributors**
2/1, Shyana Charande Street
Kolkata – 700073
**Land Mark**
#3 Lord Sinha Road
Kolkata
**Seagull Books**
26,Circus Avenue Ist Flr,
Kolkata 700017
**Thema**
46 Satish Mukerjee Road
Kolkata – 7000 26
**Timely Book Centre**
30.Chittaranjan Avenue
IInd Floor
Kolkata 700012

**CHANDIGARH**
**Capital Book Depot**
SCO, 3 Sector 17 E
Chandigarh 160017
**The Earth Store**
Sector 7C
Chandigarh 1600 07
**The English Book Shop**
S C 031, Sector 17 E
Chandigarh

**CHENNAI**
**Alpha Land Books Pvt Ltd**
12/2 Jaganathan Road
Nungambakkam
Chennai 6000 34
**Fountainhead**
Laxmi Towers
27-Dr Radha Krishna Rd
Chennai – 600004
**Odyssey Dev Agency**
6 First Main Rd
Gandhi Ngr Adyar
Chennai – 600020
**Higginbothams Ltd**
814 Anna Salai
Chennai 600002
**Land Mark Plaza**
3, Nungabakkam High
Road
Chennai – 600034
**The Book Plaza**
G-16 Spence Plaza
769 Anna Salai
Chennai 600002
**The Book Point India ltd**
160, Anna salai
Chennai – 600002
**Tulika Publishers**
7, Prithvi Avenue
Ist flr, Abhiramapuram
Chennai – 600018

**COCHIN**
**The Book Mart**
33/272Tullepady Rd
Ernakulam
Cochin 682018

**DEHRADUN**
**J K Book Dist**
Rajpur Road
Dehradun 2480 01
**Nataraj Publishers**
17 Rajpur Road
Dehradun 2480 01
**World Book**
10-A Astley Hall
Dehradun 2480 01

**FARRUKHABAD**
**Aggarwal Book Depot**
5/8 Nehru Road
Farrukhabad

**GOA**
**The Other India Press**
Above Mapusa Clinic
Mapusa
Goa 403507

**GURGAON**
**Scholastic (I) Pvt Ltd**
29 Udyog Vihar
Phase V, Gurgaon

**GUWAHATI**
**Bani Mandir**
Congress Bhawan
Hedayetpur
Guwahati 7810 03
**United Publisher**
Pan Bazar;
Main Rd
Guwahati 781001

**HYDERABAD**
**Akshara**
8-2-273 Pavani Estate
Rd, Nv 2 Banjara Hills,
Hyderabad

**INDORE**
**Badsha Book Seller**
City Centre
570 M G Road
Indore
**Jainson Book Shop**
33 Bakhi Gali
Indore 4520 04
**Readers Paradise**
16 L G Apollo Towers
M G Road, Indore
**Rupayana Book Seller**
M G Road, Indore
**Sogani Book House**
Shop No 3, Rajani
Bhawan, M G Road
Indore 1

**JAIPUR**
**Books and News Mart**
M I Rd, Jaipur 302001
**Books Corner**
M I Rd, Jaipur 302001
**Rajat Book Corner**
8 Narain Rd
Nr Trimurti Circle
Jaipur 302004

**KANPUR**
**Kitabwala**
PO box No. 468
Kanpur 208001

**LUCKNOW**
**Bharat Book centre**
17, Ashok Marg
Lucknow 226001

**British Book Depot**
84 Hazrat Ganj
Lucknow, Ph: 223250
**Dastavez Prakashan**
Masjid Lane
Hazratganj
Lucnow
**Shri Ram Advani**
BookSellers
Mayfair bldg
Hazratganj
GPO Box No. 154
Lucknow 226001
**UBDC**
A-1 Arif Chambers
Kapoorthala, Aliganj
Lucknow 228020
**Universal Book Seller**
Hazratganj
Opp. Allahabad Bank
Lucknow
**Useful Book Service**
S-3/21-23 Shastri Market
Indira Nagar
Lucknow 226016

**MADURAI**
**Tulsi Book Centre**
Town Hall Road
Madurai 6250 01

**MEERUT**
**Book Corner**
Meerut Cantt
Meerut
**Loyal Book Depot**
College Road
Meerut

**MUMBAI**
**Crossword**
Mahalaxmi Chambers
22 B Desai Rd
Mumbai 400026

**Current Book House**
Pali Hills
Bandra
Mumbai
**English Edition**
404, Ravi Bldg
189/191 D N Rd Fort
Mumbai 400001
**Lotus Book House**
516- B SV Rd
Bandra (west)
Mumbai 400050
**Strand Book Stall**
Dhannur Sir P M Rd,
Fort, Mumbai 400001


**NAGPUR**
**ISPCK Book Shop**
Residency Road
Sadar
Nagpur 4000 01


**NEW DELHI**
**Alpine Book Shop**
H 1536, Chittaranjan
Park
N D19
**Arora Book Stall**
D A V School Building
Yusuf Sarai
N D16
**Bahri Sons**
Khan Mkt, N D – 3
**Browse 'n' Buy**
O 11B Lajpat Nagar II
New Delhi 110 024
**Cambridge Book Depot**
3, Regal Bldg
Parliament Street
N D 1
**Capital Book Stall**
Gopinath Bazar
Delhi Cantt.
N D 10

**Central News Agency**
P-23 Connaught Circus
N D 1
**Cross Word**
EBONY
II nd Flr, D-4 NDSE–II
N D 49
**Dass Book Depot**
2/2, Mall Rd, Tilak Ngr
N D 18
**D K Publishers &**
**Distributros P. Ltd**
1, Ansari Rd
Daryaganj
N D 2
**D K Agencies (P) Ltd.**
4788 90/23 Ansari Rd
N D – 2
**E D Galgotia & Sons**
17 B Connaught Place
N D 1
**Famous Book Depot**
25, Janpath Bhawan
New Janpath Mkt
N D 1
**Fact & Fiction**
39, Basant Lok
Vasant Vihar
N D 57
**Faquir Chand & Sons**
18, Khan Mkt
N D 3
**Frontline Dist Pvt Ltd**
7 Palika Bazar
N D 1
**Geeta Book Centre**
JNU, Nr Ganga Hostel
New Campus
N D 67
**Genius Books**
59 A Khan Market
N D 3
**Gulati Stationery**
14, Prithviraj Mkt
Khan Mkt
N D 3

**Hem Book Centre**
JNU, Nr SSS Bldg
New Campus,
N D 67
**India Today Book Club**
Living Media India Ltd.
B 318, Okhla Phase I
N D 20
**Jawahar Book Centre**
Near SSS Bldg
New Campus, N D 7
**Jawahar Books &**
**Stationers**
179, Sarojini Ngr
N D 23
**Jolly Book Depot**
47, New Market
Tilak Nagar
N D 18
**Krishna Book Shop**
Hotel Claridges
12, Aurangzeb Rd
N D 11
**Malan Book Shop**
Lodhi Hotel, N D 3
**Manohar Pub & Dist**
4753/23, Ansari Rd
Darya ganj,
N D 2
**Midland Book Shop**
Aurobindo Place Mkt
N D 16
**New Book Depot**
18-B Connaught Place
N D 1
**New L&R Distributors**
5-B, Surya Kiran Bldg
19, K G Marg
N D 1
**Om Book Service**
1690, Ist floor
Nai Sarak
Delhi 6
**Om Book Shop**
E-77 South Extention I
N D 49

**Om Book Shop**
45 Vasant Lok
Vasant Vihar
N D
**Paramount Book Store**
88, M M Janpath
N D 1
**People Tree**
8, Regal Bldg
Parliament Street
N D 1
**Prakash Book Depot**
M-86, Connaught Place
N D 1
**Rama Book Depot**
61, Central Mkt
Lajpat Ngr
N D 24
**Ritana Books**
81 Defence Colony
Fly Over Market
N D 24
**Ritika Book House**
Hotel The Oberoi
Dr. Zakir Hussain Marg
N D 3
**Sehgal's Book Shop**
F- 38 South Extension I
N D 49
**Swayam**
H-III Sarita Vihar
N D 44
**Tek sons Book Shop**
G 5 South Extension I
N D 49
**The Book Shop**
14, A Khan Mkt
N D 3
**The Book Mark**
A – 2 South Extension I
N D 49
**The Book Review**
239, Vasant Enclave
N D 57
**The Book Worm**
B-29, Connaught Place

N D 1
**The Full Circle Book
Store**
5B Khan Market
N D 110 003
**UBS Publishers &
Distributors Ltd.**
5, Ansari Rd, P B 7015
N D 2
**University Book House**
15, U B Bunglow Rd,
Jawahar Ngr, Delhi 7
**Variety Book Depot**
A.V.G Bhawan
M-3 Con. Circus
N D 1

**NOIDA**
**Ebony**
K-5 to K-9 Sector 18
Noida, U P
**Galgotias**
G-64 Sector 18
Noida, U P

**PATNA**
**Anupam Pub and Dist**
Opposite Patna College
Patna 800004
**Books en Amee**
Booking House
Patna 800001

**PONDICHERRY**
**Books Plaza**
Rue Mahe De
Labourdonanas
Next of Chamber de
commerce
Pondicherry 605001
**Focus Book Shop**
204 Mission Street
Pondicherry

**Vak**
Sri Aurobindo Ashram
Pondicherry

**PUNE**
**Either Or**
39 Sohrab Hill,
21 Sassoon Road
Pune 4110 01
**Manneys Book Sellers**
Moledina Road
Pune 4110 01
**The International Book
Service**
Deccan Gymkhana
Pune 4110 04
**World Book Shop**
Boottee Street
Pune 4110 01

**TRICHY**
**International Books**
23 Nandhikoil Street
Trichy

**TRIVANDRUM**
**Modern Book Depot**
M G Road
GPO Junction
Trivandrum 695001
**Prabhu Books**
Old street Knateswaram
Trivanthapuram

**VARANASI**
**City Book Shop**
Godowalia
Varanasi 2210 01
**Current Book Lovers**
22 Gyan Mandal
Complex, BHU Road
Varanasi 2210 05

**Harmani Book House**
B-1/160 Assi Ghat
Varanasi 2210 05
**Indica Book Publishers**
**& Distributors**
D-40/18 Godowalia
Varanasi 2210 01
**Universal Book Co**
D-40/60 Godowalia
(South)
Varanasi 2210 01

**VIJAYAWADA**
**Ashok Book Centre**
Opp Mari's Stall College
Vijayawada 520008


**VISHAKHAPATNAM**
**Ashok Book Centre**
13-1-KST Anthony's
Church Compound
Jagadamba Junction
VishakhaPatnam

My name is
Asma. I am th[...]
My preschool
getting me
ready for
formal educatio[n]

> "I think many of our sch[...]
> in the UK could learn f[rom]
> your work and teach[...]
> methodology."
>
> – Kate Alexander, C[...]
> UK, London

## Come join ...

I am Usha. Katha
prepared my sister and
me for the govt. school
we are in now. Katha
is our family. It has
stood by us.

I shall stand by Katha
when I am a
successful entrepreneur!

MY WORLD

9Cs: Curiosity Creativity

K

KATHA

... and the 1,100
happy kids of
Katha. And see
life in a
satisfyingly
different way!

**The Non Formal
Education Centre** is a[...]
innovative mix of mod[...]
and traditional pedago[...]
which helps make lear[...]
fun, relevant. Ask the
children here. They wi[...]
you all about the
excitement of lifelong
learning.

A-3, SARVODAYA ENCLAVE, NEW DELHI 110017. katha@katha.org
PRESIDENT: ABID HUSSAIN    EXECUTIVE DIRECTOR: GEETA DHARMARAJAN

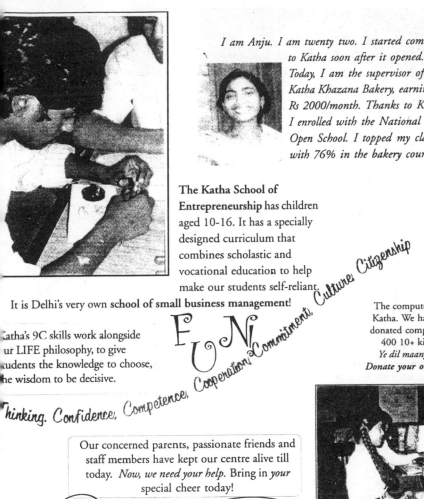

*I am Anju. I am twenty two. I started coming to Katha soon after it opened. Today, I am the supervisor of the Katha Khazana Bakery, earning Rs 2000/month. Thanks to Katha I enrolled with the National Open School. I topped my class with 76% in the bakery course!*

**The Katha School of Entrepreneurship** has children aged 10-16. It has a specially designed curriculum that combines scholastic and vocational education to help make our students self-reliant.

It is Delhi's very own **school of small business management!**

Katha's 9C skills work alongside our LIFE philosophy, to give students the knowledge to choose, the wisdom to be decisive.

**Thinking. Confidence. Competence. Cooperation. Commitment. Culture. Citizenship**

**FUN**

**SUCCESS!**

The computer centre at Katha. We have thirteen donated computers and... 400 10+ kids saying *Ye dil maange MORE!* **Donate your old computers.**

Our concerned parents, passionate friends and staff members have kept our centre alive till today. *Now, we need your help.* Bring in *your* special cheer today!

50 happy babies make **Our Creche** a happy place.

*My name's Pinkie. I am 13. I used to work as a house maid. Perveez didi brought me to Katha shala. I learn baking here. I write stories too.*

*I'm Chhoti. I am two. My mother sells ground spices. Katha takes care of me during the day. So my elder sister can go to school. I play here and Didi gives me yum...! food.*

*Volunteer today! The treasure is inside you!*

We need you! Call us at 6868193, 6521752 or 6994440 or Visit us at Katha-Khazana, Demonstration Block, Bhumiheen Camp, Kalkaji Extn., Govindpuri, New Delhi - 110019.

*My name is S...
I am 16 going ...
17. I work as
housemaid but ...
it is 12.30, it's ...
to study! I stud...*

KSE, the Katha School of
Entrepreneurship.

A large number of our teachers have been with us since 1990!

Katha, a registered, nonprofit organization was registered on September 8, 1989. Over the years, we have striven to reiterate that ...

# Katha stands for Quality

**Kathashala** was started in 1990 with six children. Today, we have more than 1200 children, from 0 - 16 years. Katha has a **creche, preschool, junior and senior schools.** An exciting mix of formal and nonformal methods makes for sustainable learning for our children. More than 5500 children, many of who have never been to school or are dropouts, have been helped to move into formal schools; we support them with **tutorials.**

**Katha School of Entrepreneurship** is an exciting one-of-its-kind programme that gives scholastic, vocational and entrepreneurial skills to young people. It is an accredited study centre of the National Open School. Our latest batch of graduates are earning up to Rs 2,500 today! We help them shape their own futures, and that of their families', too!

**Shakti-Khazana** is the women's empowerment and income generation programme which was started to facilitate women to earn, so children could come to school. Families were earning Rs 1000/month. Today our women earn Rs 2,500/ each! We believe money getting directly into their hands is one major reason why our children get to high school, and further. Katha's learning centre is in Bhumiheen, Navjiwan and Jawahar Camps, a large slum cluster of about 1,00,000 people, in Govindpuri, New Delhi. It is supported, inter alia, by DDA Slum Wing and Government of India.

FUN x 3 = Tamasha!

For the last nine years, **Shakt... Khazana** has provided incom... generation training for memb...

of the **Khazana Coop!**

Our women are teachers tod... Others are experts in baking, catering, tailoring, and food processing. Here, they get training from the Taj Mahal Hotel chef!

The Class of 1997: A great combination! Good sportsmanship and winning ways!

**Phulwari, a loving home for our physically and mentally challenged children.** They learn lifelong learning skills here.

**The Katha Maa Mandal:** 50 mothers meet regularly to discuss ideas like income generation, health, children's education, basic services. Now we also have the Bapu Mandal, at the request of the community.

**Katha Jathas** facilitate family well being, health, empowerment for the community.

*"I know Katha is sincere and honest. That's why I have been with them for so long."*

Raj Malik is a volunteer at Katha

ক

Katha ...
**Enhancing the pleasures of reading in the literacy to literature continuum!**

# DOCTOR, ENGINEER, POLICEWOMAN, MECHANIC, COMPUTER SPECIALIST ... WHAT WILL I BE?

*What happens when 1200 children, many of them working, 40 determined teachers and a whole community come together?*

*Sheer magic!*

*You'll find this excitement in the air when you enter the brick low-cost building that houses Katha-Khazana. Children running around, women entrepreneurs at work, people from the community taking a keen interest in the lives of their children. And to support their school-going activities, we started an income generation programme for their mothers in 1990. **Shakti-Khazana** helps women earn up to Rs 2500 a month!*

*The children and women of Govindpuri, a large slum cluster of more than 10,000 families, have come a long way in the six years Katha has been working with them. But there are excitements ahead. Small but sure steps towards self-confidence, self-reliance touched by the power of self-esteem, the craving for knowledge. Many of the children who come to us are working to support their families, but see where they are! Doing their BAs and BComs from Aurobindo College, Gargi ... Dreaming of becoming doctors and engineers, computer specialists and catering managers ... and more! Showing they can.*

*Would you like to be part of this excitement? Come join our world! Giving has never been easier, or more affordable! It costs just Rs 200/ month/child.*

*Or come volunteer. Your time, your experience, your ideas are important for us.*

## ABOUT KATHA

Katha, a registered nonprofit organization set up in September 1989, works in the areas of education, publishing and community development and endeavours to spread the joy of reading, knowing and living amongst adults and children. Our main objective is **to enhance the pleasures of reading for children and adults**, for experienced readers as well as for those who are just beginning to read. Our attempt is also to stimulate an interest in lifelong learning that will help the child grow into a confident, self-reliant, responsible and responsive adult, as also to help break down gender, cultural and social stereotypes, encourage and foster excellence, applaud quality literature and translations in and between the various Indian languages and work towards community revitalization and economic resurgence. The two wings of Katha are **Katha Vilasam** and **Kalpavriksham**

**KATHA VILASAM,** the Story Research and Resource Centre, was set up to foster and applaud quality Indian literature and take these to a wider audience through quality translations and related activities like **Katha Books, Academic Publishing**, the **Katha Awards** for fiction, translation and editing, **Kathakaar** – the Centre for Children's Literature, **Katha Barani** – the Translation Resource Centre, the **Katha Translation Exchange Programme, Translation Contests**. Kanchi – the Katha National Institute of Translation promotes translation through **Katha Academic Centres** in various Indian universities, **Faculty Enhancement Programmes** through Workshops, seminars and discussions, **Sishya** – Katha Clubs in colleges, **Storytellers Unlimited** – the art and craft of storytelling and **KathaRasa** – performances, art fusion and other events at the Katha Centre.

**KALPAVRIKSHAM,** the Centre for Sustainable Learning, was set up to foster quality education that is relevant and fun for children from nonliterate families, and to promote community revitalization and economic resurgence work. These goals crystallized in the development of the following areas of activities. **Katha Khazana** which includes **Katha Student Support Centre, Katha Public School, Katha School of Entrepreneurship, KITES** – the Katha Information Technology and eCommerce School, **Iccha Ghar** – **The Intel Computer Clubhouse @ Katha, Hamara Gaon** and **The Mandals** – Maa, Bapu, Balika, Balak and Danadini, **Shakti Khazana** was set up for skills upgradation and income generation activities comprising the Khazana Coop. **Kalpana Vilasam** is the cell for regular research and development of teaching learning materials, curricula, syllabi, content comprising **Teacher Training, TaQeEd — The Teachers Alliance for Quality eEducation. Tamasha's World!** comprises **Tamasha! the Children's magazine,** *Dhammakdhum! www.tamasha.org* and ANU – Animals, Nature and YOU!

## Be a Friend of Katha!

If you feel strongly about Indian literature, you belong with us! KathaNet, an invaluable network of our friends, is the mainstay of all our translation-related activities. We are happy to invite you to join this ever-widening circle of translation activists. Katha, with limited financial resources, is propped up by the unqualified enthusiasm and the indispensable support of nearly 5000 dedicated women and men.

We are constantly on the lookout for people who can spare the time to find stories for us, and to translate them. Katha has been able to access mainly the literature of the major Indian languages. Our efforts to locate resource people who could make the lesser-known literatures available to us have not yielded satisfactory results. We are specially eager to find Friends who could introduce us to Bhojpuri, Dogri, Kashmiri, Maithili, Manipuri, Nepali, Rajasthani and Sindhi fiction.

Do write to us with details about yourself, your language skills, the ways in which you can help us, and any material that you already have and feel might be publishable under a Katha programme. All this would be a labour of love, of course! But we do offer a discount of 20% on all our publications to Friends of Katha.

Write to us at –
Katha
A-3 Sarvodaya Enclave
Sri Aurobindo Marg
New Delhi   110 017          Or call us at: 2686- 8193, 2652-1752